TIME'S UP

TIME'S UP

Janey Mack

KENSINGTON BOOKS
www.kensingtonbooks.com

eISBN-13: 978-1-61773-691-9
eISBN-10: 1-61773-691-0
First Kensington Electronic Edition: July 2015

ISBN-13: 978-1-61773-690-2
ISBN-10: 1-61773-690-2
First Kensington Trade Paperback Printing: July 2015

10 9 8 7 6 5 4 3 2 1

Printed in the United States of America

To Mom and Dad

For everything. And then some.

Acknowledgments

David, a god among men. Jameson, Hud, and Grayson, for showing the patience of spiders. My terrific and true allies, Dori Lucero, Nancy, Bob, and Nicole.

James, Polly Ringdahl, Barb Pearse, Georgann Shiely, and Cristin Clark, for having my six.

Writer Les "Butch" Edgerton, for his support and guidance. Agent Laura Bradford and editor Martin Biro, whose keen eyes and enthusiasm helped make it happen.

Chapter 1

My abs were screaming. Sweat slicking between my shoulder blades, I ignored the rhythmic grunts next to me.

"Seventy-eight, seventy-nine . . ."

Gut it out. Hank's voice echoed in my head.

"Eighty-four, eighty-five . . ."

Gut it out! Gut it out! Gut it . . .

"Ninety-one."

"Time!" the PT sergeant yelled.

"Holy shit, that's gotta be a record," my counter said.

I lay prone on the mat, abs twitching like an epileptic at a rave from ninety-one sit-ups in two minutes. Fair to middling for an Army Ranger. But for me, a first in my class and a complete and total victory over jerkwad Tommy Narkinney.

Tucking my knees to my chest, I rolled up onto my shoulders and bucked to my feet Jackie Chan–style. Digging deep not to drop my head past my knees and suck air.

Hank's Law Number Five: Make it look easy.

I called over to Tommy. "How many, Nark?"

He sat on the ground, forehead on his knees, breathing heavy, straw-colored hair damp with sweat. "Eighty-eight."

"Yeah?" I said. "Good job."

Tommy frowned in suspicion. "And you?"

"Ninety-one." I raised my arms over my head, easing the fire at my sides.

He rolled his eyes and flopped back onto the ground. "Fuck me."

"No thanks."

"McGrane!" the sergeant shouted with a former Marine's perfect enunciation and eardrum-blowing volume. "Quit dicking around. Reskor wants you."

And I knew why. I was finally going to join the ranks of Flynn, Rory, and Cash McGrane. Just as my older brothers had all been awarded Top Cadet, so would I.

It took every ounce of cool I had not to skip like a little girl out of the gym.

I trotted up the stairs to Reskor's office and rapped on the thick, oak-paneled door.

"Enter."

Polished wood floors, Oriental rugs, leather chairs—it looked more like the office of a Fortune 500 CEO than the commandant of the Chicago Police Academy.

Hank's Law Number Eleven: Heavy hitters don't advertise.

I stood at full attention in front of Reskor's desk, staring blankly over the top of his balding pate.

"Miss McGrane. Please take a seat."

Adrenaline pulsed double-time through my veins. "No thank you, sir."

"Sit." Reskor pointed at the chair.

I sat.

He opened a manila folder on his desk, *M. McGrane* typed neatly across the tab. "Let's see . . . ninety-eight percent on the written exam. Scored 'expert' on the shooting range, and a first in PT, as well."

My knee started bouncing. I leaned forward, pressing it still with the heel of my hand.

"But I regret to inform you that you failed the psych review."

"Huh?" *"Failed the psych review"* didn't sound anything like *"Congratulations, Top Cadet."* "I'm sorry . . . What did you say?"

Reskor closed the manila file. "You failed."

The sweat on my forehead had dried to salt. I ran a hand over my gritty face. "There must be some mistake, sir." The room began to warp at the corners. "On what grounds?"

"As you know, failure on any exam results in immediate dismissal from the cadet program."

This can't be happening.

"Please, sir. On what grounds?"

He pressed the tips of his fingers together and gave it to me, right between the eyes. "The testing revealed you have an almost pathological need to be liked. The consensus of the peer review is that you are too thin-skinned to deal with the daily barrage of public hostility and unfriendly situations that a police officer encounters."

A pathological need to be liked? Me?

I realized I was rocking back and forth in the chair and got to my feet. "Sir, may I reapply, sir?"

"In a year, you may." His breath huffed out in a little sigh. "Reinstatement at the Academy is extremely rare. I see little point unless you can provide empirical evidence at that time to disprove the diagnosis." Reskor rose and held out his hand. "Not everyone is meant to be a police officer, Maisie."

And like some idiot robot, I shook it. "Sir, yes sir."

News of my disgrace traveled fast.

Tommy Narkinney was waiting for me in the hallway. "Tough bounce, kitty puncher."

Before I had time to tell him what a jackass he was, two academy instructors, one male and one female, escorted me to my dorm room. They watched me pack my gear and walked me out to my car in the parking lot.

What the fuck?

I sat in my Honda Accord and tried to remember how to start it, jumping when the female instructor knocked on the window. I turned the key partway and fumbled for the electric window switch.

"Hey." She gave me a sympathetic frowny-smile and said in a chipper voice, "Is there someone I can call for you?"

Jesus Criminy. My family.

"No. I'm fine. Really. Thanks." I zipped up the window and turned the key fully in the ignition.

Three miles later, I pulled into a 7-Eleven, got out of the car, and threw up.

Chapter 2

The psych review? How could I have possibly failed the psych review?

I sat in my car, blood pounding in my ears, throat hoarse, unable to wrap my head around it. All I ever wanted was to be a cop. I rubbed my eyes with the heels of my hands.

Sharpen up. There has to be a way to fix this.

I wasn't above pulling strings. Not today.

Of my five older brothers, the one I was closest to was Flynn. The oldest. And as a homicide detective for the BIS division, he sure as hell would know someone.

I dug my iPhone out of my pocket and texted him.

Where R U?

Flynn: *Working. N. Milwaukee & Hamlin. Home for dinner.*

Most murder scenes took six hours plus tech time, which meant a mid-morning homicide. I started the car and drove to the Polish district. Flynn would know what to do.

"If it ain't Baby McGrane," said a familiar thickset uniform. "Here in the flesh."

I gave a short salute. "Officer Werth."

"Not much longer till I'll be seein' you in uniform, eh?"

Oh God. Somehow I managed a wobbly smile. "Flynn around?"

"He's in the alley. Watchin' 'em load up the stiff." Werth

shook his head. "Even super-cop won't find nothing. It's a regular CSI cluster frag back there. Piss, blood, garbage, and glass, and you don't wanna know what else. Jiminey Jesus. What a place to cack."

I nodded. "If I could just talk to my brother for a minute? It's important."

Werth raised the yellow police line ribbon. "I know you know the rules, but do me a favor, all right? Stay behind the crime scene tape. Do not enter the alley."

"Thanks, Werth." I slipped under the tape. "You're a pal."

The closer I got to the alley, the tighter my chest got.

I belonged here.

The alley was filled to the gills with personnel. I caught sight of the back of Flynn's head, talking with the evidence techs while they were bagging and tagging detritus at the far end.

Up close, the victim lay in a pond of blood and alley garbage. He was a big man. Six-two, four bills, with a thick black mustache and short, coarse dark hair. A tiny woman in white coveralls with "Medical Examiner" across the back squatted down next to the vic. In her gloved hands were brown paper lunch bags and masking tape.

She raised the man's left hand, no wedding band, and clumsily got his hand into the bag before wrapping tape around the outside of the bag, and placing the bagged hand on the piece of plastic that had been taped across his chest.

Stab wounds.

And I thought I was having a bad day.

She moved to bag his other hand. On it, a class ring on steroids, gold with a bright blue stone. "Okay," she said to her partner as she got to her feet. "Let's get a board and bag under this guy."

Her partner retrieved the gear and placed it next to the body. He put his gloved hands under the victim's shoulders and heaved, grunting. No dice.

The woman came up next to him. Together, they tried to lift the vic's shoulders up enough to get him onto the board.

The body didn't budge.

"Aah! Shit." The woman jerked her hands from under the body and grabbed her lower back. "I popped somethin', damn it." Her gloves left dark smears of blood and dirt on her white coveralls. "Frigging lard monster."

Her partner snorted.

The woman straightened slowly. "Detective!" she yelled at my brother. "I need a couple of blues to lend a hand. We got a half-tonner."

The ignominy of death, presented by the Cook County ME's office.

Flynn, cop scowl of concentration on his face, turned and gave her a thumbs-up.

I slunk away from the edge of the alley before he saw me. *Jesus, what was I thinking coming here? Masochist much?*

Lupo's Cocktails beckoned from across the street.

One day I will solve my problems with grace and good judgment. Right now, however, it will be with alcohol.

Lupo's was dark and mostly empty. Opting for a front-row seat to Flynn's crime scene, I took a seat at the end of the bar and settled for a Coors Light. I was eventually going to have to drive home, after all.

I pressed the sweating bottle against my forehead. *Expelled?*

A misery-loves-company guy, gangly and awkward with glassy brown eyes, left his solo table for the stool next to mine. "Hi there."

Move along, pal. I haven't upgraded to misery yet. I returned a half nod and no smile.

He ordered a beer.

While I debated whether to chug my beer or leave it, the bartender slid Misery's Bud across the counter. Misery handed over a crumpled five. He was wearing the same gold ring with the blue stone.

The bartender pushed the five back. "On the house."

Misery lifted his beer. "To Nawisko." He drank most of it in one go and wiped his mouth on the back of his hand.

"What's the ring?" I asked.

He smiled sadly. "Amalgamated Transit Union. Local 56."

"Train?"

"Bus," he said. "See that?" He jerked his bottle toward the window at the crime scene. "That proud Polack was our union leader. But seeing as this is Chicago, not a goddamn thing is gonna happen to the assholes that ended him."

"Take it easy, Mike," the bartender cautioned.

"Gimme another beer."

The bartender glanced at me, then moved off toward the cooler. Misery Mike leaned in close. Too close. Beer wasn't all he'd been drinking today. His finger came up and brushed past my nose. "You watch. The cops are gonna say it's a goddamn mugging. But I ask ya, who the hell is gonna ice a nine-to-five joe for what he's got in his wallet? In the middle of the day? Goddamn know-nothing cop assholes."

Leaving my beer, it is.

The bartender returned. I stood up and threw a ten on the bar. "His beer's on me."

But Misery Mike wasn't letting me off the hook that easy. "Dontcha wanna know?" He caught my arm. "Who killed Nawisko?"

"Sure," I said, easing my sleeve from his fingers.

"That commie choad Coles."

"The mayor? Jesus, Mike." The bartender slapped a palm on the counter. "If that's not a sign for me to cut you off, I don't know what is."

Chapter 3

I hit the clicker for the front gate of the massive house I lived in with most of my family, feeling sorrier for myself than a skunk without a stripe.

No one was home.

It never occurred to me that I wouldn't become a police officer. Ever. The job requires a certain ability and desire, but it doesn't exactly demand every officer is the sharpest tack in the box.

Thin-skinned? Me?

Numb from the shock of it, I slunk upstairs to my room. Of course there was a way to get reinstated. I just had to think of it. I flopped down on the bed and closed my eyes for inspiration.

I jerked awake at dusk, panting and sticky with my shoes still on. *Cripes. I'm falling apart faster than an old IKEA dresser.*

Stripping down to my underwear, I left a trail of clothing to my bathroom. I turned on the shower, my bare feet sinking into the plush bath mat, the first time in ages I hadn't had to wear plastic flip-flops in the shower.

The water streamed hot on my head. I laid my cheek against the cold limestone tile and tried to cry.

Nothing.

"When in doubt, pretty it out." Grandma Pruitt's advice for the ages. When at your worst, do every possible thing you can to look good. The rest of you is sure to follow suit.

And if that doesn't work, well . . . I suppose you're an attractive suicide.

Somewhere between gluing on the short-flare false eyelashes and applying pink lip gloss I accidentally got a real look at myself in the mirror and the little flame of "everything's gonna be okay" snuffed out.

I went downstairs, getting a good look at the driveway through the transom foyer windows. Two pickup trucks, a Jag, a Jeep, and a BMW convertible were already in the driveway.

Lovely. All five of my older brothers. Home to bear witness to my crushing disgrace.

Everyone showing up was not a surprise. More often than not the lottery of overlapping cop shifts hit the rhythm of the rest of the family's lawyering, and we all converged at home.

Of course the Academy waited until today, Friday, to expel me, to give me the perception of a "normalized weekend" and ease me into accepting the sheer horror of my disgrace. And, because it's Friday, Mom cooks.

She was chopping vegetables at the kitchen island. "Maisie?" She looked up in surprise and got a load of my glam appearance. "Graduation isn't until next month. . . ."

Da and my four brothers stared at me from the granite bar that ringed the entire kitchen. My own personal Black-Irish gang. Fierce and fit, they ranged from five-eleven to six-two, all square jaws, dark eyes, and dark hair, cursed with pathological charm and the satanic ability to tan. The two oldest, Flynn and Rory, worked Homicide with Da. The twins, Declan "the sinner" and Daicen "the saint" toiled where the money was—as criminal defense attorneys at Douglas Corrigan and Pruitt with Mom. Cash, the second youngest, chose Vice.

"I failed the psych review. They sent me home."

My mother closed her eyes, shoulders sagging in relief. She dropped the knife on the counter, walked over, and hugged me tight.

Da exchanged a look with Flynn. "Well, that's that." He took a long pull from his beer.

A cold finger of humiliation slithered down my neck.

The only McGrane to fail the Academy.

"Get her a drink," Mom said to no one in particular, wrapped an arm around my shoulders, and walked me over to where Cash sat beside the twins.

Rory came back with a shot of Jameson and a Coors Light and dropped a kiss on the top of my head. "Tough break, kid. Did they say why?"

I opened my mouth, but no sound came out. *One thing's for sure. I don't suffer from a pathological need to be humiliated.*

Mom had gone back to the island and was slicing everything within reach like a Benihana chef on crack.

"You can reapply, right?" Cash, our family's very own little Mr. Sunshine, smiled helpfully at me.

"Doubtful," Declan said. "Subjective police board interviews are part of procedure and probably binding. I know they are in the FBI."

"Jayus, Dec!" Cash set his beer down on the counter. "Drive Snap into the ground, why don't you . . ."

"Don't call her Snap," Mom said automatically.

Snap. As in ginger snap. I'd adored my nickname, once. Now, at twenty-four, with my auburn hair painstakingly camouflaged with loads of blond highlights and even more brown lowlights, not so much.

Flynn and Rory nodded at each other with the same infuriating frowny-smile the woman who'd escorted me on the walk of shame gave me.

They were glad I was out.

And the sting of their relief was unbearable.

I downed the whiskey in one gulp, the scorching burn in my throat oddly settling to my stomach. Cash reached over and twisted the cap off my beer. "For God's sake," I said. "I'm not incapacitated with grief. I can open my own beer."

"Sure you can." He raised his elbow toward me, the beer cap pinched between his thumb and middle finger, and zinged the cap into my thigh.

"Ow!"

"Knock it off," Flynn said.

Cash nattered on like a deranged squirrel, the twins started arguing, and Mom kept chopping. I felt like my head was going to explode and Da just sat there, not looking at me, saying nothing.

Declan winked at me and by way of an apology, waved his beer bottle across the bar at Flynn and Rory, who were in a glowering low-voiced tête-à-tête. "So, boyos. What's eating your guts out tonight?"

"Homicide." Flynn flexed his fingers and leaned back on his stool. "Milwaukee and Hamlin. A real beaut. Middle of the morning, some beat cop finds a body in the alley. Knifed. No wallet, no ID, but this isn't some slash-and-dash robbery. This was up close and personal. Six short, sharp punctures to the upper ab and chest. Quick and quiet. Twenty seconds tops." He leaned forward, eyes bright. "A hitter or an ex-con, either way Rory and I are finally looking at something better than another goddamn drive-by."

"And?" Declan pressed.

"And nothing," Rory said. "Bastard defense attorney jammed my workweek. I've been riding the bench every day waiting to testify."

Defense attorney Declan smirked. "No offense taken."

"It's intended," Rory said. "You lot are all the same."

"Anyway," Flynn said. "The stiff's wearing this big ring. Guess who he's sweet on?"

"Amalgamated Transit Union," Rory answered.

"I text Rory a pic of the vic," Flynn said. "Fifteen seconds on the ATU website and he's got an ID."

Nawisko.

"Keith Nawisko." Flynn smiled. "An officer for the Local 56."

"Naturally, the death of any Union official must be a professional hit," mocked Declan.

"Yeh?" Rory's sharp-edged face darkened. "Then why'd the feckin' BOC swoop in and rip the file out of my hands?"

"The Bureau of Organized Crime?" Mom got her former prosecutor's look on her face. "I thought you might be stretching for the hit angle, but the BOC's interest rather seems to confirm it."

"Exactly." Flynn raked a hand through his short black hair. Chicago's labor unions were a Medusa's tangle of hierarchies, loyalties, and infighting. This was the kind of case my brothers prayed for every night before they went to bed. "Maybe the hit's a warning. Or it could be political."

"Political how?" I asked. "Infighting among Amalgamated or a bigger beef with Chicago Transit?"

"Uh . . . possibly, Snap," Flynn said, kindly.

His sweetness was an ice pick to the temple.

I am never going to make the table club.

"Or maybe the vic's just another belly-crawler who couldn't pay the vig," Da said.

"Either way, the case belongs to us," Rory said, chin set.

My father's smile was ice. "If it's drowning you're after, why torment yourself with shallow water, eh? Is that it?"

"Da," Flynn protested. "The BOC's in bed with every lowlife skell and politician in Chicago. They'll bury it. A case like this is a career maker."

"Or a one-way ticket back to Patrol." Da rapped his knuckles on the table. "Let it rest. Work the bloody cases on your desk. This is one less jacket to clear." Da set down his beer with finality and turned to me. "So, Maisie. What do you plan to do now?"

"I don't know. I hadn't ever considered I wouldn't . . ." My eyelid began to twitch. "That I couldn't . . ." The words *be a cop* refused to come out.

Mom came to my rescue. Sort of. "Law school, of course."

"Attagirl!" Declan said. "Even up the family teams—cops and lawyers."

"Uh, I don't think—"

Dad folded his arms across his chest. "You go on contract tomorrow."

"Conn!" Mom threw her napkin down on the table. "For God's sake. It only happened today."

"No plan—on contract."

"On contract" was our family's relatively easy take on the harsh reality of life. No life plan meant you paid room and board.

Flynn, Rory, and Cash still lived at home. Exempt from direct payment as they were all on the force, they paid "rent" into money market funds for their future.

"I got it, Snap!" Cash came alive from the other end of the table. He clapped his hands together and gave me a thumbs-up. "I had Jennifer on the 'cut list' but I'll keep seeing her till she hires you."

"Talk about an auspicious beginning." Daicen gave a sardonic smile.

"Yeah," I said. "That'll be great, Cash. I'm sure to be her favorite employee once you dump her."

He shrugged. "It pays well and the hours are good."

"Where does Jennifer work?" I said cautiously.

"Traffic Enforcement."

My mind whirred with potential. *State trooper? Sheriff's department?*

My dad and brothers burst into table-pounding laughter. Mom glared at them, shaking her head.

"What?" My chest got that familiar tight feeling it did when I was the butt of the joke. Which was most of the time. "What's so funny?"

Rory caught his breath first. Wiping the tears from his eyes he said, "Maisie McGrane . . . meter maid."

"Sensitivity training has worked wonders for you guys," I said. Which made them laugh all the harder.

"Sounds enticing, Cash." I stood up. "I'll think it over."

"Where are you going?" Mom said.

"Out." And because I couldn't stand them laughing at me one more second, I said the one thing I knew would shut them up. "I have a date."

It worked.

"I don't think you should be driving in your condition," Da said.

And what condition would that be? Booze on an empty stomach or a decimated life dream?

"I'll drop you off," offered Daicen. "We ought to talk a bit more about what happened."

"I got her." Flynn got up. "I have to hit the station, anyway."

I snagged my purse on the way to Flynn's spit-shined red Ford F-150. He started the truck and waited until we got to the end of the driveway. "Where to?"

"Joe's."

"I don't see your gym gear."

"I'm meeting him there." I needed to see Hank.

"Who?"

"My date," I lied.

"Have Mom and Da met him?"

"If they had, you'd have heard about it." Hank was not my boyfriend. Nor had he ever shown any inclination to be. And he definitely wasn't expecting me.

"What kind of guy do you meet in a hard-core ratty-ass gym like Joe's anyway?"

Hank was a hand-to-hand combat specialist who trained guys pushing to be Army Rangers. I'd been training with his "mutts" for over a year.

Flynn turned on the radio. Classical. We didn't talk anymore on the way to Joe's. He pulled the truck to a stop outside the front door. "I think I ought to meet this guy."

Just when you think you've hit rock bottom, you realize you can indeed, go lower.

"Please don't," I begged and my voice cracked, alarming us both.

I got out of the truck. Flynn hopped out and met me as I came around the hood. He hugged me. "Don't let it eat you up. It wasn't the job for you, Snap." He let go and got in the truck.

I heard the window go down and looked back.

"Don't do anything stupid tonight," he warned, and waited to pull away until I was inside Joe's.

Chapter 4

Joe of Joe's Gym was a mountain of Twinkie-eating flesh behind a battered black laminate reception desk with a "friggin' classy" zebra-patterned top. Joe gave me the nod and sucked a chocolate Donette out of its cellophane sleeve. "Hank around?" I said.

"Nnnnnhhh." Joe's mouth was made for eating, not for talking.

I sat on the splintery bench in the reception area and considered how long my imaginary date ought to last. The forty bucks in my wallet would get me a cab ride home but that was about it.

I could always work out. There was plenty of gear in my locker. I sighed. *Lovely. Just another overly made-up gym tramp who'd lost her way to LA Fitness.* I slung my purse over my shoulder and started toward the women's locker room.

And got stopped in a headlock. A tanned ropy bicep bulged against my throat, a heavy handheld the top of my head in optimum neck-snapping position.

Hank.

I collapsed into him, chin tucking automatically.

"Nice release, Sport Shake," he murmured in my ear.

He smelled of Paco Rabanne and leather and Hank. I turned, wrapped my arms around his waist, and squeezed. It was like hugging a building.

"They kicked me out," I said, unable to look up.

He pulled me into his chest and hugged me for real, resting his chin on the top of my head.

"Well now, Snap," Flynn said, in his old-school patrolman voice. "What do we have here?"

I spun away from Hank. "Did I forget something?"

"Yeah. Dad wanted to make sure you had some money." Flynn held up a hundred-dollar bill.

"Thanks." I snatched it out of his hand. *You'll never see that again.* "You're sooo sweet."

"Want to introduce me to your date?"

My entire body flamed red. "He's no—"

"Hank Bannon." Hank extended his hand.

"Flynn McGrane." My brother shook Hank's hand, assessing him. "Mind if I ask how old you are?"

"No."

At the lack of information forthcoming, Flynn smirked—"One of those, eh?" looks written across his face. "Where are you two going tonight?"

Hank waited a beat. "Dinner."

"She's already eaten."

I hate my brother.

"Drinks, then." Hank gave me a flash of white teeth. "Right?"

I nodded, not trusting myself to speak.

"Have her home by eleven thirty, will you?" Flynn said evenly, giving me the look. "She's got an important meeting in the morning."

We watched him leave Joe's.

He'll have run Hank's entire background before I even get changed.

"Thanks for that," I said. "Appreciate it." I started toward the locker room.

Aside from the excruciating embarrassment and my ruined life dream, things were looking up. Hank hugged me, I was up a hundred bucks, and I'd gotten under Flynn's skin like I hadn't in years. *"It wasn't the job for you, Snap." My ass!*

"Where you going?" Hank said.

I turned around. "Huh?"

"Our date." Hank jerked his head toward the door. "Let's go."

"Where's the G-Wagen?" Normally Hank drove a black Mercedes SUV.

"Seemed like a Super Bee sort of day." We crossed the parking lot to a black restored 1969 Dodge Coronet muscle car. He opened the passenger door, closing it after me. I tried not to hyperventilate as he went around and got in. "Talk or music?" he said.

I was way too nervous to talk. "Music."

Not a stickler of restoration for restoration's sake, Hank pushed a button beneath the video screen in the dash and said, "Brazil mix." A Jobim samba filled the car.

I couldn't stop smiling. A tear slid down my right cheek.

Great. I'm the human embodiment of A Tale of Two Cities.

I wiped it away without his noticing and snuck a glance at Hank. Clean-shaven. Unusual for him at this time of night. I spent the ride pondering that. It was a lot kinder than living through the Police Academy expulsion loop.

Hank drove like he did everything else—with speed and precision. He drove us into the city and stopped in front of an unremarkable limestone building with a simple black awning. A valet collected Hank's keys, while the doorman opened my car door as well as the door to the building with flourish. "Good evening, Mr. Bannon, miss. Welcome to Blackie's."

I was used to Hank's hands on me from training. Even so, it was hard to hide the happy shiver as his hand went to the small of my back. We took an elevator to an upper floor of the private club and he led me into a dimly lit bar trimmed in mahogany and leather. Pure swank.

A tuxedoed waiter appeared at his elbow. "The usual, Mr. Bannon?"

Hank held up two fingers. The waiter disappeared.

"You all right?" he said.

"No." I stared into his sleet-gray eyes. "I'm not." *But being with you under any circumstance is pretty terrific.*

"Why'd you get the boot?"

"Commandant Reskor called me in and told me I failed the psych review." I winced. "Apparently I'm too thin-skinned to deal with an antagonistic public."

"And?"

"I don't know." I rubbed my eyes. "He gave me the bum's rush and I . . . I folded like a lawn chair."

He reached over and gently tapped his finger against my temple. "Lizard brain."

Hank's Law Number Three. Don't let your lizard brain go rogue. Lizard brain is the leftover primitive fight-or-flight bit of your brain that takes over in times of extreme duress and makes you believe you're acting rationally when you're not. It usually gets you killed. "Yeah."

"Mad yet?" he said.

"Noo-oo."

"You will be." He tapped his temple. "Keep the lizard under the rock."

The waiter returned with a pair of vodka martinis on the rocks with olives. I took a sip and gazed out the window at the twinkling city lights. Just another reminder of the flashing lights I wasn't a part of. Like the crime scene today. "Hank?" I trailed a finger across the rim of my glass. "What do you know about the Unions?"

"Enough."

"Does the Mob really own them?"

"The Veteratti family has been known to exert some influence."

Influence. The way he said the word fired a synapse in my brain. "You knew I got expelled before I told you, didn't you?" I said slowly. *Maybe before I did.*

"I keep tabs on all my mutts."

"But I'm not one of your mutts, am I? Not really."

"No." His mouth quirked up at the corner.

That hurt. "Thanks a lot. You look real broken up for me."

"I'm not." He lifted his glass to me in salute then took a drink.

My throat tightened. "Oh? Why?"

"I don't date cops."

What?

I blinked, taking my time to sort that pertinent piece of information. But even now, at my lowest of lows, it didn't matter. I couldn't lie to Hank. "Hell or high water, I'm going to get reinstated."

A shadow crossed his face. "It's not the only game in town."

"To me it is."

"Well . . ." He rested his forearms on the table. "You're not a cop yet."

My eyes dropped to his mouth. He had a thin, cruel upper lip, with a full lower one. The same shaped mouth as every Batman and Captain America comic book I'd ever read. A superhero mouth. It would be so easy to just lean in and . . . Flynn's voice echoed in my head. *"Don't do anything stupid, Snap."*

I sat back in my chair. "I think maybe I should go home now."

"Okay."

We finished our drinks and left. Too soon, Hank pulled onto my street and stopped a block away from my house.

"Um, my house is—"

"I know where you live." He got out, opened my door, and held out his hand.

I let him help me out of the car. When I went to take my hand from his, he laced his fingers through mine. "Why are we walking?"

"I like it."

The automatic outdoor lights turned on as I opened the gate and we went up the driveway. At the sidewalk I stutter-stepped and stopped. "There's something I ought to tell you. . . ."

Hank smiled at me in equal parts irritation and indulgence.

"The story of 'Hang 'em High' July Pruitt and Conn Mc-Grane?"

He knew.

Of course he did.

Our birth mother died the night I was born. Killed by a multiple-offender fat cat in a DUI collision. When the Chicago machine let him off with a warning, the assistant state's attorney, the young black high-flier July Pruitt, quit and joined the powerhouse firm of Douglas and Corrigan on the condition she work *McGrane v. Westbrook* pro bono. July won a twelve-million-dollar civil suit, Da's heart, and adopted the six of us to boot.

I pinched the bridge of my nose. *It wasn't . . . I just couldn't bear the thought of Hank looking surprised when he saw Mom.* "I'm sorry."

"Don't be." We walked up the front steps and stopped at the front door.

"Law Number One, isn't it?" My vision blurred. "I am defined by my disasters."

"Baby, your disaster is only beginning." And then he kissed me. Hard, possessive, and . . . fleeting. "Mutts are running the bleachers tomorrow. St. Mary's. Oh-six-hundred."

"Yeah," I said, trying to catch my breath. "Okay."

He reached around and opened the door. I went in. "Good night," he said, closing it behind me.

The house was unusually dark and quiet. I walked to the back hall to drop my purse and heard the faint whine of the lathe. Da was still up. I went into the garage. The farthest of the six stalls had been converted into my father's workshop. I opened the door to the warm smell of sawdust. He stood at the machine, laboring over his latest project, a pair of George Nakashima–inspired walnut chairs for Daicen.

I waited until he finished. "Hi, Da."

He turned and flipped his protective glasses up onto his head. "Hullo, you."

My smile turned watery. "I'm sorry I let you down."

"You could never." He set down the wood and sandpaper and came around the workbench to hug me tight. He let go. "Bah, I've covered you in dust."

"That's the least of my problems."

He didn't take the bait. Instead he picked up the spindle and began to sand. "How was your date?"

"Awful and wonderful."

"What's he like?"

I brushed the powder-fine dust off my chest, thinking. "Us," I said finally. "He's like us."

"Jaysus, Mary, and Joseph!" he said in a thick brogue. "Then stay the hell away from the lad."

I grinned. Everyone did when Da went all-Irish. "Easier said than done."

He smiled back and his eyes softened. "Maybe I was a wee bit hasty putting you on contract. How about you make your mother happy? Sign up for law school and I'll give you the summer off."

"Law school's never going to happen."

"You've suffered a mighty disappointment. Don't discard a bright future out of hand."

"What are you saying?" The unfairness of it all hit me like a baseball bat to the chest. "I don't have what it takes to be a cop?"

"I'm not the one saying it."

"Oh no?" I could feel my lizard brain scrambling out from beneath its rock. "You're glad I'm out."

"I'm not crying in my beer if that's what you're asking."

"Maybe you think I should take Cash up on his offer. Be some lame-ass meter maid?"

Da looked down the length of the spindle, rotating it. "Mightn't be a bad interim job for the summer. Take some of the shine off the fantasy you've created."

Try the world I've grown up in.

He raised the sandpaper again. Touching up perfection. "Dealing with the public's resentment, oceans of paperwork . . ."

Holy cat! There it was, like a diamond ring in a gumball machine.

I'd ticket my way into reinstatement.

Blood pulsed in my ears as I fought to keep the delight from my face. "Fine," I said, somehow managing to keep my voice paper-flat. "I'll be the best damn meter maid you've ever seen."

"You do that, luv."

Chapter 5

I trotted down the stairs, the house still mostly dark at five thirty. I pulled my hair into a high ponytail, a hard knot of resentment burning in my belly. I'd grab a PowerBar to eat on the way to St. Mary's.

Thank God for Hank. And bleacher stairs. Cash met me in the hallway, finger across his lips. He crouched and motioned for me to come toward him. We snuck around the back side of the kitchen. Mom and Flynn were at the dining room table.

"He's thirty-one," Flynn was saying. "Seven years older than Maisie. Christ, he could be her—"

"Brother? Uncle? Cousin?" Mom flipped the pages on two separate briefs she had spread out on the table.

"Mom. An ex–Army Ranger? And who knows if that's even true? His records are inaccessible. Age-wise he's at the physical apex of his career. So you tell me. Why is he training guys in some dump of a gym?"

My mother took a precise bite of poached egg and arugula.

"Mom," Flynn said. "You can't let Maisie go out with this guy. He has a house worth about 1.2 million, no mortgage, and only token credit card purchases. It's like he doesn't exist."

Cash turned to me. I waved him off.

"He sounds fiscally responsible to me," Mom said. "Your sister's a grown woman and can date whomever she pleases. I see no reason to overreact."

"He has at least three vehicles, multiple gun licenses—"

"Nor do I believe brotherly concern constitutes a legitimate reason to run Mr. Bannon through the system."

"I ran him through the family sources." Flynn sat back in his chair and folded his arms across his chest. "Like Maisie should have had the sense to do in the first place."

"Who says she hasn't?" Mom set her knife and fork across her plate. "Your sister is devastated at losing her place at the Academy. And while I gently reveal to her that law school is indeed her destiny, I'd appreciate it if you kept your big muddy feet off my clean floors."

"Fine. But—"

"And while we're on the subject, Flynn McGrane, perhaps if you focused more of your energies on your own love life, your father and I would finally get the grandbaby we so richly deserve."

Cash curled up in a ball behind the couch, shaking with soundless laughter as Mom continued to give it to Flynn. I left him there and went to St. Mary's to run stairs.

Ernesto Padilla, my usual partner and best pal since elementary school, was waiting for me at the edge of the field, drumming his hands on the surrounding chain-link fence. A good-looking Latino, he was short, lean, and whippet-fast. I could almost hear Nicole's voice in my head: *Skin the color of a Kraft Caramel, just begging to be licked.*

I hadn't seen Nicole in over a year. I missed her—just like all my former friends who were girls. But it was always the same. One visit to my house and they fell in love with one or more of my brothers, who either dated and dumped them or never had any interest in the first place. One more reason arrow-straight Ernesto was my best friend.

Hank was at the far end of the football field, running through knife blocks and parries with the rehabbers. Hard cases. Different from cops. Different from criminals—at least the ones I'd been exposed to. These guys were soldiers, living at the next level of violence. Totally focused, Hank didn't so much as glance in my direction.

"Hey, *chica*." Ernesto punched me in the arm as soon as I got within reach. "Hank told me you're back. What happened?"

"I'm out. Don't ask," I said darkly.

"Ah—fuck 'em."

"Yeah. Whatever." I stretched my sides. "So, pally. Cheer me up. What've you been up to?"

He pulled down the corner of his shorts, exposing a scorpion tattoo curled on his hip bone. "Check it. My new ink."

"Fierce." I eased my iPhone from my jacket pocket. "Hurt much?"

"Hell, no! I'm weak? Is that what you think?"

"No. I *think* your mom's gonna be pissed."

He looked up in surprise, and I snapped a picture on my phone. "Shit! You better not!"

I took off running down onto the field, zigzagging as I yelled over my shoulder. "Sending it right now."

He tackled me at the knees, knocking me to the ground, the phone flying from my hand into the grass. Ernesto scrambled over my legs, picked it up, and started scrolling to delete his picture. I rolled onto my back laughing.

Across the field Hank gave a short, sharp whistle through his teeth.

Ernesto gave me an arm up, and I dumped my jacket and phone as we hustled to the bleachers and joined the other mutts, the half-dozen or so young guys pretraining to be Rangers, on the stairs, waiting for Hank and the rehabbers to join us.

No sign of anything from Hank. Not a wink or a smile. Not that I could have seen anything through the blacker-than-black sunglasses he wore.

Stairs. Obstacle course. Basic cals.

I busted it out, as mad as a hornet in a rainstorm, beating guys I'd barely been able to keep up with, finishing only just behind Hank and one especially scary rehabber.

Afterward Ernesto and I lounged on the bleachers. "So, what you gonna do?" he said. "You're more than qualified for armed forces, state trooper, U.S. Marshals."

"Failing the psych review is pretty much the ultimate black-ball. Anything else I'd even consider is pretty much shot to hell." I cracked my neck. "Except maybe the fire department."

"Nah." Ernesto pulled a pack of smokes and a lighter from his jacket pocket. "All those fire boys do is work out and chase women. It's all about the hose." He lit the cigarette and took a single long drag. "Be a paramedic."

"Like you?"

"Eight-hour shifts, plenty of action, overtime, and speed. It's fun and every now and again you go home feeling kinda saintly."

"I'm not giving up," I said. "I'm going to be a cop."

"How?"

"I figure a stint in an enforcement-style job might be enough for reinstatement."

"As what? A mall cop?"

"Shoot right for the stars, don't you?" I laughed. "I'm aiming at something a little less glamorous. Parking enforcement."

"As in *meter maid?*"

I nodded.

Ernesto rolled his eyes, stubbed his cigarette out, and flicked it beneath the stairs. "You gotta be kidding me."

I clasped my hands behind my head and lay back on the riser. "It won't be forever."

He hooted with laughter. "That's what they all say, *chica.*"

A shadow fell over us. Hank, holding a body-sized gear bag. "Pads and I are hitting the range. Want to ride along?"

"I didn't bring anything," I said.

"I'll spot you."

"Shotgun," called Ernesto, already trotting down the stairs to Hank's G-Wagen.

"Have an extra cap on you?" I said.

Hank unzipped a side pocket on the rucksack and flipped me a ball cap with "Army" embroidered across it. "Keep it."

"Thanks." As we walked to the car, I adjusted the band and pulled my ponytail through it.

"Nice hustle today, Angel Face," said Hank. I glanced up, but he was looking straight ahead.

We got to the truck. Ernesto leaned across the hood, pretending to sleep. Hank unlocked the doors by remote and opened the rear passenger door for me before stowing his gear in the back.

Ernesto waited until we reached all the way to the end of the parking lot before screwing with me. "Heard the news? Our little girl's gonna grow a curly tail and suck the public teat."

"Thanks a lot, Ernesto," I said, wishing Hank wasn't in the truck so I could tag him in the back of the head. "It's not a career choice. Just a means to an end."

"Ah, *chica*. Keep telling yourself that. Joining the Traffic Enforcement Bureau's worse than making a deal with the devil."

Hank tipped his sunglasses down and caught my eye in the rearview mirror. "Once you've paid the Danegeld, you never get rid of the Dane."

"Kipling? So uplifting, sensei." Ernesto put his hands together and gave a deferential bow to Hank before he turned around in the front seat. "Listen up, Little Grasshopper. Dig the well *before* you are thirsty."

I stuck my foot under Ernesto's seat and kicked hard.

Twenty-five minutes later, geared up, and Glock'd, we stood at the end of the shooting lanes at The Second Amendment. "You *chupas* done warming up?" Ernesto slapped three five-dollar bills on the counter behind us. "Three rounds. I choose first."

I reached my hand into the inside pocket of my gym shorts for my emergency twenty. Hank put his hand on my arm. "I got it."

Ernesto whistled as Hank anted up.

"Don't know why you're bothering, Pads," Hank said. "Merely an exercise in futility."

"Yeah? We'll see 'bout that. Twenty shots at twenty-five feet." Ernesto waggled his brows. "Closest grouping."

Nothing feels as good as shooting a gun. Ear-numbing blasts—even when doubled up with plugs and muffs—and the faint acrid hint of propellant in the air beat a mani-pedi anytime.

We pressed the buttons and the paper targets zipped up the line to meet us.

Too close to call. Ernesto swept three of the fives off the counter anyway.

My turn. "Accuracy. Single shot. Fifty feet."

Ernesto nicked the bull's-eye lower left. Hank dead center. I got up, ready to pull a Robin Hood and shoot through the same hole. Hank smiled at me and, like some dorky puppy, I pulled right. *Goddamn it!*

"Shit, *chica!* Just 'cause he spots you a couple bullets, you don't have to let him win."

"Quit crying," Hank said. "Fifty feet. Twenty rounds. Combo scoring, time and accuracy."

Ernesto danced in place. "Oh yeah. Oh yeah."

"Opposite hand," Hank said.

Ernesto groaned.

"God, you're such a show-off," I said.

It didn't take long for Hank to clean our clocks. We spent the rest of the hour burning through ammo. I rode shotgun as we drove back to St. Mary's, Ernesto lounging in the backseat, singing loudly to Lynyrd Skynyrd. We dropped him off at his pickup and drove to my car at the lot on the other side of the football field.

Hank put the SUV in Park, turned the radio down, and twisted in his seat to face me. "Traffic Enforcement?"

I nodded and readjusted my ball cap. "Civil Service. Hard to find something more unpleasant."

Hank cocked a brow. "A college degree in criminal justice."

"And a meter maid on Monday."

His mouth twitched. "I'll pick you up Friday at eight. To celebrate." He got out of the SUV, came around, and opened my door while I sat immobile in elation. "I'm heading out to Cali this week. On business."

"Oh yeah?" *What kind of business?* "Don't get too much sun." I climbed in my car. "Thanks for today, Hank."

He winked and shut my door. I put the key in the ignition.

Well, that was . . . anticlimactic.

Hank rapped on the window. I zipped it down. He leaned in, caught my face in his hands, and pressed his mouth to mine. Searing and sweet. "Friday night. I'll pick you up at eight."

It was going to be the longest five days of my life.

I knocked on Cash's open door.

He lounged in his beanbag playing Xbox. "Yeah?" he said, not looking away from the enormous flat screen.

"Can I talk to you?"

Fingers tapped the controls double-time. "Uh-huh."

I went into his room. Two years older than me and he lived like a seventeen-year-old TV star.

There was an aura about Flynn, Rory, and Da. Hard and forceful, they were cops through blood and bone. Cash was equally intense about work, but somehow surfed along on a playful happy-go-lucky wave of man-boy. The fact that he didn't wear his cop on his person was what made him such a standout asset to Vice. If I hadn't seen Cash in action on a ride along, I'd have never believed it.

I crossed the room, pulled the drapes aside, and opened the window.

"God dang it." Cash hit the remote. "What are you doing?"

"Trying not to pass out from the stench of AXE body spray and Doritos."

"Ha-ha. Very funny. And it's Brut, by the way."

"That's like . . . grandpa cologne."

"Which is why it works so well. The girls already have a built-in fondness for the smell. They just don't remember why."

"Speaking of girls," I said.

"No, no, no, Clarice. And you were doing so well," he said in a passable Hannibal Lecter. "You were courteous, you had been receptive to courtesy, you had established trust . . . Oh wait, you hadn't." He punched Pause, tossed the remote down, and started throwing hand signs. "Busting in my crib, yo. Messin' wid my concentration. Knockin' my stank."

I flopped down on the bed and folded my arms across my chest, refusing to pay attention to him. Cash lasted all of forty-five seconds before he bounced down next to me, landing on his stomach.

"Is your offer still good with Jennifer?" I asked, with barely a tinge of shame. Hank knowing had pretty much neutralized the cringe factor. It was way harder to be an idiot in front of Hank than my brother who actually was an idiot.

His dark eyes widened and for a moment, he actually did look seventeen. "Are you freaking kidding me?"

"No."

He rolled onto his back and we lay there, staring at the ceiling. "Jaysus, Maisie. There has to be something less . . . less *humiliating* out in the great wide world. I mean, even working at the movie theater would pretty much at least ensure you wouldn't be running into slags like Tommy Narkinney every day."

"Will you do it?" I rubbed my eyes as though I were tearing up.

Cash cleared his throat. "Yeah, well. Maybe I wasn't serious."

"I am."

"Jennifer's kind of a pain in the ass. Which is why I'm cutting her from the team." He yawned and cracked his knuckles. "Ah, well. I suppose I can hold off for another week." An evil smile spread across his face. "But it's gonna cost you."

Chapter 6

Jennifer Lince of the Traffic Enforcement Bureau was a slight and sharp-faced white-blonde, attractive in a repressed school-teacher sort of way. Her fishbowl office was pin-neat; the only objects on the sleek Herman Miller desk were a closed laptop, in and out trays, and an eight-by-ten frame facing her.

She stood up and offered her hand to me like a trained poodle for one of those weird girly handshakes. "And you must be Maisie. How nice to finally meet you." She pointed at the two red fabric chairs in front of her desk. "Please, have a seat."

"Thanks." I sat down, leaning a little too far forward on the way to catch a peek at the picture on her desk. Cash grinned back at me from the silver frame.

A million bucks said he had no idea his face was on her desk.

"I must say I was pleasantly surprised to hear from Caiseal. He's been as elusive as the Invisible Man lately. Then three calls last night."

My brother. The master of subtlety. "Uh . . . yeah, he's pulling double shifts at the station. It's just that Cash is—"

"Cash?" she asked sharply and pulled a manila folder marked *Interviews* from the in tray.

"Cash, short for Caiseal," I said.

She stared at me, unblinking.

What is her problem? "You know, like when people call you Jenny?"

"People don't. My name is Jennifer. If my parents had wanted people to call me Jenny, they would have named me Jenny."

"O—kay." I sat up a little straighter. "After my . . . er . . . falling-out with the Police Academy, *Caiseal* thought a job in Traffic Enforcement—"

"Yes. Why is that exactly?"

"I've always had a great respect for parking—"

"No. The Police Academy. You had high marks. Why did you quit?"

"Excuse me?"

Jennifer paged through my application. "The fax I received from the Academy states 'subject declined to continue academy post psych interview.' Why?"

I suppressed a sigh of pure relief. At least my future employers weren't to be informed of my pitiful lack of emotional regulation.

"Ms. McGrane?"

"Maisie . . . Yes, I did," I said, scrambling to invent a reason why I didn't want the best job in the world. "I realized the . . . uh . . . some elements of police work were too . . . intense for me."

"I see." She nodded. "Although I would be remiss if I did not caution you that occasionally, you may be dealing with unhappy or even hostile members of the public."

Thank You, God. "I can imagine."

The interview slowed to a slog as I waded through endless generic questions designed to reveal personality and suitability.

Ms. Lince closed the folder on her desk. "Now a little about us. The Traffic Enforcement Bureau is a branch of Dhu West, a privately owned LLC. We are not a government agency, nor do we partner with any other state or municipal agency."

I nodded.

"The Traffic Enforcement Bureau has garnered a hundred-year lease of the City of Chicago's downtown parking meters. We maintain and operate over thirty-six thousand meters and generate approximately twenty-eight million dollars a year in revenue."

My eyes began to glaze over.

Jennifer folded her hands primly on the desk. "What interests you most about the TEB family?"

Nothing. "Its reputation and opportunity for advancement."

"Dhu West and the TEB strive to help employees achieve their goals. I'm proof of that." She held up a finger, putting me on pause, and signaled for someone to enter her glass office.

Her secretary extended a clipboard. "Dean resigned."

Jennifer frowned, signed it, and turned her attention back to me. "There is a high level of turnover in this position. That, combined with your brother's impeccable recommendation, have me wishing I could put you on the roster today. Unfortunately, the training session started this morning. The next one won't begin for two weeks." She turned to the secretary. "Give her a requisition for the next class."

Two more weeks plus a week of training? Holy cat, a fifty-two-week meter maid prison term was stretching into a fifty-five-week eternity. "Is the training a legal requirement or company policy?"

She thought for a moment before answering. "Policy. But you'd never pass the test without it. Even after training, the median score of first-time test takers is sixty-eight percent."

I could pass the test. I just needed to take it. "That has to be stressful for you. All the interviewing, waiting for them to cycle through training only to fail—"

"Or drop out after the first unpleasant encounter." Jennifer sat back in her chair for a moment, then flipped open her laptop and clicked a few keys. "What's the closest distance you can park to a fire hydrant?"

"Fifteen feet."

"A fire station driveway?"

Dinnertime entertainment at the McGranes'. The more obscure the violation, the more points scored. "Twenty."

They used to call it "pulling a Conn McGrane" in Vice. Vice cops were too cocky to write parking tickets. But when Da had an untouchable perp in his sights, he'd paper-trail the guy—ticketing everything from too close to a stop sign to more than twelve inches from a curb. And in little more than a month he'd have a built-in arrest warrant.

She sat back in her chair, a speculative gleam in her eyes. "Perhaps, just this once, I could make an exception."

I took the test.

Two hours later I was back in Jennifer Lince's office. "A ninety-seven percent," she said. "Impressive."

What did I get wrong?

"Thank you. I won't let you down."

"The thing is—" She hesitated. "It really is against company policy to bypass the two-week class session." Her french-tipped fingernails tapped an ivory card that lay on her desk and sat back. "If only I could think of a way . . ."

She looked from the card to me. Twice. Before I caught on and picked up the card. *You are cordially invited to Dhu West's Annual Gala . . .*

So that's how it is. I pimp out my brother and get the job.

And just to make it a complete pig's breakfast, the gala wasn't for two months. Eight weeks of dating and a black tie event. *How skeevie does she think I am?* "I . . . Uh, Caiseal's low man on the totem. He doesn't have much choice for shifts."

"I'm sure you could help him understand how important this is to you."

And I thought picking up his room for a month was bad. This was going to cost . . . I didn't want to imagine how much. Then again, I never did pay him back for shaving my eyebrows off in tenth grade. "No problem."

Jennifer rose and extended her hand. I stood and shook it. "Welcome aboard."

"Thanks." I held the card out to her.

"Keep it. As part of the TEB family, you're invited, as well. In fact, I'll make sure we're seated at the same table."

"That'll be . . . great."

"All righty, then." Jennifer gave me a perky smile. "I'm assigning you to Leticia Jackson for ride-along instruction. My secretary will supply you with everything you need and direct you to Dispatch." She opened a desk drawer, removed a silver badge, and slid it across to me. The words *Traffic Enforcement Bureau* stood out in relief across the top, the number *40506* engraved in the bar at the bottom.

The taste in my mouth turned bitter as I picked up the Mickey Mouse corporate fake. I should have been getting my real shield.

"If you're as ready to become a parking enforcement agent as I think you are, and of course pending Leticia's evaluation, I'll be proud to assign you that very badge next Monday."

Chapter 7

Dispatch was a helpful nerd named Obi in a tricked-out *Star Wars* wheelchair. He drew me a map to the magical mecca of meter maids on the back of a pizza flyer and handed me a key card, radio, and AutoCITE ticketing machine before warning me to never, ever punch in more than four minutes before my shift. "Dhu West has a strict policy about overtime."

"Oh." And because I couldn't help myself, I asked, "Is that your name, really?"

He grinned, showing a set of choppers that had never seen a retainer. "You bet. Obi-Wan Peter Luke Olson." He pushed smeary glasses up the bridge of his nose. "I had it changed last year."

"Cool."

"Yeah. I kept the Peter and Olson for my mom. And Facebook." He wiggled his brows. "'Cause you never know when an old girlfriend's gonna look up for a hookup. Am I right or am I right?"

"You know it," I said, studying the map. "Why's Dispatch so far away?"

"Radio signal requirements." He pulled a paper packet from beneath the counter. "You're new here, so let me give you a little advice. PEAs don't get much respect, so don't go looking for it. And"—he slid the packet to me—"keep the Loogie hidden when entering and exiting."

"Loogie?" I opened the package. Inside was a reflective traf-

fic vest the color of neon phlegm. *How sublimely revolting.*
"Thanks, Obi. I appreciate it." And I did. I turned to leave.

"So, Maisie? Uh . . ." He chewed his bottom lip.

Please don't ask me out.

"I'd lose the hat."

Whew. Except now I was getting fashion advice from a basement dweller. "Not a good look?" My hair was slicked back
with gel beneath the black PEA ball cap, ponytail swinging
through the adjustable strap. No way was I gonna be seen without it.

"No, it's fine. Great." He shrugged. "It's just Miz Jackson
doesn't much care for hats."

"Thanks for the intel."

He pointed at his Darth Vader LEGO wristwatch. "You have
time to leave it at your car."

Hardly. In a sick sort of irony, the Traffic Enforcement Bureau didn't provide parking for its employees. It had taken me
fifteen minutes of searching before I gave up and parked six
blocks away from Dispatch.

Hank's Law Number Seven: Never be late.

I had less than twenty minutes to find the TEB's PEA's working office, my locker, and Leticia Jackson.

"I can hold it for you, if you like," he offered hopefully.

"I got it. Thanks again, Obi." I gave him a small salute and
left.

Three blocks and two alleys later, I swiped my key card
through the security lock of a nondescript office door in a squat
cement building. The empty reception area smelled like a combination of fried rice, burnt microwave popcorn, and two-day-old
tuna salad. I decided to pass on hunting for an administrator to
get my locker assigned. Purse free, my cargo pockets held thirty
bucks and a couple of protein bars. Against Obi-Wan's advice, I
was keeping the cap.

I followed the stink down a gray hallway. I turned the corner
at the sound of chatter. Twenty-three uniformed parking agents,

milling around the time card punch, stopped and gave me the walleye.

"Hi," I said. "I'm looking for Leticia Jackson?"

Crickets.

A chubby Hispanic snorted and whispered something behind her hand to a lone and much heavier white male with an eighties metal-band haircut. They laughed.

Whatever.

This job was turning out to be as much fun as actually doing time. Or worse, revisiting junior high. Same rules still applied. *So, whose ass do I have to beat to not become everybody's bitch?*

A chime over the PA system started a jostling of black and blue uniforms, pushing to the punch clock. I waited, trying to make eye contact.

Zip.

I took my turn, then followed the pack through a tight maze of hallways to the back of the building, where three sets of glass doors opened onto a pristine razor-wired parking lot full of . . . golf carts.

The lot was double-gated, tire-spiked, with a lot attendant in a snappy little bulletproof guardhouse and a dozen visibly placed security cameras. Which meant, of course, there were more. I located car number 13172 and waited for Leticia. The others drove out of the lot, waiting to snap on their flashing yellow lights until they hit the end of the block at a peppy twenty miles per hour.

Alone in the lot, I circled the blue and white, two-seater enclosed cart. It had a mini covered bed, like a pickup. Which, according to the official *Parking Enforcement Agent Manual,* should contain at least three of the despised bright yellow boots. The metal grille and hubcaps were stamped Westland Utility Motors. Across the back of the bed in five-inch letters above the city worker license plate were the words "Interceptor–4."

Seriously, how wasted were the dudes at Westland to name a three-wheeled covered motorized trike the "Interceptor"?

It was a beautiful day. Even if I was dressed in black cargo pants and a knockoff blue police shirt littered with patches and a fat silver bar that read "Trainee" over my left breast.

Leticia Jackson was now nineteen minutes late.

Utilize wasted minutes to hone your edge. I straightened into military attention. Chest lifted and arched, stomach in, legs to-gether—straight but not locked. As close to Buddha as I could get, and concentrated on something pleasant. My date with Hank.

I'd asked him once what he did when he wasn't training.

"The occasional 1099 consult."

Ooo-kay. After that, I ran Hank through the system. For no other reason than my moon-eyed infatuation. And I'd been far more disappointed than Flynn to come up empty.

My stomach muscles quivered. I remained motionless.

I had tonight, tomorrow, and the next day to get my hair highlighted, get a spray tan, and figure out what to wear on Fri-day night.

Perspiration prickled on my forehead. Probably best not to start the day in a covered golf cart smelling like a New Age soap-and-water-conservationist hippie. I relaxed and looked at my watch. Again.

At twenty-six minutes past the hour, a four-foot, eleven-inch black woman walked onto the lot with an intricate updo metic-ulously pinned in and around her PEA visor. A solid one-eighty, she was apparently trying to make up in width what she lacked in height.

She sauntered across the asphalt, ticket machine swinging from her black cargo pants, radio bobbing against the poly-blend shirt.

I'd seen looser casing on a sausage. "Leticia?" I asked.

"You can call me Miz Jackson."

If I'm nasty? "Nice to meet you."

"Mmm-hmm." She eyed me up and down. "My, my, my. Well, ain't you just a bitty-bit of a thing."

The perverse prejudice of reverse weight-ism. I should've

been ready for it as the only one in the break room with a BMI still on the chart.

Ms. Jackson stepped in front of me and leaned into my personal space. The trick's effectiveness diminished somewhat by the eight inches I had on her. She pointed a decaled nail in my vague direction. "What's that on your head?"

"A TEB issue cap, ma'am."

She cocked a pierced brow. "What does it say on the cap?"

"PEA."

"And are you a parking enforcement agent at this time?"

"No, ma'am." *A safe bet her favorite movie is* Cool Hand Luke.

"Then I suggest you take it off, Trainee."

I did, stowing it in one of my cargo pockets, but not before I caught Leticia's combination smirk and head bob.

Hank's Law Number Eight: If they ask for the rope, give it to them.

I let it slide, waiting as she unlocked the door to the cart. Leticia got in. The Interceptor uttered a small wheeze in protest as she leaned across and unlocked the passenger side door. I climbed in.

It smelled like tater tots.

The Interceptor-4 wasn't a bad ride for a souped-up go-cart—plummy blue vinyl seats, padded armrests, and an AM/FM stereo. Leticia staked the entire console with a water bottle in one cup holder and her pink clutch in the other. She snapped on the radio and pressed the AM button. Mark Levin joined us in the tiny cart, delivering clarity to the great unwashed. Leticia cocked a brow and waited.

Unsure of what she was waiting for, I kept my mouth shut.

"Did you read the manual, Trainee?"

"Yes, ma'am."

"How 'bout the handbook?"

Pretty much memorized them both. You can't win the game if you don't know the rules. "Yes, ma'am."

She started the cart and we pulled up to the guardhouse.

An old Asian man with a dried apple face slid open his Plexiglas window, and leaned way out to get a good look at me.
"What we got today, Miss Jackson? Salt-N-Pepa?"

Leticia gave him a boob-jiggling shimmy. "More like Pepper
Shaker and Saltine."

Was that a cracker reference?

The old man gave a barking laugh of delight, closed his window, and opened the gate. We drove out onto the downtown
city streets of Chicago.

Leticia did not buckle up.

I tugged my seat belt. "Optional?"

She snorted. "Last time I checked, there weren't no seat belts
on a motorcycle."

"What's that?" I pointed at one of the dials in the dashboard.

"An LTI reader." Leticia slid on mirrored aviator sunglasses.

I waited a beat. Nothing. "What's that?"

"State-of-the-art G-force detector." Leaning forward, she
scanned the meters looking for red flags. "It tells you if you're
going too fast to make a turn."

"You're kidding."

"Hell, no. Dhu West docks two days' pay for every tip over.
Cheap-ass bastards."

I nodded in agreement, wondering how many times she'd
beached it.

"It's not like driving a car, you know."

"Didn't think so." I eyed the cart around me. "It's a trike."

"Mmm-hmmm." Leticia reached up and tapped her knuckles
on the metal ceiling. "But the City of Chi gives the carts a free
pass on account of they're covered. Truth is, they don't wanna
pay for us being Class B licensed drivers, as that would count as
a skill and raise our hourly wage."

She shook her head and flipped on the AC, cranking it up to
its highest setting. On one of the few decent days in the state of
Illinois.

"Don't the windows work?" I asked.

"I'm not messing my 'do." She double-parked in front of a

red Mercedes SL at Starbucks and turned on the flashers. "Now, go get me a white chocolate crème Frappuccino, whole milk, whipped cream, and a couple of them raspberry scones."

Seriously? Shanghaied for Starbucks?

"And I'd do that because?" I said, careful to keep my voice even and non-confrontational.

"On account of your being so grateful and shit at my impartation of my parking knowledge to you during this training session."

I pressed my lips together in a polite smile. Her sense of entitlement irked me, but not as much as knowing I'd fall in line because I needed her approval at week's end.

Ms. Jackson graciously cleared that up for me with combination brow cock and head bob. "You plan on sittin' here all day?" She flicked her fingers at me, shooing me out the door. "Out. I got tickets to write."

I wish I hadn't worn the "Loogie" into Starbucks.

I stood in line, getting snake hisses, about as popular as a sex offender at a PTA meeting.

Two suits in front of me decided to rethink their order. Idiot metros.

God, could this take any longer?

Under silent protest, I put in Leticia's order and started to pick up a sugar-free Red Bull from the open case. And stopped. A hit of caffeine was not going to help me keep my mouth shut under my supervisor's misanthropic tutelage.

I waited.

The green-aproned black-shirted manager's lip raised up in a sneer. "Venti white choc Frapp, whole and whipped for the parking Nazi."

"Excuse me," I held out my hand for the white-lidded cup. "But Himmler also had a couple of raspberry scones to go."

Green-apron black-shirt didn't like my smart reply and barked at green-apron white-shirt. Another minute and the scones appeared, in an overdesigned tan sack crafted from tree-saving eco-friendly paper of peace.

$14.78. God only knew what she'd want for lunch.

I went outside. Leticia had circled the block back to the red Mercedes, and was having a chest-to-chest with its driver, a skeletal white woman in a suit and four-inch stilettos.

"You dissin' my behind took this to a whole new level."

The woman's chin rose even higher, but not before I caught the glint of fear in her eyes. "Just give me the ticket."

"You didn't say please." Leticia raised the AutoCITE ticketing machine and typed a rapid staccato. "Well, looky here. Four outstanding parking tickets. Who'd a thought . . ."

Leticia pressed the radio bar on her lapel a couple of times. "Obi? Unit 13172. We're gonna need a boot removal crew and tow at Wabash and Madison."

"Roger that, Ms. Jackson," came Obi's scratchy reply.

"Oh no. You can't—" The woman stepped backwards, hand at her protruding collarbone. "You wouldn't dare!"

Without turning, Leticia said over her shoulder, "Get the boot, McGrane."

"Keys," I said. Leticia tossed them to me. I put her Starbucks in the cart and opened the white trunk.

"Ooooh! You—you horrible little troll! I have a client meeting in forty minutes. What am I supposed to do?"

Call a cab, lady.

I lugged out the Wolverine—a thirty-five-pound, bright orange spiked boot, closed and locked the trunk and hauled it over.

"Rear wheel away from the curb," Leticia said. I put the heavy metal vise near the tire. Now what? I looked at her and turned my palms up.

Leticia rolled her eyes and walked over muttering, "Goddamn know-nothing trainee." She squatted down next to me. "Keep her outta' my action while I'm putting this on." I stood up. Leticia handed me her ticket gun. "Print out the ticket and give it to her."

I stepped onto the curb and pushed Print. I handed the woman—cheeks scarlet with impotent fury—her ticket.

"And what exactly happens now?" she demanded.

Leticia grunted and looked up from the boot. "You march your fake-ass red-bottomed Christopher Les Boo-tins down to Impound, pay your tickets, tow, and impound fees, and get your car back."

"Oooh!" The woman genteelly stomped her high heel on the sidewalk. "I'll have your head on a pike!"

"Don't you mean plate?" Leticia said.

I gave a strangled cough of laughter. The woman made a move toward Leticia. I stepped between them. She stopped short and took her cellular from her purse.

"You—putting that . . . that *thing* on my car. What's your name?"

"Parking Enforcement Agent Leticia Jackson at your service."

The woman entered the information into her BlackBerry.

Finished with the boot, Leticia stood up and dusted her hands. "Y'all have a nice day now, you hear?"

Chapter 8

"So how many tickets are we required to write a day?"

Leticia looked over her sunglasses at me. "I thought you read the manual, Miss Know-Everything-Except-How-to-Put-on-a-Boot-Trainee."

"I did. There was only some vague reference about the Traffic Enforcement Bureau and how its agents exist only to enforce the parking laws of the City of Chicago."

"That's right. There's no such thing as a quota. Don't ask me again." Leticia gave a warning look. "And don't ask me for a booting lesson, neither."

For the next two hours and ten minutes, I watched Leticia write tickets. Waiting like a starved child for her chicken nuggets of wisdom.

"There are four kinds of public we deal with," she said, adjusting her visor in the reflection of a Corvette window she'd just ticketed. "Wishers, waiters, vandals, and haters."

Well, that sounds promising. "What's a wisher?"

"A wisher is a fish that knows their time's up on the meter, but they just stay where they are, wishing their watch was wrong, wishing they'd called in sick today, wishing they'd parked somewhere else, but not coming back. Not paying their due."

I see.

"Here we are. Fifth Street. Doctor's office central. Easy as taking pie from an anorexic." Leticia reached behind her for a black metal pole. She affixed a lump of chalk in the tip, retracted her side door open, and telescoped the pole. "One of the few zones left with coin ops."

We drove down the street, Leticia leaning halfway out of the Interceptor, bracing herself on the steering wheel, driving, and chalking tires. "Nobody reads the signs."

The LTI gauge must be hitting the red zone. I couldn't check. I was too busy trying to even the weight load, sitting off the edge of my seat, hanging my elbow and shoulder out the opposite window. "Why are you chalking tires at meters?"

"A Dhu West special. The Two Hour Limit Parking Zone." She grinned. "When the doctor runs late, and doctors always run late, all of these fish'll come running out to feed the meter. But you can't feed a meter with a two-hour limit. You need to move your damn car."

Three saps ineffectually refilled their meter box. We circled around the block.

"Mmm-hmmm. I love getting me a little Escalade." Leticia ran a ticket on an expired.

I waited a short distance away in front of an old Chrysler minivan. Faded blue with a little rust and a couple of dents. Two minutes left on its digital reader. I glanced inside. Three infant car seats and all the goop that accompanies a fleet of small children. But it was the half-empty carton of Luvs diapers that did it.

I edged a quarter out of my pocket and slid it into the slot.

"I know I din't just see you fill some fish's meter, McGrane."

Busted. "No, ma'am."

" 'Cause that would result in your instant termination," Leticia said.

"Yes, ma'am." I kicked the meter box lightly with the steel toe of my black work boot.

For lunch, Leticia had a Big Mac, large fries, and two apple pies on her own dime plus a large chocolate Yoo-hoo I bought her during another regulation fifteen-minute break at the 7-Eleven.

I ate a Protein Plus PowerBar. Leticia watched me in curious disgust, like I was a chimp eating my own poo.

Really? If I'd eaten what she had today, I'd be stretched out

*on the street in a food coma like an anaconda that'd gotten
ahold of a small deer.*

We pulled up in front of a large brown building. "Game
time," Leticia said.

Ten stories of office and apartments. Old style with iron-
trimmed windows. Pricey. Full of "save the history" dwellers
who told everyone how great it was to live within walking distance of downtown, never letting on about the lack of parking
and closet space or the homeless guys pissing in their doorway.

Leticia stopped in front of the parking meter pay box. The
third space on the display was blinking. "You wanna write a
ticket?" She held out her AutoCITE machine.

Finally.

Time to figure out how to make my way on the program. I
got out and went to the offender. A MINI Cooper with a Union
Jack on the roof.

I tried to type in the license plate. It didn't work. I hit the
Reset button. It asked for operator ID. I went back to the cart.

Leticia leaned across and rolled down the passenger-side window of the Interceptor. "What's the problem?"

"I need your operator ID."

"Give it here."

I handed Leticia the machine. She entered her code and
passed it back. I typed in the license of the MINI Cooper, then
went to the meter box to enter the ID.

A heavy wet weight rained down on the top on my head.

I staggered backwards. Gasping and spluttering and trying to
catch my breath, I smeared viscous liquid from my eyes.

It was pink. Thick and sticky. An old strawberry milk shake.

A very old one.

Wolf whistles and cheers rang out. I spun and looked up at
the building, just in time to see a couple of black-trimmed windows on either the seventh or eighth floor swing shut.

Inside the protective cover of the Interceptor, Leticia trembled
and shook. Laughing so hard no sound came out. Her eyes were
squinched together, tears streaming down her cheeks. "Oh!
Oh." She clutched her sides.

I wiped a clotted curd off my cheek and walked to the cart. I grabbed the door handle.

It was locked.

I took a deep breath and gagged from the stink of sour strawberry milk. "This isn't funny, Leticia." I jerked on the handle.

"Whoo-eee!" Leticia grinned and fanned her hand in front of her face. "Girl, you are rank!"

"Yeah. I get that." I knew the answer, but I asked anyway. "This ever happen before?"

"Only the second Tuesday of every month," Leticia gasped, wiping her eyes. "For the past three years. Haven't been able to catch them yet."

"Open up."

"You're outta your mind if you think I'm letting you in my fine ride."

I gritted my teeth. "What do you suggest? I trot alongside you for the rest of the shift?"

"Nah. This is what we refer to as an 'incident'. You go on back to the lot, write up a report, and I'll sign it. You'll get your full eight hours."

Sweet. Only fifteen blocks to walk, smelling as bad as a cartoon character with the wavy lines coming off me.

I jogged back to the lot and swiped my sticky key card.

There was no shower in the PEA locker room. Not that I had any clothes to change into anyway. I took off the Loogie and my shirt. The strawberry stink had sunk into my sports bra and pants. I cleaned up as best I could at the sink, put the smelly blue poly back on, and punched out.

I figured I could strip down at my car. But first, I walked the five blocks back to Dispatch.

"Hey, Obi-Wan."

He took a sudden interest in rolling a chewed-up yellow pencil across the counter. "Hi, Maisie."

"Thanks for the tip about the hat. At least I didn't have to request another one."

"Even Yoda is powerless against Miz Jackson," he said, unable to make eye contact.

I took pity on him. "I'm not mad. I mean, I'm mad at the jack-hole that did it, but it's not like you could have stepped in."

Except you could have.

He peeked up at me.

I let him off the hook. "It's a rookie thing—right?"

"Yeah. That's it. Screwing with the new kid."

I smoothed my gluey hair behind my ear. "Can I ask you something?"

"Of course. I'm always here for you."

Only slightly creepy. "What's the deal with quotas?"

Obi's brow furrowed. "What did Ms. Jackson say?"

"There aren't any," I said.

"And she's correct."

"But someone as sage and wise as you would be aware that . . ."

He smiled. "The same traffic patterns combined with years of standardized data are accurate enough for Dhu West to estimate the overall quantity of offenders per given week. Which means—"

"They have a pretty good idea of exactly how many tickets I should be writing a day."

Obi nodded and put a finger across his lips.

A conversation for another day. "Um . . . Do you think maybe I could borrow a boot? To get the hang of it?"

"I'm on early tomorrow. I start at five thirty." Obi fingered the sparse hairs on his chin. "I could show you the basics at six o'clock."

"Oh-six-hundred it is."

I left Dispatch and started jogging as soon as I hit the sidewalk. I arrived at my Honda, which thankfully did not have a bright orange thirty-dollar ticket on it, and took off my shirt. My sports bra was soaked and pink, but the stink eased a little. I put the reflective vest and shirt inside a plastic grocery bag I found in the glove box and tossed them in the trunk. My pants were sticky. My hair stunk. And I was a good half hour from home.

But only eight minutes from Joe's Gym.

"Hey, Joe."

He bared his teeth showing a mouthful of Cheez-Its at my sports-bra top. Then the stench hit him and he grunted, wrinkling up his nose.

"Hear anything from Hank?" I said.

"Nuh." Joe turned his head trying to get away from me. "You smell."

I hit the locker room, took a shower and scrubbed off the slime, but I couldn't rinse away the little feeling of freak that a person I never met dumped a rotten milk shake on my head.

Working out didn't make it go away, but it got my dander up enough to want to get even. No way a little curdled milk was going to keep me from getting back to the Academy.

I finished with the speed rope, cleaned up again, pulled on sweatpants and a Joe's Gym T-shirt, and dragged my overstuffed gym bag to the car.

I caught a look at myself in the rearview at a stoplight. By Friday, the milk shake story would definitely be funny.

And there was nothing I liked better than making Hank laugh.

Chapter 9

The gooey pink milk shake–covered uniform went into the washing machine with a double dose of Tide. A sharp pain zinged the middle of my forehead. I still had to talk to Cash about Jennifer. And the Gala.

Hoping to soften him up with ice cream, I went to the kitchen, stopping short as I heard Flynn's voice. "N-A-W-I-S-K-O. Obits, memorial services, anything you see in the papers."

"Yes. I will do," answered Thierry, our dapper cook/housekeeper.

I came around the corner. "Don't let Da find out." I leaned against the bar next to Flynn. "Hi, guys."

"'Allo, Maisie." Thierry set the Post-it with Flynn's request aside and returned to the box lunches he was making for my parents and brothers.

Flynn sat back on the stool. "How goes the job, Snap?"

Aren't we sweet? "Sunshine and lollipops. What do you think?"

My brother rubbed the back of his neck. "Sorry. It's been a rough couple of days."

"Tell me about it, Kettle." I gave him a playful shove. "I'd like to help, if you'd let me."

"Thing is, Pot—" Flynn stood up. "It's hard to hire you as a junior officer, when you're dating a criminal."

He left the room.

"Who is this criminal?" Thierry shot me a sideways look. "What is he like?"

"Hank." I smiled and thought about our housekeeper's obsession with *Game of Thrones*. "He's a younger, darker Nikolaj Coster-Waldau."

"*Dieu,* a man. No wonder Flynn dislikes him so. When do I meet this Hank?"

"He's taking me out on Friday."

"Typical." He lifted a shoulder in a Gallic shrug. "Why not a day of my work?"

"Because"—I rounded the counter to the fridge and opened the freezer—"I don't want you to steal him."

"Bah. No cardboard tonight. Come, I make you something."

"Actually, I was thinking of ice cream for Cash."

"Sit," Thierry ordered. "I make you a bribe worthy of consideration."

"That bad?"

"Cash, he looks like the thunder." He shook his head and laughed. "Is no good for you, Maisie."

I carried the silver tray with two rectangular plates of tropical banana splits up to my brother's room. Empty. But his Xbox was on pause.

Twenty-to-one, he was sitting in my room, in the dark, waiting to pull a gangster moment and turn on the light as soon as I entered. I nudged the door open with my foot.

Cash flipped on the light. He was sitting in one of the taupe microfiber armchairs nestled in the bay window. I set the tray on the coffee table, put a spoon on the ice cream plate and offered it to him. He ignored me, removed a folded-up piece of paper from his shirt pocket, and tossed it across the table.

"What's that?"

"Our contract."

I held out the ice cream again. "You want some, or do I get both?"

Cash took the sundae and started eating.

I sat down and unfolded the paper.

*   *   *

> *I, Maisie Lee McGrane, do solemnly swear*
> *to fulfill the following duties until so directed*
> *by my generous brother Cash McGrane.*
>   *1) Be Cash's thrall.*

He and his best pal and partner, Koji, had been worshiping at the *Lord of the Rings* altar again. There was no number two. "Nice," I said.

Cash flipped his dark hair off his forehead. "Not as nice as the four-page text I got from Jennifer talking about what she's wearing to the Gala. Jaysus." He tossed me a pen. "Sign it."

I did. He shoved another enormous bite in his mouth.

How can he not get a brain freeze?

"Apparently I'm also taking Jennifer to some idiotic art house movie tomorrow night." Cash pulled out his car keys and tossed them on the table. "You've got a busy night ahead of you. Detailing my car." He scraped the rest of the ice cream off the plate and licked the spoon.

I felt a twinge of guilt. Real guilt. The sick, twisty kind in the bottom of my belly. "You bet. I'm sorry about this. I just . . ."

"Yeah. I know." Cash set his empty plate on the tray. He picked up mine, took a bite, and said around a mouthful of mango and banana, "I'm a prince of a guy."

Wednesday morning I hit Dispatch at the crack of dawn.

"Is it just me or did you time travel to Florida for a vacation?" Obi said, maneuvering his *Star Wars* wheelchair around the counter.

It took me a minute to catch his reference to my spray tan. "Cost me thirty bucks this morning."

"You're the first PEA I've ever met with a fake tan."

"Thank the gods I have one. Otherwise you'd be blinded by my pure and unholy whiteness."

He gave a thin, braying laugh and motioned me back. I followed him up the handicap ramp and out the back door of the Dispatch office.

"I had one of the guys leave a boot out back on this fine

Wednesday morning." Obi wheeled over to an apple-red Toyota Prius with tinted windows and a giant white X-wing decal on the rear window. The license plate read "RED LDER."

"Nice ride," I said.

"You're telling me. The ladies love it."

Yeah, all the ones named Princess Leia.

In front of the Prius sat a bright yellow boot. "How come this one doesn't have the spikes?" I asked.

"The Wolverine's only for show. Truth is, you'll wreck your car just as fast trying to drive with any boot on, spiked or not." Obi took a laser pointer from one of his black wheelchair saddlebags and twirled it between his fingers.

"What's that for?"

"You didn't think I was going to get down there with you, did you?"

For the next fifteen minutes, Obi gave me an in-depth lesson with the boot, explaining the parts and how to affix it.

"Okay," I said. "I'm ready. Let's give it a whirl."

"Do or not do. There is no whirl."

I set the boot up next to the rear tire and affixed the large yellow disk to the hubcap. "Thanks, Obi. I hate looking stupid in front of Leticia," I said, tightening the back bolt with the key.

"It won't only be Miz Jackson you look stupid in front of if you don't secure the hubcap plate. A fish swimming away with a boot is almost as bad as losing your AutoCITE."

"Does that ever happen?" I said. "The AutoCITE?"

"About as often as a cop loses his gun. And when it does, it always makes the news." He adjusted his glasses. "Now, young friend. Tell me all that you have learned about the power of the boot."

"Any car with two or more tickets one day past due can be booted. The average PEA boots nine vehicles a week. After affixing boot to said vehicle, I radio Dispatch for boot removal crew and tow."

"You have learned well, young Jedi."

"Do you need to get back in?" I asked. "I wouldn't mind running a couple of speed tests."

Obi took an iPad from his saddlebag. "Check it. The coolest stopwatch app ever."

Five times I dragged the boot from the curb and affixed it to the tire, then took it off and put it back.

"The fourth was your fastest at nineteen seconds. Man, you got some pipes on you." Obi smiled shyly. "Who'd you get the tan for, Maisie? Hot date?"

"A little personal, don't you think?"

Obi's face flushed. "I wasn't—"

"I'm just kidding." I wiped my forehead on the sleeve of my hoodie. "His name's Hank. He finally asked me out, after I flashed him the googley heart-eyes for over a year."

Obi's face wrinkled in disbelief. "What's wrong with him?"

"Not a single thing." I sighed.

"Yeah, right."

We went back into Dispatch, with me lugging the thirty-five-pound boot.

I got over to the PEA building, changed, and entered the break room to a warm reception of zero eye contact and step around. I took a hard yellow plastic chair in the corner and listened to the chatter. Working for the Traffic Enforcement Bureau seemed to rate lower in job satisfaction than the lost luggage department of any major airline.

The milk shake incident was starting to feel like a warm and playful welcome.

I only waited ten minutes at car 13172 before Leticia zipped us off to Dunkin' Donuts. Sans Loogie, I placed her order for a blueberry waffle and maple sausage sandwich, hash browns, chicken biscuit, and a large vanilla bean Coolatta and thanked my lucky stars training only lasted a week. She was waiting for me in the passenger seat. "You drive."

Now we're talking. I got in and started it up. "Where to?"

"Michigan Avenue." Expensive retail shops with an obscene lack of parking and people who weren't afraid to get in your face.

I wonder how long it takes before confrontation starts to be fun.

Leticia started on the chicken biscuit. "You writin' a movie or something?"

"Huh?"

"That crap you left in my box this morning."

My one-and-a-quarter-page incident report?

"All typed up and shit." She shook her head. "What you trying to do? Mess everything up for everybody?" She grunted. "Redo it. One paragraph. Handwritten."

"Yes, ma'am."

"Damn straight, yes, ma'am," she muttered and took a slurp of Coolatta.

Ticketing a yellow Porsche 911 double-parked in front of the Prada store, I heard the two most embarrassing words in the world.

"Hi, honey!"

I looked up. My mom waved at me from inside her custom-painted "British racing green" Jaguar XJ. She was in a yellow No Loading Zone.

Please. Not now. "Hi, Mom," I mouthed and gave her the "move along" wave. She rolled her eyes and turned on her hazard lights.

Leticia pulled in behind her, got out of the cart, and stepped in between us. "What do we have here? You wanting to run in and pick up something?"

"Oh no. I just want to say hi to my daughter."

"You can't park here. Or wait here. It's a No Loading Zone," Leticia said.

"I know, but—"

"Look, I'm no hater," Leticia said. "The last thing I wanna do is write a ticket on a sister in a fine ride, but you can't wait here for your girl."

"But she's right behind you."

Leticia turned. Scanning, I'm sure for someone . . . tanner. I gave a small wave.

"No shit! That's your momma, McGrane?"

"I most certainly am," Mom said.

Leticia went around to the driver's-side window and held out her hand. "Leticia Jackson, parking enforcement agent supervisor."

They shook hands. "July Pruitt McGrane, nice to meet you."

I dragged a hand over my face. Eventually, after several cell phone pictures with Leticia—whom my mother promised she'd e-mail copies—Mom left.

Well, that was almost as fun as performing my own appendectomy.

Leticia gave me the once-over. "I know you be wearing a fake tan. So tell me. 'Xactly how white is your daddy?"

Chapter 10

Thursday. Day three, and I was back in the passenger's seat. As a supervisor, Leticia spot-drove everyone's route. Today it was the Fulton River District warehouses at the far edge of Chicago's downtown, Dennis Miller filling in for Jesus as our copilot.

"Hold up," I said. A silver RX Hybrid Lexus sport sedan was parked in a No Standing, No Loading Zone in front of a hydrant. A triple with the fish still in it. I grabbed the AutoCITE from the center console.

"Put the gun down, McGrane. Ain't nothing to see here." Leticia's red-glossed lips lifted in contempt. "That's a Dhu West Special. A member of the Lexus League."

I replaced the gun in the console. "I don't get it."

"Our Mayor Coles slapped on a personal privilege when he sold off the Parking Enforcement Union to the Saudis. Silver and black hybrid Lexuses get unhassled, unrestricted, unticketed parking. All his staffers drive 'em."

Yeah, right. "No way ordinary street cops are giving those cars a free ride."

She gave me a head snap of irritation. "I let you enter that plate into the gun, it'll read 'do not ticket.' This is Chi-town. We ain't had a Republican mayor since 'Big Bill Thompson' in 1931. So what's that tell you?"

I flashed my palms, at a total loss.

"It tells you to get your lily-white onion out of the damn cart and make that freeloader move hisself to a legitimate parking spot."

I approached the car slowly, the milk shake incident lingering in the corner of my mind, although Leticia's disgust was real enough.

The driver was slumped low down in the seat, napping, Sox cap low on his face. I stepped around a large oil spot that was still live enough to leave a partial shoe print and rapped on the window. Nothing. The guy didn't even flinch.

Uh-oh.

I knocked again, then leaned over the side mirror to peer through the windshield. I jerked backwards in surprise, not fear. I'd been surrounded by crime scene photos my entire life. Full color and grotesque.

The driver had two bullet holes in the chest of his very bloody white dress shirt. A brown-red syrupy puddle pooled in his lap. His face looked as if it had been carved from gray wax and his eyes were cloudy marbles.

Poor bastard.

Moving in as close as possible without touching the car, I examined the victim. White, early thirties, slim, light brown hair. The top two buttons of his shirt were undone. Folded neatly on the seat next to him were a yellow plaid necktie and a lanyard with his Mayoral Staffer ID. His name was Thorne Clark.

My first McGrane table club stiff and I didn't even own the case.

I had a BS in criminal justice, but it was the lifetime of listening and looking at my parents and brothers' cases that had my brain processing and synthesizing details as easily as if I'd been at a thousand crime scenes.

The amount of blood in his lap was unusual. When a person dies, the heart stops pumping. The holes in Mr. Clark had done enough damage to immobilize him while he bled out. *Hollow point?*

I circled the car and looked in from the rear window. The camel leather back of the driver's seat was intact. Hollow points would have ended up in the backseat or even the trunk.

Wadcutters.

Revolver rounds made for paper target practice. When used on live targets, the bullets made nice holes going in and didn't come out.

Holy cat. I sprinted back to the cart. "Call Dispatch. The guy's been murdered."

"Get in the cart, McGrane." Leticia put the Interceptor in gear. "Not our bidness."

"You're kidding, right?"

She swiveled to face me head-on. "Do you have any idea what kind of paperwork you have to fill out on a stiff? Supervisors have to take a three-day PTSD half-pay leave for counseling." She wagged a blinged-out nail at me. "Nuh-uh."

"It's a crime scene."

"You wanna be a Girl Scout? Get your own ride home." Leticia pressed a button in the console. The passenger window slid closed and away she went.

It took me half a minute to fumble my iPhone out of my cargo pocket. I thought I was calm but the adrenaline was kicking in, my fine motor skills decreasing.

Stay chilly.

"Call Flynn," I voice-dialed.

"What's up, Snap?" His voice was short, still ticked off about the bus driver case.

"I got a body for you and Rory."

"What?"

My voice went all squeaky. "I think I'm standing in front of a contract hit on a mayoral staffer in the warehouse district. Do you want it or should I call it in?"

"Are you safe? Secure enough on your own to wait?"

"Yeah."

"Is he fresh?"

"Not too. At least I don't think so."

"Text me your GPS co-ords. We'll be there in ten. You know the drill."

*   *   *

My brothers arrived like rock stars in an unmarked black Dodge Charger. I walked over to their car and waited as Rory called it in on the regular channels, watching as they examined and video-recorded the scene with their phones.

Time ticked by slower than a one-legged dog on tranquilizers, as I figured I'd pretty much cracked it and couldn't wait to spill.

"Nice find, Snap." Flynn came over wearing a huge grin. "This one's a peach."

All at once, the scene was deluged in a flash flood of evidence techs, beat cops, the ME crew, impound tow truck, and the ever-present public notification team.

"About the scene—" I started.

Feeling magnanimous, Flynn sat down on the hood of the car, all encouragement. "Lay it out for me."

"Did you see the print at the edge of the oil?"

He nodded, with barely a hint of superiority. Rory came over to listen as he supervised the activity surrounding the Lexus.

"It's a Haix boot. Most cops wear Haix boots. I'm thinking the perp—either someone impersonating a cop or even a cop—gets the vic to pull over and roll his window down, pops him twice in the chest with a wadcutter-loaded revolver. After, the perp opens the door, closes the window, and turns off the car."

"Expelled from the Academy and your first drop is a dirty cop." Flynn folded his arms across his chest. "Sweet."

"What's your read?" I said, throwing down the gauntlet.

His hand came up. "Aside from the fact that the oil, as well as the print, may have been here for days, you're wearing Haix boots. So do paramedics, firemen, and security guards, to name a few."

"Tech!" Rory snapped his fingers at a woman in white coveralls.

The evidence tech jogged over. "Yes sir?"

Rory pointed at my feet. "Bag her boots."

"Yes sir." She withdrew a permanent marker and a couple of large plastic bags from one of the pockets in her coveralls.

"No. No way," I said, backing up. "You're kidding, right?"

Rory shook his head, straight-faced.

The tech scribbled across the labels while I struggled to undo my boots. "But there's no oil on these." I stepped out of them, gingerly planting my pure white athletic-socked feet on the grimy asphalt. "Besides, my boots have a crosshatched toe tread. And that print is way too big to be mine."

Flynn's mouth contorted as he tried to keep a straight face. "SOP, Snap."

"Yeah." Rory snorted with laugher. "Watch your socks, kid."

The tech opened each bag for me to drop my work boots into, closed them, and trotted off with the bags to the evidence van.

"Is this you guys thanking me for calling you instead of calling it in?" Heat burned up my throat. "Mom's gonna love this."

"Jaysus," Rory said. "Still can't take a joke, can yeh?" He walked away and started talking to a uniform who'd just finished cordoning off the area.

"Tech!" Flynn shouted. The woman turned around. "Bring her some booties." He put a hand on my shoulder. "Eighty-twenty you're right about the wadcutters."

Even though he'd taken my shoes, I couldn't help the smile. "Can I stay and watch you guys work the scene?"

The uniform came over. "Excuse me, miss? Detective Mc-Grane asked me to give you a ride home."

Flynn shook his head. "Scram. I'll fill you in at dinner."

The scent of sugar and eggs and flour filled the early afternoon air. Thierry was at the stove, whisking Genoise cake batter over a bain-marie. Petite madeleines. He took the batter off the water bath and folded it into a pastry bag.

"Hi, Thierry." I slumped on the stool and watched him layer in row after row of tiny scallop-shaped pastries. "Pistachio?"

"*Oui.*"

Da's favorite. A manila folder lay on the counter. I flipped it open, idly. Inside were obituaries from the *Sun Times* and the *Tribune*.

Keith Nawisko, Chicago bus driver and
officer of the Amalgamated Transit Union

Local #56, died Friday after a brutal attack near N. Milwaukee Blvd.

"I find for Flynn." Thierry clicked his tongue against his teeth.
The buzzer dinged. He removed a batch from the oven and
flipped the tiny cakes nimbly from the pan onto the cooling rack.
"Is sad, no?"

"Yeah." There wasn't any funeral or wake information listed
on the obit. The BOC probably hadn't released the body yet.
Thierry offered a madeleine from across the counter. I bit into
the scalloped cake and started for the office. "Perfection."

*Hmmm. Perhaps a complimentary background report on
Keith Nawisko would release my Haix boots from the evidence
locker.*

"*Attends,* Maisie." Thierry removed a folded piece of paper
from his apron and held it up. "From Cash."

I eyed it dubiously. "What is it?"

"A list of the chores?"

Oh brother.

It took me an hour and a half to finish Cash's thrall duty. I
cleaned his room, his bathroom, paid his bills online, put away
his laundry, made his Saturday morning tee time, and e-mailed
the rest of his foursome with the requisite sign-off: *Please e-mail
your answer to Maisie McGrane, personal secretary to Mr. Cash
McGrane.*

Finally, I set up in the workstation next to Mom's office and
logged on to what the McGranes called the family system. Since
Mom, Da, and all my brothers spent their entire lives working
with and around unpleasant and dangerous people, we sub-
scribed to several stealthy, expensive, and not entirely legitimate
information brokers.

After pulling and printing the hundred pages the system had
to offer, I went through Amalgamated Transit's event pages, vision blurring as I skimmed through the names in the photos
searching for Nawisko. *Johnson, Kolarov, Andersen, Boyko,
Peterson, Lindgren, Verba* . . . A prime requisite to hold transit

union office seemed to be possession of a Slavic or Scandinavian surname.

The printer kicked into high gear as I queued up pictures of Nawisko, screen pulls of his Facebook account, the union's org chart, and summary backgrounds on all the Local #56 board members. I added them to Nawisko's obit and system reports. By the time I'd finished, the file was an inch thick.

Time to work my vic. Mayoral staffer Thorne Clark. I tracked down his SSN and loaded it into Integral Search. A set of gear icons began spinning on the monitor.

"What are you doing?" Flynn asked from the doorway.

"Investigating. You put Thierry on obituary duty, so I thought I'd help out. Background and financials on Nawisko." I waved the manila folder. "Don't worry, I won't tell Da."

"Maisie—" His voice was tired and loaded with warning.

"Did you know bus drivers make $28.64 an hour? Which is nothing compared to how much Nawisko pulled down as an officer of the Local #56."

Flynn came over and hiked a hip onto the desk. He ran a hand over his eyes and sighed. "Why are you a meter maid?"

I cleared my throat and tried not to wince. "To prove I don't have a 'pathological need to be liked' and that I'm not 'too thin-skinned to deal with a hostile public' so I can reapply for reinstatement to the Academy."

"So, to combat the psych review you took the most vile job you could find?"

"Yeah."

His lips curled in a rueful smile. "That just might work." He picked up my research and flipped through it. "This is good, Snap. Real good." He closed the folder and tapped it against his palm. "Been at it long?"

"Couple hours."

"You could do this professionally."

"I'm no desk monkey."

"Aren't you?" He reached over and clicked the mouse. The monitor woke up with Integral Search's series of mini-windows showing Thorne Clark's social networking for the past thirty days. He scrolled through some of Clark's Facebook musings and said absently, "Your boots are in the mudroom."

"Thanks."

"For what it's worth, I think you got a raw deal."

Me too. A tear bubble expanded in my throat.

"How'd you like to be an unofficial consultant?" Flynn held up the folder. "You pull and print everything and anything. I can't shake the feeling these vics are connected."

He wasn't throwing me a bone—this was an entire skeleton. "Really?"

"In return, I'll show you the case jackets, walk through how I'm working them, and maybe write a letter for your reinstatement file."

I jumped up and hugged him. "You're the best brother ever!"

"Just make sure you say that in front of the rest of them."

Chapter 11

The logical detachment I had when I found the murdered Mr. Clark didn't make it all the way to my subconscious. I shot up in bed seeing blood and bullet holes at 4 a.m. With no hope of going back to sleep, I went to Joe's to clear my head.

I grabbed a speed rope, warming up with side swings and singles. Today was going to be a great day. My last training day with Leticia. And in fifteen hours and twenty-five minutes I was going out. With Hank.

My life rocks!

I switched to double-unders, thinking about how I'd talk the scene with Hank. Maybe he'd help me surprise Flynn even more. Finishing with crisscrosses, I chanted in time as the rope snapped on the gym floor.

"Game on. Game on. Game on . . ."

Friday was bagel breakfast day for Leticia. I sat in the Interceptor watching her eat while getting lectured.

"I punched your insubordinate ass's time card out yesterday and I don't do that shit for nobody." She wiped her mouth on a Bruegger's napkin. "That was a one-timer."

"Thank you, ma'am."

"Still. You pretty frosty, for a rook." She flipped on the radio, dialed in AM 560, and swallowed the last bite of her second everything-bagel with lox and cream cheese. "I love me some Prager on a Friday. Especially that goddamn *Happiness Hour*."

She shot me a sideways look. "You know who I'm talking about?"

"Yeah. Sure," I said. "Dennis Prager. Nice voice. Logical."

"And Jewish."

"Are you?" I asked, "Jewish, I mean?"

"No." She looked at me like I was crazy. "But I sure do appreciate them on a Friday."

Ooo-kay. I tucked my hair behind my ear and looked out the window. "Where are we going?"

"It's a surprise," she said happily, and cranked the radio even louder. We turned onto a residential street, quiet except for the corner where it looked like a drunken car dealer had opened shop. Cars were parked helter-skelter—on the sidewalks, hanging out of driveways, double- and triple-parked, blocking hydrants. No residential stickers were the least of it.

"Oh yeah, baby." Leticia gave a high-pitched girlish giggle. "I hope you're ready to boot, McGrane, 'cause we're carrying eight in the caboose and I'm sure as hell not bringing 'em back."

Leticia parked the cart, tossed me the trunk keys, and got out. Fingers flashing on the AutoCITE before I'd unbuckled my seat belt.

"Boot." She pointed at a '79 Monte Carlo, and continued down the sidewalk ticketing with a speed and quickness that was truly a sight to behold. "Boot here," she said and slid an orange violation beneath the windshield wiper of an Isuzu Rodeo.

I had hit my stride by the fourth boot, barely registering annoyance at unlocking the trunk, pulling the boot, locking the trunk and lugging the boot down the block. Leticia's enthusiasm was as contagious as a preschooler with the flu.

"Heavy hitter, $750 in unpaids." Leticia tipped her head at a maroon Oldsmobile.

I lugged the boot down the curb, walking up into a yard to boot the car on the sidewalk.

Lazy idiots. Parking on a city sidewalk instead of walking a half block.

"Stop right there, you motherfucking meter bitch!" shrieked

a black man, late thirties, five-eleven, two-forty, run-walking toward Leticia.

She marched out to meet him in the street. "Stay on the boot, McGrane."

Hank's Law Number Nine: Confidence is not competence.

I dropped the boot on the ground and stood up, trunk keys laced through my fingers.

Leticia got right up in his face, or more accurately, chest. "You got a problem, *sir?*"

"Yeah. *You,* woman!"

"Is that right? Well, why don't you tell me all about it, Marcus. You Ahmad-Rashad-Muhammad-Ali-wannabe."

"You mock me? Mock Allah?" The man raised his fist. "Infidel bitch."

Leticia gave an incendiary head bob. "Go ahead. If you think you're man enough."

I hit the radio on my vest. "Dispatch, this is car one-three-one-seven-two."

Two men burst out of the apartment building and down the steps. Which, I realized, was not an apartment building. According to the small handwritten cardboard sign Scotch-taped to the cracked window, it was the Brothers of Allah Prayer Center.

A dozen more men came out of the building. A few in robes, most in jeans and various designer logo'd T-shirts. Cursing and gesturing, they moved toward Leticia and Marcus.

Jaysus, Mary, and Joseph.

"Dispatch?" I said again. "This is car one-three-one—"

My radio squawked. "Maisie," Obi said, "—on—way—"

"Say again, Dispatch." I started toward Leticia.

Leticia caught my movement out of the corner of her eye. "Affix the damn boot, McGrane," she called over her shoulder.

"The cops," Obi said, amid the static, "there soon."

The first two men grabbed Marcus and dragged him—still yelling at Leticia—back to the building. The rest of the crowd, arguing and swearing, collected around Leticia. She pushed her way through the mob and sashayed past me like Naomi on the catwalk, punching license numbers on her AutoCITE, ticketing.

I squatted down and clamped on the hub plate.

A litter of boys ranging in age from six to twelve followed her, pulling tickets off the cars, ripping them to shreds, spitting on them. Leticia ignored them and placed another ticket.

The men were following at a distance, complaining. With an extreme gesture, she pointed a fuchsia, blinged-out nail at a silver Honda Civic. "Boot it."

No worries, then. Who cares about a couple dozen rabid inner city guys screaming religious persecution?

I followed Leticia's order. Went back to the cart, unlocked the trunk, pulled another boot, locked the trunk, and jogged after her.

Three of the men broke off from the mob following Leticia and came toward me, threatening but keeping their distance.

I ignored them and dropped the boot at the rear wheel of the Civic. Sweat dripped off my forehead, staining the sidewalk. I fumbled with the boot, getting nervy watching Leticia while also trying to watch my back.

Marcus—swearing like a guy from a Tarantino movie—got away from the men restraining him and charged toward Leticia.

Leticia jammed a ticket on the windshield of a Chrysler LeBaron, and spun back to face Marcus, arms extended, chest thrust out, like one of the girls on *The Price Is Right*, loving it. "I'm sorry, *sir*. I don't believe I heard that last racist remark."

"I said," Marcus shouted, "get that skinny-ass cracker away from these cars."

"What do you think, McGrane?" Leticia called out to me. "You wanna knock off early, maybe go get us a couple of crispy bacon sandwiches and beers and wait for these sorry-ass brothers to learn how to read and quit parking on the sidewalk?"

I finished tightening the hubcap plate and held two fingers against my thigh. Two boots left.

Leticia nodded.

I got to my feet and turned to retrieve another boot. Three men blocked my way, faces bent with contempt. I widened my stance, transferred my weight to the balls of my feet, keys in one hand, lug wrench in the other.

Insanity.

I could hear Hank's voice in my head. *"The only standard of a fighter is his fight. Not just the fights he picks, but the fights that pick him."*

With my hand holding the lug wrench, I hit the radio on my vest. "Dispatch, boot removal crew and tow—"

The smallest of the three ripped the radio from my fingers, tearing my vest. He threw it on the ground.

A lifetime of training kicked in. I dropped the lug wrench, drove my forearm into his throat, and stomped on the instep of his foot. He fell forward and I grabbed his arm, jerking it up hard behind his back, forcing him to kiss the hood of the Civic as I kicked his legs apart.

"Oh, you done it now!" Leticia shouted in jubilation. "You crazy sons of . . . Assaulting a PEA is a felony!"

"This is fucking ethnic profiling," Marcus said. "Allah will stomp your fat ass, Leticia."

Leticia laughed. "Ain't you just a walking TV commercial to convert?"

I had my assailant pinned to the hood and two surprised and pissed-off guys behind me. *Cripes. Now what, Lizard Brain?*

The blurp of a police siren sounded.

Thank God.

"Is there a problem here, *Miss* McGrane?"

Of all the losers to walk into my gin joint . . .

"Last time I checked," Tommy Narkinney said in my ear, "meter maids don't have the authority to manhandle and appre- hend private citizens."

He slapped his hand on the hood of the Civic next to the man's head I had pinned. "Especially Academy washouts. Let him up."

I did.

My assailant retreated to the safety of his two pals.

Narkinney glanced over at his partner, a chunky forty-something white male in the thick of it with Leticia, Marcus, and a crowd of angry men, and snorted. "Jesus, can't you do anything without putting on a show?"

I pointed at the man. "He assaulted me. Tore my radio off and broke it."

"Yeah?" Tommy laced his fingers together and flexed. " 'Cause from where I sit, it looks like you're the one doing the assaulting."

Jerk. "I'm filing, Nark. There ought to be plenty of paperwork for a Class D."

"Not today, you're not," Narkinney said.

Emboldened, my assailant pointed at me. "That—that woman did not even ask us to move our cars!"

Narkinney fake-coughed over his chuckle.

"It is Friday prayer. A holy time. They do this to us because we are Muslim!"

"No member of any religion is immune to the traffic laws of Chicago," I said. "You need more parking, file for a permit."

"Hey, McGrane," Leticia shouted at me, grinning. "The boys in blue are gonna stay here while we finish. Get me a boot."

I pointed at my broken radio on the sidewalk. One of the three men had crushed it. "And who's gonna pay for that?" I said to Narkinney.

"It's not like you can't afford it." He turned to the men. "Other side of the street or in the building. Now."

They scuttled away.

"You better get back to work." Narkinney grinned. "Peterson and I ain't gonna hang around all day."

I booted two more cars. A Kia and a Chevy. Getting the business from Tommy Narkinney the entire time, while Leticia flirted shamelessly with Peterson as she ticketed, dawdling like a fat man at an all-you-can-eat buffet.

The boot removal crew and tow trucks showed up. Finally.

I walked back to the cart with Leticia. "Now this is what I call a damn fine Friday," she said.

The squad car pulled up as we were getting back in the cart. Narkinney hung out the passenger window. "Call me anytime you need your meter filled, McGrane." Laughing, they drove away.

Leticia started the cart and we drove off. An unholy excitement still sparked in her eyes. "I used to date that broke-ass son of a whore until he impregnated my sister. My baby sister."

"And so you do this?"

"Every third Friday the good Lord gives me." She grinned. "Makes life worth living. Asshole Marcus don't pay Sharelle a dime of child support. So a'course she and Shanice are living with me."

Putting us at risk over a grudge. Jaysus.

"Leticia, that was a powder keg back there."

"Bullshit. Do you know Marcus the Molester only converted just so's he could have his new baby mama—she only fifteen— wrapped up like a wooly burrito, cooking and cleaning and signing her checks over and not having any say in her life. Makes me sick."

"That may be, but that's not the point."

Leticia pulled over, put the cart in Park, and angled the rearview mirror. "The hell it ain't." She carefully unpinned her PEA visor and patted a tissue between the cornrows. "He's working on another one now. Poor brainwashed bitches popping out welfare babies, slaving away for his scrub ass. He don't need four wives. He need a job."

"What if they file a conduct complaint?"

"I have an exemplary record with the public." Leticia reattached her visor. "And you can bet your ass Dhu West don't want any more attention around the fact that they're an Arab company in an Arab country running Chicago's Traffic Bureau."

"Seriously?"

"Damn, girl, don't you watch the news? Our mayor and the Mob humped that deal to get him in office. Selling our city off piece by piece for who knows how much campaign money." She shook her head. "A cryin' shame."

"I'm feeling a little light-headed," I said. "Can we go get something to eat?"

"I wasn't kidding about that bacon sandwich." Leticia grinned. "It's a tasty treat."

"My radio's busted."

"Leave a report in my box. I gotta say, McGrane, you ain't that bad for a trainee. In fact, I'm gonna set you up proper—just like the prize baby white elephant you are."

"Thanks."

I think.

Chapter 12

I never dated much. Oddly enough, guys weren't all that interested in going out with me once they realized I lived in a house
full of guard dogs armed with badges and law degrees. Friday
night, I went downstairs dressed to the nines with a bellyful of
butterflies. Mom and the twins were at the far end of the bar arguing over their latest defendant, an obscenely wealthy and connected child molester. Cash lay on the sectional in the great
room, texting in front of the Angels playing the Cubs.

Mom gave me a once-over. "You look terrific." The twins
grunted in agreement, not looking up.

7:50 p.m. I lounged against the arm of the couch and tried to
watch TV. The Angels are my favorite team, but I couldn't follow the game at all. I got up and fetched my mail from the mudroom and brought it into the kitchen. *National Review, Vogue
Paris,* two offers for credit cards, a dental cleaning reminder
postcard, and a single white envelope hand-addressed with the
crimson Loyola law school crest in the return address corner.

Terrific.

"What's this, Mom?" I held up the letter.

"I've secured a place for you at Loyola," she said in a happy,
easy tone. The one that always came before the hammer. "I want
you to quit Traffic Enforcement. Use the summer to recharge. Re-
focus."

Declan and Daicen exchanged a look, scooted back their
stools, and fled the room.

Gee, thanks for having my back, guys.

Hank's Law Number Seventeen: Deescalate. The true fight is won without fighting.

"Mom, I'm just about to go on a date with the guy I've been crushing on for a year and a half. Could we please talk about this later?"

"Absolutely. You're in at Loyola and that's all that matters."

My lizard brain strangled the calming breath in my throat and took a swipe at Mom from under the rock. "You want me to be a lawyer? Really? You're getting a child molester off and you're sick about it."

She stood up and smiled grimly. "I'm more than sick about the Schumer case. But there are many different kinds of law to practice." She marched into the kitchen and began to rifle through the freezer. "But if you think for one minute I'm going to let my college-educated daughter squander her future writing parking tickets for minimum wage, you've got another think coming." She slammed a box of salmon filets on the counter and whirled on me. "Where are the molten lava cakes that Thierry made for my Sunday luncheon group?"

Instantly, the tension left my neck and back. This was not about me. The case was really getting to her. "He hid them in the box marked 'sea bass.' "

"Typical," she muttered.

Living to fight another day, I left my mail on the counter and flopped down next to Cash.

8:02.

Hank was never late.

Ever.

Cash wiggled his empty beer bottle at me. "Were you gonna get a beer, Snap?"

Eight weeks of serving Cash's every whim was starting to feel more like eighty years. "You bet." I popped up and went to the wet bar. "Want anything, Mom?"

The lava cake heating in the microwave had all her attention. "No thanks, baby."

I brought Cash his beer, wanting one but holding out.

"What's the matter?" he asked. "You get stood up?"

Mom carried her lava cake back to the table. "I fail to see how that remark is of any assistance to your sister."

"Just curious," he said with a cheery smile.

8:16. The phone rang. The caller ID on the bottom of the TV screen read "Hank Bannon." "I got it." I ran to the phone. "Hello?"

"May I please speak with Miss Maisie McGrane?" a woman's smooth, well-modulated voice seeped into my ear. The kind of voice that embodied the word *sultry*.

"Uh, this is."

"Miss McGrane, I'm calling on behalf of Mr. Bannon. He regrets he will not be able to attend your conference this evening."

Conference? My throat tightened. *Standing me up. And having his phone sex operator deliver it on his cell phone.* "Why is that, exactly?"

"I'm afraid the negotiations he's involved in require more of his attention than he originally planned."

"I see." I said nothing, letting the silence stretch, waiting for her to fill the void.

She didn't.

"Thanks for the call," I said.

"Is there a return message?"

"No." I hung up.

Mom kept reading her files, eating cake. Pretending she hadn't heard every word. Cash's texting hit warp speed.

"He can't make it," I said, trying unsuccessfully to shrug off the disproportionately crushing disappointment.

"That's too bad," Mom said. "I was looking forward to meeting him."

"Yeah." I slunk over to the bar fridge and got a Miller Lite. Cash grabbed the beer out of my hands, making me jump. "Gah!" I hadn't heard him get up.

He grinned smugly at me and said loudly over his shoulder, "You look too good to stay home, Snap. I'm taking you out."

"That's sweet of you, honey," Mom said.

"Get changed, thrall." He popped the top on my beer and took a swig. "The guys and I need a designated driver."

Nothing like petting a kitten before stomping on its head.

Wearing jeans, a black Mack truck tee, and motorcycle boots, I jangled the keys to Cash's Jeep in the doorway. "Are we going or what?"

"We're waiting for Koji," he said, glued to Halo mayhem on his TV.

"Well, why don't we just go pick him up? I'm your designated driver, aren't I?"

"Yeah, but he's staying over. We're taking his MDX."

Cash's best friend loved his shiny red Acura more than anything in the world. It was unimaginable that he'd let me hold his keys, much less drive it. "And Koji is aware of this fact?"

"You bet. He suggested it."

"Riiight."

Cash laughed. "He's not so hot and heavy about his baby since some idiot rear-ended him. And anyway, it's the only car that'll hold all six of us . . . And you, of course."

Six totally wasted hotshot cops. This was going to be worse than Jersey Shore *meets* Hooking Up. "How long till he gets here?"

A half hour later, Cash shouted from the front door, "Mai-sie! Let's go. Koji's here!"

I got my cell from the charging station and met Da coming in from the garage. "Hullo, luv," he said. "Heard the bad news. A no-show, eh?"

He didn't exactly look torn up. Which was probably where my brothers got the idea that my life would be better off without any dates, ever.

"Yeah. He had a work thing."

"What does he do again?"

"Uh—"

"C'mon, Maisie!" Cash shouted from the foyer. "We don't have all night."

Yeah, I wish. If we get home before 4 a.m. it'll be a miracle.

Da set his briefcase down. "I hear you and Cash are two peas in a pod lately. Looks like the job's already giving you some patience." He hugged me and kissed the top of my head. "I like it."

If he only knew.

"Snap!" Cash yelled from the front door.

Da swatted me on the butt as I walked past. "Have fun tonight."

Koji, an athletic Asian with a dancer's body, reluctantly held out his keys. "I suppose you might as well drive it under my sober supervision." He got in on the passenger side, my brother in back.

"Where to?"

"The pack's joining up at Tom's house," Cash said.

I started the car and drove down the driveway, Koji stomping on the floor as I eased to a stop before turning onto the street. "Maybe you and Cash should switch seats."

"You planning on ticketing me for backseat driving, *meter maid?*" Koji said, to Cash's hoot of delight.

"No," I said, "but I'll sure as hell make sure I ticket your double-parking peanut butt, the second you stop to run in and get a Cinnabon."

"Promise?" Koji asked, "Baby, you'll be my Monday morning trifecta. Cinnabon, you give me a ticket in that cute lil' neon vest, and then I get to drop it on Jensen's desk to clean up."

Great. They're gonna force-feed me crow all night. With chopsticks. I tapped the brakes. Hard.

"Hey!" Koji said. "Treat my baby with respect, ticket tyrant."

Cash leaned up in between us. "Got it out of your system, Koji?"

"Dude, you can't tell me—"

"Zip it," Cash said. "You want her to screw with our hookups?"

I shrugged in agreement. "I mean, it's not like you'd care if I told them you both still live at home, right?"

"Damn, Maisie." Openmouthed, Koji stared at me, aghast. "Now, that's just cold."

I shrugged and glanced in the rearview.

Cash winked. *Only a McGrane can torture a McGrane.*

Lithium was packed. Half-naked women shivered in the cool night air, waiting for access. Cash's wolf pack had no such problem, waved in by the bouncers. I trailed behind, surprised as much by the pals they invited along as the clubs we were hitting. Then again, maybe cocky hotshot cops were the only ones they could drum up after scoring me as a designated driver on such short notice.

I hung at the bar, counting the bubbles fizzing in my third Diet Coke, the *oontz-oontz* of techno numbing my brain. Koji bought the pack, minus himself and Cash, yet another round of shots. My Spidey sense started tingling. He wasn't exactly the spread-it-around kind.

A girl blew water vapor from an electric cigarette in my face, as she reached across me for a handful of nuts. *Why is it when you're drinking, the mixed nut bar bowl is a tasty treat, but sober, it's more disgusting than a swab of the inside of a McDonald's Playplace tunnel?*

My steel G-Shock watch read 22:30. Women swarmed around my brother and his gang like honeybees to a cone of cotton candy.

And they haven't even flashed their stinking badges yet. Ugh.

"Yo, *chica*," Ernesto said in my ear. "What's my favorite hard-ass doing in a pop-tart lounge like this?"

"My date stood me up so I'm stuck designated-driving for Cash."

"Date? You?" Ernesto's eyes popped. "With who?"

"Who do you think?"

Ernesto's eyes got even wider. "Huh. Really? I mean . . . I guess I just didn't think he'd ever—"

"Well, he didn't. His girl Friday gave me the Heisman."

"Her." He gave a low whistle. "Oh yeah. I could talk to her all day."

Thanks a lot, Mr. Sensitive Best Friend. "Ever meet her?"

"Nope. But with a voice like that . . ." He gave a happy shudder.

"She's probably sixty-five, topping the scales at two-fifty with a ratty old beehive."

"Not a problem. I'll keep my eyes closed as long as she keeps talking."

"Aig!" I tapped my temple. "Thanks for that."

Ernesto took a sudden interest in his shoes. "I'm glad, actually, you didn't go."

"What? Why?"

"Hank started asking me to fill in for him around the time you took off for . . . you know."

The Police Academy. I waited.

Ernesto put his hands in his back pockets. "Some of the re-habbers—they're not so quiet when Hank's away."

"Oh?"

"I've heard some things. Bad things."

Part of his appeal. "I need a little more than that."

Ernesto chewed a thumbnail, trying to break it to me gently. "How about *wet work?*"

"Oh my God, Ernesto." I rolled my eyes. "Those guys were totally jerking your chain."

"I dunno. I don't think so. You've grown up in a house full of Clint Eastwood macho badasses, so of course you're gonna go for the toughest guy around, but Hank's a killer. Straight-up."

My fingers clenched into fists. "He was an Army Ranger, not a Boy Scout."

"This training he's doing? It's more like recruiting for whatever Blackwater/Academi organization he's working for." Ernesto shook his head. "I like Hank. I do. But he's carrying some fucked-up black-cloud baggage, is all I'm saying, *chica.* He's one dark guy."

Cash slung an arm around my neck, making me jump. "Sorry to interrupt, Pads. But our driver's on the clock."

Gee, having a brother is so awesome, I just want to share him. With someone else. Forever.

Ernesto gave me a small wave with a sympathetic smile chaser as my brother and Koji hustled me toward the exit, where the wolf pack was waylaid by a bachelorette party wearing more perfume than a Glade factory makes in a month.

"Who'da thought?" Cash said in my ear. "Flynn was right."

"About what?"

"Your Mr. Wonderful. Ernesto the Earnest disapproves, as well."

"Ooh, burn." Koji squealed. "Squee!"

I glared at him. "Settle down, Preteen Patty."

Koji laughed. "Don't get mad at me. I showed up."

"It's a good thing we're leaving. I'm done for the night."

Cash put his nose to mine. "You're driving if you wanna be working on Monday." He jerked a thumb at an opening in the crowd. "Let's go."

We hit two more bars—phone numbers dropping on the guys like confetti at a ticker-tape parade. All the while, Cash and Koji nursed their beers like they had nipples attached. They were up to something—hamming it up like they were as blasted as their crew when they were stone sober.

The MDX reeked of aftershave and alcohol. "Where to?" I asked the wolf pack. "Home?"

"Not!" Koji said. "How about Hud's?"

Really? We'd spent the night trolling twenty-dollar-cover techno clubs only to end up at a knockdown dive?

Chapter 13

I pulled into Hud's parking lot. Pickups, Crown Vics, a few Tauruses and even a couple blue and whites. *The ultimate cop bar.*

Smoky and dark and packed to the gills, Hud's was corner booths, wobbly scarred tables, and the only place in town where Clapton, Fleetwood Mac, and .38 Special still played on a coin-operated juke. The wolf pack bellied noisily up to the bar while my brother and his best friend drifted casually away.

"McGrane." A densely muscled man in a black T-shirt raised a hand at Cash from a corner table. "Plenty of room here." He sat in the leather booth that ringed one side, two men sitting in chairs across from him.

"I'll wait." I pointed at the bar.

"No way." Cash put his hand between my shoulder blades and gave me a short shove toward the booth.

The man slid out. "Hop in." He was handsome in the way that all hard, über-fit guys are good-looking. About twenty-eight, five-ten, brown and brown, with the thick, defined muscular build that only a shorter guy can carry. Clean-cut and tatt-free, he still had that lil' something extra that screamed badass.

Cash slid in first, I went next, and the tough guy sat next to me.

"Lee Sharpe." He held out his hand and jerked his head toward Cash and Koji. "What're you doing with these knockarounds?"

I shook his hand. "Maisie McGrane."

Lee leaned forward and said to Cash. "Sorry, man."

My brother's eyes closed halfway. "She's my sister."

"Well, that's okay, then." Lee smiled and rested his elbow behind me on the booth. "What are you doing with these knock-arounds, Maisie?"

The other men laughed.

Lee Sharpe was a master of the friendly banter that talks most girls into bed before they realize they're already naked. I flirted with him distractedly, unable to get off the squeaky hamster wheel of Hank standing me up.

My unintentional disinterest only fired Lee's interest in me. "Your brother and Koji," he said. "They're definitely riding at the top of the heap."

For what? "Yeah?" I said as I got a load of the *AT* on one of their Windbreakers hanging over the back of the chair. *AT as in SWAT.*

Holy cat. Cash and Koji, the Vice Kings, were applying to SWAT.

The night fell neatly into place. What better way to set yourself apart than to show up with your competition drunk off their asses? Across the table, Koji and my brother were already in the thick of it with the two other SWAT guys.

Free at last. I covered my mouth with my hand, trying to squish the grin off my face. The silver lining to being stood up by Hank. Cash's run as Master Slaver was over. Almost as quickly as it had begun. *Mom and Da are going to kill him.*

I realized Lee was talking to me. "Huh?"

"I said, how—"

"You gotta be fuckin' kidding me!" Tommy Narkinney's voice splattered over me like hot grease. He was sitting at the head of six little tables pushed together, surrounded by blue-shirted beat walkers. Nine of them. "If it isn't our favorite meter maid."

Cash set his beer down. I gave him an imperceptible head shake.

"Mai-sie Dai-sy McGrane!" Narkinney yelled in a singsong

voice. He smacked his thigh with his palm. "Why don't you come on over here and write me a ticket?"

Lee's mouth twitched, but he said nothing.

I rubbed the bridge of my nose. *Shake it off. Narkinney's not worth it. Hank's Law Number Seventeen: Deescalate. The true fight is won without fighting.*

I gave Koji a tight smile. "Hey. How 'bout them Cubs?"

"Yeah." Koji nodded and put his hand on Cash's arm. "Crazy how bad they always suck."

"Meter maid!" Narkinney stood up. "I'm talking to you."

Lee looked lazily across the table at his two teammates, letting it unfold. Koji kept up the Cubs chatter, his hand never leaving Cash's arm.

Narkinney crossed the bar, headed straight for me. The beat cops tight behind, backing him up. Of course they would. He'd been drinking with some of these guys in his backyard probably before he could even spell beer. Nark was beat-born. A beat cop from a long line of beat cops. All with the same bellyful of disdain for rank, division, and don't even get them started on specializeds like SWAT.

He stopped at our table, leaned over, and rapped his beer bottle against the table in front of me. "Jesus, you sad little wannabe washout."

I rolled my tongue in my cheek, willing myself not to respond. Not staring, not ignoring, not escalating.

He was drunk. And judging from his chubby partner's glassy eyes, so was Peterson. Celebrating my comeuppance at the Brothers of Allah Prayer Center. The rest of the blue shirts all wore the same smug smirk. They'd heard all about me. In great, embellished detail, no doubt.

Deescalate.

"Hey, Tommy. How you doing?" I said in the calm voice I'd cultivated for a run-in with a *Deliverance* hillbilly. "It's really nice of you to come over and say hi."

That stopped him. His brows knit together, trying to figure my angle.

Caveman not understand nice.

Lee's hand slid down onto my shoulder. Marking me as his as surely as pissing on my leg.

Damn.

Narkinney eyed Lee's hand with a leer. "Humping SWAT ain't gonna get you reinstated at the Academy."

Lee was on his feet, chest inches from Narkinney's. "I don't like your manners, son."

"Fuck you, Sharpe." Tommy Narkinney had four inches on him, but that was it.

Lee Sharpe had twenty pounds, Hank's same thousand-yard stare, and all the cussedness of a wolverine. "Back off, flat-foot," he said, wanting Nark to push it, looking for a scrap.

His two SWAT buddies got up from the table. Cash and Koji followed suit, engines revving.

"So it is true," Narkinney said. "You SWAT ass-wads can't do anything without holding each other's dicks."

The beat cops laughed, feeling pretty good about the odds.

I got to my feet. "Hey, Tommy. C'mon." Palms up, I edged Lee backwards. "You got your licks in."

"I haven't even started to *lick* you, McGrane," he said, loud enough for everyone to hear.

Cash's wasted wolf pack got up from the bar.

I closed my eyes and blew out a slow breath. I asked for that. A lousy choice of words. Deescalate. I opted for what had saved my butt more times than I could count with furious brothers.

I jerked my elbow uncomfortably above my shoulder, letting my wrist and hand dangle limply. "Ouch! Uncle. Lemme go. Uncle!"

I almost had him.

But the beat-cop hyenas behind him wouldn't let up, egging him on. Narkinney thrust his face inches from mine. My nose filled with the stink of his beer-sweat cologne.

Narkinney smiled at Lee. "So you being team lead—you get first crack?" He waved his finger between us. "Does she fuck like a boy, too?"

And with that, deescalation was off the table. My lizard brain crawled out from under the rock and turned velociraptor.

"You got something to say to me, Nark?" I bit my index finger in mock flirtation. "Or is your dick in a twist because I can do more push-ups than you?"

Cash's wolf pack erupted into hoots and catcalls.

Narkinney's nostrils flared. "I'm the one with the shield, bitch."

"Yeah," I said, ready to throw down. "But that doesn't mean I can't kick your ass."

The wolf pack began chanting, "Kick his ass, kick his ass."

Narkinney's cheeks turned a splotchy red, hands balling to fists. "I don't hit bitches."

I mouthed the word "pussy."

Nark spat in my face.

In one fluid motion Lee shoved me toward the booth and smashed his fist into Narkinney's face. I fell back onto the vinyl banquette as Tommy's nose collapsed in a sickening squelch.

He hit the floor like a 190-pound sandbag.

The bar exploded.

Wiping Narkinney's spit from my cheek, I slid off the banquette. He wasn't moving.

Seriously? Even with a broken nose, no guy ever goes down in a bar fight with one punch. Ever.

I squatted down beside Narkinney and rolled him over. His nose was mashed to one side of his face, blood running down his chin faster than a spilled half gallon of milk.

Son of a bitch.

He needed to get up so I could kick his ass.

Cash and Koji traded blows with a couple of beat cops. Thirty feet away, Lee was back-to-back with another SWAT waist-deep in blue uniforms, throwing crisp brutal punches.

A thing to see.

And I just stood there, a useless mixture of fury and adrenaline churning in my gut. I'd escalated for . . . nothing. Lee popped what should've been my cherry, and won me a lifetime's supply of Narkinney's petty revenge to boot.

Aww, hell.

A hand landed on my shoulder. I spun and Peterson—that fat fuck—actually took a swing at me. His ringed knuckles glanced off my mouth, splitting my lip.

I responded like Hank had taught me.

Three short, distracting jabs to the face and a heavy left with everything I had to the underside of his potbelly.

Peterson took a couple wobbly steps back and sat down hard in one of the chairs. "Meter bitch," he croaked, holding his girth.

Whatever.

I went back to Narkinney—still prone—and kicked his foot with my boot.

Out cold.

The wolf pack was holding their own, adrenaline-fueled egos giving them the Drunken Master edge. Something whistled down past my cheek. I ducked too late and it cracked against my collarbone.

Oh my God, that hurt.

I dropped to my knees, hand on my shoulder. *What was that?*

"You fucking asshole!" Cash shouted in my general direction as he drove his fist low and hard into some guy's kidneys. "That's my—" Punch. "Sister!" Punch.

I crawled under the bar table. Needles of fire zinged up and down my useless arm. I couldn't feel my fingers. Who the hell did that to me?

"Knock, knock." Peterson leaned in.

He grabbed the front of my shirt and dragged me out from beneath the table, making sure to crack my head on the table on the way up. *Damn it.* I scrambled to get my feet beneath me.

Peterson raised his arm.

Jesus H. He hit me with a goddamn beer bottle.

And he is going to do it again.

I popped up and nailed him with a side kick to the leg, making sure to aim downward and chamber the knee. Bruce Lee–style.

Peterson's leg gave way and he collapsed against the table.

The beer bottle fell from his hand and shattered on the floor. "Stupid whore!"

I grabbed him by the back of his head and slammed his face into the table. He swore and whipped back a chunky elbow, clipping me on the chin. I took a power step and drove my knee up hard into his groin.

Peterson wheezed like a dying accordion and lay there, face-down across the table. I stood over him, panting. Fingers curling and uncurling, the feeling finally coming back to my hands.

An ear-bleeding air horn blared until the fighting stopped.

Hud's bartender stood on the bar, aerosol can in hand. "Dudes. Disperse. I'm sure you don't want to spend the night writing each other up and who the hell else am I gonna call to stop this shit?"

The wolf pack went hands-up, wearing the same I-didn't-do-nothing look as a bunch of second-grade boys, and went back to their places at the bar.

"Jaysus, Maisie." Cash came up behind me. "Nice work." He reached over and took ahold of Peterson by the collar and jerked him backwards off the table.

Peterson landed on the floor on his well-padded butt and rolled onto his side, hands buried in his groin.

"A fucking career-ender, that's what this ought to be." Cash ran a raw and swollen hand through his dark hair. "Peterson. What an asshole! Using a beer bottle on another cop—" He shook his head impatiently. "Whatever."

Cash's slip was a knife to the heart. *I should be a cop. Instead I am a whatever.* I looked at Peterson squirming around on the dirty floor in agony. I felt nothing. No anger. No remorse.

"Christ, Snap. When Flynn, Rory, and Da get an earful of this . . ."

I bit my split lip without thinking and winced. "They won't."

"Like hell," Cash said. "Hud's probably already called Da himself."

"I'll take the heat," I said.

"Riiiiiight." He snorted in disgust. "Da's so not gonna be okay with this. And Flynn . . . Jay-sus. I'll have to think of something to keep us *in* the frying pan."

Lee and his buddies came back. He jerked his head at the unconscious Narkinney. "Want an apology?" he asked, completely serious. "I'll wake him up."

"Um, no. I think breaking his nose was probably enough."

Lee bounced on his toes and rolled his shoulders in regret. "Hey—flat-foot," he called to a uniform with a purpling eye. "Get these guys outta here."

A couple of beat cops helped Peterson to his feet and dragged Narkinney away.

Lee caught my chin and took a good look. "You're sporting a couple of dingers." His voice turned nonchalant. "Who hit you?"

"Does it matter?" I smiled, not daring to give him another spark. "This is my first official bar fight."

Lee's eyes narrowed. "Sit down, okay?" He went to the bar.

A couple of bar-backs came by, sweeping up broken glass, mopping up spilled drinks, righting tables and chairs. I slid in the booth next to a glowering Cash, arms folded across his chest. Koji—the Eagle Scout—already had a round waiting at our table, including a beer for me.

I took a drink, the frosty cold Lite stinging my torn lip. *Delicious.*

Lee returned with ice in a plastic bag, wrapped in a towel. He held it out to me.

"That was sweet," I said, taking it. "Sweet but unnecessary."

"Yeah? You'll thank me tomorrow." Lee put his hand on mine and lifted the makeshift ice pack to my lower lip and chin. "So, tell me. Is what Nark saying true?"

That I'm a complete loser who got kicked out of the Police Academy? Yes. "Huh?" I said, making him actually ask it out loud.

"That you're a parking enforcement agent?"

Not bringing up my fall from grace was one thing. But not calling me a meter maid? That was old-whiskey smooth. The kind of cool that gets a string of women trailing along behind.

"Yes," I said, leaving the ice pack in front of my mouth, waiting for the washout part.

It didn't come.

"How do you like it?" Lee said.

"It's interesting."

"Working with the public always is. It's why I became a cop." Lee grinned and took a drink of his Stella Artois. "You ever date anyone on the job?"

"No." I said. "Never."

"We're not all like that jackass."

"What?" I asked, catching up. "Oh no, I'm not opposed to law enforcement or anything. But my father and three brothers apparently traded in the sacred partner don't-date-my-ex card for the don't-even-look-at-my-sister/daughter one."

"McGrane." Recognition dawned on Lee's face. "Your clan's Detective Division, Homicide, yeah?" He looked at my brother. "Except for Cash in Vice."

I nodded.

"That's okay, then." Lee said. "I don't think they'll enter into the equation."

Equation?

He gave me a look. And it was a good one. "How about dinner?"

"Thanks, Lee. But I don't think so."

My head hurt and I felt sick. Sick from adrenaline, a dozen Diet Cokes, getting kicked out of the Academy, Tommy Narkinney, Peterson, the PEA in general, and most of all, Hank.

Lee let me out of the booth, and I signaled to my brother with the keys.

After the last of the wasted wolf pack was dispatched, Cash, Koji, and I headed back to our house. Inside, Koji split off, going to the main floor guest room he normally stayed in, while Cash and I went upstairs and quietly crossed the hallway to our rooms.

"Hey!" Cash whispered and waved me into his room. "Make sure you wake me and Koji up at eight thirty tomorrow. We want to hit the range before our tee time."

"No."

"Excuse me?" Cash put a hand to his ear. "I didn't hear a *yessir*."

"And you won't," I said. "The deal's off. You're going to continue to see Jennifer Lince. And I'm a free woman."

"Oh yeah?" He sat down on his bed.

I pressed my hands dramatically over my heart. "Mom will be so proud you applied to SWAT."

The color drained from his face. "I don't know what you're talking about."

"Best of luck with that one. After I tell Da, you'll be off the list faster than you can blink in denial."

"You don't know that."

"Yeah? Then why haven't you told them yourself?"

Cash flopped back onto the bed and said to the ceiling, "God, I hate you."

I gave him a poor baby pout and walked toward the door.

"Okay, wait," he said scrambling. "I'll—"

"You'll keep seeing Jennifer until after the Dhu West Gala. I'll cover your chores. But no more thrall duty."

Cash nodded. "Deal."

I made it to the door before he asked, "What'd Lee Sharpe say?"

"You and Koji are at the top of the heap."

Chapter 14

Saturday dawn, I woke up with a throbbing shoulder, tender chin, and a headache. I got dressed and surveyed the damage in the bathroom mirror. I owed Lee Sharpe big-time for the ice pack. The bruise on my chin was pretty much undetectable, unless someone was looking for it. My lip didn't look that bad, either, slathered with Aquaphor and surrounded by Dermablend concealer.

Way too early, I started down the stairs, prepared to beg Thierry for a smoothie and a poached egg, and halted at the sounds of protest.

Cash and Koji were already up and in the hot seat, fibbing away like mad. "Honestly, Mr. McGrane. You should have seen those idiot beat cops begging SWAT for a throw-down."

"And Maisie was with you?"

"Jaysus, Da," Cash complained. "Nothing happened. She's totally fine."

"Pretty feckin' thoughtful, taking her to Hud's," Rory said, "seeing as she's just been scotched from the Academy."

"Give it a rest, Rory. She was happy to go. In fact," he embellished, "it was her idea."

"Maisie, darlin'," Da called. "Come down off the stairs and tell me your version of last night's shenanigans."

Burnt toast.

Cash and Koji were still arguing with Rory as I skulked into the dining room.

Flynn's phone buzzed. "McGrane." He snapped his fingers and held up his palm. The squabbling stopped. "On our way." He hung up and looked at Rory and Da. "Triple homicide in Ashburn. One juvenile."

"This isn't over," Da said, following Flynn and Rory out of the dining room.

Minutes later, Cash, Koji, and I watched from the window as they tore out of the driveway, dash, deck and grille lights flashing.

"Bullet officially dodged." Cash took a bite from his makeshift breakfast burrito. He'd wrapped a pancake around his bacon and scrambled eggs so as to not stop eating for a second. "I mean—" He sucked some falling egg back into his mouth. "How lucky are we? Mom and the twins, stuck in the city, slaving away on their pedo case. Da and the guys gone till the wee hours." He smacked me in the arm. "Let's have a party."

"You're an imbecile."

"Dude," Koji said. "Get real. We're working tomorrow." He looked at his watch. "C'mon. Two hours till tee time and I gotta hit some balls."

I spent the rest of the day culling through Thorne Clark's solitary, squeaky-clean life, looking for connections to Nawisko that didn't exist.

Sunday I went to Joe's Gym, telling myself I'd trained there for the last twenty-two months and I had every right to be there.

Hank wasn't there, either.

Monday morning, bright and early, I waited in Dhu West's Traffic Enforcement Bureau reception area for Jennifer Lince. Today was the day she'd hand over the coveted keys to the golf cart and bestow upon me the Barbie-replica shield. The little piece of aluminum that the TEB believed gave their minimum-wage earner a sense of righteousness and pride.

I drummed my hands on my black cargo pants–covered knees. Dhu West ran with the efficiency of a clock dipped in maple syrup. Eventually, Jennifer's sullen secretary led me back to her office.

Ms. Lince, phone wedged between her ear and shoulder, was hard at work, fingers flying across her computer keyboard. "Yes. I understand. I see." She stopped typing and pointed at one of the red fabric chairs.

Everything in her office was exactly as it had been when I'd seen her a week ago, including the silver eight-by-ten framed photo of Cash, except for two things. The pony keg–sized mug of coffee that could flush out the digestive tract of an elephant and a little scrap of paper sticking up from her keyboard.

Oh jeez. The stub to the art movie Cash took her to.

Finally, she hung up the phone, took a manila folder with my name on it from her in-box, and began to read. "My goodness, Maisie." Jennifer smiled pertly at me over the folder. "I have never known Leticia Jackson to give such a glowing recommendation. Caiseal must not be the only one with charm to spare in the McGrane family."

I smiled politely, not taking the bait.

"In fact," Jennifer said, "if I wasn't so well-acquainted with her illiterate scrawl, I'd have said you wrote it yourself and, quite frankly, overdid it."

I hadn't seen that one coming. "A lot in common, I guess."

Jennifer's eyes narrowed. "Such as?"

"Uh . . . Dennis Prager?"

"Really? A mutual friend?" She tipped her head in relief. "Okay then." She closed the folder, hefted her giant cup of coffee to her lips and took a long slurp. "I think you have what it takes to become a Dhu West player. A can-do attitude and a certain level of . . . *understanding*."

"Ma'am?"

"Dhu West only recently acquired the Chicago contract. As one of the single non-union-run city departments, Dhu West focuses on two things the unions don't—profit and efficiency. Which is why I've assigned you to a senior agent."

"PEA agents don't have partners," I said automatically.

"Normally that's correct." Her lips rolled back in a prim smile. "Your new partner, Eunice Peat, has had a long career with the

TEB. Unfortunately, she's operating at the barest minimum standard while her age and health condition are causing a drain on the entire PEA benefit package."

Uh-oh.

"Dhu West believes an early retirement would best suit all parties." Her blue eyes lit with an unholy glee. "Naturally, when you find your partner's not performing to company standards, or is physically incapable of properly executing her duties, you will immediately bring that to my specific attention."

Argh. A partner Dhu West wants fired.

There isn't enough Excedrin in Walmart for this kind of headache.

"I believe in respect, and I think you do, too, Maisie. Respect that you have a higher loyalty to Dhu West, above whatever affinity you may have for a partner." Jennifer opened a desk drawer and removed an AutoCITE machine, Traffic Enforcement Bureau shield, and an eight-and-a-half-by-eleven laminated route card. She slid them across the desk to me. "With Leticia's recommendation and effective performance, the sky's the limit for your career here." She stood up and extended her hand. "Welcome aboard, Maisie."

"I heard you'd made the cut and I was, like, so totally jazzed," Obi said, wheeling around the counter of the Dispatch office building.

Oh Obi. No one says jazzed.

He handed me a boot requisition form on a clipboard. "Usually you have a standard two boots per vehicle, unless you have Friday specials like—you know." He leaned in. "Hey! I heard about the boots you laid at the Brothers of Allah Prayer Center. Those guys are complete assholes."

"You can say that again."

He chuckled. "Miz Jackson said one of the cops who showed up was just as bad."

"Yeah." I looked the form over and signed the bottom.

His face scrunched up in question. "Why didn't they arrest the guy who broke your radio?"

"Officer Narkinney and I aren't exactly what you'd call pals."
I forced a smile. "More like mortal enemies."

"Oh," Obi said. "Stormtrooper?"

"Romulan."

Obi rolled his eyes. "Ix-nay on the ek-Trey."

"I thought Stormtroopers were pretty much silent. Narkinney is loud and obnoxious."

"Ahhhh." Obi stroked the wispy fuzz on his upper lip. "Tusken Raider."

"Now you're talking." I handed the clipboard back, not letting go until he looked me in the eye. "From now on, Ms. Jackson should arrive with an escort every third Friday."

Obi nodded. "I'm on it." He slipped the clipboard into one of the *Star Wars* saddlebags on the side of the chair.

"Where do I get the keys?"

"You don't. Ms. Peat's the driver." He wheeled backwards up the ramp, showing off.

"Can you give me the lowdown on my new partner?"

Obi smiled sadly and shook his head. "The Force is strong within you, my young friend, but even I cannot reveal your destiny."

Gee, thanks.

I swiped my key card at the TEB entrance, stopped in front of the time clock, and punched in.

"Told you I'd set you up, McGrane," Leticia Jackson crowed from the hallway. She marched into the break room, black shoes squeaking on the waxy gray linoleum floor. "Get me a Cherry Coke and some Cheetos and come sit your scrawny ass down." She sat down at one of the stained Formica tables while I pulled out a couple bucks and fed them into the vending machines.

Today was not the day to skimp on a bribe. I threw in a Snickers, as well.

I brought the snacks over and sat down. Leticia wiped the sweat from her neck with an orange bandanna. "There's a couple things we need to get straight, McGrane."

"Should I be taking notes?"

Leticia squinted at me to see if I was kidding, decided I wasn't, and opened the chips. "Hell, no! This is James Bond, CIA kinda shit." She leaned across the table, eyes wide. "This is one hundred percent under-the-table radio silence."

Unable to help myself, I faked a look of intense interest. "Wow."

Leticia cocked her head and eyed me suspiciously. "You ain't wearing a wire, is you, McGrane?"

"No."

"Okay." She shook out a couple Cheetos and popped them in her mouth.

"Of course, as a civilian, I'm under no obligation to tell you the truth," I said helpfully. "Nor would I have to tell you if I was a police officer."

Leticia stopped mid-chew and gave me the look one of those hippos on the Discovery Channel does just before it charges the cameraman and rips his leg off. "You're blathering." She finished chewing. "Cops can't lie. That's entrapment."

"Nope. The law does not prohibit officers from lying in the course of performing their duties." She raised a skeptical brow and I continued, "Entrapment's when someone's persuaded by police to commit a crime that they had no previous intention of committing."

Leticia shook her head and thrust her stubby fingers back into the bag. "You sure do know a lot of useless shit."

She was attractive in that cute-potential chubby-faced way. I wondered what she'd look like sixty pounds lighter. Smoking hot, or would that aura of would-be attractiveness evaporate into the ether with the lost weight?

"We're going to talk about your new partner, Eunice Peat," Leticia said. "And before you ask, it's Niecy, never Eunice." She raised her palms ceiling-ward. "Lordy, what kind of back-country hillbilly gives their baby girl a homely-ass name like Eunice?"

I shrugged. Maisie McGrane was not exactly the moniker of a cosmopolitan sophisticate.

"Anyhow," Leticia said, "I got a warm spot in my heart for Niecy. She brought me up through the ranks, when the TEB was still owned by peeps who actually lived in this goddamn country."

"Um, I don't really see—"

"Niecy's got a touch of the Parkinson's," she said.

"How bad?"

"Bad enough that Dhu West has the Ice Bi-otch Lince looking for every way to Sunday to throw her ass out."

"Why?"

"Bottom line, why you think?" Leticia rolled her eyes. "Niecy hits thirty-five years in three months. If she can hang in, it's another ten thousand a year in pension. She can't quit. On account of she's too young to get Medicare and she don't qualify for the Medicaid with her pension."

I had the distinct sensation of needing a double scotch and I don't drink scotch.

Hank's Law Number Ten: Keep your mouth shut.

"Naturally, after you and me kicked Marcus-Mohammed in the balls at the House of fuckin' Burka Oppression, I thought of your skinny-ass hopping in and out of the cart, booting like nothing I've ever seen."

I folded my hands on the Formica table, ignoring the need to pull at my shirt collar. *When trying to befriend a suspect, show them you're on the same team.* I couldn't remember if it was a cop-ism or a lawyer-ism, but it meant I was screwed. Totally.

"I wrote you up aces so Lince would have to choose you." She took a swig of Cherry Coke. "Are you hearing what I'm saying to you, McGrane?"

"Yes, ma'am."

"Well, you just sitting there. Not nodding. Not moving. Nothing."

"I'm waiting," I said.

"For what?"

"The other shoe to drop."

Leticia sat back and grinned at me. "Other shoe . . . That's a good one. You make that up?"

"No, ma'am."

She nodded and slit open the Snickers with a baby-blue airbrushed thumbnail. "Look. She ain't that bad. Only a couple times Chen—the gate dude—and me had to load her into the trike."

I didn't say a word.

Leticia sucked in a breath through her teeth and set the Snickers down untouched. "What you're gonna do is hop in and out writing tickets like you're supposed to, only sometimes you might pick up the wrong AutoCITE. And by the time you get all the way to the meter, you just ask Niecy for her number, on account of you want to do your best for Dhu West and don't wanna waste any time."

Not only against company policy, but actually illegal. "Jesus. I can't—"

"Like hell you can't. You're my little marine." She gave me a fist pump. "Boo-Yah!"

Ooh-Rah.

"How many tickets a week?" I asked.

Leticia's chin came up, all trace of good humor gone from her eyes. "That sounds real close to you asking me about a quota."

"Hell, no." I sighed. *Complete and total FUBAR.* I slid over the route card Jennifer had given me. "Any tips?"

It was the closest I've ever seen to someone going apoplectic. Leticia ate the entire Snickers in two bites. "Oh no, she di-n't, oh no, she di-n't."

Huffing in fury, she finished the Cheetos next, gnawing each chip down to nothing with the tiny mincing bites of a maniacal chipmunk. "The Ice Bi-otch thinks she can run me, she got another think coming."

Food gone, Leticia took a cleansing breath. "That's a dead route, McGrane. You couldn't lay twenty tickets a day between the two of you."

"Now what?" I said.

"You drive your route once a day. Then you free." She smiled grimly. "I'm givin' you license to poach."

"Huh?"

"You and Niecy write and boot on any route, whenever and wherever. I guarantee ain't no one gonna complain."

To our face, maybe.

"That's what I thought." She smiled at me. "Don't worry 'bout a thing. I'm gonna set you up cherry. You're my baby white elephant, McGrane. I'll keep you on board. No matter what." Leticia spit in her hand and held it out.

Oh gross.

I did the same and we shook on it.

I went out on the lot to meet my new partner. Eunice "Niecy" Peat was a tiny, early sixty-something with a sparse halo of violent orange hair and skin as white as school chalk. She blew a plume of smoke out the open passenger window of Interceptor 13248.

"So you're the effing cavalry," Niecy said in a voice forged of whiskey sours and three packs a day. Her small face screwed up in displeasure as she waved a shaking hand at me. "Back up. Let me get a gander at ya."

I stepped away.

"You a God-fearing gal?"

I shrugged. "Lapsed Catholic."

She nodded. "Fair enough. It's those with no religion at all who got no charity in their hearts. No loyalty, neither."

No longer surprised why Leticia idolized her, I scrounged up one of Ernesto's kung fu quotes. "All can know good as good only because there is evil."

Niecy took another drag, considered my fortune cookie wisdom, and nodded in agreement. "Get in."

I climbed into the driver's side of the Interceptor. It reeked of smoke and Aqua Net. I fastened my seat belt and glanced at my new partner.

She was tiny. Minute. *What is it about the TEB that attracts the vertically challenged?*

"Leticia explain the way things work?" she said. "I hold the keys, but you're driving."

"Yes, ma'am." I handed her the route card.

Niecy looked at it and scratched the back of her neck. "Piss for lemonade. This ain't good."

"Leticia also gave us a license to poach."

"Jiminy Christmas, of course she did." She reached out a trembling hand and snapped on the radio. Sean Hannity. "I used to hate this shizzle." Niecy nodded at the radio. "But Leticia, danged if she didn't wear me down till now I'm used to it. She says the only way to stick it to the man is to become the man. Not take anything from anyone and make decisions for your own self." Niecy gave a derisive snort and took another drag on her cigarette. "So you tell me. What kinda decisions does a meter maid make?"

I thought about it for a second. "To ticket or not to ticket."

Niecy flicked the cigarette butt out the window. "Are we gonna sit here all day or what?"

She back-seat drove us through the first half of our route, where the ticketing was nonexistent. "We're tied to the stake while the Ice Bitch is out looking for a blowtorch."

We left our route to hit up Agent Lucero's office park sweet spot.

"Stop. A twofer." Gripping her gun, Niecy eased out next to a red Nissan Maxima. "Eyeball the other side and meet me at the end of the block."

Midway up the street, a black armored Lincoln limo was illegally parked in front of a cinder-block office building. A huge black guy, wearing the fabled chauffeur's uniform including silver-buttoned jacket, knee-high boots, and jodhpurs as seen only in the movies, wiped something off the windshield and got back into the vehicle. So tragically ridiculous, I felt nothing but sympathy for the driver. Needing a little angelic interference myself, I decided to pay it forward.

I pulled over, left the Interceptor, and went and rapped on the limo's window. It slid smoothly down. Halfway.

The chauffeur tipped down his mirrored shades and gave me the once-over. "A hundred. Go 'round back and wait for me to unlock it."

Yeah, that's me. Your friendly neighborhood meter maid hooker.

"I don't think so." I smiled politely. "You're in a No Standing Zone."

"A what?"

"Look, I don't want to bust your chops, but you're in a No Loading, No Standing Zone among other things. With a Class D license, you know and I know that you sure as hell know what a No Standing Zone is."

Unimpressed, he pushed the mirrored sunglasses up. "And what's that?"

"A sixty-dollar fine if I'm feeling generous enough to disregard your other violations."

"Damn, you're a cold piece of work." He rolled the window down all the way and squared his immense shoulders to me. "Do you know whose car you be messin' with?"

"No."

"The mayor's."

"Okay," I said. "As I don't see any flashing service lights, no city service vehicle permit stickers, and no diplomatic plates, you'll have to move if you don't want to be ticketed."

He laughed, exposing teeth rode hard by Camels. "Oh yeah?" He pulled ahead, filling the two empty handicapped parking spaces. "Is this better?"

That's what I get for trying to be nice. "Actually, you were better off before. No Standing Zone plus a disabled curb cut plus a fire lane blockage had you at $285. Now you're in two handicapped spaces and still blocking the disabled curb cut. $575."

"Go on and write it then, bitch." He closed the window.

As a member of the Traffic Enforcement Bureau, a parking enforcement agent is always willing to aid and assist members of the public.

I stepped up onto the curb, typed the ticket into the AutoCITE, printed it out, tucked it into its Agent-Orange envelope, and went back to the car.

The window opened a sliver. I popped the ticket in. "Have a nice day," I said, already moving toward the Interceptor.

"Yo!" The driver's window rolled all the way down. I stopped and returned to the Lincoln.

The crumpled-up ticket hit me square in the chest. "Go fuck yourself."

I left the ticket in the street and concentrated on walking slowly back to the Interceptor. I climbed in, a little trembly and kind of freaked.

The traitorous thought that perhaps I was, indeed, "too thin-skinned to be a cop" turned over and over in my mind.

I put my head down on the steering wheel.

"Eegh." Niecy grunted and turned down the volume on Mark Steyn. "Whassa' matter, kid?"

Only fifty-one weeks to go, God help me. "I need a minute."

"You'll get used to it." Her thin orange hair quivered as she shook her head. "The times when someone ain't just pissed to heck to get a ticket—they actually want to cut your danged guts out."

Please. Stop helping.

"Take all the time you need." Niecy turned the volume back up and snuggled into her seat.

I sat staring at the armored Lincoln limo, wondering what I would have done if he'd been a perp.

Hank's Law Number Six: Don't fear fear.

As I reached forward to start the Interceptor, a black Benz S class limo pulled into the handicapped spaces behind the Lincoln limo and flashed its headlights.

The black chauffeur got out and walked to the rear of the Benz. The window lowered. The chauffeur twitched. The window went up. The chauffeur walked stiff-legged mechanically back to the Lincoln. Whatever he'd been told, it wasn't good. He got into the limo and drove away, mouth stretched in a mirthless grimace.

Niecy pointed at the Mercedes. "You gonna ticket that whale, too?"

"Maybe."

The driver of the Benz got out and opened the door for his passenger. An olive-skinned, masculine-looking woman with a swath of expensive blond hair stepped into the street. She raised a cell phone to her ear, said a single word, and disconnected.

"Are we gonna sit here all day or what, McGrane?"

A white Ford van emblazoned with the words *Allied Meat*

Packing screeched to a stop next to the Benz. "Shhh. Something's happening."

The blonde nodded to the two men in the van and got back in the Benz. As the limo pulled away, the men in the van pulled on surgical masks and got out. They wore stained white coveralls, caps, and work gloves and went around to the back of the van. Three more men in identical clothing jumped out. Together they unloaded ten five-gallon pails and pried off the tops, flipping the lids onto the sidewalk.

The van driver opened the office door and held it while the four-man crew, each lugging two pails apiece, disappeared inside the building. I rummaged around in the center console for a pen and wrote the van's plate number on my wrist.

"What is this place?" I said.

"How the eff should I know?" Niecy pressed her nose against the window. "Why are they taking those buckets inside?"

Alone on the sidewalk, the van driver picked up one of the two remaining pails and splashed its contents high onto the plate-glass window. A grayish-whitish liquid splattered and dripped down the window.

The noxious stink of putrefied ammonia permeated the air vents of our cart.

"Jeebus crispies on a cracker!" Niecy gagged.

I covered my nose and mouth with one hand, snapped off the AC, and flipped the vents closed. My eyes watered. The driver picked up his second pail and hurled its contents onto the building. He dropped the empty pails on the sidewalk, got behind the wheel, and gunned the engine.

"Holy criminey." Niecy bounced up and down in her seat. "This is Mob shizzle."

"Shizzle is right." I'd smelled that stink once before. The time I'd visited a henhouse. "Chicken shizzle."

The coveralled crew, now pail-free, hustled out of the building, got into the van, and took off.

The office door burst open. Men and women, heads and shoulders coated in dripping white liquid, ran out of the building, coughing and gagging, trying to wipe the guano sludge off their faces. A woman shrugged off her sweater and scrubbed her face against the inside. The T-shirt she wore underneath was emblazoned with Talbott Cottle Coles's campaign logo.

"Get us outta here!" Niecy barked.

I called Flynn as soon as my shift was over. The chicken shitting wasn't exactly something I could just call in. Nor did I want to report it to some no-load beat cop like Narkinney.

He answered on the first ring. "What's up, Snap?"

"I just watched a crew of men from an Allied Meat Packing van cover one of Coles's campaign offices in chicken shit. Literally."

Flynn was silent for a moment. "Did you get the plates?"

I gave him the number.

"Nice work." He hung up.

I skip-walked the remaining six blocks to my gold Honda, equal parts ecstatic—Flynn, and depressed—Hank, wanting to go to Joe's and clear my head, but I just . . . couldn't. Ten miles on the basement treadmill watching *Callan* DVDs, however, sounded like a decent alternative.

My phone vibrated. I scrabbled it out of my leg pants pocket. Unknown Caller.

Hank? I leaned against the car. It took two more rings before I felt calm enough to answer. "Hello?"

"Maisie? Lee Sharpe," said a terse staccato.

"What's up?" I asked, not bothering to mask the disappointment in my voice.

"I was wondering if you'd reconsidered."

"What?"

"Dinner. With me."

Lee may be SWAT cool, but he was a hotshot all the same. The fact I hadn't fainted at his feet Saturday must've grated like a sandpaper shirt.

I rubbed the back of my neck. "Look, Lee. That's not such a good idea."

"Why not? Cash said you aren't seeing anyone."

Ouch. I tried to formulate a response, but all I could think of was ways to maim my brother.

"Benny's Chop House. Friday night. We'll hit the Berkshire Room and maybe the Violet Hour after."

Expensive, trendy places. Not a casual, get-to-know-you kind of date. Although I doubted he ever went on more than a couple dates with the same girl. Or needed to.

"Lee—"

"Come on. It's just dinner. It's not like I'm asking you to move in or anything." I could hear the smile in his voice, and for some reason it made me smile back.

"I'll pick you up at eight," he said.

I let my head loll back and banged it gently on the car roof.

"Maisie?"

There was no way anything good was going to come from going out with Lee Sharpe. "Sure," I said. "Why not?"

Chapter 15

Poaching was where the action was. First thing, we hit the end of Sanchez's route—a full city block of doctor's offices next to an always full, fifty-dollar-a-day ramp and two blocks of snooty brownstones with nary an all-day meter box to be seen.

But even after scoring three dozen tickets, we'd be hard-pressed to hit quota. Niecy was worse than deadweight with a bladder the size of a peeled grape. The morning passed pilfering between pit stops, and me wondering how I could possibly talk her into wearing Depends for the rest of the year.

"The senior PEA always chooses where to go for lunch," was the single thing she said, besides telling me her operator number.

At eleven we putt-putted a dozen blocks away from our route to Butch's Beer Garden, a skuzzy little joint where no one gave a flying squirrel about the illegality of secondhand smoke.

"Butch," Niecy called out as we walked in.

"Niecy, baby, where you been?" The bartender set a bag of Lay's plain potato chips on the bar and poured out a Diet Coke.

"Rehab." Niecy gave a squawk of laughter, took the chips and soda, and headed with shaky but determined strides to the back of the bar. I trailed behind like a stray dog.

She planted herself on a red vinyl stool at the rear counter and slapped down two ten-dollar bills. A dumpy waitress counted out twenty pull-tabs and swiped the money off the counter.

One wall of Butch's back room was haphazardly stacked

with ancient TVs all set to off track betting. Three obese guys, wearing the ugliest White Sox crap I'd ever seen, sat chugging beer and bitching about disability restrictions, ripped tickets lying in a pile in front of them.

Niecy grunted, struggling to get her fingers to close on the little paper tab of the gambling ticket. Too painful to watch, on several levels, I wandered back to the front of the bar, ordered a tonic water and lime, and ate my protein bar.

We'd written seventy-three tickets in five hours. I knew we were low, just not how low. I was in desperate need of information. And I knew just where to get it.

Out came the iPhone. Hello eBay.

Ten minutes of surfing and I found it. The perfect bribe. The offer Obi could not refuse.

Thirty-five cents' worth of green plastic.

An original Kenner "Greedo" action figure, N.I.P. (new in package) with a *Buy It Now* price of one hundred and five dollars.

A bargain at twice the price.

I swiped through the PayPal screens. Did I want to pay an additional twenty bucks for overnight delivery?

Hell, yes.

Niecy was in a jovial mood the rest of the afternoon. Coming out five dollars ahead at Butch's made for a banner afternoon. Back in the cart, she rolled down her window and, after misfiring the lighter seven or eight times, lit a cigarette.

She exhaled in my direction. "What's that crap on your boots, McGrane?"

I looked down at the thin slivers of navy blue hockey-stick tape I'd adhered to my boots. "Tape."

"I can see that," she carped. "I got the Parkinson's. I ain't blind."

Perhaps "jovial" had been a little overreaching.

"I put it on," I said. "Inch marks. The quickest way to measure distances from curb, planting strips, and two-inch maximum hang-over into yellow zone lines."

"Not bad, kid." Niecy gave a jerky nod of approval.

I wrote up another fifty-seven tickets. Not a good day, not nearly enough to keep us in the berries, but I was praying I'd hit the lower side of average at least.

Niecey looked at her Timex. "Miller time."

I turned the Interceptor around and drove back to the motor pool.

"Drop me at the gatehouse," Niecy said. I pulled the cart through the gate and stopped at the back of the gatehouse. Chen, the gate guy, was already out of his Plexiglas hut and had Niecy by the arm.

I parked the Interceptor in space 13248. I'd have liked to leave the doors open and air the thing out, but that was against regulations.

C'est la vie.

I took the AutoCITE ticketing guns inside, plugged them in to the computer, and dumped the operator data. Afterward, I loaded the guns into the chargers and went to punch out.

Two women gabbing about baby daddies blocked the time clock. I snapped my time card across the back of my hand over and over. The big one gave me a dirty look over her shoulder and went back to talking. Not moving an inch.

It took a hideous amount of self-restraint not to shove past them.

Forty seconds later, the minute hand clacked on the time clock and they punched out. I took my turn and ran-walked for the door.

I stank of smoke. The PowerBar I'd eaten for lunch sat in my belly like a lump of lead. I was not cut out for breaking the law—any law. Engaging in criminal activity was proving to be an overwhelming amount of work for little reward. Hank or not, I was going to Joe's. I needed to work out or my head was going to explode.

My fingers grabbed the door handle.

"Not so fast, McGrane," Leticia Jackson said.

You gotta be kidding me. I turned and smiled at her.

"Well?"

"One hundred forty-eight. No boots."

"That's it?" Her face crinkled in disapproval. She adjusted the waistband of her pants. "No fish today?"

"Plenty that got away. It's too bad I couldn't just drop her off at Butch's."

"Niecy does love her some pull-tabs." Leticia laughed and waved a hand at me. "I told you I'd take care of you. Just make sure you leave Niecy ahead of you in total. Dhu West'll let you slide a month or three easy with you being new and all." She pointed a finger at me. "You got a cell phone?"

"Yes."

She snapped her fingers. I got it out and handed it to her.

"This be my *personal* number, so don't go handing it out to everyone like it's Halloween candy."

"No, ma'am."

She entered her number into the phone. "Your only job is making sure Niecy's square. Day or night, I don't give a goddamn what time, you call me if you're not coming in. You think you're getting the stomach flu? You call me at three a.m. before you start heaving up that cardboard crap you think is food. You dig?"

"I dig."

Two things were waiting for me on my bed the following day. A FedEx box and a navy blue folder. I opened the folder. Inside was the ME's preliminary report. The final autopsy report would follow in six weeks. And just in case the detectives couldn't remember, the warning "The findings of the scene investigation are preliminary and no final conclusions should be drawn from them" was stamped across every page.

I flipped through multiple photos of Thorne Clark's entry wounds, estimated line drawings of the bullets' angles of entry, and approximate gun distance from the body when fired—more than two feet, less than ten—based on the wounds' abrasion collars. I skimmed through organ and tissue damage. Four type-written pages to confirm that yes, the vic had taken two to the chest and it had killed him.

Approximate time of death was between 11 p.m. and 3 a.m. A few pages of scant victim background—driver's license, address, credit report. A couple more pages of the crime scene photos and drawings and then the prelim ballistics report. The bullets were Buffalo Bore hardcast wadcutters. Shot from a .38 revolver.

Oh yeah.

Flynn knocked on my open door. "You were right. Wads in a revolver. If it was a hitter, he might've used a snubbie. Maybe an S&W K-Frame."

"Hi to you, too." I squinted at my brother. "What's the matter?"

He sank into one of my armchairs and put his feet on the cof-fee table. "The BOC was sniffing around today."

"What'd they have to say about the chicken er . . . waste?"

"I must've forgot to put that in the case file," he said inno-cently. "Coles's office hasn't made a peep, either."

"Fifty gallons of toxic chicken guano." My nose wrinkled at the enormity of the sheer awfulness. "You can't file an insurance claim without a police report."

"Funny, that," Flynn said.

New-in-package Greedo in hand, I went to see Obi. At 5:30 Thursday morning, he was where he always was, control central. I hiked my hip up onto the counter. "I seek your help, Obi-Wan."

He jerked upright, a manga comic of mostly naked women dropped out of his route binder onto the floor. I hopped off, picked it up, and held it out.

A dark red blush climbed his throat. He snatched it from me and secreted it away in one of his wheelchair pouches. "Er, what's up, Maisie?"

"I seek what every young Jedi searches for. Guidance."

Obi looked furtively around, his smeary glasses sliding down his nose, and whispered, "Did you know the tallest man in the world is on average *sixty-eight* inches taller than the shortest? Imagine if the guy was a foot taller."

Eighty short? Holy cat. Leticia wouldn't be able to save our butts. No one could.

"Obi, I'm . . . I didn't know . . ." I sniffed and let out a shuddering breath.

Eighty tickets short of average and the idea of washing out as a meter maid—it wouldn't be too hard to start crying for real.

Obi spun his wheelchair around and pointed his elbow toward the door. "You look like you could use a little fresh air."

Outside, I sat down on a cement parking stop. Obi wheeled up close to me. He was wearing red leather driving gloves. The fingerless kind with venting holes over the knuckles.

"Cool mitts," I said.

"Yeah." His lips parted in a goofy bucktoothed grin. "I really like you, Maisie."

"I *like* you, too, Obi," I said carefully. "And I need this job."

He wheeled nervously back and forth, staring across the parking lot.

I moved into his line of sight. "Niecy does, too."

"Yub, yub. Look, there's a couple things I know that might help."

"Like what?"

"Like all tickets are not equal. On the spreadsheet, a boot is equivalent to two dozen meter tickets. Yellow zones are worth three. Parking in block, auxiliary lane, planting strip, are worth four. Water meter blocking and reserve zone are worth five. There's a bunch more, but mostly, anything on the meter box is only worth one ticket. Even triple tickets on overtime parking meters are worth only the three written."

"So with that hit of Leticia's at the Brothers of Allah . . ."

"Yeah." Obi nodded. "For the month."

"Thanks, Obi. That clears up a lot." I took out the tissue-wrapped Greedo and handed it to him.

"Ohhh!" he breathed, his fingers trembling as he reverently

traced the plastic-covered action figure. "I can't. Maisie, this is too much. It's so special, I—"

"You deserve it." *He'll be in my debt forever.*

I gave him a short salute and turned to go.

"Maisie, wait! There's one more thing. . . ."

Obi's "other thing" was an AutoCITE hack, from that day forward only to be known as *Greedo's Code*. By pressing the eight, three, shift, and reset keys at the same time, I was able to bypass the AutoCITE's system and illegally prefill five tickets. I only had to hit the select key, type the number, and *voilà*, the prewritten ticket loaded and printed with the current time.

We loaded our guns at the meter banks, drove around looking for yellow paint violations, and returned at the time Niecy noted on the Post-it on the dashboard. Technically, I never gave a ticket that wasn't earned. But I felt greasy and dirty and not like a good person anymore.

We circled the block on Donna Brown's route like a couple of starved sharks. Two large apartment buildings faced each other. One a six-story, the other a four. And only one had a private garage.

We'd hit quota by midafternoon.

Niecy took the north side's four meter boxes, picking up two cars hanging over into yellow zones.

I took the south side. As I approached the first meter box, a dark, flapping cloud fell past my head. I ducked behind one of the fenced-in elm trees on the sidewalk.

A pile of clothes. Some clean, some not so clean. *Ugh.*

Next came the shoes. One at a time.

I peered out from beneath the tree. A skinny woman in a hot pink satin bra leaned out the window, holding a Nike in optimum pitching position.

A grubby, shirtless guy in sweatpants and bare feet rushed out of the building. "Jenna!" he screamed. "You bitch! Don't you dare!"

"Bite me!" Jenna threw the Nike.

Screaming Guy tried to catch it. The shoe bounced off his shoulder. "Goddamn it! It's my goddamn apartment! *You* get the hell out!"

"Make me, you cheating piece of shit!" An armful of CDs and DVDs were next, clattering and scattering as they hit the cement. Screaming Guy scuttled back and forth across the sidewalk, trying to gather his junk while avoiding projectiles from above.

I hit my radio when Jenna hefted a heavy, ancient Diehl table fan up onto the sill. "Dispatch! This is Car 13248. Dispatch!"

She shoved it out. It hit the cement with a loud, metallic thud.

"Obi, here," came the voice from my radio. "What's up, Maisie?"

"We're on Fifteenth and Jefferson. Call a squad car. We got a domestic in progress."

The radio hissed with static. "I don't think that's a good idea, Maisie."

A tray full of silverware rained down from the fourth floor. "Call them," I said. "Now! Someone's going to get hurt." *Or killed.*

Screaming Guy ran back up the steps to the apartment building and frantically punched the call buttons to get buzzed in. Nothing. He kicked the glass doors, swearing.

"Don't say I didn't warn you," Obi said.

A television imploded on the sidewalk.

"Call, Obi!"

Cans of food shot out the apartment window, bouncing off the sidewalk, dinging into parked cars.

Screaming Guy ran back down the stairs. "Throw me down the keys, Jenna, so I can come up and cut your fucking throat!"

A can of Campbell's soup dented the hood of a red Kia Soul.

"Jenna! Goddamn it! Not my fucking car!"

Another can hit the sidewalk, clanging against the wrought-iron fencing of the elm I was crouched behind.

Unfazed, Niecy crossed the street and walked up beside me. She stood in front of the Soul and punched in the license plate.

"Get back to work, McGrane. All these friggin' fish are illegally parked."

Screaming Guy caught sight of Niecy sliding the bright orange envelope under the Soul's windshield wiper. "You bitches! You motherfucking Nazi meter bitches!" He ran toward us.

Niecy held up a Taser.

"Yeah? Oh yeah?" he screamed, backing up. "Piss on a guy when he's down, huh?"

A siren sounded from the street.

The last voice in the world I wanted to hear sounded over the loudspeaker. "What'd you do now, 'Meter Maid McGrane'?"

Dammit.

Tommy Narkinney got out of the squad car, wearing a metal splint over his broken nose. Peterson gingerly exited from the driver's-side door, looking murderous. Apparently the bar fight at Hud's was not yet water under the bridge.

Niecy, on a roll, kept ticketing.

"You don't need us." Narkinney pointed over my shoulder, laughing. "You need a car wash."

Screaming Guy was peeing on the Interceptor. Aiming high, letting his hot yellow stream spray across the driver's-side window and down the door handle.

Aw for cripes' sakes.

Peterson let loose a phlegmy chortle.

Screaming Guy, realizing the cops were on his side, danced around the back of the Interceptor, grooving toward me, pants around his knees.

"You two-timing asshole!" Jenna yelled from the window. "Pull your pants up!"

Mostly-Naked Screaming Guy danced closer to me. Peterson and Narkinney howled with laughter.

"Incoming!" I shouted.

A frying pan hurtled through the air, barely missing Peterson. It landed on the patrol car windshield with a sickening crunch.

"You're gonna fuckin' pay for that, McGrane!" Peterson said as he and Narkinney grabbed Screaming Guy, whose pants were now down around his ankles, and dragged him up onto the sidewalk.

The good humor garnered at my expense long gone, Narkinney and Peterson each took a wrist and cable-cuffed Screaming Guy to the wrought-iron fence surrounding the elm tree, face out.

Prolonged indecent exposure, courtesy of the Chicago Police Department. Our tax dollars at work.

Narkinney and Peterson tore up the steps of the apartment building, catching a break as a jogger held the door for them.

"Hey, you! A little help!" Screaming Guy yelled at me. Bare-assed against the fence, dink swinging in the breeze.

A lot of nerve for someone who just peed on my door. I stared at him. "Seriously?"

"For fuck's sake!" he complained. "Gimme a break!"

"Yeah." I bent down and picked up one of the cleaner shirts Jenna had thrown down onto the sidewalk. "Helping you is at the top of my list." I took the shirt over and wiped his pee off the window and door handle of the Interceptor.

"That's my friggin' shirt, meter bitch!"

I walked over to him. "Want it back?" I threw it in his face.

"Arrgh!" He jerked his shoulders, shimmying to get the sodden T-shirt off.

Turnabout, baby.

My smug smile faded to sickly. *Turnabout, indeed.* Narkinney would hold me the rest of the day, under the guise of taking my statement as a witness to Screaming Guy's indecent exposure, public urination, disorderly conduct, domestic violence, and Jenna's attempted assault against a police officer.

We couldn't afford a day of failed quota because he wanted to bust my chops. "C'mon, Niecy," I said, itching to leave. "Let's get out of here."

She started toward the cart and stopped. "Hell. I can't leave him like that."

"Are you kidding me?" I said.

Screaming Guy gave a braying laugh. "The ole lady's got a heart, unlike you!"

Niecy walked over to Screaming Guy, pulled out her cell phone, and took a couple snaps of his exposed unit. "Danged if you don't got yourself a crooked little pisser," she said.

Screaming Guy's face twisted in outrage. "What kind of sick bitch are you?"

Niecy smirked as she walked back to the Interceptor. "The gals in the break room are gonna love this."

Chapter 16

In a relatively good mood after work, I gave Joe a salute as I passed by the zebra-patterned reception desk, not even asking if he'd seen Hank.

"Eeghhh," he said, chewing on a Little Debbie Apple Flip. He held up a finger for me to wait, and took a chug of Yoo-hoo. He pulled a remote out of the drawer and slid it across the counter. "New *Supers*. TiVo'd."

"Wow, thanks! You're the man, Joe."

He grunted and went back to the Apple Flips.

The treadmills were full, as were the ellipticals, which left . . .

Ancient stair stepper, prepare to feel my Supernatural-ized wrath.

I hopped on, set the TV input to Joe's TiVo signal, the stepper to eleven, and watched Sam and Dean battle demons to eighties music, chasing away any thoughts about anything. Near the end of the third episode, my towel damp with sweat, I stepped off and ran smack into Flynn's chest.

"I thought I'd find you here," he said with a mean smile. "Home. Now."

"Let me grab my gear." I trotted to the locker room. Flynn's smile was even meaner by the time I met him in the lobby. He shoved open the front door and grabbed my bruised collarbone with a vise-like grip that put Spock to shame.

"Ow!" I squirmed, trying to duck away. *Bastard Peterson.*

Who hits another person with a beer bottle anyway? "Jeez, what is your problem?"

Flynn grunted and frog-marched me down the sidewalk to where he'd parked next to my car. He peeled out of the parking lot, and I followed him home and into Da's study.

"Sit," he commanded, his posture a study in barely leashed bad cop.

I rubbed my gritty arms as the chill of a real bad feeling settled in.

"What the hell did you think you were doing?"

"Huh?"

"Leaving the scene? Of multiple offenses directed at police officers?"

Oh shit.

"Come on, Flynn." I tried to laugh it off. "A domestic gone awry. Cripes, it was my cart that got peed on. My eyes scarred by the peenie."

"You're not funny," he said. "First Hud's, now this? For God's sake, Maisie. That woman threw a frying pan with enough force to crack a windshield. She could have killed someone."

"Nark's been gunning for me since the Academy and Peterson . . ." My self-righteous complaints dissolved in my throat as I remembered the mile of lies Cash had paved over the incident at Hud's.

"This is not about your *SWAT Gone Wild* fabrication. Nor is it about the ludicrous grudge you have with Narkinney, you selfish, spoiled little—" Flynn broke off and dragged a hand over his face.

A slow exhale and he began again. "This is about respect for the uniform. For those who protect and serve. Someone I thought you aspired to be."

That hurt. A lot worse than the Spock grip.

"You have no idea how lucky you are," he said. "I caught the tail of it from some rookie running his mouth. Three hours of damage control later and now I'm working Thanksgiving. Thanks a whole helluva lot."

"I'm sorry."

Please don't shut me out of the case.

"Oh, it gets worse. Much worse." His dark glare had me squirming. "While I was saving your ass, the BOC stopped by and swiped the Clark case."

Dammit. Dammit. Dammit. "I'm so very sorry."

"And you're going to be more so."

He let me wait for it. Knowing the suspense itself was an additional punishment.

I bit the insides of my cheeks to keep from pleading. Anything I said would be used against me. I glanced ceiling-ward, waiting for the Wile E. Coyote safe to fall on my head.

The corner of his mouth curled. "You're going to call Narkinney and Peterson and apologize for leaving the scene."

"But—"

"And you're going to offer to do whatever it takes to repair the situation." He took his iPhone from his pocket and set it on the coffee table in front of me. "Right now."

Hank's Law Number Thirteen: Anyone can endure expected pain.

I picked up the phone.

"Just hit Call." Flynn said helpfully. "And leave it on speaker." *The bastard.*

I tapped Call on the screen and set the phone on the table between us.

It rang three times. "Narkinney here," he answered in a voice so pleasant I wondered if I'd called his father by mistake.

"Um, this is Maisie McGrane."

"Why, hello there, Maisie. I'm so glad to hear your voice. I was worried something happened to you."

"Oh really?" I said, acid burning a hole through my tongue.

Flynn held up a finger in warning.

"Yeah," Narkinney said. "You tell me. Why would a Police Academy cadet who could not shut up about scoring a ninety-five on procedure ignore said procedure and leave the scene?"

Jerkwad. "My partner and I were certain that with two such accomplished officers as you and Mr. Peterson on top of the situation, the public would be better served by us returning to traffic management."

He chuckled. "Mmm-hmm. I guess it's a good thing you washed out, your memory being so short."

Blood pulsed behind my eyes.

Suck it up.

"At any rate, I'd like to apologize," I said, forcing the words out like a guy having to ask for directions. "If you'd like me to come in and make a statement, I'll do so immediately."

"No need," Tommy said in a lecherous voice that he wouldn't have dared use face-to-face. "I'll just take it in trade, Maisie-Daisy."

My brother's lip curled in revulsion. He grabbed the phone and turned the speaker function off. "Narkinney?" He sat back in his chair, a wide smile on his face making him sound friendly while his eyes were as empty as a shark's. "Flynn McGrane. Impressive, volunteering alongside Peterson to become a liaison for the Traffic Enforcement Bureau." He nodded. "A big commitment from a rookie." He turned his flat gaze on me. "Maisie will be submitting a letter to her supervisor commending you and your partner's quick response to the situation, as well as copying your CO."

For crying out loud.

"Yeah . . . Sure . . . Appreciate that." He put the phone back on speaker and set it on the table. "Is Peterson there? Maisie would like to speak to him, as well."

"As a matter of fact, he is."

There was a slight scuffling sound. "Peterson."

"Officer Peterson, this is Maisie McGrane." *You remember, the girl you assaulted with a beer bottle last Friday night, you son of a bitch.*

Walking Flynn's way, I pasted a cheerleader's Vaseline smile on my face. "I'm sorry for any inconvenience I may have caused you and your partner."

Peterson grunted. "Pull this shit again and I'll throw your ass in jail."

"Okayee," I said perkily. "'Bye." I clicked off the phone.

"This stays between us," Flynn said. "Only because Mom and Da don't need the aggravation right now."

"Thank you."

"Go write the letters." He picked up the TV remote. "And for chrissakes, Snap, shape up." He clicked the TV on. Talk over.

I went upstairs to my room, belly full of crow casserole and skin coated in a combination of dried sweat and humiliation ooze. At least I hadn't showered before fake-apologizing.

I had to hand it to Flynn. Rocking the guilt almost as well as our Irish grandmother. He really ought to get married, have a baby, and make its life hell.

Chapter 17

Daicen, the saint, didn't become the family mediator by accident. Cunning and wise and surprisingly candid, he had a theory on groveling. "When you're forced to crawl on your belly, facedown in the muck, it's best to inhale great heaping gasps of it, letting it fill your nose, mouth, and lungs. Not because it gets any easier, but because you sure as hell don't want to do it again."

I addressed and printed out three copies of my letter of mucksuck. One for Narkinney and Peterson's CO, one for Jennifer Lince, and one for Jennifer's supreme supervisor, Dhu West's PR manager Sterling Black. Might as well bank a little goodwill.

Friday morning, I swung by Dhu West's office in the Paxton Tower before work and rid myself of my elephantine burden of shame. Two letters of false praise secured with the reception desk's early morning guard and the dreaded muck-suck into the outgoing mail slot.

Equal parts relieved and ticked off, I went to work.

Niecy and I spent the morning poaching Kay Moody's route. At least my partner wasn't smoking. With all the Aqua Net and Jean Naté fuming off her, one match and *whooomph!* The Interceptor would erupt in flames like something out of a cheap Chinese action movie.

"Eh!" Niecy said. "Where the effin' hell you taking us?"

I kept my eyes on the road. "The route we were assigned."

"Puck it. The strip in front of City Hall's a dead zone." Niecy snorted. "Swing by Butch's instead. Early lunch."

I didn't bother responding, just kept driving.

"Crap, you're a hardheaded little bastard."

"Me?" I turned onto the strip. There he was again. Mr. Lincoln. Begging for a throw-down.

"Take a gander at that holier-than-heck piece of crap," Niecy said.

"You gotta be kidding me," I muttered under my breath and squared my shoulders. "Uh, Niecy? We ran him a $575 ticket a couple days ago."

She smiled big enough to reveal some serious dental work and slapped her hand on her thigh in applause. "And we're gonna do it again."

"Yeah, about that . . . It's the mayor's limo."

"So? I didn't vote for that lil' pink monkey boner. His office has to file forgiveness paperwork and we still get credit. Nail him."

"Roll down the window." I hopped out. "You're gonna love this."

I approached the limo and knocked on the illegally tinted driver's-side window. It slid down whisper-quiet to reveal the uniformed chauffeur leering at me. "You back to boss me up?"

I wasn't exactly sure what that meant, but my answer was an emphatic no. "Not today, sir. You're standing in a fire lane, blocking a hydrant, with a rear tire on the curb. $310." I smiled at my reflection in his mirrored shades.

"Don't you give a shit about the environment, girl?"

"As much as the next third-world nation."

"Then why you want me rolling these rims all over town burning up the fossil fuels?"

"Actually, idling for hours does *more* harm to the environment," I said, lying like a salesgirl in a plus-size shop. "It puts greater wear on the engine, which will need to be replaced sooner, and idling still burns gas."

A good bluster backs down plenty of bullies. He seemed to like it. "You got a name?"

"Agent McGrane."

"Whoot! *Agent.*" He chortled.

"How'd the mayor like his present?" I asked.

He stopped laughing. "What you talkin' 'bout?"

"The chicken shitting."

He sucked his teeth, reassessing me. "You cattin' off, girl. Coming at me like that."

"Am I?"

"You is."

Perhaps baiting him had been a bit hasty. I held up my AutoCITE. "Gonna move?"

"No. Go on and write it, girl. It's your neck in the noose."

I held out the ticket. He grabbed my wrist. "They call me Poppa Dozen." He ran a thick tongue over his tea-colored teeth. "I'll show you why anytime you wanna take a look." He twisted my forearm, forcing me in closer, my head now inside the car. "You best watch yo self, bluebird. When I need to handle someone, I do it up close and personal–like. You dig?"

I yanked my arm free, ticket fluttering to his lap, and staggered back from the car. "Have a nice day," I said, proud the shake in my knees wasn't in my voice.

"Yo! McGrane!" He ripped the ticket in half, then in half again, and tossed the pieces to the ground. "You gonna ticket me for that?"

"Not my department, Poppa Environmentalist." I turned and walked back to the cart.

Niecy's face was screwed-up bitter-beer tight. We took off. She made it to the end of the block before folding over with laughter.

Butch's was starting to seem like a great idea.

"Agent McGrane." The radio on my reflective neon vest crackled. "This is Dispatch, over."

I clicked it. "Go ahead, Obi."

"Orders from Ms. Lince. You're to report to Dhu West immediately."

Jennifer Lince, in a dark pink Donna Karan suit, put a finger to her lips, pressed a button, and let me listen in on speakerphone. "Yes, Mr. Black. A perfect example of how efficiently Dhu West can work together with regular city employees."

"That's exactly the kind of forward thinking that drives the positive press we need. Great work, Jennifer. And keep an eye on this McGrane character. Unbelievable. A PEA who can write in complete sentences."

Jennifer trilled a girlish giggle. "Will do, Mr. Black."

He disconnected and Jennifer punched the phone off. She turned to me, hands clasped to her breast. "The mayor's PR director called Sterling Black today." She pressed her hands to her cheeks. "It seems Officer Narkinney's lieutenant is the brother of the mayor's chief of staff."

"Neat," I said, getting that sinking feeling. *Poppa Dozen's tickets haven't hit yet.*

She tossed her head, her pale-blond french twist remained motionless, shellacked in place with hair spray. "Why, I'm so happy I can't even think!" Closing her eyes, she blew out a long breath, placed her fingertips on the edge of the desk and turned her full focus on me. "While that was a complimentary letter you penned, it was very naughty to send it out without the proper supervisory approval."

Really? You're having a conniption of joy like some dingo on a baby and I'm getting the scold?

I had a sudden urge to crack my knuckles. "It won't happen again, Ms. Lince."

"Jennifer. No need for us to be so formal."

"Yes, ma'am." *I prefer formality, it keeps me alert. Ready for when someone is going to come up behind me, carve out my kidney, and sell it on the black market to some wealthy second-rate foreign national saddled with socialized medicine.*

"Maisie, Maisie, Maisie."

There was just something about the way she said my name—like two pieces of Styrofoam rubbing together. She picked an invisible lint speck from her skirt. "Do you remember the conversation we had when I assigned you your badge?"

I nodded. Sweat broke out between my shoulder blades. *Here it comes. The shrapnel from Jennifer Lince's "Bust Niecy's Hump" land mine.*

She lifted the lid of her laptop and clicked a few keys. An

Excel spreadsheet opened onscreen. "Surprisingly, you and your partner's numbers are dead-center average." She gave me a withering smile. "I'd hate to have to rethink this assignment."

What do you want me to do? Take a tire iron to her hip?

Jennifer folded her hands on the desk and said wistfully, "Eunice Peat is the PEA's misfortune."

Silly me. It wasn't the crappy poly-blend uniform, the ostracism of everyday citizens, or even the random bits of horror propagated by lunatics when we've no recourse at hand.

The misfortune was Niecy.

"A ticking time bomb, I'm afraid. Have you taken note of any improprieties?"

It was a challenge not to shudder. "No, ma'am."

Jennifer rolled her chair back from the desk and crossed her thin legs. "Who are you wearing?"

"Huh?" *Last time I checked it was Kale Uniforms for the PEA.*

"To the Gala, of course. I've just had the final tailoring done to the most gorgeous Mark + James shell-pink gown." She smiled.

Oh goody. Girly chat. Just the thing after trying to coerce me into betraying a coworker.

"It's black-tie optional and while obviously Caiseal would suit perfectly in a tuxedo, I believe that when one is in a position of authority it's best *not* to wear black tie, as it keeps one more relatable to the rest of the employees."

How can she say that without puckering?

"Caiseal has been absolutely impossible to get in touch with the last few days. I cannot understand what drives someone to work in such a dangerous profession, with terrible hours and barely adequate pay."

Funny, I could think of a million reasons.

She gave a tremulous little shake, like a dove after coming out of a magician's sleeve. "Do you know which color suit he's going to wear? Black or navy?"

I coughed to keep from laughing. "I'm not sure."

"Black, probably. He wears enough blue during the day."

Wrong. There's no such thing as enough blue.

Jennifer held up two black ties, one with pale pink flecks in a black-on-black paisley print and the other with subdued pale-pink stripes. "Which would he prefer?"

Neither. "I honestly can't say."

She laid the ties back in the cover of the Barneys box, rummaged through the tissue, and held up two navy ties with pale-pink detailing. "Or these."

Cash is going to kill me.

"So who are you bringing?"

"Uh . . . Gosh, Ms. Lin . . . er . . . Jennifer, I haven't quite decided yet."

"You shouldn't leave it too long, you know. Who you bring says as much about you as your outfit."

Chapter 18

At five o'clock I found myself with a couple of hours to kill. Plenty of time to go to Joe's, hit the jump rope, speed bag, and spend a good long time getting ready in the empty women's locker room. On the way to my car, I scrolled through my incoming call list, found Lee's number, and pressed Call.

"Lee Sharpe." He had a nice voice.

"Hi, it's Maisie."

"How you doing?" he said casually, but I could hear the question of *are you cancelling last-minute?* in his voice.

"I was wondering if you could pick me up at Joe's Gym tonight?" *You never know. There was the miniscule chance Hank might turn up and it would serve him right.*

"A little too early for me to meet the family?"

"Not at all. Feel free to drive over and introduce yourself. I'll be at Joe's. Self-preservation."

Lee laughed. Warm and charming. "You bet. See you at eight."

In the locker room, I started to worry that going out with Lee was a mistake. A big one.

A lonely little piranha of hope nibble-gnawed at my brain. Hank wasn't the kind of guy that would stand me up. And not call. Not for a week. Not without a reason . . .

I blew out a breath and put on some lip gloss.

I sure as heck am not wearing my heart on my sleeve for a

guy who's just not that into me. I mean—I am, but I sure as hell am wearing a jacket over it.

My mother had taught me every man was a lesson unto himself. *"Use the ones you're not interested in as practice for the ones you are."* A little cold-blooded, maybe, but July McGrane's dating advice was a highly coveted commodity.

Karmic *quid pro quo* for a player like Lee Sharpe.

I'd chosen my clothes accordingly. Black high-heeled, strappy Stuart Weitzman sandals, slim black pants, and a fluttery sheer-sleeved, high-necked black blouse. Completely covered up in form-fitting but not tight clothes. The antithetical outfit for a guy used to scantily clad women throwing themselves at his feet.

Perfect.

A raven-haired waitress in a low-cut top served us two Ketel One martinis on the rocks with olives, lingering in front of Lee. I watched her leave. He didn't.

"It's your game," I said. "You go first."

"Brad Thor, *Predator,* Lynyrd Skynyrd, Captain Crunch, and Under Armour," Lee said.

"Hmmm," I said, scrambling. "Dick Francis, *Kill Bill Volume 1*, Cake, Cocoa Puffs, and Nike."

"Acceptable." He smiled and tipped his hand back and forth. "Nike's a little iffy, but I'll let it slide." He took a drink of his martini. "Worst date ever?"

"Can't say. Ours isn't over yet."

"Oh, you're a funny one, you are." He drummed his fingers on the table, bongo-style. His barely contained energy, strangely endearing. "Okay, *again*, I'll go first. My worst. Eighth grade. Getting caught naked in my tenth-grade girlfriend's bedroom."

"Ehhhgh. You were having sex in eighth grade?"

Lee cocked his head. "I didn't say I was having sex. I said I was naked."

"Stop." I laughed. "I don't want to know."

"I do. I want to know about you. C'mon, tell me."

I ran a hand through my hair. "My worst dates were just *too.*"

"Two?"

"Too boring, too skeevie, too geeky, too—*too*."

Lee fell back in his chair and shook his head in disappoint-ment. "That is the most feeble answer I've ever heard."

"I didn't realize this was a competition." I tapped my cheek with my finger. "Gosh, any guy who wasn't scared off by my Da, Serpico, was threatened and/or tortured by my brothers."

Lee pursed his lips in mock agreement. "Yeah. That's right. Nothing to tell."

I rocked my head from side to side, shaking loose a few of the hundreds of cringeworthy memories. "Okay. How about my brothers dumping a trash can full of water on my homecoming date? No, hang on—the time Rory showed up and dropped the guy's juvie rap sheet on the table at the restaurant in front of all my friends. Or maybe when Declan set up a fake IRS audit on a junior investment banker I really liked." I picked up my drink and set it down again. "I got it." My lips curled in a wicked grin. "Hands down, best-ever worst moment. Flynn tagging my date in the back of the head with a paintball gun, sniper-style at the make-out bluffs."

"Okay, okay." Lee laughed. "You win. Or they do."

And so it went. He was fun to talk to, smart, with a cavalier edge of confidence that said "Of course you like me, because I like me."

And I did, I realized, like Lee.

As I hadn't gone on a real date since I first laid eyes on Hank, the inevitable comparisons between them ran across my brain like the stock ticker tape on the Fox Business Network. Hank maintained a strong ten-length lead of pure chemical infatua-tion. But where Hank was unattainable, Lee was accessible. Scarily open, even.

"Thrill me with a little shoptalk," he said.

I did, telling him all the stories I'd planned to tell Hank. Lee, laughing his warm laugh in all the right places. "—so Poppa Dozen grabs my arm and says *I take care*—"

An edge of a thought eddied in my brain.

"Maisie?"

"Sorry." I crinkled my nose and shook my head. "He says, 'I take care of business up close and personal–like.' What does that sound like to you?"

"A threat." He rested his chin on his hand. "Or a hit."

I tapped my nose and pointed at him.

"Charades, is it?" He tapped his nose and pointed back at me. "I take it the McGranes are a game-playing family."

"Is there any other kind?"

"I wouldn't mind playing some." Lee twirled a spoon between his fingers. "How about dessert?"

Hank may own the Laws of Combat, but my mother has the Rules of Engagement. Of course, in a year and a half, I never quite got close enough to use my mother's rules on Hank, but that didn't mean they didn't work.

Which was why after dessert I made Lee take me home instead of moving on to the Violet Hour.

July McGrane's Rules of Engagement Number One: Leave while you're having a wonderful time.

Check.

Lee didn't put up much of a fight, too intrigued by where I wasn't taking the date.

July McGrane's Rules of Engagement Number Three: Maintain a sense of mystery.

Check.

Lee and I waited at the valet stand of Benny's Chop House for his Bullitt Mustang. Once Mom got a gander at Lee's Steve McQueen highland green, she'd melt like chocolate in the sun.

"You really want to go home?" Lee asked, as he handed the valet a twenty.

"Yes."

I slid into the seat, Lee closed the door behind me, and rounded the Mustang in quick strides. The backseat was littered with jackets, sweats, ball caps, and black duffel bags jammed with gear. Not filthy but messy. And it made me feel more at ease somehow.

We stopped in front of my house. He revved the car as though he was going to pull up to the keypad and camera.

"Seriously, Lee. Stop. We'll have half of Homicide out here if you pull into the gate."

"It's only eleven thirty. It's not like I kept you out all night." Lee parked on the street, in front of the driveway. "In fact, I barely spent any time with you at all."

He popped his seat belt and turned sideways in his seat to face me, forearm propped on the steering wheel. I undid my seat belt.

Lee crooked a finger at me. "C'mere."

"Why?" I asked, and leaned the slightest bit forward.

He grinned. "I want to kiss you."

I drew back, hand at my throat, and laid on the thickest Southern drawl I could muster. "Why, Mr. Sharpe! I accepted your invitation to dinner. But an improper advance? And to think, I *trusted* you."

"Did you now?" Lee laughed. "That was silly." He didn't move, waiting for me to, enjoying this. Because there's nothing a player likes more than a new game with new rules.

I held out my hand. He took it.

"Thank you for dinner," I said.

"So that's it?" he asked and kissed the back of my hand, brown eyes crinkling at the corners. "You're just going to go in and go to bed?"

"Oh no," I said, perfectly serious. "First, I'm going to kneel down beside my bed and say ten Hail Marys and five Our Fathers for impure thoughts."

"Catholic school?" he said.

"St. Ignatius. And the uniform still fits."

"You're an imp, Maisie."

"And you're only now figuring that out?"

Lee got out of the car, came around, and opened my door.

"Thanks," I said, as he closed it behind me. "But please, don't walk me to the door."

He flashed his palms and backed away around the hood of the car. I giggled. He drummed his hands on the driver's-side roof. "I'll be thinking about you tonight."

"In a plaid skirt and school tie, no doubt."

Lee laughed and got in the car. I typed the code into the gate and it swung open. He sat in the car, waiting. I waved him on with mock flourish, feeling flirty and cute.

The taillights of the green Mustang faded into darkness, and I walked toward the house—the lightness of Lee carrying me up the driveway—and then, like hearing the losing number on a lotto ticket, the happy feeling was gone.

Who am I kidding? I'm a lawbreaking meter maid Police Academy washout. Flynn was still mad as hell at me, my reinstatement was about as accessible as a trip to Mars. And Hank . . .

I stamped my heels in a little not-gonna-go-there dance and walked up the sidewalk.

"Gah!" I clattered backwards at the dark shape of a man leaning against one of the portico pillars, recognizing him before I even regained my balance.

He pushed off the pillar and stepped into the light. His close-cropped hair had gone slightly shaggy, and stubble covered the hard line of his jaw. He looked tired and untouchable and perfect.

"Sorry I'm late, Doll Face." His deep voice vibrated in my chest, and the part of me that is unfamiliar with the word *pride* thrummed with pure delight.

I glanced at my watch. "Only a week and three hours."

Raised on film noir, I'd dreamt of this moment. Fantasized about it the way most girls plan their wedding. A tough guy with a dark side walks through the door, and I am the jaded siren, as smooth and cool as window glass in winter.

"How are you?" he asked.

Be cool.

"Glad to see you," I said a little too earnestly.

Not cool at all.

Why-oh-why did I have those martinis with Lee?

His grin flashed white in the darkness. "I'm glad to see you, too. How's the job?"

"It's been a series of diverse learning experiences. So far, someone dumped an old milk shake on my head, a guy peed on my cart, I found a dead body, and had a front-row seat to a low-budget *Godfather*-style retaliation."

He laughed. "And you're certain law school is a terrible idea."

"Where were you, Hank?" The words popped right out of my mouth. *From lame to pathetic in six-tenths of a second.*

"Cali."

"Oh?" I said archly. "And there're no phones in California?"

"Not clean ones. Not in Cali, Colombia."

Oh. "What were you doing there?"

The smile faded from his face. "Things other people won't."

"Okay." I nodded. "Okay. I don't need to know." The words turned to ash in my mouth.

"That's the first lie you've ever told me."

"Oh yeah?" A perverse spark of happiness danced in my brain that he'd noticed. "What happened?"

He gave his head a slight shake and put his hand on my shoulder.

Of course, you can't tell me. "Is that why you're here? Looking for a little absolution?"

"Maybe." Hank's hand slid up the back of my neck, sifting his fingers through my hair. "Does it matter?"

It felt so good, my vision blurred. "Real people don't live like characters in a Vince Flynn book."

"I do." He closed the distance between us and kissed me. Fierce and hot, his fingers tangled in my hair, my brain liquefying into melted honey. His hands slid down around my hips, his teeth closed on my ear.

Oooh. I shuddered and the alarm in my head went off. "Hank—"

He nuzzled his scruffy chin against my collarbone and trailed a line of nipping kisses up my neck. He raised his head, the muscles around his gunmetal-gray eyes tight. "Come home with me."

Every atom of my body screamed yes. But I just wasn't built that way. With a shaky breath, I stepped back. "I c-can't."

A shadow flickered across his face. "How was your date?"

I shoulda, woulda seen that one coming. "Uh . . . nice," I said, with the slow concentration of a punch-drunk boxer. "Real . . . nice."

"Good," he said. "That's good for you."

"Is it?" *Please please please tell me it's not.*

Hank's mouth quirked up at the corner. "Yeah. It is."

For a split second I thought he might touch me.

He didn't. Just walked away to the Super Bee, parked in the shadows, invisible from the street.

What's so great about tough guys, anyway?

Chapter 19

I lay awake all night thinking about Hank, feeling more naïve and coddled than ever. Unfathomable. Along the lines of explaining molecular nanotechnology to a baboon. And I was the baboon.

I spent the early morning moping around and got roped into playing tennis with Daicen, Declan, and Mom at the club. Forgetting that playing anything with three lawyers is about as much fun as waiting for license tabs at the DMV.

Afterward, they enjoyed a long, arguing brunch while I glugged two glasses of Riesling and began giggling uncontrollably. Side aching, I suggested that since they were basically playing the legal version of Dungeons & Dragons, maybe they'd have more fun finishing up with a bunch of twenty-sided dice in the basement.

Unamused, they dropped me off at home and went back to work.

Flynn and Rory were in the kitchen. I wasn't exactly their favorite person, either.

A Band-Aid ripper at heart, there's no point in skulking about. "Hi, guys."

Nothing doing. They didn't even look up.

Neato. The Silent Treatment. "I'm sorry about what happened."

"It's not your fault," Flynn said.

Rory gave a derisive snort.

"Neither of us could have stopped the BOC from commandeering the case." Flynn blew out a breath. "Da could have. Maybe."

"Like feck he would. He's just as fast to roll over as the rest of 'em. It's all a pile of political shite." Rory rolled his tongue in his cheek. "Mebbe we've outgrown the CPD, eh?" He shoved away from the counter. "I'm going out."

Flynn and I watched him stalk away.

"He's all talk," Flynn said. "It takes a toll, you know? Kids killing kids. For drugs, for money, for the hell of it. So when you finally get a real case . . ." He shook his head. "Heck, we were only in Clark's house for about fifteen minutes before we got called out on a drive-by. We had the techs bag what little we could and beat it. The BOC's been there, cleared the place out. Probably found exactly what we were looking for."

"And what's that?" I asked.

"The connection. The link between Keith Nawisko and Thorne Clark. There is one. Has to be. Two pro hits."

"Different weapons," I said.

"Both public places. Close contact. The lack of fear . . . They're linked. I'm certain of it."

"What if they didn't find it? What if it's still in Clark's apartment?"

"If Pollyanna were a Valkyrie . . ." He reached over and ruffled my hair. "Sorry your unofficial consult won't make it into your jacket. I'll put you on the next one, though, Snap. I won't let you stay a meter maid forever."

His magnanimity cut me to the quick.

I was going to find a link if it killed me.

9:30 p.m. I parked a couple doors down from the small, brownstone apartment building. Late enough that most people weren't going out, but early enough that no one took any notice of a little extra noise.

I checked my gear and caught my reflection in the rearview. I was really going to do this. Looking forward to it, even. My green eyes danced with excitement, cheeks pink with risk.

"Screw this up," I warned myself, "and you'll never ever become a cop."

Well, then. Best not screw up.

I pulled the black hood of my jacket over my ponytail, made sure the dome light was off, and got out of the car. A gibbous moon lit the empty sidewalk. I sidled up to the apartment building, climbed the first two steps, and bent down to tie my shoe. I tied it twice before a hand-holding couple left the building. Someone was on my side, angels or devils, I wasn't sure. They even held the door for me.

Inside, I skipped the elevator and took the stairs to the fourth floor two at a time, glad to expend some nervous energy.

Clark's apartment, A, was at the opposite end of the building, closest to the elevator. I padded down the hallway, stopping at the three other apartments, D, C, and B, listening at the doors. TV blared from C. The others were silent.

An eight-and-a-half-by-eleven police seal sticker had been sloppily pasted across the door and jamb.

I took a razor blade from my back pocket and slit the fibrous paper along the door seam. I glanced down the empty hall and pulled the Shomer-Tec lock-pick gun from my jacket. It resembled a flattened cap gun with a long thin piece of steel protruding from the barrel.

With five brothers who liked to lock me in as well as out of everything, the snap gun had proven to be the smartest fifty bucks I ever spent growing up. Contrary to the movies, picking a lock was tough, not the technique as much as having steady hands under high adrenaline.

It was called a snap gun for a reason. It was damn loud. My hands were sweating.

Hank's Law Number Four: Keep your head.

I freed the tension wrench, a slim bent piece of steel, from the handle of the gun and slid it into the lock. With the wrench in place, I put the needle nose of the snap gun into the lock, took a quick breath, and then pulled the trigger fast and hard.

The gun jumped in my hand, as the needle nose struck the

pins upward to hit the shear line. The metallic clicks blasting like fireworks, ringing in my ears.

It took eleven snaps—twenty-three seconds—to unseat the lock.

Olly olly oxen free.

With a final look down the hallway, I twisted the tension wrench, opened the door, and stepped across the threshold. The stopwatch in my brain started ticking, drumming, actually, as I closed the door behind me.

With a flashlight, gloves, and infinite care, I rapidly searched the kitchen. I checked the freezer, the fridge, cabinets, and under the sink. I even pulled the liner in the kitchen trash can to see if Clark had squirreled something beneath.

Zip.

Flynn was sure these hits were connected. I needed something, anything, that showed Thorne Clark and Keith Nawisko were related.

I cycled through the dining room—the table the only furniture to show signs of life with a bowl of wrinkling apples—and made my way into the living room. West Elm cream-colored sofas with red pillows and CB2 artwork. Design magazines in a galvanized tub. A stop sign hung above the fireplace mantel.

Tick. Tick. Tick.

The apartment was a modest two-bedroom remodel with open kitchen, dining nook, and great room that wasn't great enough to hide something Flynn and Rory might have overlooked.

The BOC's evidence team had paid the most attention to the smaller bedroom/office. Thorne's computer and laptop had been removed, as evidenced from the dust pattern and cords left behind on the desk. The file cabinet had been emptied, as well. I went into the bedroom. A flick of the flashlight showed a low profile bed, with a pair of New Balance mule sneakers serving as slippers on one side of the bed.

I went to the dresser. Aside from a giant Mason jar of change on the dresser, an ancient kitschy kangaroo ring and wallet caddy, Ray-Bans, and a stack of catalogs, nothing. I checked under the mattress, as well as the bed and pillows. No photos.

Zero.

The only signs of personality left in the apartment were the clothes in the closet. Brooks Brothers shirts and suits, Levi's, pithy Threadless tees, and Target underwear.

Tick. Tick. Tick.

Clenching the flashlight between my teeth, I went back to the dresser and started rifling through the dresser drawers, running my hands along the undersides. Talking myself down in looped internal monologue. *Nobody lives here. Keep calm. Room by room. There has to be something.*

Except that I'd been in the apartment almost ten minutes and had turned up less than nothing. I gagged on my flashlight and kept looking.

Apprehension prickled my skin. The eerie feeling you get that someone is watching you, because someone is.

I clicked off the flashlight and crouched down beside the bed.

A hulking black shadow loomed in the doorway.

I skittered backwards, tripped over the tennis shoes, and crashed into the bureau, tipping over the giant Mason jar of change, which rained onto the floor in a hideous symphony.

Oh Jesus. Game over.

"A little noisy for a cat burglar," Hank said.

It took me a good thirty seconds to catch my breath.

"You through here?"

"I don't know," I said, buzzing from the heady cocktail of shock and mortification with a twist of relief. "Am I?"

He grabbed my arm and manhandled me into the kitchen. "You want to get hurt? Caught? Or both?" He smacked the tension wrench I'd left in the door on the counter.

I winced. I'd left the wrench in the door so I wouldn't have to use the snap gun again to lock it. A stupid and lazy mistake.

Hank tossed a crumpled piece of paper on top of the wrench. I turned on the flashlight. A computer screen shot: grassed.com. *Top Twenty Places to Hide Your Stash.* "What's this?"

"Clark's web history."

"But the CPD has his computers."

"More than one way to skin a cat, Sunshine." He moved to the center of the dining room table and reached beneath it. "Number sixteen."

#16: The drop leaf in the dining room table.

The ingenuity of drug addicts is sadly impressive.

Standing at either end, we pulled the table apart. Four bank-wrapped stacks of fifty-dollar bills sat atop a composition book on the unused wooden panel. Hank slipped the book into his jacket and pocketed the money.

"What is it?"

"No," he said.

"But—"

"What are you doing here?"

I pressed my lips together. *Two can play at this game.*

"Goddammit," he muttered and moved in tight, his face inches from mine. "Wise up. You may be a McGrane, but you'll never be one of the boys."

Funny how not much in life is crueler than the truth.

A sigh squeezed its way out of my chest.

"Let's go," he said.

"I, uh . . . think I'll clean up the pennies, first."

"Always look for the smoothest point of ingress." Hank climbed out of the window onto the fire escape. "Basic recon. I'll leave the stairs down."

I walked back into the bedroom, lifted the fallen jar off its side, got down on my hands and knees, and started scooping change into it as quickly and quietly as possible.

It wasn't as though I could tell my brothers about Hank or what he found in the table.

Suck-tastic.

Tonight definitely made the top ten of Most Imbecilic Things I've Done Lately.

Finished, I stood up and nudged the kangaroo caddy to make some space for the jar on the dresser. It didn't move. I bumped it harder, and it tipped.

I set the jar down and picked up the caddy. A silver ring hung from the tail, the belly held two pair of cuff links, one set with the mayor's election logos, the other his fraternity. I slid a finger underneath.

A photograph fluttered down to the dresser. It had been taped to the base. Thorne Clark smiling with his arm around a hard-looking blonde with sly eyes.

I'd seen her before.

The woman who gave the nod to the men who'd dumped the guano in Coles's campaign office.

I flipped over the photo. A phone number was scrawled across the back.

Maybe tonight's adventure hadn't been so stupid after all.

Chapter 20

I woke up the next morning to a mostly empty house. Flynn and Rory were sandbagged at work with a murder-suicide. Da had locked himself in the office, which meant no access to the family system to try and figure out who the blonde was or back-trace the phone number. I took a picture of both sides of the photo and debated texting it to Flynn.

Working out did nothing to lessen the thoughts ping-ponging in my brain. What to tell my brothers? What not to tell them? And Hank. Always Hank. I got off the treadmill.

When the universe is against you, it's best to hunker down and hoark out.

I spent the afternoon on the couch in Da's den, drinking sugar Coke, eating sea-salt pita chips and Milk Duds, while binge-watching old episodes of *Wire in the Blood*.

"What's going on in here?" Da poured himself a whiskey and eased down next to me.

"Guilty pleasures."

He ran a hand over my hair, then took the box of Milk Duds off my lap and shook some into his hand. "Aye. We two haven't had a proper sit in donkey's years."

My Coke caught in a choking snort. "Who are you, king of the leprechauns?"

He smiled and waggled his brows. The phone rang. Da glanced at the caller ID and handed it to me.

Hank Bannon.

I let it ring twice more. Eyes alight, Da nestled deeper into the couch.

"Really?" I said, but I was secretly glad he was staying. I'd be less . . . *less*. I clicked the phone. "Hello?"

"Miss McGrane, please," said the sultry voice I was pretty sure I despised.

"Speaking."

"Mr. Bannon would like a meet."

Oh, would he? I chewed my lip and glanced at Da. "When?"

"A car will be there in fifteen minutes."

That sounded ominous. I angled for a hint. "Dress code?"

"Come as you are."

Gee, thanks. "Okay." I hung up and tossed the phone on the coffee table.

"So the fella says jump . . ." Da said.

I put my hands on his cheeks and tried to salvage some self-respect. "Ach, me poor, innocent Da. Cain't ye see I aim to run the lad to ground, all the while making him think it be his idee?"

Da rolled his eyes and shouted at my back as I sprinted from the room. "That's the worst brogue I've ever heard."

Upstairs, I got cuted-up as fast as possible before throwing on a girly dress with a flouncy skirt and battered Frye cowboy boots. I twirled once in front of the mirror. Fresh and innocent when I felt anything but.

A strangely familiar man in a suit and sunglasses assisted me into the back of a navy BMW 5 Series and drove me to the ship-yard warehouses. He didn't speak. A single word. Which didn't exactly aid in my quest to ID him.

He stopped in front of a crumbling brick building with the single weathered word *Refrigeration* legible. Sunglasses opened my car door and together we walked to the entrance. He un-locked the door and I followed him down a shadowy hallway. Overhead, the few working fluorescent lights buzzed and snapped.

Talk about showing a girl a good time.

We stopped at a steel door. Sunglasses knocked twice, then inserted a key and swung open the door. Hank waited in front of a white tiled wall, wearing a grimy white T-shirt, torn desert camo pants, and black boots.

My mouth went dry. Filthy and sweaty never looked so primal-sexy. I scanned the rest of the room, trying to get frosty.

A bare bulb on a wire hung above a card table with a laptop and two chairs. "Nice." I raised my chin. "I like the *Saw VI* vibe you got going on here."

Hank smirked.

Sunglasses moved behind me to the card table. As he leaned forward to pull out the chair, I caught sight of the thinnest of lines that ran along the edge of his hairline, down the temple, and around his ear. The penny dropped. He'd trained with Hank. One of his short-stint rehabbers. Only when I'd seen him, his face had been littered with shrapnel.

"How was the drive in?" Hank said.

"Silent." I crossed the gritty cement floor and took the proffered seat.

Hank jerked his head at Sunglasses, who walked toward the door.

"Salvatore looks terrific, though," I said. The slight hitch in the driver's step confirmed his identity. The door opened, closed, and locked behind him. "Where was he? Beverly Hills?"

"Brazil." Hank walked over to the table. "The best reconstruction guys are in South America now." He sat down and pushed the closed laptop in front of me.

I opened the computer. The browser was open to www.hill buzz.org, Kevin Dujan's underground city gossip column. The webpage had the operator's coding open. The blog hadn't been posted yet.

> Will Windy City bus drivers soon be wearing
> burkas? Chi-town's illustrious mayor Talbott
> Cottle Coles is poised to sell off yet another

bite-sized chunk of Chicago Labor to the Saudi
invasion known as Dhu West. Why? To fund
his reelection, of course.

Squawk on the street says Eddie V cried
"fowl" in spectacular fashion.

"The chicken shit at Coles's office," I said softly. *Duh. Times
a thousand.* I rubbed my eyes with the heels of my hands.
"Who's Eddie V?"

"Eddie Veteratti. Runs Chicago's Labor Union. Runs it exactly
like Tony Lombardo did for Capone in the nineteen-twenties."

I kept reading.

But slinging shit is all the rage this time of
year. So while the Local #56 staunchly denies
any and all rumors, it makes you wonder. Is
Monday night's memorial service for murder
victim (sic) Keith Nawisko or the bus drivers'
union?

Hank reached across the table, pushed Delete, and the post
disappeared. He closed the laptop.

"Flynn and Rory caught the Nawisko case," I said. "The Bureau of Organized Crime took it over."

"Naturally." Hank ran a hand along his jaw, his scruff making a faint rasping sound. "They know who did it."

Whoa. "Do you?"

"One of Coles's enforcers." He leaned back in his chair. "It
wasn't a sanctioned hit."

And you know that how, exactly? I pulled the picture of
Thorne and the blond woman from my pocket and flipped it
onto the table. "Who is she?"

Hank's breath came out in a soft hiss. "Violetta 'Vi' Veteratti."

"Eddie's wife?"

"Sister."

"Thorne Clark was Flynn and Rory's case." I tapped the photo. "The BOC took that one, too. What's the connection?"

"There isn't one. Maybe they'll get it back."

"But Clark was a professional hit." My nose crinkled in confusion. "According to the ME's report, they used hardcast wadcutters. Low muzzle flash and signature. Limited power but up close, a buzz saw through bones and meat."

"Placement?"

"Right between the pockets."

Hank shook his head. "An old hitter's trick doesn't an assassin make, Sport Shake. The Union sell-off was never going to happen." He picked up the photo and put it in his pants pocket. "Clark was working for Vi."

"Then who killed him?"

"Freelancer. Not connected." Hank shrugged. "Ex-military, maybe. Dangerous."

"Why are you telling me this?"

"You're a nice girl." His voice deepened. "I don't want to see you get hurt."

Poke me in the eye with a stick, why don't you? "Me, neither."

My knee started bouncing under the table. I wasn't going to roll over that easy. *July McGrane's Rules of Engagement Number Four: Keep them off balance.* I took a deep breath. "Will you go to the Dhu West Gala with me?"

He hadn't been expecting that.

The best cops and lawyers are proficient when it comes to the ask-and-wait. I, however, had not inherited my family's mad skills and had to count so as not to prattle on like a drunken parrot on crack. I tapped my fingers on my thigh, keeping time.

Ten seconds.

Twenty.

"When is it?" he said.

"Two weeks. Friday." I started counting again. Sixteen seconds.

"What about the guy with the Bullitt?"

"I'm not looking for a *date*, Hank," I fibbed. "I just need someone to watch my back."

More silence.

"Maisie . . ."

"Forget I mentioned it." I felt sick. And small. And stupid. Tears blurred my vision. I sighed. "There's blood on your shirt."

Hank looked down at the fine mist of red across his left shoulder and back up at me. "It's not mine."

I know that.

"Please." He reached out and ran his knuckles down my cheek. "Let it alone."

"I-I can't."

He dropped his hand. "Salvatore!"

The door unlocked and opened.

I guess that's my cue.

Chapter 21

St. Hyacinth Basilica was a magnificent redbrick three-towered Polish cathedral with an opulent Baroque interior. A spectacularly lofty backdrop for bus driver and Union leader Keith Nawisko's memorial service.

Thanks for the tip, Hank.

While it wasn't his intention, he'd given me a real lead and the time and place to pursue it. One of Coles's crew murdered Nawisko, and Eddie V's guys hadn't killed Clark. But just because they weren't linked in a way that Hank cared about didn't mean the cases weren't connected.

I knew in my gut Flynn was right. Someone who knew Nawisko and/or the Local #56 would have plenty of motive. A person who might even be at this memorial service.

Dressed in a dark and demure Carmen Marc Valvo wool crêpe jacket and pants, I'd capped off my look with a pair of clear glass, rim-free spectacles. Which weren't glasses at all, but an innocuous forty-megapixel Tech-Secure camera that took panoramic pictures by remote—a fake MP3 receiver that also served as 30 gigs of storage with an LCD playback screen.

One of the best things about living in a house full of men are the toys.

Two hours early, I'd discreetly reconnoitered the basilica. The arched stone entry of the western transept was the ideal vantage point to take pictures of the attendants in the nave.

I meandered into the sanctuary. A pair of old ladies knelt before St. Joseph, votive flames glimmering in the dim light.

Couldn't hurt. I put a twenty into the little brass collection box and hedged my bets, lighting a candle in front of St. Anthony, patron saint of seekers of lost articles, and another in front of the patron saint of justice, St. Francis.

A trio of suited ushers wearing St. Hyacinth Basilica name tags passed through en route to the nave. I ran a final equipment check in the bathroom and took my place. Organ music filled the church with a swelling, powerful sadness.

It wasn't difficult to locate members of the Local #56. Those who weren't wearing blue nylon jackets were pulling at their shirt collars flashing gaudy blue-stoned union rings, faces full of impotent anger.

I snap-snapped away, tipping my head back to catch the non-Catholics who'd taken the stairs and watched from the eastern wing. The service went on. Coughing sounded above me. The only blind spot. I'd have to swing all the way around to the opposite transept to get a shot.

The priest intoned in a severe and caliginous voice, "Only those who have appropriately prepared themselves are to receive the Eucharist."

Catholic guilt overtook my undercover cool.

Forgive me, Father, it's been a couple years since my last confession and I'm here pretending to be James Bond.

The back of my neck grew hot and my throat started itching. "The guilts," Da called it, that smidge of self-realization that rears its head in a high-pressure situation.

There I was, looking for hell in church.

I slipped out the side exit into the cool night air and cleared my throat again and again before realizing that for as glorious a building as the basilica was, it was definitely in a nasty part of town. I hot-footed it to the front of the church and entered quietly through the giant brass doors on the farthest east side.

Poster-sized photographs of Nawisko rested on easels. Several blue jackets and a couple cheap suits prowled the lobby like caged coyotes, talking in low, guttural voices. "I tole you there was no goddamn way Eddie V'd sell us out."

"You say that like he's some kinda saint. Like an intern and some chicken shit are supposed to make good for Nawisko?"

"It's that asswipe Coles trying to sell us to the goddamn A-rabs."

Grunts and nods followed that assertion. "Only shit Coles cares about is his reelection."

Eyes averted, I turned my head slowly past the men, pressing the remote a nickel's worth in succession.

Hank's voice sounded in my head, "Get moving or get noticed." I went to the heavy door of the nave and reached for the handle when the door shoved open, almost hitting me.

A fat, balding man with wispy reddish-brown hair came out, pressing a handkerchief to his eyes, blue nylon jacket straining across his bulk. "Our Keith. A goddamn betrayal, is what this is."

A thick-fingered hand landed on the fat man's shoulder. "Time for a drink, Pop." Peterson.

I scooted behind the door, holding it open. He hadn't seen me. Couldn't have seen me. *Ergh.* The guy gave me the feeling I was wearing a shirt full of ants. The latent effect of his assault, I suppose. *Please, please don't let Narkinney be with him.*

A steady stream of blue jackets filled the lobby, grousing and lamenting. My arm ached from holding the door. An usher came by, kicked down the doorstop for the stragglers, and began herding the mourners into the refectory for refreshments.

I said four Our Fathers and left.

"Toughy dickens, McGrane." Niecy reset her AutoCITE. "You look like you spent the night in the ass-end of a dump truck."

"Gee, thanks." I glanced at myself in the Interceptor's rearview. A little bleary-eyed from downloading and cropping more than three hundred photos from the memorial, but it wasn't like I hadn't showered for a week. "Lunchtime. Where to?" I asked, preemptively flipping on my hazards so I could pull a *U.* "Butch's?"

"Frack, no."

Well, that's unfortunate. I'd planned on Niecy burning an hour or so at the gambling ticket counter while I sussed out IDs from Nawisko's memorial.

"It's uniform day at IE's," she said.

Whatever that meant. "Nifty."

A twenty-five-minute traffic-logged and ticket-free trip landed us in front of Irwin Edwin's Burger Joint. "Best butter burgers in Chicag-ie," Niecy said. "Third Tuesday of every month is half-off for anyone in uniform. Which is why you're gonna park around the block and not write one effin' ticket."

"Trying to garner a little public goodwill, are we? Does that actually work?"

"Cuss, yeah!" Niecy was out of the cart before I'd even popped the Interceptor into Park.

Super-duper. Shorting out our day for a bargain burger. Am I the only one who gives a rat's ass about your benefits?

I ended up parking three blocks away. I pulled my copy of Thorne Clark's case file and the bulging 24-Hour Walgreens photo envelope from under my seat.

My iPhone chirped.

Lee Sharpe.

I set my papers on Niecy's seat. "Hello?"

"Finished scourging yet?"

"Ooh! Now there's an opening line," I said. "An archaic reference to self-flagellation doubling as a backhanded knock on my Catholic upbringing. That's hot."

Lee laughed. "I went to a significant amount of trouble looking that up, you know."

"Yeah, typing's tough without opposable thumbs."

"That wasn't much of a date last week. How 'bout we give it another go?"

I wanted to say yes. To want to play games and get that churning feeling of excitement and anticipation. But nothing came out.

"C'mon, Maisie. Lighten up. The world's one big, happy place."

"Lee—"

"How about I take you to that party? You know, the one you roped Cash into."

Oh. My. God. Talk about karma biting me in the butt.

"This is a one-shot deal," I warned.

"Sure," he said. "And I promise to hold it against you when you change your mind."

I stowed my iPhone in the cargo pocket and fastened the flap. I reached over for the case folder and photos. *The hell with it. I want a hamburger.*

I got out of the cart and jogged over to Irwin Edwin's.

Burger basket and Dr Pepper in hand, I scanned the restaurant for Niecy. She was holding court from the middle of a long and crowded picnic table, looking like an ad for the United Colors of Uniforms.

The entire table ate with one hand while manipulating their smartphones. Niecy looked up from her screen long enough to point a shaking finger at me and say to no one in particular, "That's my partner, McGrane."

A guy wearing a T-Mobile oxford made eye contact. "Who're you following?"

"Where?" I asked, squeezing in between two UPS employees.

"On Twitter. IowaHawkBlog, AdamBaldwin, ILoveScienceSexually, Ace of SpadesHQ, YeahNickSearcy, Dennis Miller? Who?"

"I don't do Twi—"

"McGrane's so old school"—Niecy cackled—"she thinks a phone is for talking."

A handsome kid wearing an A-Agents pest control polo smacked his hands down on the table and stood up, fists raised in triumph. "James Woods is following me."

T-Mobile's mouth dropped open. "The actor? No way, Bob."

"Check it." He flashed his phone at the table. "I tweeted, Hated you in *The Specialist*. Love you on Twitter. Now he's following me."

"You snot-nosed mutha-lucka," Niecy screeched. The table burst into laughter. I ate my butter burger, getting schooled in the ways of Twitter and Twitchy and loving every minute of it.

After lunch, we walked back to the cart, Niecy lecturing all the way. "You gotta understand, kid. The shizzle's on the griddle. You gotta step up. Get informed. If it wasn't for Leticia, I'd be—"

She skidded to a stop, grabbing my shirtsleeve. "What the *frack?*"

Chapter 22

Our Interceptor was thrashed. Tires slashed, *bitch-cunt-whore-slut* keyed into the paint, and every window, turn signal, headlight—even the flashers—were smashed.

The anger behind it was staggering.

Niecy sank down onto the curb and rooted in her purse for a cigarette. "Jeezy-creezy. Ain't this a fuggin' kick in the head."

"Sucks to be us." I took my cap off and ran a hand through my hair before putting it back on.

A gang of teenagers, maybe? They're always pissed off.

I moved in for a closer look. The stink of sour milk and rotten fish filled my nose. An empty garbage can lay behind the cart. Safe to assume its contents were inside.

Aw shit. So were my case report and the photos.

I peeked in the broken window and sprang backwards, banging my head on the door frame and staggering over my feet.

Ow ow ow!

Pressing the back of my head with one hand, I wiped my eyes on my sleeve.

It can't be. It just can't.

I shook my head hard and took another look. Trash covered the passenger side of the cart. The driver's side was empty except for a single brass bullet with a flattened lead end. I didn't need to pick it up to know it was a Buffalo Bore hardcast wadcutter.

Holy fuck.

I hit my radio. "Dispatch, this is car 13248. We have a non-emergency situation—"

"Hold up, McGrane." Niecy took a drag. "They're already here."

I looked down the street. A blue-and-white approached at a snail's pace, slowing to a crawl after they were good and sure we'd seen them.

Really? I mean, the only thing that could make it worse—oh wait, it can't get any worse.

Tommy Narkinney hung out of the driver's window, a giant, shit-eating grin on his face. "Maisie-Daisy McGrane. Here we go again."

"Nice of you to drop by," I said. "Funny how we didn't even call it in yet."

"Just passing through." Peterson leaned forward and held up a half-eaten hamburger and a white bag with Irwin Edwin's blue print on it. "Uniform day."

A hundred bucks says you passed it on the way and came back around to bust our chops.

"What the fug are you so happy about? Smilin' like a couple of effin' Mongoloids." Niecy flicked her cigarette at the squad car. "Get off your lard-butts and write a friggin' report."

Tommy's smile warped into a sneer.

Still eating, Peterson got out of the car, paused to hike his pants up beneath his big gut, and moseyed over to the Interceptor. He jammed the rest of the hamburger into his mouth, crumpled up the white wrapper, and threw it on the ground. He wiped his hands on the belly of his shirt, laid a hand on the Interceptor's roof, and stuck his thick, crew-cut head into the window.

"What's this?" He reached his hand in the window.

"Don't!" I shouted. "It's a crime scene." *For chrissakes!*

He held up the bullet between two fingers. "You wanna explain this?"

"It was evidence."

"Fuckin' wannabe." He snorted and tossed it back into the window. "Tell 'em," he said to Tommy as he got back in the car.

"Thing is, gals, this is a contracted city vehicle. You don't own it. If Dhu West wants to file an insurance claim, they come down to the station and fill out a report." He waited for Peterson to get in the car before starting it.

Tommy put his fingers to his mouth like he was blowing a kiss and flipped me off instead.

Well, that's adorable.

I called Dispatch for a tow truck. Niecy called Leticia.

Leticia got there first and took a good, long look. "This some nasty, fucked-up shit, you know what I'm sayin'? We're going to Butch's. Now."

"I'll wait for the tow," I said as Leticia loaded Niecy into her cart. "Meet you there."

Before they hit the corner, I'd found a stick and started shifting the smelly debris on the passenger seat.

The case file and memorial photos were gone.

Flynn and I sat on the curb watching the evidence tech bag the bullet and take some pictures. I told him about my recon at Nawisko's memorial service and the now missing photos and ME report. He hadn't liked it, but he'd lump it.

"Rory and I got the Clark case back today," he said. "In the BOC's esteemed opinion, it's a whut-whup."

Wrong time, wrong place. "That's good."

His eyes narrowed. "You don't seem real surprised."

"I'm not." I rubbed my hands on my pants. "Thorne Clark was working for the Veterattis."

"The Mob? And you would know this how?"

"Um . . . A little bird told me?"

"More like a hawk." Flynn loosened his tie. "Anything else you want to share?"

I pulled out my iPhone, scrolled to the photo I'd snapped of the picture of Vi and Thorne and the other I'd taken of the phone number on the back. I handed it to him.

"How—"

"Don't ask. Please."

Flynn texted himself the photos. "What else did the hawk tell you?"

I wanted to tell him Nawisko wasn't a sanctioned hit. Instead I said, "The Veterattis weren't happy to lose Clark."

"Jaysus." Flynn ran a hand through his hair and stood up. "Stay the hell away from Bannon." He tossed the phone in my lap. "I mean it, Snap."

"McGrane!" Leticia shouted.

I might have missed them at the only inhabited table in the joint, drinking pitchers of frozen margaritas for a five spot. No salted rims or fancy glasses, just a salt shaker and beer mugs, each with an anemic slice of lime.

Argh, me pirating PEAs, there'll be scurvy aplenty.

"What the fug took you so long?" Niecy said.

I sat down. "Waiting for the tow to show."

Leticia slid me over a mug of tequila slush. I took a swig and blanched. The margarita was carrying enough citric acid to rust out a battleship.

Leticia popped a mini–corn dog in her mouth. "You hungry?" She pushed the red plastic basket of mini–corn dogs in my direction. "Eat up."

Before I could grab one, Niecy shoved the basket back at Leticia. "What the fug you thinking? The kid won't eat that crap."

Leticia twisted in her chair and yelled at the empty bar. "Butch! Bring us some o' them fried zucchinis and chicken tenders." She turned to me, gave me a mini–head bob. "Healthy enough for you?"

"Perfect," I said, weirdly hungry.

Butch stood up slowly from behind the bar. "Got it." He went into the kitchen.

"What is he doing back there?" I asked, not sure I wanted to hear the answer.

"Bad back. He be layin' down, doing his chiropractical exercises," Leticia said.

We drank for a while, not talking. I wasn't sure how to broach the subject that the killer was on to me. "Niecy, maybe you ought to take a couple days off."

"Who the hell are you? My effing wet nurse?"

No, I'm not. Because Jesus loves me. "Whoever did this to our cart wasn't kidding."

Niecy squawked and rapped her mug on the table. "Jeebus, the kid's got her panties in a bunch cuz some Grade-A A-hole tagged our cart.

"Damn." Leticia whistled. "Imagine if she'd come back to Sanchez's cart."

They chuckled. Niecy clarified, "Someone took a giant dump in the driver's seat."

"Bleah." I grimaced. "What is wrong with the world?" My phone chirped. "McGrane," I answered.

"Long time, no talk," Ernesto said. "Where are you?"

"Uh, Butch's Beer Garden."

"I know that dump. Jeez, it's not even three o'clock yet. You must be having one hell of a day."

"Yeah, well . . . Our cart was vandalized today."

"No shit?"

Leticia and Niecy stared at me with laser focus. "Yeah," I said, staring back. "No shit."

Niecy howled a scratchy coyote laugh. Leticia's cheeks puffed out as she pressed her lips tight together, trying not to spit out a mouthful of mini–corn dog. She slapped her hand against the table, the other unable to let go of her mug of margarita.

"I'm heading over to Joe's later," I said. "See you then?"

"It's a plan."

I hung up as Butch came over with the food. The fried zucchini was appallingly delicious.

Twenty minutes later, he brought us over a round of four Dos Equis with limes.

"There's only three of us," Niecy said, "and we didn't order no south-of-the-border crap."

"He did." Butch jerked a thumb over his shoulder.

"*Chica.*" Ernesto put his hands on my shoulders. He let his voice purposely carry across the table. "You going to introduce me to your *bellas damas?*"

"Mmmm-mmm-mmm," Leticia said, letting her eyes take the slow boat up and down Ernesto's fit form. "Who we got here?"

"Ernesto Padilla, at your service."

Leticia fell away in a fake faint, hand at her breast, back arched. "Ain't you just a fine piece of *smexy*. What you hanging out with McGrane for?"

"Cuz she's got such good-looking friends."

Niecy tittered while Leticia vogued him a scorching pout.

"I'm gonna steal her for a sec, okay?" He gestured toward the back room. "*Chica?*"

I got up and took two of the beers. Leticia's hand shot out and grabbed my wrist. "You bring El Guapo back, you hear?" she hissed.

"Loud and clear." I followed Ernesto into the back room. He bought thirty dollars' worth of pull-tabs, dropped a five-dollar tip, and chose a small table in the corner. "Man, this place brings new meaning to the word *dive*."

"Why are you here?"

He tossed me a couple of tabs, and picked up one, talking as he concentrated on tearing apart the fragile paper. "You didn't sound like your normal happy self. And now that I see you, I gotta say, you don't look like your normally happy self, either."

I wedged the lime down into my beer and brought him up to speed on Flynn, the case, and the warning left on the seat of the cart. I tipped my head at the girls. "Think I should fill 'em in?"

Ernesto thought it over. "No. Flynn would've told you to tell them if he thought it was necessary." He took a long swallow of Dos Equis. "You all right?"

"Pretty much lost in the jungle, swimming in quicksand." I picked up a pull-tab and tore off the strips. Zip.

"Figure out Hank's not Tarzan yet?"

"I never thought he was, Cheetah."

"Keep your distance." Ernesto punched me in the shoulder and picked up another tab. "How's meter-maiding?"

"Pick up those ratty things and I'll introduce you to two reasons to keep your day job."

* * *

Niecy was the big winner. Two hundred dollars on one of Ernesto's pull-tabs. She fell further in love with him when he refused to split the winnings. Leticia was in love with Ernesto for an entirely different reason. His "smexy" ass. Whatever that was.

Irritated and itchy, I threw a couple twenties on the table. I needed to get to Joe's and find my center. "Sorry, guys. That ol' highway's a'callin'."

"Need a ride to your car?" Ernesto asked.

"Nah. Already texted a cab to take me back to Dispatch to pick up my car. I'll risk the six blocks to Joe's."

He stood up. "Save my chair, ladies?"

"For as long as it takes, El Guapo," Leticia said.

We walked outside, blinking in the bright afternoon sun. He gave a low whistle. "That Leticia's something else."

"Cripes, Ernesto. Don't even joke about that."

"I wouldn't mind tapping a little of that chocolate."

"She weighs like two hundred pounds!"

"A chick like that . . . It just adds to it." He cracked his knuckles. "She's like one of those waxy little doughnuts Joe's always eating at the gym. Nasty and yet . . . sometimes necessary."

My cab pulled up to the curb. "You're a sick man," I said. "Sick."

Chapter 23

Joe wasn't alone behind the front desk. An oily-looking guy wearing a gold crucifix and an open-necked black-on-black striped Goombah shirt leered at me.

Swell. One more guy who owns a boxed set of The Sopranos.

"Hey, Joe," I said.

Joe gave me a tip of his chin and raised an orange and white Unjury bottle to his lips.

A protein shake? It's a world gone mad.

I flipped him a thumbs-up. "Good for you, Joe."

"He's getting the lap-band," the skeevie guy piped up. "I'm Ronnie. His nephew. While he's incapacitated I'll be managing this"—he raised his hands toward me and rotated them in tiny circles, feeling me up by air—"fine establishment."

Ewwww.

Ronnie was the kind of skeeve a girl's careful not to smile at. The kind that has her jamming a chair up under the doorknob even though her door is locked. Just because.

"What's your name?" he asked.

Simmer down, Guido. "McGrane."

His lips pooched out in disappointment. He wiped his hand on his shirt and held it out. "Pleased to meet you."

At least he hadn't adjusted.

I shook hands as fast as I could. As I pulled my hand away, he flicked his finger across my palm.

I gagged up a little margarita.

Heading through the double doors to the locker room, I stopped, pretended to tie my shoe, and palmed one of the brown rubber doorstops.

I jammed it under the women's locker room door. With less than a handful of women working out at Joe's, I wasn't worried about inconveniencing anyone. And as Da drilled into my head, "Never *ever* ignore that uneasy feeling."

After I changed, I put the doorstop above my locker and hit the elliptical machine. A regular on the elliptical next to mine started a TiVo'd *Red Eye w/ Greg Gutfeld*. Fine by me. I plugged in my headphones and channel-surfed to his input. Working out with a buzz comes with its own little charge—knowing I can party and still take names.

Except for today. Butch's margaritas were giving me the acid reflux of a Ridley Scott alien. Or maybe it was the wadcutter chaser I couldn't quit thinking about.

At least Hank's not here.

Five and a half miles the hard way, I got off wobbly-legged, feeling like I could use a little Pepto.

"Hey, Sport Shake," said the devil, leaning out of the metal doors of the basketball court. "Wanna play?"

God, he's handsome.

I didn't usually take part in Hank's low-level hand-to-hand classes. The newbies made too many allowances for my size and sex. "Why not?"

"Thanks, Peaches," Hank murmured in my ear, circling around to talk to the eight men sitting on the scuffed hardwood of Joe's court floor in front of us.

Those nicknames. Man-oh-man, how they send me.

The best part of sitting in on Hank's class was the opportunity to just stare at him. All smooth fluid muscle, power, and control. And that voice . . .

"For context, China," he said. "The average Ranger is five-eleven, one-eighty pounds. A PRC infantryman is five-five, one-fifteen. McGrane and I are taller, but about the proportion we're after. The PRC are strictly Qinna Gedou, utilizing a hand-to-hand system effective against a larger, stronger opponent. Qinna Gedou relies primarily on throws and sweeps. Watch for the drop plant of the left leg, the spin . . ."

Hank's words blurred together, unintelligible. Warm ripples of loveliness traveled down my spine.

Why-oh-why hadn't I gone home with him when I had the chance?

I exhaled in a slow sigh of infatuation.

Hank's foot drove into my stomach with the force of a sledge-hammer.

I landed on my butt three feet away. Rolled over onto my hands and knees and threw up chicken tenders, fried zucchini and margaritas on the hardwood court.

"Christ, Maisie." Hank's hand was on my back. "I'm sorry. I thought you were paying attention."

Oh, like that doesn't make it worse. I couldn't stop retching. *At least my hair's in a ponytail.*

"We're done for today," he said to the mutts. "One of you guys send Ronnie in here to clean this up."

I heard them leave.

"Easy now. Easy." Hank stroked my back with a slow, heavy hand, petting me like the dog I was. "Nothing left. Shallow breaths."

I wiped my mouth on my shirt and let him help me to my feet. There wasn't a hole deep enough for me to crawl into. "I'm gonna clean up," I said and fled.

I showered and got fixed up. Everything I needed was in my locker: mouthwash, toothpaste and brush, makeup, and clothes.

A knock sounded on the locker room door.

"Maisie?" Hank said. "You okay?"

"Yeah," I croaked. "Fine."

"I want to see for myself."

I looked at my bra and pantied reflection in the mirror and winced. Aside from the rapidly darkening bruise under my ster-num, my retch-fest had left behind a queasy tint that makeup couldn't quite fix. "Hank. Please. Go home."

"No."

For the love of Mike . . .

I braced myself over the sink. "Beat it, will you? I want to take my time and I can't if I know you're hanging around."

Nothing. "Hank?"

"Okay." He hit his palm twice on the door. "Okay."

I took a long time. Mostly because my guts had been kicked through my spine and I couldn't move any faster if I wanted to and partly to ensure he'd gone.

The gym was practically empty by the time I got out. And thankfully Hank-free.

I passed by Ronnie and Joe at the reception desk. "See you guys."

"Errrrgh," Joe said, slurping down another protein shake.

Ronnie just glared at me over Joe's shoulder. Upper lip stretched back from his teeth in pure revulsion.

I guess puking has its privileges.

Or not.

Hank was leaning against the hood of his G-Wagen, looking a little pale around the gills himself. "How are you?"

"Aside from the egg on my face?" I tried to maintain eye contact, but it was beyond my capability.

"I hit you hard. Too hard." He ran a hand through his hair. "Let me see."

"Not necessary."

"Now," he barked in a command that had me raising my T-shirt before I knew what I was doing. I hesitated and lifted it all the way up. He took a knee, his fingers barely grazed the rapidly darkening bruise that ended just below my sports bra, and a tiny mortifying whimper slipped from my lips.

Hank eased my T-shirt down and got to his feet. "You're getting checked out."

"No. No way." *Is it too much to ask to let me go home and die?* "I'm gonna get in my car, go home, and pretend this never happened."

A pulse ticked at the corner of his jaw. "Not funny."

I closed my eyes and let out a sigh. "Okay, Hank. Here's the deal. I had a couple of margaritas before working out. You caught me off guard, which was embarrassing. I puked in front of the mutts, which was humiliating. I took forever in the locker room because I was hoping you'd go home and let me solo my shame."

"I did that to you." He leaned down, his face inches from mine. "And you're getting checked out."

I took a stutter-step backwards and bumped up against my car, which hurt bad enough to have me suck in a breath. I didn't know he could get so . . . angry.

"It was an accident, Hank. Entirely my fault." I threw my best *kitten-left-out-in-the-rain look* at him. It had a fair-to-middling success rate on my brothers. Head down with a wobbly smile and a shy, searching glance up through my lashes. The first time I ever felt it for real on my end. "If you care about me at all, you'll let me handle this on my own. *Please.*"

Hank raised his palms. I dug my key out of my pocket and pressed it, unlocking the Honda. He opened the door for me, closing it after I got in.

He knocked on the window. I put the key in the ignition and rolled it down.

"Maisie, about the Gala . . . I can take you. If you like."

Aww, sweet. A pity date. And I thought worm's belly was as low as I could go. Still, hope springs eternal. Maybe if I take a fist to the face we'll get engaged.

"It's okay, Hank. I got a date."

His jaw slid slightly to one side. "Who?"

If I felt a little better, I might've held back. "The Bullitt."

Hank smiled, but he didn't look happy. "Okay." He rapped twice on the roof of my car. "Go home."

"'Allo, Maisie." Thierry looked up from cutting vegetables next to the sink. "You are in luck. I make one of your favorite today. Japanese shabu shabu."

Well, that sucks. It was going to be a long time before I felt like eating again. Days, maybe.

He removed an index card from his apron pocket and handed it across. "From Flynn."

I tried not to groan as I took it.

> *Snap,*
> *Bad news. The only prints on the cartridge*
> *were Officer Wesley Peterson's. I had an*
> *evidence tech pick up the reprint of your*
> *photos and start ID.*
>   *Time for you to be smart. Be safe. Take a*
> *step back.*
>   *P.S.*
> *Da needs to know. Two days, tops.*

Thierry's brow bent in concern. "Is bad news?"

Hell, yes. The worst. "Nothing unexpected."

"Maisie?" Mom's voice echoed from the phone intercom system. "Maisie? Would you please come into my office immediately?"

The word *immediately* was code for big trouble. Because this day couldn't get any worse.

Mom's office was an extension of her personality. Cool and sophisticated, done up in creams and whites with the barest touches of icy blue. She got up from her desk, stepped around, and hugged me gingerly.

"Are you all right?" I said.

"Perhaps that is what I should be asking you."

Uh-oh.

"Oh?"

Mom folded her arms across her chest. "Your recent lack of transparency is beginning to grate, sweetheart."

My stomach cramped.

"I just got off the phone with Mr. Bannon."

What the—?

"Raise your shirt, please."

I did. A grapefruit-sized bruise sat directly above my navel.

"Good Lord." Mom looked away and motioned for me to put my shirt down. "If I didn't have a conference call with the ASA in twenty minutes . . ." She shook her head. "Thierry will take you to Urgent Care this instant."

"I'm fine, Mom. Doesn't hurt a bit," I fibbed.

"Oh really?" She leaned against the corner of her desk. "Is that why you refused to accept Mr. Bannon's polite and generous offer?"

"No."

She folded her arms across her chest. "As I recall, you were pining away for him as recently as yesterday."

Never play mind games with a former prosecutor. They miss the punitive side of criminal court too much.

"Because you know, Maisie—"

"I know. I know. I know." *July McGrane's Rules of Engagement Number Five: Always let a man take care of you.*

Mom nodded. "I expect a call right away, and if there is anything, you will go directly to the Emergency Room."

I nodded and walked to the door, trying hard not to hunch over. Mom called after me, "Tell Thierry to take the Range Rover. You'll be more comfortable, baby."

Chapter 24

Getting out of bed had me Lamaze-panting like a pregnant woman. Bruised pancreas, my ass. It felt like my guts had gone through a drill press. Finally upright, legs over the side, I saw my high-lace steel-toed black work boots on the floor and almost decided to lie back down. Only then I'd have to get up again to get my cell phone out of my purse to call Leticia. And I sure as hell wasn't going to go through that again.

I stood and went to the closet. *No oxy for the driver today.* I rummaged around in my drawer for a compression tee, whimpering as I eased the tight spandex down into place. "Don't be such a crybaby," I told myself, and groaned as I pulled on the cargo pants.

The boots took forever.

The stairs down to the kitchen even longer.

Not gonna be early today.

I stood in front of the battered clock, searching for my punch card. As I reached for it, someone gave me a sharp shove between the shoulder blades. I fell forward, knocking my forehead against the buff sheet metal.

"Yo, bitch," said a heavily accented voice. "You looking to make us all late now, too, *besaculos?*"

Clinging to the card holder, my abs spasmed and my throat hitched. I breathed in short huffs to keep the vomit down and slowly pivoted to see who was rattling my cage.

Sanchez.

I shouldn't have tried so hard not to puke.

She got right up in my face, giving me the microscope's view of her thick makeup, several shades too light for her skin tone. Her fingers were stiff in gang signs. "Keep your ass off my route, *pinche fresa.*"

Calling me names I don't understand. Will blessings never cease? "Let me tell you how it works, Sanchez. If Niecy and I score a boot or three off you on the way to our route, well, I guess that's just your tough luck."

She raised a fist to my face.

I didn't flinch. No cause. Even if she were able to hit me, there wouldn't be much behind it. Her feet were too close together. "Don't like it?" I said. "Take it up with Ms. Jackson."

Her face twisted in a sneer. "Oh, you think I'm ascared of the *mayate, puta?*"

Those names I did know. "Yeah. I do," I said, getting owly. "And I think you're *ascared* of Niecy, too."

That hit the mark close enough. The pancake foundation couldn't hide the red that mottled her cheeks. Sanchez threw her fist over my shoulder and grabbed her card, punched it, and jammed it back in the rack behind me.

She hissed in my ear, *"El que la hace, la paga."*

Now that sounded ominous. "Oh yeah?" I said. "What's that mean?"

"The one that does, pays, bitch." She spat on my boot.

I haven't wanted to hit someone so bad since Tommy Narkinney.

Hank's Law Number Two: Respond to threats with complete confidence.

I leaned in to her. "Now, let me tell you something." Tone flat, Dirty Harry–style. "I'm already paying. Double."

Her eyes clouded in confusion, unable to keep up with her own allegory. She snorted and pushed past me out of the break room, shooting a parting forearm at my throat.

I ducked. Her elbow banged into the time clock. It left a hairline crack in the ancient plastic cover. She didn't turn around, just strutted off.

That must've hurt.

I didn't laugh. I couldn't. After moving that fast, it took everything I had not to whimper.

Niecy and I were trolling Jeanne McGill's route—thankfully not Sanchez's—and the going was as fast as a snail on a salt lick.

"Eh, kid! Snap the frig to it. We got us a big, fat one." Niecy raised a wavering finger toward a crusty blue Chevy Malibu.

I was too sore—worthless, actually. I eased out of the cart, unable to decide who I hated more, Niecy or the knucklehead that couldn't obey basic parking laws.

It even hurt to open the Interceptor's trunk.

"Don't be such a wimp," I said, trying to psych myself up into lifting the boot. "Gut it out."

Dear God.

The compression tee might have been made out of tissue paper. I was sweating raindrops and jelly beans by the time I got the boot up and onto the side of the Interceptor's trunk.

"Jeebus. What the fug's taking so long?" Niecy carped from the window. "You think I got all day to stand around holding off the fish for you?"

Says my pint-sized, crippled bodyguard.

With extreme caution, I bent my knees and lifted the boot in my arms, cradling it awkwardly like a Transformer's infant off-spring.

I walked to the rear of the Malibu. Hard to believe it had ever seen a day with a shine and polish. I stubbed my toe on the lip of a manhole cover and, gasping like a sorority girl, dropped the boot.

Its orange metal arm grooved a fat, eight-inch key mark down the door.

Cripes. I leaned against the Malibu, bent over at the waist, breathing in short pants.

"Well, that's a big ol' pool of piss," Niecy said from behind me, making me flinch. "How do you wanna swim in it? Incident report or put the boot in the frigging trunk and get the heck outta here?"

"Incident report," I said without hesitation.

"Ain't you the Good Samaritan?"

"That's me." But my halo was tarnished. I'd rather fill out a hundred IO4-753's than bend down and affix the boot.

Niecy sucked her teeth. "You wanna mess up our numbers so you can sleep at night? Swim in the shizza and shaft our week?"

I shrugged.

"Put the effin' boot on." She snorted. "And don't think I'm cleaning up after you. You can write your own frigging IO4."

I alternated between vomiting and passing out as I maneuvered the boot into place.

Jeez, Hank. Why couldn't you just have broken my nose?

My partner lounged in the cart listening to Michelle Malkin on Laura Ingraham's podcast. I secured the last nut, pulled myself up by the Malibu's door, and wiped my face on my sleeve, looking forward to writing a note of apology and filling in the report. Fifteen solid minutes of rest.

"Kid!" Niecy leaned out of the Interceptor window, my cell dangling from her hand. "El Guapo wants a word. You in?"

"Yeah, sure." Clammy as a sick salamander, I took my iPhone from Niecy's hand.

She'd changed my screen saver to her PEA badge. *Would the hijinks never end?* "Hello?"

"*Chica.* You busy?"

"Same old," I said.

"Wanna work out tonight?"

"I'll take a pass. I'm, uh, not real fast on my feet today."

"So it is true. Joe told me Hank freaking served you one right in the chops."

Please don't tell me to man up.

"Are you sure you should even be at work?" Ernesto asked sweetly, giving me a complimentary guilt towelette. "I could take you to the movies, that's pretty relaxing. . . ."

I sighed. A beaver with a birch sapling was less tenacious. "I'm beat. Wanna hang out at my house on Friday?"

"I'm there." He hung up.

"Knowing you live at home like you do . . ." Niecy gave an exaggerated, openmouthed wink. "I'm fine to look the other way if you wanna meet him for a little *bow-chicka-wow-wow*." She gave a couple of arthritic thrusts and tittered. "Just drop me at Butch's."

"Thanks, but no." I blew out a breath and searched the clipboard file for the Incident Report. "Besides," I said, "we have one boot left."

"Do what you gotta do, kid." She made a cawing sound that passed for a laugh, leaned forward, unplugged her iPod, and tuned the radio to Rush Limbaugh.

There was something soothing about Rush Limbaugh. His velvet overtones of virtue flowed over us, amping us up with righteousness. There were plenty of fish, but not a one to lay off the orange anchor on. We wrote tickets all afternoon, walking the walk of the sinless—we were public servants. Commendable, even.

I don't know if it was Rush or the six Tylenol I sucked down with a sugar-free Red Bull at our Walgreens pit stop, but I was starting to feel better.

Niecy looked at her watch. "Crap, we're over. It's almost five o'clock."

Overtime equals points against PEAs.

"We're laying this boot if it kills us." I turned onto the street and—as dependable as the creepy homeless dude spanking it under the stairs at the Morse Red El stop—there he was.

Poppa Dozen and his black armored limo, standing-zone pretty across two handicapped spaces. Traffic was in full swing, so I pulled up and parked a good twenty yards behind him, alongside the alleyway.

The tickets I'd written were only a week old. He had a good four or five more weeks before the boot would activate. That is, if no one caught them in the system and made them disappear before then. After hearing Lince gush like a lovesick tween over the mayor, our tickets wouldn't last past the first complaint from His Honor's office.

May as well take it while we can get it.

One week short of ten more months to go, and silver linings were in short supply.

I got out of the cart and knocked on the opaque limo window.

The window retracted six inches. Out came a thick black middle finger. After a beat, the finger disappeared and the window closed.

Good day to you, too, unnerving personal enforcer, sir.

Da's favorite motivator was, "Life is ten percent what happens to you and ninety percent how you react to it." He failed to clarify, however, that the 10 percent could happen all at once. AutoCITE at the ready, I loaded the $430 ticket for parking in two handicapped spaces, blocking a hydrant, and hit Enter.

The word *Scofflaw* blinked on the scuffed LCD screen.

Yeah, baby!

I trotted back to the Interceptor and tapped on the window. Niecy rolled it down. "What?"

"I'm gonna boot this bulletproof orca."

"Hit him curbside." She grinned. "I'll keep watch."

I fastened the orange Wolverine on the rear wheel of the limo lickety-split. Remembering as I tried to stand up, that yes, indeed, I did have a bruised pancreas and shouldn't be lifting anything.

"Oh my gawd, we're so gonna get an A!" On the front steps of City Hall, a posse of Midwestern-Italian tank-topped, hair-hopped junior college girls gathered around their diminutive teen leader.

Niecy honked the Interceptor's horn.

Poppa Dozen came around the front of the limo to the sidewalk. Weirdly, the horrible jodhpurs, jackboots, double-breasted jacket, and chauffeur's hat made him look kind of . . . scary.

Shit.

I pulled myself up by the rear tire.

He strode toward me. Definitely bigger than I originally thought. Hulking, actually. "You wanna get active with me, baby?"

"Huh?" *Criminy. Where was Hank when I needed him?*

"You better step, bitch." He tipped the mirrored aviators down his nose and glared at me. Eyes bloodshot and fierce. "And take that motherfucking boot off. Now."

Perhaps my actions had been a bit . . . rash.

"Bluebird." Dozen pushed the sunglasses back into place. "This ain't no joke. The mayor has hisself a big-time appointment."

The ghastly realization that I may have just booted away my future skittered around in my brain like a cockroach on a kitchen counter.

"I can't." I shrugged helplessly. "Only the removal and tow unit has the key."

Poppa Dozen took a switchblade out of an inside pocket of his jacket, opened it, and snapped the fingers of his other hand.

What the hell is this? West Side Story?

He held up the knife. "Call whoever the fuck you need to get it off."

"Settle down, Dozen." I hit the radio on my vest. "Agent McGrane requesting an immediate boot removal."

"Negative, over," Obi replied.

"Yo," Dozen said, putting his mouth to the radio, face at my breast. "Meter bitch tagged the wrong fucking car. The mayor's car. You better recognize and get your ass down here pronto and unlock it."

"I don't know who you think you are, sir," came Obi's astonishingly crisp reply, "but it is unlawful to touch a parking enforcement agent and/or his or her equipment, over."

Dozen raised his eyes from my radio with a baleful glance, face inches from mine. He riffled the scruff under his chin with the blade of the knife.

"Hey, metah-maid!" the teen leader called from the stairs, in a Bronx singsong. "You in some kinda trouble ovah there?"

Dozen looked over his shoulder. All five girls aimed their smartphones and best Mafioso glares at him.

"Cuz, lady," the girl said, not backing down, "it looks to me like you might be needin' some help, if you know what I mean."

Dozen swung his head back to me.

"Do I?" I said, giving him the flat cop stare. "Need help?"

He blew a snort of air through his nose. "Hell, yes."

I leaned around him and called, "Everything's fine. Thanks, girls." I hit my radio again. "Obi. Connect me to Lince, now!"

A whine of feedback, then, "Jennifer Lince's office, go ahead."

"This is Agent McGrane. There's been a big mistake. I need an immediate boot removal, over."

"Negative." The glee was unmistakable in Lince's secretary's voice. "The Traffic Enforcement Bureau will not remove a boot without payment. There is no protocol for mistakes."

"That your boss?" Poppa Dozen said. "Damn, girl. You need a new job."

You're telling me.

He laughed. "You'll be looking for one tomorrow, that's for damn sure."

"You, too, smart ass." *Talk about a crash-and-burn.*

Poppa Dozen twirled the switchblade between his fingers and looked down at the tire. "What if I punch it—let the air out? I can change a tire in two flat."

"Nope," I said. "The jaws are tight and the plate's secure—no access to the lug nuts."

"Bitch, I'm sticking my neck out for you, and this is what you give me? Negativity?"

"Seriously? Try moving the car next time, Mr. Save-the-Environment."

"You got no mofo idea—"

"Ohmigod! Ohmigod! I can see him coming through the glass doors!" scream-whispered one of the mini-Mafia.

"Spread out," the little one ordered. "Pay attention to where you are, and don't break the visual plane! No cross-cut angles."

Out of the glass doors and from between the marble pillars of City Hall, strode His Honor, Mayor Talbott Cottle Coles. The new breed of politician—slim, six-foot, one-sixty-five, blandly attractive with a *Zoom!* white smile and salt-and-pepper hair.

Coles's hair-trigger temper and penchant for quoting *The Untouchables* made him a media darling. Bluster and attitude are always embraced when it's for the *correct* side. Otherwise he'd have been tarred and feathered while they wound his guts out inch by inch on an intestinal crank.

He started down the flat stone steps, safely surrounded by his staff of Brooks Brothers– and J.Crew–suited clones, trailed by two goons in black. The little Italian girl juked her way to him like Walter Payton and blocked his path on the first landing.

"Hiya. I'm Allegra Luciana Maria Gaccione from Westwood College, and I'd like to interview you about the increasing tuition costs of junior college," she said in less time than it took a Southerner to spit.

Coles shot a look of irritation at one of his aides, then smiled down at Allegra. He turned to face the smartphone camera Allegra's friend was recording them with. A consummate professional, he waited a moment and said, "Hello, Westwood College. Talbott Cottle Coles here, and where there's a will there's a way. Westwood's a place where *you* can succeed." He gave a thumbs-up.

The dogface. He even recalled the school's TV commercial motto. Ugh.

A small crowd formed around the mayor's latest camera-op flirtation.

"An interview, please!" Allegra said.

"I like your moxie, young lady." He snapped his fingers at a woman in a navy pantsuit with an idiotic retro droopy bow. "Give her ten minutes, next week."

The aide, a fake smile plastered on her face, opened her date book and tried to wrangle Allegra off to the side.

Like that was ever gonna happen.

"How'm I gonna know you won't back out?" Allegra said. "I got some pretty tough questions."

"You wound me." Coles clutched his jacket at about his heart. "No faith in your humble public servant?"

The crowd, growing larger by the second, hooted and clapped, eating it up.

"But, Your Honor, sir," Allegra said. "Can't you just answer a couple a questions right now?"

Again, he looked directly at the camera instead of Allegra and said, "I'd love to, Ms. Gaccione, but I'm on my way to a very important meeting."

Instant name recall. The Red Bull gurgled loudly in my stomach.

"Nice." Poppa Dozen nodded toward my midsection. "Your belly knows it even if your brain don't." He closed the blade, swapping it in his jacket for a cell phone. "You on your own." He walked away toward the front of the vehicle, phone at his ear.

Allegra sidestep-shuffled to stay in front of Coles. "If ya don't mind me askin', who's so's important, you don't have time for your constituency?"

Whoa. Allegra boned up for this interview.

"Just between you and me?" He gave Allegra a spirited wink. "How about the vice president of the United States."

Oh shit.

"Yeah, okay," Allegra stepped aside, nodding. "For him—I'll take a rain check."

Oh no. Oh no. Oh no.

The crowds parted as the mayor of Chicago and his minions came down the steps. I stood in front of the limo, reflective Loogie vest blazing shamelessly in the sun.

Coles eyed me curiously. "And who do we have here?"

There's always time for one more photo op.

"Agent McGrane, sir." I stepped to the side.

Let's get ready to rumble.

His mouth opened at the sight of the orange boot, color flushing his cheeks, before he caught himself mid-frown. "Okay. I get it." He nodded and grinned, looking for the TV cameras. "Hot meter maid. Boot on the limo." Coles chuckled and turned to his staff. "You punk'd me. Funny."

Punk'd? That show's deader than mesh trucker hats.

"I'm afraid not, sir," I said.

He approached me and laughed again, a big, brassy laugh, and got in too close. I could smell Dentyne that almost but didn't quite cover the garlic falafel he'd had for lunch. "You get that thing off my limo immediately, or you'll be out of a job before the end of the day."

I hit my radio. "Dispatch? Jaysus, Obi. It's the mayor of Chicago. Call in any goddamn favor you can."

"On it, McGrane. Already en route. Twenty minutes out."

I turned to the mayor and raised my palms in an apology I actually did feel. "I'm sorry, sir."

"I'm going to be late for the vice president of the United States, and you're *sorry?*" Coles's face darkened to brick. He reared back and said in a second-rate De Niro doing Capone, "You're nothing but a lot of talk and a badge! You hear me? You're nothing!" He reached out and ripped the PEA badge off my vest and threw it at me. "Nothing!"

The crowd broke into wild cheers.

So this is it. The hill I'm going to die on. Littered with a poorly referenced movie quote and a public flogging.

"I get it," I said. "You're the mayor. But even an elected official isn't entitled to block a fire exit, hydrant, and two handicapped spaces."

"You overzealous, mall-cop impersonator," he said, playing to the crowd in a polished public speaking voice that seemed to carry for blocks.

The crowd began to chant. "Coles! Coles!"

"Seeing as you're the man who personally doubled parking fines to raise revenue for the city," I said, mildly, "I figured you knew better."

The crowd quieted a fraction. Make that a fraction of a fraction.

Coles held up his fist, sideways, thumb extended. He held up his other hand palm-up. "What say you, Chicagoans?"

The only thumbs not pointing down belonged to the mini-Mafia girls, whose fingers were clenched around their smartphones, recording every second.

"The people have spoken," he said and turned his thumb down. "You're fired." Talbott Cottle Coles clasped his hands together and waved them by his head like some old-timey prizefighter, to the crowd's applause.

Four bright blue–helmeted police officers on shiny white motorcycles pulled up in front of City Hall.

"See that, bluebird?" Poppa Dozen returned to my side and pointed. "Tha's our mutherfucking motorcade."

"Maybe one of them has a sidecar," I said.

Coles stiffened but kept up the show and signed a few autographs. Waving, he turned, and before I could move out of the way, he put his hands out and gave me a short, sharp shove, hitting the bruise under my sternum with a horrible, unerring accuracy.

I stumbled back, falling hard against the limo and burbled up a throat-full of Red Bull vomit water. It trickled down the front of my reflective vest.

Was there no end to Hank's gypsy curse of insta-hurl?

Poppa Dozen snorted a muffled laugh that dissolved into serious throat clearing. He knew his was coming.

Coles glared at me over his shoulder, brown eyes victorious. "Nobody likes a meter maid."

Moments later, Poppa Dozen drove off in one of the mayoral staff's commandeered non-environmentally conscious Cadillac Escalades from the parking ramp, taking Al Capone Jr. to meet the vice president.

There'd been plenty of rage behind the mayor's badge snatch. A large flap of reflector material hung loose on my vest. While Coles didn't have the outright authority to fire me, it wouldn't take more than a phone call to make it happen.

And it was going to happen.

I can't even say it was fun while it lasted. This job sucked worse than knocking my car keys into a gas station toilet.

Niecy and I waited around silently until the removal crew showed up an hour later. I eased out of the Loogie—the water-repellent reflective vest held up pretty well, considering—and got into the Interceptor.

"Talk about going to hell in a fast car," Niecy said.

"I prefer to travel by SST." The pooch was officially screwed. Six ways till Sunday.

"What the eff is that?"

"Never mind." I started the Interceptor. "Let's get out of here."

"This ain't little, McGrane. We gotta powwow with Leticia."

"Not me. I've had enough." *And I think I finally did. Have enough.* Nothing was going to save me from Talbott Cottle Coles's wrath. "I'm going home."

To be alternately coddled and teased beyond bearing by my family that loves me.

Chapter 25

That was that.

No sense in getting all het-up over what happened. Nothing to be done but take it as it came.

I will never ever be a cop.

I turned off the car, hit the garage door opener, and got out. Deep pain in my upper abdomen radiated through the middle of my back and up into my shoulders. All I wanted was an oxy and a shower.

The second day was always the worst. *Hooray. Something to look forward to tomorrow.* I hauled my carcass into the house.

An enormous collection of dense blossoms took center stage on the kitchen counter.

Creamy dahlias, white Lisianthus, bone-colored roses, and ivory hydrangeas skillfully arranged in a thick glass rectangle the size of a large shoe box, inset with another glass, slightly smaller rectangle, smooth white beans pressed between the two vases, hiding any trace of the stems.

Pure art. Transcendent and beautiful even in its decay.

"They're gorgeous," Mom said, coming into the kitchen. "Thierry already took pictures."

I lifted the flap of the thick ivory envelope and removed the card.

Every pearl has its oyster
H

If he only knew . . .

I grinned, not quite sure what to make of it—his intention, no doubt—and that pleased me just as much.

Mom picked up the envelope and examined the brown script on back. "The Dilly Lily. The man has taste."

I handed her the card. She read it and smiled. "And a sense of humor." Her brown eyes flickered over my stomach. "How badly does it hurt?"

"Bad enough."

"You called to let him know about your bruised pancreas."

I cringed, only half-kidding. "Texted."

"Coward."

No argument here. "Seriously, Mom. One cannot maintain a relationship based on pity alone."

"A three-hundred-dollar floral arrangement doesn't exactly scream pity, baby. You make your brothers look like Mensa versions of Dr. Phil," she scoffed. "My God, have I taught you nothing?"

"I know, I know, I know."

"You may think you do." She stroked the spiky petals of a fist-sized dahlia. "How was work?"

"Horrific and exhausting." *And not without impending repercussions.* "Yours?"

Mom went to the fridge and took out a bottle of Pinot Grigio. "Not quite that good." She poured a balloon glass almost to the rim. "Take this up and have a soak."

Icy-cold white wine and a hot bath. Mom's favorite cure-all.

Throw in a couple of oxys and it works pretty well.

"Maisie?" Mom's voice came through the phone intercom. She refused to have people yelling back and forth. Not when our house was so large, there were so many of us, and she did so much work from home.

I picked up the phone next to my bed. "Yes?"

"Mr. Bannon's on line two."

The second of four light-up buttons was blinking. I clicked it. "Hello?"

"How you feeling, Scout?"

"I've been better."

"I'm sure," he said in a serious voice that had me wanting to hang up. Caring commiseration would destroy my fictive dream. My current survival strategy was taking a page from the TV show *I Didn't Know I Was Pregnant*. One hundred percent denial.

"Thank you for the flowers," I said. "They're amazing. Spectacular . . . And undeserved."

"I don't know about that." I could hear the smile in his voice. "You made me look good in front of the mutts."

I laughed.

"Maisie?" Mom hesitated over the intercom. "Leticia Jackson is on line three."

"Uh, Hank? That's my boss."

"I'll hold."

"I'd rather you didn't." *Well, that came out about as wrong as anything could.* "I mean, I'm afraid it's going to be a long, unpleasant conversation."

"Sure," he said, as unreadable as ever. "Take care." He hung up.

Rats.

I took a deep breath and clicked line three. "This is Maisie."

"Where the hell you live, McGrane?" Leticia said. "Some kinda office building?"

"Hey, Leticia—"

"Don't you 'hey, Leticia' me. Not when you bring a shit storm like this raining down on our heads—"

My cell phone chirped. A text from Ernesto. I let Leticia vent on speakerphone and opened the message.

Ernesto: *Chica. What's up?*
I think I got fired by the mayor today.
Ernesto: *No shit? Guy's a complete prick*
The prickiest
Ernesto: *WTF? Ur not kidding!*
What?
Ernesto: *Ur on Ch. 5.*

"Leticia?" I interrupted. "Are you in front of a television?"

"I'm in my damn home, McGrane. Of course I'm in front of a TV."

"Turn it to Channel Five."

Local TV news—twenty-two minutes consisting of fourteen teasers for stories that were shorter than the tease itself, a semi-accurate weather report, sports scores, and Mike's Moan, an Andy Rooney–style segment where Chicagoans called or wrote in with their gripes about anything and everything Illinois.

Looking like an obese version of Daniel Tosh sporting a thick mustache and glasses, Mike always wore a Chi-town sports team jersey. "Lately you've all been moaning to Mike about the highway robbery known as city street parking. But what comes around, goes around."

The TV cut to a series of stills of the orange-booted limo.

"Even our own Mayor Talbott Cottle Coles can't escape the boot of anguish." The picture changed to a clip of PR video of Coles waving in front of the American flag. "Nope," Mike said. "No one's free from the ticket tyrants. The meter fascists. The heartless harlots."

Okay. This isn't so bad. Of course, there'd be fallout, but it's not radioactive or anything.

"But get a load of this," Mike said to the camera. "Saint Ditka be praised, even the meter maid didn't feel too good about sticking it to our mayor." Up flashed a still of me sliming my vest.

At least it was a still.

"That's all from Mike. Go Bears. Go Bulls. Go Sox. Go Blackhawks. Go home, Cubs."

The TV cut to commercial.

Ouch.

"Humph," Leticia said. "This is worse than I was considering. You best take tomorrow off, McGrane. Let me see how the land is lying and shit."

"Okay. 'Bye Leticia." I hung up.

The cell chirped again. Ernesto.

*   *   *

Ernesto: *Chica. Want me to come over?*
No. U'll only interfere w/suicide attempt
Ernesto: *Ha. Ha. Tomorrow nite?*
Sure. We'll get wasted!
Ernesto: *Just checked ch. 2 and 7. Only talked about the boot. No video. @)- -,--x12*

Talk about a sign things were circling the drain. Ernesto was texting me flowers.

Thanks, E.
Ernesto: *Xo xo*
Xo urself.

I woke up Friday morning, wondering how I was going to get fired. I went downstairs, where Thierry was making liver and onions and French fries for me for breakfast. I took a seat at the bar.

"I hear you are a TV star," he said. "I make liver for the bruise, yes?"

And because I adore it. "Thanks, Thierry." He set a glass-bottled Coke in front of me. "Anyone else around?"

"*Non.*"

I sighed in relief.

Thierry flipped the liver in the pan. He glanced over his shoulder with me and ducked. "Enough are coming tonight, that I stay and cook."

Great.

"Add me and one more."

"You bring Hank, yes?" He set my plate in front of me. Heaven. Beef fat–fried shoestring fries with sea salt and a side of seasoned mayonnaise took half the plate while the rest held liver with a butter-blackened crust and caramelized onions.

"No, just Ernesto."

"You will want the ketchup?" He moued in resignation.

I nodded.

Shaking his head, he placed it in front of me. In the bottle—
so I could feel his disappointment.

Join the club, baby.

"I make pizzas tonight." Thierry's pizzas were cooked in the
wood-fire oven Mom had expressly commissioned for him. He
tossed the crust and everyone loaded their own. No matter
what, it was a night that always turned rowdy. And hell, if anyone deserved a party, it was me.

"Perfect," I said and tucked into my heavenly breakfast.

Afterward, I took a long shower and wasted the early afternoon cute-ing up while watching David Niven in *Stairway to
Heaven* on TMC and then redoing my eye makeup after crying
through the entire second half.

"Maisie?" Thierry said on the intercom. "Jennifer Lince is
telephoning you."

Crap.

I drove downtown to the TEB building and parked in the
$11.50-an-hour ramp.

*Why not? I'd be back on Mom and Dad's dime in law school
soon enough.*

I threaded my way through the fleeing corporate stream and
spent the elevator ride hoping I wouldn't have to sit and sweat
the mandatory half hour in reception before getting fired.

Fired. Cripes.

I'd never been fired from anything. Although I guess expelled
from the Police Academy probably counted. Well, at least after
Jennifer canned me, I had something to fire back—*Golly gee,
I'm so sorry that Cash won't be able to make it to the Dhu West
Gala after all.*

Bing. Silver lining present and accounted for.

Jennifer Lince's secretary was waiting for me when I stepped
off the elevator. "This way, Miss McGrane." She led me back,
all polite smiles and seriousness, and opened the door without
knocking, closing it before I got all the way inside.

A good-looking man, late forties with blond hair slicked

back, excellent caps, and a manicure waved me in. He was sitting behind Jennifer's desk, Ferragamo-shod feet propped on top, right next to Cash's eight-by-ten. "So this is Agent Maisie McGrane."

Jennifer sat on the edge of her seat, chipmunk-tense, an enormous frozen smile on her face. If she'd had whiskers, they'd have been bristling with excitement.

The man twirled his finger. "Let me get a look at you."

Jennifer nodded at me so hard I thought her head might fall off. I turned around in front of him, feeling ridiculous.

"She's cute," he said approvingly to Jennifer. "Tight. Fit. Not just attractive but actually pretty." He smiled and spoke to me. "Attractive's code in my business for 'not Quasimodo,' but it doesn't guarantee much more than a step away from the freak show." He dropped his feet off the desk and sat up. "I'm Sterling Black. I run public relations for the Dhu West Corporation. And you, Maisie baby, have gone viral."

Chapter 26

"What?" I said.

"You're at 31,750 hits and it's only been up 140 minutes." Sterling gestured to Jennifer. "Show her."

Jennifer brought over a MacBook Pro with fifteen-inch screen open to a YouTube video. She set it on my knees, tapped Play, and stepped back.

Choppy cuts of the local Chicago news stations talking heads were jammed together, bantering in an understandable edit. "Even our—great mayor—Talbott Cottle Coles—isn't immune—from the boot." It ended on a still shot of the orange Wolverine clamped to the rear limo tire.

A chrome logo *GN* spun into view. A gorilla knuckle-walked across the screen and lobbed a grenade at the logo, which melted in a fiery explosion with the voice-over, "Guerrilla News. We're not afraid to throw *bleep* at anyone."

Juvenile, but slickly produced. I looked up at Sterling. He pointed back at the screen. The explosion faded to black, and up came a familiar face, wearing a maroon military beret and fatigues, seated behind a steel desk with a camouflage-netting backdrop. "This is Allegra Luciana Maria Gaccione reporting for Guerrilla News, and I'm gonna blow you away."

The video cut to Talbott Cottle Coles asking my name and ended with him ripping off my badge.

God, I made a Care Bear look macho. Surprising, how much worse it felt watching it happen.

Allegra smiled at the camera. "This is what the mayor and the MSM don't want you to see. Let's take another look."

The screen froze, dimmed except for a large circle showing Coles's hand on my vest. The video rolled and re-rolled as he ripped it off again and again. Allegra said in a serious voice-over, "Threatening a parking enforcement agent is a felony." The picture cut to Allegra in studio. "And this is just the beginning of the indignity that our own mayor dumped on poor Miss Maisie McGrane."

I gripped the sides of the laptop to keep from covering my eyes.

What followed was a PR bloodbath. Five camera angles expertly spliced together, showed Chicago's wunderkind playing my demise to the crowd with the occasional shot of me, pale-faced and pathetic.

Allegra folded her hands on the steel news desk. "How's that work, exactly? A powerful leader, man of the people, throws a city employee—*a defenseless young woman*—to the wolves? Publically berating and embarrassing her because he can't handle the fact that his limo got booted for parking in not one but two *handicapped spaces?*" Allegra shook her head piously, but the gleam in her eye was undeniable. "Watch closely, the best is yet to come."

The Guerrilla cameragirls had captured Coles's hands to my chest in excruciating multi-angle detail, and ran it in slow-mo, graciously returning to normal speed for my Red Bull puke-up.

"Did you know touching a parking enforcement agent is *felony aggravated battery?*" Allegra demanded. "Three news stations push a puff piece. The mayor got a boot. Where's the outrage, Chicago? Where's the DA? I'm guessing he's throwing back a couple of thirty-dollar scotches with Talbott Cottle Coles at the Standard Club, weaving a damage-control web."

She saluted the camera. "This is Allegra Luciana Maria Gaccione reporting for Guerrilla News, and I hope I blew your mind." The Guerrilla News gorilla crossed the bottom of the screen and lobbed a grenade at Allegra. The screen exploded in flames, then cut to black.

The YouTube counter read 37,035 hits.

I closed the laptop, leaned forward, and set it smoothly on the desk. *Amazing, really, seeing as I'd just been beaten with a sack of oranges.*

"I'm going to hire that kid," Sterling said. "But first I'm going to make you famous."

The most vicious, callous thing anyone's ever said to me. A choking gasp forced its way out of my throat. Sterling Black— whisking my reinstatement off the table without even knowing it.

Arrgh.

"Imagine the potential, Maisie," he said. "Fame and the inevitable fortune that follows it when properly managed."

Jennifer put her hands together and fingertip-clapped.

What potential? The only famous cops aren't cops at all but retired FBI profilers and that lemon-sucking D-lister Steven Seagal. Cops aren't famous because they don't want to be.

Sterling kept talking. I didn't hear him. My tongue was stuck to the roof of my mouth, tasting a vile combination of sweet and ammonia as though I'd taken a straight shot of antifreeze.

Sterling gave me the raised brow and half smile. Waiting for my gratitude.

I was fresh out.

"I beg your pardon, Mr. Black—"

"Sterling," he said.

"Okay . . . Sterling . . . I don't want to be famous. You can have my fifteen seconds."

"Minutes," he corrected.

Seriously, dude. I'm praying my time is running in Planck units.

"Instant celebrity. If you're lucky, Maisie, really lucky, an opportunity like this knocks on your door. And do you know how many people ignore that knocking?"

"The few of us who rank reality TV lower than class action lawyers and used car salesmen?"

Jennifer Lince sucked in a breath. Terrified or in awe of Sterling Black, most likely a combination of both.

"Irreverent. Smart." He pointed at me. "I like you."

The Don Draper worked for him well enough.

Sterling tipped his head toward Ms. Lince, and without taking his eyes from mine, said, "Jenny, sweetheart, why don't you go get a massage on me?" He winked at me, but Jennifer took it to be hers as he'd intended.

Snaps for smoothness.

"Yes, sir, Mr. Black, sir." Jennifer got jerkily to her feet, adjusted her skirt, and left the office.

He waited until the door closed behind her, spade-shaped fingers drumming on my manila personnel file. "Not a lot in here for me to get to know you." He toyed with the corner of the file. "Are you a fan of Talbott Cottle Coles, Maisie?"

"I didn't target him, if that's what you're asking."

"I wasn't," he lied with a smile. "Nice to know, nonetheless. Did you vote for him?"

"No."

He chuckled. "Me, neither."

Great. Let's ride off into the Republican sunset together, Sundance.

"Maisie McGrane." Sterling leaned toward me. "I want *you* to be the new face of the TEB."

"I'm sorry?" I clenched the edge of my chair so hard my fingers went numb. Which was all right, as they now matched the rest of me.

"This is the perfect opportunity to springboard into a positive Parking Enforcement Agent campaign." Sterling started the soft sell. "Put the candy-coating on the necessary evil of public safety, etcetera."

Focus. Hank's Law Number Four: Keep your head.

There had to be an escape hatch.

"That's ummm . . . wow . . . really flattering, but I'm just not that kind of a girl."

"Of course you are. My next big thing."

How about the old, "it's not you, it's me"?

"Look, Sterling. I've never taken a decent picture. Ever. And when I'm not stuttering, I lip off. Absolutely the last person in the world you want to be the spokesmodel for feeding the meter."

"No worries, Maisie," Sterling said, a practiced look of concern on his face. "Every journey begins with a little self-doubt."

"Maybe I'm not explaining this right." I wiggled my fingers. "I want this to fade away."

"There's only one way that's gonna happen." He shrugged. "You quit."

So, that's how you wanna play it, huh?

"I'm not going to quit." *Not yet.*

"And I don't want you to. But I'm not going to lie to you, either," Sterling said. "With that video, the cat's out of the eco-friendly shopping bag, and Talbott Cottle Coles is gunning for you."

I settled back in my chair and got comfortable. "He won't get far with video evidence of aggravated assault with a side of battery. An open court case against the city's top official probably won't look so good for Dhu West's parking poster girl."

Sterling's eyes went opaque.

Time for the heat. "I have eighteen months to press charges."

"But you won't."

I knew why I wouldn't. But why was he so sure? "Oh?"

"Ah-ah-ah." He wagged a finger at me. "I *know* you. An aggressive little up-and-comer." He gave me a couple grooving nods. "And I'm digging the wide-eyed innocent routine. It's cute."

"I'm not interested."

"You're scared. I get it. And hey, I'm impressed that you have the sense to look ahead—imagining the worst-case scenario and all that. Clever. But you won't be going this alone. I've got your back."

Sure, you do.

Sterling held out his hands, holding an imaginary bounty. "I'm offering you money, position, and the potential for more. A lot more. You can write your own ticket."

Cute. "What's in it for you?"

He ran a finger across his lower lip. "Let's just say Dhu West has been a very close friend of the mayor's. But there comes a

time when a public separation is preferable to one or both parties. Dhu West feels that now is that time."

*One sacrificial lamb, coming right up. You want Pepsi with
that?*

"And let's not forget who's really at stake here." His face
drew into a good-looking frown. "All the other parking enforcement agents." He shook his head sadly. "Your reviled,
spat-upon sisters and brothers watch as one of their best and
brightest takes it on the chin from an elected city official. Assaulted. By the mayor of Chicago, no less. Why, it practically
screams 'Come beat the shit out of us! Everyone hates us!' to the
general public, doesn't it?"

I could almost hear the theme song to *Rudy* playing in the
background. I smiled as though it didn't matter—could never
matter—but of course it did. For me the job was the means to
an end. Even now, I could leave it any time, take my chances
with law school or whatever else I could think of. But Leticia?
Niecy and the rest of those poor stiffs?

It was their life.

A small groan came from the back of my throat. Amazing really,
how those who possess no conscience are so adept at pressuring
those of us who do.

"I do things two ways, Maisie. The happy way or the hard
way. With the happy way, there's space to adjust, make re-
quests—everyone's happy. The hard way's exactly that." He
made a clicking sound against his teeth. "Hard."

According to Hank, there are more than twenty-two ways to
kill a man with your bare hands. I know of a dozen. But bashing
Sterling Black over the head with his MacBook Pro until his
brains leaked out of his ears had an appealing sort of Zen sym-
metry to it.

Sterling leaned back in the Swedish desk chair and put his
hands behind his head. "Which way do you want it?"

"Happy." A little time was better than none.

A knock sounded at the door.

"Enter," Sterling said.

In came his Charlie's Angels squad of personal assistants—a

blonde, a brunette, and a redhead all in tight short skirts and low-necked blouses. Twentysomethings with Bluetooth earpieces attached, walking that fine line between sexy and slutty and owning it.

The auburn beauty faced down Sterling across the desk. The tip of her tongue slipped out and touched her upper lip, her green eyes alight. "The big three plus plenty of cable." She put her hands on the end of the desk and leaned way over, giving him the cleavage shot. "Who do you want most?"

Unaffected by what my brothers would deem a stellar rack, Sterling put his hands behind his head. "Who's hungriest?"

She beamed and said in a voice that hummed, "They all are, baby."

"*Good Day USA*." Sterling turned to me. "Do you know what spin is?"

"As in O'Reilly's No Spin Zone?" I said.

"That geriatric spaniel couldn't spin his way out of a paper sack."

Sterling's aides giggled on cue.

He grinned at me. "I'm the top *top,* baby."

"The Caesar of spin," oozed the brunette.

I'd like to get off now, please.

He turned to the blonde. "Contract."

She whipped out an iPad and began tapping and dragging on the screen with a slim black stylus.

"Standard, one through sixty, add on 4 clauses A through F, rights clauses 35 A through R, print and video 75A through 78C," Sterling said. The blonde clicked and tapped, then nodded at the brunette, who disappeared from the office.

The redhead took the chair next to mine and said in a soft voice, "You have no idea how lucky you are to have Sterling."

The brunette returned with a thick stack of paper, secured with a black binder clip, and set it on the corner of the desk closest to me. Red Post-it flags marked with *Sign Here* were scattered among its contents.

Sterling gestured for me to pick it up.

"What is it?" I asked, not reaching for it.

"Standard PR contract. Boilerplate, you know how it is."

Boilerplate. The single word that raised the hackles of any decent lawyer. "No, actually I don't."

Sterling smiled. "You need representation at a higher, more specific level for this opportunity." He uncapped an ebony Waterman pen and set it on the contract.

I shook my head.

"Can't or won't?" he asked, clearly tired of this.

"There are three lawyers in my family," I said. "I'm sure you can understand I don't feel comfortable signing *anything* without one of them taking a look-see."

He raised a brow and nodded grudgingly. "Okay. Tomorrow morning. Here. Seven a.m. Signed or ready to negotiate."

Saturday morning? Seriously?

Sterling picked up the contract from the corner of the desk and held it up. The brunette took it. The blonde held her stylus and tablet at the ready, while he put the cap back on the pen and replaced it in his suit coat pocket. "Remove A through F on 4 and add S through V on 5. Addendums 1.A through G and D include the fee-split with all the minis."

She tip-tapped his contract alterations on the iPad and nodded at the brunette, who left.

Sterling may as well have been speaking Japanese, but I got one thing out of it. Ready to take advantage, he'd been even quicker to back down. Sterling Black wanted me for something more than the new face of the PEA, and that might just be my way out.

Chapter 27

Talk about an unpleasant development.

I drove home with the contract screaming at me from inside my purse on the passenger's seat and fourteen hours to figure a way out of Sterling Black's media tar pit. *Or else it'd be me on TV, accompanied by the hideous and final death rattle of my dream of becoming a cop.*

What campaign did Sterling envision? *My Goodness, My Meter Maid? Got Tickets?*

And as if that wasn't enough, our driveway was full of cars. *Super-duper.*

I had to park on the street. I came in through the back garage door trying to rev myself up. A party, Ernesto, and the slim but real possibility that no one had seen the YouTube video yet. *Chin up.*

At the moment, I still had my job and three top-notch lawyers who sure as hell should be able to get me out of Sterling's stranglehold.

I went through the mudroom, dropped my keys in the dish, and heard Allegra's nasal voice-over from the family room. *There is no God.*

They were all watching it. On the Sharp one-hundred-eight-inch screen LCD TV with Wi-Fi. Da, Flynn, Rory, Declan, Daicen, Cash. Howling with laughter.

Declan, the devil, as was his specialty, imitated me to perfection as the Guerrilla News video rolled. The room was plugged to the gills with pure testosterone. Ernesto was there. So were Koji and several other cops I'd known for years. All laughing so hard tears rolled down their cheeks.

"Hi, M-m-m-meter Maid, M-m-Maisie!" Declan said in a stutter-blurp fake throw-up voice, making everyone laugh even harder.

Except me.

I dropped my bag and jerked my shirt up. "See this? It's called a bruised pancreas. I had it *before* the mayor shoved me."

The laughing choked to silence at the sight of my gruesome torso-covering bruise, which had turned a spectacular mottled black and violet.

"Jaysus, Mary, and Joseph," Da whispered. "Who did that to you?"

My five brothers stared at me in white-lipped fury.

"I did," Hank said.

The whip-crack of necks almost audible as everyone jerked to look at him.

He stood in the doorway from the living room, a beer in one hand, my mom on his arm. His black Gucci shirt was open at the neck, rolled up at the sleeves, and tucked into black pants with a black canvas military belt. All daunting sinewy hardness and cruel good looks.

Breathtaking.

"Hank?" I squeaked. *For the love of Mike . . .*

"I stepped into a kick during training," I said hastily, yanking my shirt back down. "I wasn't paying attention. One hundred percent my fault!"

Too late. The nine cops in the room giving Hank the eye had already decided it was a domestic and were wondering when the blanket party was.

Thierry clapped his hands from the kitchen. "Are we making the pizzas or are we not?"

Cash quit texting and sent his Italian music mix through the stereo—everything from *The Godfather* sound track to Ennio Morricone's spaghetti westerns. Rory shot Hank a last suspicious once-over before heading to the kitchen, throwing his arms around two other guys, getting the traffic flowing.

Flynn changed the input on the television to a ball game. I caught his eye and glanced at Da.

He shook his head, then tapped his watch.

He hadn't told Da about the Clark case. Time may be ticking, but I'll take as much of it as I can.

Ernesto came over and got right in my face. "Where the hell you been, *chica?* I've been calling and texting you the last two hours."

"Dhu West. I turned my phone off."

His face crumpled in commiseration. "How'd it go?"

"Not good," I said. "I'm getting a promotion."

Across the room, Daicen joined Mom and Hank.

Ernesto held up his empty glass. "You need a beer, my friend. And so do I."

"Damn straight." We walked over to the wet bar. I put a glass under the tap. Thierry had changed the keg to Moretti in honor of pizza night. I took a sip. Icy-cold goodness. "How long has Hank been here?"

"A while," Ernesto replied. "We got here before the cops got off shift and showed up."

"We?"

"I didn't think you'd mind Hank tagging along. Not to mention, he's not the kind of guy you say no to."

Hank. Here. In my own home. Talking to my mother. WTF?
"I better go say hi."

"Hey," Ernesto said, "gimme your phone, will ya?"

I picked up my bag, tossed him my cell, took out the contract, and walked over to Mom, Daicen, and Hank.

"Where've you been?" Mom said.

"Dhu West." I handed my brother the contract. "Sterling Black wants me to be the new face of Parking Enforcement." I let that sink in and turned to Hank. "Could you give us a minute? I need a little legal advice."

"I don't know, dear. Mr. Bannon may be able to provide

some interesting insight into your situation," Mom said. "Shall we adjourn to my office?"

Once we were seated at the conference table, Mom asked, "What did Sterling Black say exactly, Maisie?"

"The video is too tough to spin. Dhu West wants to publicly separate from Talbott Cottle Coles."

Daicen passed the first few pages to Mom. "Coles's options are limited to a public apology and anger management classes." He turned another page of the contract. "I've seen the video. The only thing in Coles's favor is the fact that his member remained in his trousers."

"I don't know." Mom rolled a pen between her teeth. "Dhu West has been in bed with Coles since before his first campaign, and the Saudis want to dump him now? On the edge of reelection?"

Maybe the Saudis were ticked the Bus Driver's Union sell-off didn't pan out.

"If it is a setup, I don't see it. Maisie's as clean as they come. And this"—Daicen tapped the contract—"comes with handcuffs."

"I'm not going on TV."

"Why are you balking?" Mom said. "This could be a springboard to a new career." A wily gleam sparked in her eyes. "What do you think about running for office?"

"Don't be ridiculous," I said.

Mom scanned another paragraph. "Dhu West seems to consider your refusal to participate as insubordination and thereby a firing offense. Your options are to appear or resign."

"I'm not quitting. C'mon, guys," I rasped. "You gotta get me out of this. Please?"

"Want a paper bag, killer?" Hank said.

Cute.

He ran a hand along the length of his jaw. "Requesting a veteran team member accompany her on set seems reasonable."

"Cogent, even." Daicen's eyes crinkled at the corners. He crossed his arms over his chest, dark eyes narrowed in thought. "Any ideas?"

Mom smirked. "I vote for Leticia Jackson."

Great. Apparently no one in my twisted plane of reality was offering the blue pill today.

Hank and I left Mom and Daicen going over the contract line by line and stepped out of the sound-baffled office into the hallway. The party was in full raucous swing.

I led him down the hall into the study. I hit the remote and the art lights flanking the stone fireplace came on, as did the flat screen, set as usual to the Rat Pack music station.

Hank leaned against the door frame, filling it. Uniquely able to make me feel tense and awkward.

Impressive.

"You've been playing at this meter maid thing for a while now," he said.

"I've got my eye on the prize."

"Yeah?" Hank moved in close. "You sure it's not a case of 'I have my own matches and sulphur and I'll make my own hell'?"

Always with the Kipling.

"Going on a PR tour—with whatever scheme your murder of lawyers comes up with . . ." His voice turned husky. "No good will come of this."

"Clairvoyant, are we?" I said.

"This is Chicago, Sweet Stuff. What goes over the devil's back will be paid for under his belly, and Coles and Dhu West are riding in a continual loop." He touched his forehead to mine, and, in spite of myself, warm happy spread throughout my chest. "Quit."

Why? A weird little buzz started in the back of my mind. Like a honeybee trapped in a jelly jar. I tipped my head back to look at him. "Are you *asking* me to quit?" I said, careful to keep the hopefulness out of my voice.

"What if I am?" he said.

Wow. Well, then . . .

I pretty much almost might even consider it.

Hank let go of me. I turned to see my father stride into the office, all Irish smile and hot eyes.

There wasn't enough Botox in the U.S. to keep my face from contorting into a twisted-up cringe.

"Hank Bannon." Hank held out his hand.

My father shook it. "Conn McGrane," he said in a friendly brogue. "You wouldn't mind giving me a minute with me gel, eh, boyo? Seeing as you already kicked the living shite out of her and all."

Hank smiled thinly. "Of course." He left, closing the door behind him.

"Thanks, Da. That was cool." *Can't anyone in my family act normal for once?*

Da flipped his fingers upward. "Show me."

I raised my shirt.

"Nasty." He whistled at the expanse of dark bruise. "What were you thinking, going to work like that?"

I jerked my shirt down. "I'm on contract."

"Jaysus, Maisie." Da dropped down onto the couch and covered his eyes with his hand. "You'll be the death of me."

"You haven't heard the good news yet," I said, all sunshine and rainbows. "I'm Dhu West's new face of Parking Enforcement. Neat, huh?"

"Why are you doing this?"

"I don't have much choice." I sat down in the chair opposite. "Aside from the fact that my absence as good as declares open season on my coworkers, if I don't go I'm fired."

"Hanging yourself over a half-assed job."

"A means to an end, Da."

"And what end would that be?"

Really? You honestly have no idea? "Reinstatement. At the Academy."

"For chrissakes." He rubbed his temples. "Wake up. You failed the demmed psych exam. It's over."

A pale red haze coated my vision. "Maybe I can make a deal with Coles," I snarked. "Tell him I'll drop the aggravated felony battery if he gets me reinstated."

Holy cat! Did I just unwrap the Golden Ticket?

My father's expression turned to pure granite. "Stay the feck away from Coles."

Dropping the f-bomb? On me?

"You have no idea what Chicago's corruption machine is capable of," he said, using his perp voice, making my pulse hammer like a sapsucker on a Scotch Pine.

"I can guess—"

Da was off the couch, looming over me before I could finish. "No, you can't. Keep away from Coles."

He still wins for pretty much the scariest guy ever.

"It's my life, Da," I said, jerkily.

He nodded and glanced around the room. The words "is it?" unnecessary to speak. He stood up. "Why don't you go find that roughneck you call a fella and ask him what you should do?"

Chapter 28

Hank lounged against a stacked-stone column in the foyer.

The doorbell chimed. I ignored it. *Ask me again if I want to go home with you.*

The doorbell rang again.

"Gonna answer that?" he said.

"Uh, sure." I pulled open the front door.

"How's my favorite multimedia star?" Lee Sharpe asked, looking cut and powerful in an olive-drab tee and jeans. A dozen long-stemmed pink roses in his hand.

Why do I ever even bother getting out of bed in the morning?

"Uh . . . Hi, Lee," I said, stiff with shock as he thrust the flowers into my hands. "You shouldn't have."

Lee stepped inside, dipped his head, and kissed my cheek. "I didn't." He smiled and clicked his tongue. "They're for your mom."

Seriously? Just for tonight, could one guy around here not *be the epitome of cool?*

"Hiya," Lee said throwing a two-fingered mock salute to Hank over my head.

Hank tipped his head back in a half nod.

Lee glanced back at me, eyes narrowed. "Ooookay," he said, chucked me under the chin, and walked right on into the family room. "Hey, Cash!"

I guess he's been here before. I shrugged at Hank.

"Bullitt?"

"I don't know why he's here." I put my hand on the door and started to close it.

"I do." Hank caught the door above me. He leaned down and kissed me, slow and easy and the world stood still.

He lifted his head and I swayed. *Imperceptibly, thank God.*

"Quit." And then he was gone.

Ernesto hustled out of the family room into the foyer. "*Madre de Dios*, Maisie." He looked at the roses and rolled his eyes before jerking open the door. "What the hell is happening with you?" He shoved my phone into the flowers and, not bothering to wait for an answer, went after Hank, slamming the door behind him.

How the heck should I know?

I slumped against it, the iPhone warm in my hand. *And what exactly have you been up to, Ernesto?*

I tapped the call log on my phone. He'd made a fifty-six-minute-and-fifteen-second call.

To Leticia Jackson. *Madre de Dios* was right.

I took one of the two empty seats left at the far end of the kitchen counter. Thierry slid a plate of pizza and glass of beer in front of me.

"Here she is, lads," Declan the sinner called from the pool table. "Put it up, Cash. Let's see how many hits she's up to."

He did it without so much as a blink of conscience.

"Whoo-hooo!" shouted a friend of Flynn's as Allegra's video trumped the game on the big screen. "134,238 hits. Bigger than Miley, baby!"

Lovely.

Amidst the catcalls and wolf whistles, Allegra's three-and-a-half-minute story played again for what felt like thirty years. "Yo, Maisie! What's Allegra's number?" Koji called out as it finally ended, deflecting some of the ribbing. "I'll take her on a ride-along."

Whatever.

I felt a hand on my back and turned on my stool.

"How you doing?" Lee sat down next to me and gave me a considering once-over.

"Great." I raised my beer. "Embracing my infamy as the up-chucking meter maid."

"Not to be PC or anything, but I think Puking Parking Enforcement Agent has a nicer cadence."

I socked him in the arm with a decent amount of pepper.

"Aw, Maisie." Lee drummed his fingers on the bar. "Was that insensitive? There's no such thing as bad publicity, baby," he said, sounding eerily like Sterling Black. "Have you even considered where it could take you?"

"Thrill me."

"Maisie brand airsick bags." He grinned. "You could pitch Dramamine—no wait—ipecac."

I laughed. "Aren't you as sweet as an angel's sigh?"

He's a little funny. A very little.

His face turned serious. "Maisie, I—"

Daicen's head popped in between us as he draped an arm over each of our shoulders. "All hail Maisie's legal representation." He playfully ground his chin into the top of my head. "Sorry to cut this short, Snap, but it's time to turn in. We've got some heavy-level negotiating tomorrow." He straightened and faced the sprawling family room filled with guys playing pool and video games, eating and drinking, Italian music blaring with ESPN muted on the multiple television screens.

I showed Lee the splayed fingers of resignation and slid off the stool.

Lee caught my wrist. "Sleep tight," he said, voice smoky. "Don't let the bedbugs bite."

"Funny," I said. "I was sort of hoping they'd eat me alive."

The party, as expected, was still going strong at 5:45 a.m. I could hear the faint clatter of Foosball and echo of deep voices from the basement rec room. Guys who work the third shift never know when to go home.

I got into Daicen's silver sedan, jittery as a junkie, nerves vibrating off the windows "Dai, about this meeting . . ."

He put his sunglasses on and backed out of the garage. "You want the video buried so you can serve out your meter maid sentence, which you hope will overturn the psych diagnosis, eventually leading to your reinstatement at the Police Academy?"

"How did you—"

"I am the clever one." Daicen flexed his fingers. "Although I highly doubt the rest of the clan's in the dark." He started the car and waited until I was latched before driving out of the gate.

"I will extricate you from this circumstance with a minimum amount of fuss." Daicen tuned his iPod to static. "White noise," he said. "Remarkably effective for focus."

Works for me. I didn't feel like talking anyway.

Daicen hummed sporadically along, thriving in the not quite quiet, which I hoped was working like a shot of Adderall to his Einstein.

We pulled into the parking garage. He took off his sunglasses, face grave. "Wherever I lead, you follow. Clear?"

"Crystal."

We rode up in the Dhu West elevator. Me wishing I felt as fierce as I looked in my black on black Nanette Lepore suit, and Daicen, sleek and keen in navy Calvin Klein with a crisp white shirt, navy and silver rep tie, and black Jack Georges briefcase.

I shifted my weight from side to side on my stilettos.

Would whoever took my life, please return it to its full and uptight position?

The tiniest creases appeared at the corners of my brother's ebony eyes and his mouth twitched. He was an eye-smiler, never with his mouth. Like our grandpa. "A piece of cake, Snap."

The elevator dinged when we hit the thirty-second floor. The doors opened. Sterling's brunette led us into a stylish meeting room where we shook hands, traded shark smiles, and after accepting unwanted cappuccinos, sat down.

"So." Sterling's gaze drifted over Daicen, sizing him up. "What firm do you work for again?"

"Corrigan, Douglas and Pruitt."

"Haven't heard of them." Sterling shrugged in an attempt at nonchalance. He craned his head toward the blonde. "Why don't you ask Bliss to sit in?" He turned back to Daicen. "What do they specialize in?"

"A little civil, a little criminal. Nothing fancy," Daicen said.

"Don't be modest," the redhead said, slinking into the room. "Corrigan, Douglas and Pruitt are one hundred percent badass."

My brother got to his feet. "Daicen McGrane."

"Bliss Adair."

And I thought Maisie was bad. At least my parents hadn't named me with the lofty aspiration that I might one day become a stripper.

She eased down into the chair across from my brother and slowly crossed a pair of great legs.

"A close family," Sterling said. "I like it."

"That's not entirely all." Daicen let his eyes slide over Bliss. Almost insolently. Which was weird. Because he was definitely *not* that guy. "I've always had an interest in celebrity representation."

Since when?

"Where better to start than family?" Bliss teased. "It's not like they can fire you."

Sterling flipped open a black leather portfolio. "Let's get down to it, shall we? I take it there are some contractual agreements you'd like to discuss."

"With less than two months' experience," Daicen said, "Maisie's not qualified to represent the Traffic Enforcement Bureau on a national stage."

"I disagree. Your sister is one of Dhu West's rising stars," Bliss purred at Daicen. "And more importantly, we are talking about a physical altercation with a prominent city official. If she doesn't go on and present her side of the story, the backlash against the other parking enforcement agents will be devastating."

"An astute observation." His eyes never left hers as he continued in a soft, offhanded voice. "Of course, filing formal charges against Talbott Cottle Coles will have the same effect."

"Unfortunately, it won't," Sterling said. "And Dhu West would prefer you didn't."

"Oh?"

"We're severing ties with Coles. We'd prefer a clean break." Sterling gave my brother an appraising look. "This is a tremendous opportunity."

"Alone? On a national stage? I consider that a tremendous risk."

Bliss took the bait. "What if someone accompanied her?"

Daicen turned to me. "How does that strike you?"

I bit my lip and raised a shoulder. He put an arm around me and pulled a patronizing face at Sterling and Bliss. "Is there an office we could step into for a moment?"

"Don't be silly." Sterling stood. "I need to check a couple calls. Take as much time as you need."

Daicen half-rose out of his chair in politeness and they left, closing the door behind them. He glanced pointedly at the ceiling. Camera'd and mike'd, no doubt.

Let the show begin.

"This is a once-in-a-lifetime opportunity. Who would you like to accompany you?"

He hadn't found any wiggle room.

"Jennifer Lince." She'd appropriate my interview faster than a scalded dog.

"A non-starter," he said. "Dhu West will want to present a more *diverse* ethnicity."

"My only other supervisor is Leticia Jackson and they won't want her."

"Why not?"

"Leticia's about as colorful as a steamroller in a gay pride parade and twice as loud." I folded my arms across my chest. "I won't go on alone."

"I'll do my best." He nodded, face solemn, eyes crinkling at the corners. "Why don't you run along, tell Mr. Black and that heavenly Bliss I'm ready, and wait for me in the lobby."

* * *

An hour and a half later, Daicen walked out—all handshakes and smiles and let's-play-squash.

Bliss slipped out as Sterling went back in the office, sidled up to Daicen, and placed her business card in the breast pocket of his jacket.

Daicen covered his pocket with his palm.

You want some cheese with that ham sandwich?

" 'Bye, now." Bliss threw him a pose that would've earned the Snap-on Tools calendar stamp of approval and sashayed back into the conference room.

Dream on, Reddi-wip.

Daicen covered his mouth, half-laughing until we hit the lobby. He waited until we were back in the car in the dim underground parking ramp before saying anything. He took Bliss's card out of his pocket, flicked it back and forth across his finger. "Exactly as expected."

"Oh yeah?"

He held up the card. "Shall I pass this on to Declan? Let him rattle her cage a bit while we fly to New York tomorrow?" He tossed it onto the dash.

"What?" I banged my head against the headrest. "I thought you were going to get me out of this." Cold sweat filmed on my back.

Nice. My new Nanette Lepore would be taking the nonstop straight to the dry cleaners.

"I said I'd extricate you from the situation with the least amount of fuss. What did you think?" He sighed and put his sunglasses on. "That I have the Time Bandits locked in my trunk on retainer? That we'd nip back in time and unhook the boot?"

"Me going on a national morning show is nothing *but* fuss," I ground out.

"You still have your job and a shot at reinstatement." He fished a pack of Wint-O-Green Life Savers out of the cup holder, put one between his teeth, and offered them to me.

"No thanks."

"Maisie," Daicen said around the candy he held between his

teeth. "If you do as I say, your celebrity will last no longer than the triboluminescent effect of this Life Saver." He crunched the candy, emitting a tiny blue-white spark.

I wish.

I let my breath out in a slow exhale. "Thanks for today. I'm sorry, I really do appreciate your help."

"Now, now," he said pleasantly. "I am the nice one."

"Gosh. There's got to be *something* I can do to repay you . . ." I picked Bliss's business card off the dash. "Why, I know! I'll have Mom invite Bliss over for dinner."

"As your preferred brother and newly signed agent, I was prepared to charge you a discounted rate of ten percent." He plucked the card from my fingers and slipped it into his shirt pocket. "I've changed my mind. I'll take thirty. Gross."

I laughed as we drove out of the parking ramp. "Now what?"

"Call Leticia. Tell her the good news."

Chapter 29

"This better be good, McGrane," Leticia warned. "Calling me so early an' shit on a Saturday morning."

It was five minutes to ten. "Have you seen it?"

"You mean the video where Mayor Coles assault-n-batteries your weak ass and you throw up on yourself to get him back?"

"That'd be the one."

Leticia laughed. "How 'bout I get Niecy and meet you at Butch's to figure out how to save your lily-white onion?"

An infinitesimal lump formed in my throat.

"Hold up." Leticia's voice turned suspicious. "You ain't thinking about quitting on me, now? Cuz, I ain't in the mood to go shopping for another marine, you dig?"

Easily swallowed.

"Are you in the mood to fly to New York tomorrow and appear with me on the *Good Day USA* show Monday morning?"

Silence.

A lot of it.

"You comin' at me correct?"

"Yes," I said.

Her scream of excitement was so shrill I dropped the phone.

Daicen met us on the sidewalk, opening the gate. He stowed Leticia's bags in the trunk, installed her in the front seat, and closed the passenger door behind her.

"Damn, you know some fine-looking boys, McGrane," Leticia said, watching my brother come 'round the hood.

"Anyone in particular?" I asked innocently, opening the door to talk about Ernesto.

"Wouldn't you like to know?"

Yes, actually, I would.

Daicen got in and started the car.

"You're rollin' in a tight whip." Leticia ran her hand along the center console. "What do you do, anyways?"

"I'm a lawyer."

Leticia shot me a look over her shoulder. I nodded in confirmation that he was, indeed, a lawyer.

"We be grown women, so why 'zactly you coming along to New York?"

My brother tipped his head up and looked at me in the rearview mirror. Even though I couldn't see his eyes through his Smith Optics, I knew he was smiling. "I'm Maisie's agent."

"Her what?" Leticia's chin hit her chest.

She wrestled around in her seat, fighting the seat belt to face me. "I thought this was all Dhu West. You didn't spill you be getting famous." She threw a small head bob my way, then readjusted herself back in the gray leather seat. "Needin' an agent. Shit, what am I? The jankey-ass Robin to your Batman?"

"Not at all, Ms. Jackson," Daicen said calmly. "Maisie's humiliation is merely one of those moments where others find it necessary to offer her an opportunity to further her embarrassment for money."

"Is she payin' you?"

Daicen on the hot seat. I shivered with silent laughter.

"Of course," Daicen said.

"How much?"

Or not. My brother wasn't laughing. "Ten percent."

"Oh yeah? I heard agents take fifteen."

"It's a discounted rate. We are related, after all."

Leticia rolled her tongue in her cheek. "You think I need an agent?"

"I don't know," Daicen said. "Do you?"

She smoothed the orange fabric of her capris. "What would you charge to represent me?"

He drummed his fingers on the steering wheel, considering. "Ten percent."

Leticia chewed that over for a minute. "No. You best take the fifteen."

"That's up to you, Ms. Jackson." He gave me another rearview mirror full of sunglasses. "May I ask why?"

"Cuz I don't want no strings if I gotta fire your ass for salting my game."

"Agreed." Daicen held out his hand and Leticia shook it.

"You got any talk radio in this ride?"

Sterling Black's PR machine had muscle behind the makeup. We flew to New York first-class, had the Dhu West limo at our disposal, and spent the night in the gorgeous James Hotel. At least I did. Leticia couldn't fathom staying in, and my brother was more than happy to entertain his new client.

I called Flynn after a decadent room service dinner. "Hi."

"Hi yourself, Snap. Calling for a case update or just to hear my voice?"

"Both."

"Sure." He snorted. "The memorial IDs are a slow slog. I swung by the Local #56 and got a reception colder than dry ice."

"Surprised, were you?"

"Hardly." He chuckled. "I traced the phone number on the back of the picture."

"And?"

"It belongs to The Storkling. A private club owned by a shell corporation with ties to the Veterattis. But it's a helluva thing, trying not to trip any of the BOC's alarms. Or Da's."

There was a long pause. I knew exactly what he was thinking. "I've told you all I can, Flynn. Hank and I aren't exactly seeing eye to eye lately."

"Well, I guess that's something. Good luck tomorrow."

* * *

3:50 a.m., feeling bizarrely flippant in a navy blue Marc Jacobs suit, I went down to the lobby of the James Hotel. Leticia and Daicen were already waiting in the limo, dressed for the day in fuchsia and black respectively, their eyes ablaze with the adrenaline and excitement of a couple of raccoons caught in a Burger King Dumpster.

I got in the car.

"Oh my God! Oh my God!" Leticia said, fanning herself with her hands. "We saw them both! Megyn Kelly *and* Sean Hannity."

"When?"

"Last night—" Daicen started.

"You snooze, you lose!" Leticia said. "My agent got me a private tour of Studio J."

"Studio J?"

"The Fox News building." Daicen's eyes creased at the corners. "It might have gone a bit smoother if Leticia hadn't completely lost her mind."

"It's true." Leticia shook her head in unremorseful delight. "I was screaming like I'd won the Showcase on *The Price Is Right.* Whaddya expect?" She waved frantically at her partner in crime. "C'mon, c'mon. Show her the pictures!"

Daicen handed me his iPhone.

"Hannity even took us on set and threw me a football."

I scrolled through a roll of Leticia hugging and posing with her celebrity crushes. I held out the phone. "Niecy'll turn grass green when she sees these."

"Won't she, though?" Leticia grabbed the phone, laughing in pure delight. "Can I? E-mail?" she asked Daicen.

"Certainly." Leticia started e-mailing the photos. My brother caught my eye. "Dhu West may have finished with Talbott Cottles Coles," Daicen said, "but the mayor remains a media darling. And you, sister dear, are not."

Was reinstatement really worth this level of disgrace? Were my coworkers? Was anything?

"The secret to ending this or any other type of celebrity is . . ."
He leaned forward until his forehead almost touched mine and

whispered the sacred secret of the ages, "Boredom. Do not raise your voice, smile, frown, or shrink away. Remain stone-faced and monotonous."

"And then?"

"They'll cut to commercial and toss your bromidic being to the curb before the break's ended."

"Genius," I croaked.

The limo slowed to a stop in front of the broadcast building. We stepped out into the blazing lights, a small crowd of out-of-towners already gathering for the chance to wave at their friends back home on *Good Day USA*'s weather segment.

Inside, studio aides in maroon blazers met us at Reception, issued us passes, and delivered us to the place where the morning magic happened. The set.

Good Day USA was shot on two large and two smaller gold-and-orange-colored stages. Leticia elbowed me. "Over there!" She gave a tiny squeal. "Victor Cruz."

Sure enough, the Giants wide receiver in jeans and a T-shirt, crossed the set and disappeared down a hallway.

"Oooh-eeee." Leticia danced several yards after him in a three-two clave rhythm. "I'd salsa with him any day."

I started back toward Daicen and stopped.

Bliss Adair appeared out of nowhere in a crisp white shirt—going French with black lace bra exposed underneath—and a taupe skirt so short it was made for standing only. She sauntered up to my brother, took his face between her hands, and kissed him right on the mouth.

Ergh?

She tipped her head back. "Good morning, darling."

Well, that happened faster than a knife fight in a phone booth.

"Hello to you, too." Daicen said, with as much emotion as a slab of concrete.

OMG. He likes her!

"I've got a treat for you." Her lips parted in a smile. "Bruce, the producer, has promised to take you into the control room during the live shoot. A real behind-the-scenes experience. Isn't that delicious?"

"Yes," he said.

Leticia stayed at a distance, crossed her arms, and gave Bliss a hard once-over. It was clear the auburn-haired beauty had come up lacking.

Bliss waved over a man one sandwich away from emaciation wearing a Band of Outsiders ultra-svelte suit. After a serious ogle at my brother, he asked, "Bliss, who is this cool drink of water?"

"Daicen McGrane," she answered, slipping her arm through his. He held out his hand.

Bruce took it in a genteel shake. "I hear you're a real up-and-comer."

My brother cocked a brow at Bliss. "Don't believe a word she says."

Wow.

"Bliss and Sterling are the gold standard when it comes to locating talent," Bruce said gallantly. "Come, I'll take you back. Things will start moving around here pretty quickly."

"I'd like to see Maisie and Leticia settled first, if I may," Daicen said.

Bliss's teal eyes and pink lips went round in sweet surprise. "That's why I'm here, of course. Hair, wardrobe, and makeup. If you're really that worried, darling, you can check on them in the green room."

Daicen let Bruce lead him away.

Bliss, all business, took several quick steps on the shiny floor in the opposite direction. She stopped and spun on her heel, fist on hip. "Let's *go*, ladies."

Leticia trotted to catch up, firing questions at her like an Uzi on full automatic. "When do I meet Alec Anders? An' Juliana Tate? How much time till we on TV? Can I get Cruz's autograph?"

I lagged behind, a pulsing pressure building behind my eyes, and heard Daicen's voice slice across the set, "You know what they say, Bruce. No matter how beautiful she is, some guy some-where is sick to death of her."

The producer laughed and clapped his hands. "*Love* it!"

From the way my brother was endearing himself to Bruce, I must be in a lot more trouble than even I thought I was. Something jabbed at the back of my brain as I hurried to catch up with Leticia and Bliss.

Hair and makeup took forty-two minutes with a chatty young man with blue hair named Chazz, whose life's dream was to become the next Alexis Vogel. "Just one more set of false eye-lashes and you'll be perfection."

"Another?" I said. "Chazz, you're making me look better than I ever have before, but can't we tone it down a bit? I mean, it's a little intense for a parking enforcement agent."

"A what?"

"A meter maid."

He giggled.

Bliss opened the door and peeked inside. "She looks perfect, Chazz. Absolutely perfect."

I looked at my reflection in the mirror. On the plus side, I was almost unrecognizable in full *Playboy* Bunny hair and makeup.

Bliss snapped her fingers. "Up, up. Let's go."

"Where?" But even as I asked, I already knew the answer. *Wardrobe.*

Chapter 30

You've got to be fucking kidding me.

"I look like the naughty meter maid from a Frederick's of Hollywood catalog," I said, trying to pull the pale blue poly-nylon blend shirt closed.

"It's perfect," Bliss said. "A smidge snug. But just what we're looking for."

"A smidge?"

"Huh." Her teeth gleamed in an insincere grimace. "I was sure you were a double zero just like me."

Sure you were. "Try a four."

"Not possible." She shook her head in baffled amazement. "Go figure."

The wardrobe woman batted my hands away, put ginormous squares of double-stick tape on the tops of my breasts, and none too gently pressed the blouse tight to my skin. "If you don't mess with it, the tape'll last fourteen hours." She slung a fluorescent-orange 1970s-style crossing-guard belt around my waist, complete with matching sash that sliced across my far-too-exposed cleavage.

The wardrobe woman left the room, leaving Bliss and me alone, staring at my reflection in front of the full-length mirror. A toss-up as to which was more disturbing, the abject horror in my eyes or the satisfaction in hers.

The shirt, so tight I could barely breathe, was tucked into a navy blue pencil skirt that had gone to war with a sharpener and lost. Badly.

Apparently rock bottom isn't low enough. Cave diving, any-one? "Um, seriously—"

"You look great," Bliss said. "Far more approachable."

For what? A hand job?

The dressing room door flew open, slamming against the wall. Leticia stomped in, wearing a brand-new, freshly pressed PEA standard-issue uniform. "Yo, Bootsie. You wanna 'splain to me what's wrong with my pink suit?"

"Oh Leticia. I know, it's been a whirlwind, hasn't it?" Bliss bit an impossibly full lip in sympathy. "Why, I'm sure Daicen hasn't had a second alone with you to discuss the dress clause on your contract."

He hadn't with me, either. And he could be damn sure I'd take my pound of flesh—with sandpaper and a spackle knife—layer by agonizing layer.

Leticia got a load of me. Her eyes bugged. "Holy shit. What the hell you got on, McGrane?"

"Pure genius." Bliss said. "It's part of Sterling's 'make friends with the public' campaign."

"Yeah, right." Leticia snorted. "She be makin' all kind o' friends lookin' like a ho'."

Bliss crossed the room to the wet bar. "The City of Chicago will vote on your uniform. One of several we'll be unveiling over the Internet, on billboards, and in magazines."

"Hold up," Leticia said. "Are you telling me, a bunch o' rootie poos can pick a hoochie suit like that? And I'll have to wear it?" She rolled her eyes. "Oh hell, no!"

"Obviously it would be cut to your size," Bliss said with her back to us.

"Oh yeah?" Leticia's braids began to shake like a rattler's tail. "And what *size* do you think I be?"

A cork popped. Bliss turned, holding a green bottle of champagne. "What do you girls say to a little preshow Bolly?"

Leticia's eyes lit up.

"I don't think so," I said. "I'm guessing Sterling won't want us acting like a couple of *Maury* show refugees."

Bliss poured a glass to the brim, handed it to Leticia, and said to me, "Well, aren't you just a big ol' wet blanket?"

Leticia took a sip as Bliss poured a glass for herself. "Break a leg." She held out her glass to Leticia.

They clinked glasses. "I'll break both."

A soft knock sounded on the door, and the wardrobe woman reappeared. She held up an old school–style stewardess cap. "Almost forgot."

Oh hell, no!

I sat down and let the wardrobe woman bobby-pin the cap into my hot-rollered overteased 'do.

Leticia laughed so hard, champagne came out her nose. "Damn, that hurts!" She snuffled into a handful of tissues.

Bliss set her glass down. "Ready to shine for Dhu West and Sterling, ladies?"

Does Bear Grylls drink his own pee?

"Sure," I said, in a voice so flat it'd been ironed. "Let's do it."

The green room wasn't green at all.

Leticia grabbed the sleeve of our maroon-jacketed page, startling him. "Yo, you're supposed to take us to the green room. This here's pink."

Drunk tank pink.

"Yes, ma'am," he said. "It's Baker-Miller Pink."

Holy cat, it really is.

The page continued, "The studio looked to the American Institute for Biosocial Research and found that this particular shade of pink helps suppress anxiety and puts people at ease. It can even slow heart rates."

Subliminal Xanax. A safe bet it was not the on-deck color at the *Maury* show.

I perched gingerly on the edge of a pink fabric couch.

Leticia followed the page to the craft services table, where a watermelon swan floated in a pond of tropical fruit and breakfast rolls. Another bottle of Bollinger wrapped in a white towel waited in an ice bucket.

The page poured a glass for Leticia and with great deference asked if Bliss and I would care for any.

"Actually, would you be an absolute lamb and double-check on our meet and greet?" Bliss said breathily to the page.

The page nodded his head like he was trying to hammer a nail into his chest with his chin. "Yes, ma'am, right away, ma'am." He left.

Bliss pointed a finger at Leticia and me. "The two of you are not, I repeat, *not* to leave this room for any reason. Do you understand me?"

Leticia took a bite of kiwi from the plate she'd dished up. "Where you think we're gonna go?"

Bliss tapped the toe of her nude-colored Jimmy Choo.

"You're the boss," I said.

"That's right, I am. I'm going to check on Daicen, then I'll be right back." With a final warning look, Bliss va-va-voomed away.

Leticia tossed back the rest of her champagne and poured some more. "You seriously ain't letting that ho-bag date our agent, is you?"

"I'll get right on that," I said with a mock salute. "I can't think of a thing Daicen'd like more than relationship advice from his baby sister."

Leticia settled in next to me on the pink leather couch. "I'm not feeling 'zactly copacetic in here." She puffed out her cheeks. "Color's startin' to mess with me."

"I know. I feel like a strand of E. coli trapped in a bottle of Pepto-Bismol."

"Jesus, McGrane. Don't say any o' that crazy shit on TV, a'ight?" She leaned back and crossed her legs. "I got my peoples recording this."

"I'll do my best."

"That's all we ask for around here," said Grade-A celebrity morning-show host Juliana Tate from the doorway of the pink green room. She had the bizarre anthropomorphic shape required by all television newscasters and live show hosts—the Tootsie Pop—a giant melon of a head on a tiny stick-like body.

Leticia made a gargled squawk, thrust her plate and champagne onto my lap, and got to her feet. "Miz Tate?"

Juliana Tate walked into the room in high heels and a fitted black suit. "You must be Leticia Jackson."

Leticia nodded slowly, mouth ajar, as mooney-eyed as a Hare Krishna.

I set her plate and glass on the pink end table.

"I'm so pleased to meet you." Juliana turned and flashed me her trademark toothy smile of oversized Chiclet caps. "And you must be Miss McGrane."

"Guilty." I got to my feet, wishing Leticia would quit gawping at her.

Juliana shook my hand. "I can't tell you what a pleasure it is to make your acquaintance, Maisie. That video—" She tucked the perpetually loose strand of her pert bob behind her ear and puffed a short but empathetic exhale. "It took real guts to do what you did."

How long is this going to take?

"It's a thankless but important job, serving the public." Juliana's sympathetic smile didn't quite cover the exploitative spark in her hazel eyes.

Oh, please don't make me this week's kitten-in-the-well.

Leticia finally found her voice. "Picture?" She held out her cell phone to me.

"Don't be silly," Juliana said, taking Leticia's phone. "Page!"

The maroon blazer young man reappeared with a professional digital camera with paparazzi-sized flash and a clipboard.

Juliana handed him Leticia's phone, her voice saccharine-sweet as she bared her teeth at the page. "Looks like *someone* forgot to acquire all electronic devices."

His nose twitched like a gerbil's on blow. He pocketed Leticia's phone and looked at me. "If I might collect—"

"It's with my things in Wardrobe," I said.

"I don't know if you know this," Juliana gushed, "but *Faces of USA*, my pictorial book of my interviews, hit the *New York Times* best-seller list this week."

"Girl, you killin' it." Leticia high-fived her.

"I know, isn't that fantastic?" Juliana clasped her hands. "So, of course my publisher's demanding another." She inclined her head at the page.

He offered the clipboard and pen for Leticia to sign. "It's a photo release, ma'am," he explained. "For the book. I'll e-mail you a copy of the photo immediately."

Leticia signed her name without so much as a glance at the paper and offered me the clipboard.

"No thanks," I said.

Juliana Tate tipped her head back and laughed. "In less than fifteen minutes, you gals are going to be on-screen in front of one-point-two million viewers. Now is not the time to go camera shy, Maisie."

I took the clipboard. A standard-issue photo release. "Would you mind if I sign it after my agent okays it?"

"Certainly." Juliana's smile didn't waver. "Let's take the picture now, though. The *Good Day* set is a busy place."

"Where would you like the photo, Ms. Tate?" the page said.

Juliana pursed her lips thoughtfully. "Out by the logo, I think."

Leticia and I posed with Juliana Tate in front of the gold and orange sunrise set of *Good Day USA*. To Leticia's complete delight, co-host Alec Anders and his mostly shaved enormous balding head hopped in the photo op, and then, to her displeasure, so did Bliss.

Ten minutes later, prepped and polished, we waited like racehorses in the starting gate.

"Joining us today," Alec said as Bliss pushed us out on set, "are two of Chicago's parking enforcement agents, Leticia Jackson and Maisie McGrane."

"Welcome, welcome," Juliana Tate said, meeting us midway. "Ms. Jackson, would you like to take a seat by Mr. Cruz."

Victor Cruz gave a small wave.

"Oh, I got that, Juliana." Leticia salsa-danced toward Victor and Alec on the main set. "It's all good."

"Ms. Jackson," Juliana said into Camera Three, as Leticia crossed the set, "is wearing the current parking enforcement agent uniform." She grinned into Camera Two as it pulled back, giving America a good look at me. "And Ms. McGrane, what is that you're wearing?"

Hooters meets Police Academy.

"Dhu West, the company that oversees Chicago's Traffic Enforcement Bureau, wants its employees to feel at their best when working with the public," I said. "I'm wearing one of the test uniforms that both my fellow workers and the public will be voting on to represent the Windy City."

"Now that's my kind of retro," Alec said from the stage where Leticia and Victor Cruz sat.

At weather guy Raine Ledoux's chuckle, Camera Four's green light went on at the faraway green screen set. "Didja know Australia's Gold Coast meter maids wear bikinis?"

"No, Raine, I didn't," Alec said. "How *is* the weather Down Under?"

"Sixty-seven, Alec." Raine rotated his hand over the top third of the green screen and said in a poor Australian accent, "As you can see, the precipitation levels are pretty high. I'm afraid those *Sheilas* might be a tad bit chilly."

"Poor things probably all huddled up around the *barbie*," Alec said.

Ooof. Who watches this garbage?

Camera Three's green light came on just in time for Juliana's two-count laugh. "Brrrr. When we come back, Ms. McGrane and I'll be having a cozy chat about her job and how she came to be here."

Neato.

A swarm of people in jeans and wireless headphones descended upon us, touching up hair and makeup, checking my mic as Juliana and I made our way to the living room set—two armchairs and a coffee table in front of a fake set of windows on New York.

"What about Leticia?" I said, watching her flirt outrageously with Alec forty yards away, as Cameras One, Two, and Three moved in and set up around us.

"What about her? Oh honey," Juliana pouted in sympathy. "You had to know we'd show the video."

The floor manager called for quiet. "And three . . . two . . ." He pointed at Juliana.

"I'm here with parking enforcement agent Maisie McGrane. Do you mind if I call you Maisie?"

Seeing as you have for the last half hour, why not? "No, not at all, Juliana."

"Many of our audience might not know why you're here today. Would you like to tell them, or should I?"

"Be my guest."

Juliana swiveled her seat to face Camera Two. "Maisie Mc-Grane is at the center of Chicago's roiling controversy with the honorable mayor of Chicago, Talbott Cottles Coles. Roll tape."

The video was chopped to a merciful thirty seconds, vicious in its representation of the situation. I actually looked even worse, if that was possible.

"Goodness, Maisie," Juliana said, hand at her breast. "That was quite a show."

Boring equals off-air. Stay frosty.

"I have to ask"—Juliana leaned forward—"were you—had you been drinking? Perhaps feeling ill?"

Whiskey Tango Foxtrot?

"He barely touched you—brushed up against you, really, and you vomited on yourself? Honestly?"

Let the games begin.

One . . . two . . . three. "It didn't feel like nothing," I said calmly.

"It looked more like you spit up a mouthful of soda."

I blinked and said nothing.

Juliana crossed her legs. "How long have you had a vendetta against Mayor Talbott Cottles Coles?"

In the last year, did you kill more hobos, more puppies, or was it about the same?

I paused, tilted my head, and looked quizzically at my attacker. "I beg your pardon?"

"It's not my pardon you need to be begging," Juliana replied smartly. "It's his."

I don't think boring is going to work.

"You didn't vote for Coles, did you?" Juliana pressed. "You're a registered Republican."

That's me, the Antichrist.

"Yes, I am," I said. "I didn't think journalists released details like that about the general public."

She scoffed. "You lost that right when you set up Coles with your own personal camera crew."

"I didn't," I said mildly. "I've never met nor spoken to any of the people associated with the making of that video."

"You knew Coles had an appointment with the vice president."

Jesus, are they ever going to break for commercial?

"It's illegal and unlawful to park across two handicapped spaces," I said.

Juliana swiveled in her chair for a Camera Two soliloquy, tucked the errant strand of bob behind her ear, and leaned in to the camera. "This was an obvious and heavy-handed hit job—a journalistic setup. And frankly, I find it disgusting." She shook her head in wounded contempt and swiveled back to face me. "It's people like you, Miss McGrane, who tarnish the integrity of journalism. An insidious, pernicious thing to do to our profession for your own personal gain."

Ooooh. Pulling out the big words.

"I don't see how," I said pleasantly. "I'm not a journalist."

"And for all your scheming, you'll never become one." Juliana smirked. "You really think you can fool us? That we'll stand idly by as you try to discredit an honorable man?"

"I don't know where you got your information."

"Really? You have a bachelor of science in criminal justice from the University of Illinois. A second major in journalism."

"Actually, I only minored in journalism." My mouth disconnected from my brain. "I chose it because it had the easiest credit load."

Stupid, stupid! Blood in the water. Just what the barracuda ordered.

"Me-ow-ch!" Alec chuckled from the other set. Camera Four zoomed in on his vanilla, semi-attractive face. "Watch out, Juliana. That kitten has claws."

"Three months ago you were the top cadet at the Illinois Police Academy and you withdraw, in an election year? To become a meter maid?" She smiled, closing the trap. "How stupid do you think we are?"

Extremely?

Juliana took a paper from the folder and waved it in front of me. "I have here a release from the Police Academy, signed by your own father. Dated two weeks prior to you leaving the academy."

"Wha . . . What?"

The bottom fell out of my world, and they cut to commercial.

Chapter 31

Having successfully eviscerated me in front of a million viewers, queen bee Juliana spun in her chair for the hair and makeup minions. The evidence of my father's betrayal lay abandoned on the coffee table, no longer useful.

An announcement sounded overhead. "Extended commercial break. Three hundred thirty seconds. Start on Set One."

I didn't pick up the papers. I didn't need to. My father's signature was on it, as horrifyingly visible as a black beetle in a bag of white rice. So was Commandant Reskor's. Each dated in their respective handwriting a week *prior* to the psych evaluation. Two weeks prior to the day Reskor called me into his office and expelled me.

I felt floaty and drifty, my blood somehow sublimated to helium.

Bliss Adair crossed the floor toward Set Three. "Good morning, Juliana."

"Hello, er . . . a . . . Belinda?" Juliana guessed unconvincingly.

"Bliss. Ooooh." She snapped her fingers. "Almost got it right this time, Ju-ju Bee." Her smile turned sunnier as Juliana's lips crimped at the nickname. "Wow. What a show."

"You know me," Juliana said. "I can be a bit of a terrier when I uncover a good story."

Bliss nodded. "A regular bitch with a bone."

Juliana tossed her chic bob. Chat over.

Bring It On 6: The After Years.

Bliss bent, collected the papers off of the coffee table, and looked at me. "Maisie?"

"Hmmm?"

She leaned close to me and put her mouth by my ear, "Get up." Bliss grasped my arm right above the elbow and propelled me behind the fake windows on NY. She let go to reach around behind me and unplug the microphone cord from my transmitting pack. "Move."

We crossed behind Set Two. Bliss muttered to herself in a hot little whisper, "Who the hell does she think she is, playing gotcha with me?"

Instead of stopping at Set One, we kept going, disappearing into one of the Habitrail hallways, Bliss hissing and spitting like an old humidifier. "Christ, her ass is flattening faster than her ratings. If she thinks she's gonna screw up everything I've built, not to mention mess with your agent——the first great guy I've met in like forever—she's got another think coming."

It felt good to walk.

"The Honorable Talbott Cottle Coles." She stamped her heel. "Oooh!"

She stopped short, and I bumped into her. "Maisie! Are you listening to me?"

Am I? Her words hadn't penetrated the Tempur-Pedic cocoon of my brain, which was busy swaddling my father's betrayal like some deranged butterfly.

Bliss slapped me smartly across the face and put her perfect nose inches from mine. "You're going to get back on that set and put a smile on your face and give it right back to that slandering cow, you hear me?"

I nodded.

"Good." Bliss reached out and touched my cheek. "Sorry about that."

"Sure," I said thickly.

* * *

"Forty seconds!" the director's assistant shouted. "Places."

Victor Cruz had left the set. I took his place on the couch next to Leticia. A grip reached over the couch behind me and reattached my microphone.

"Shit, McGrane. Why you let her go barkin' up in your personal business?" Leticia rolled a walleye over Juliana and Alec, knee to knee in their chairs across from us, conversing in urgent murmurs. "What happened? You get all stage-frighty an' shit?"

I shrugged.

"Be cool." She popped me in the ribs with her elbow. "I got you."

No, really—please don't.

The set director shouted, "Twenty seconds! Ten . . . five . . ."

"Welcome back, America, to *Good Day USA*," Alec Anders said. "If you've just joined us, we're talking parking tickets, fines, and a conspiracy to try to destroy an honorable man."

Juliana Tate smiled, turning up the radiance factor an extra hundred watts. "We've been talking to Chicago's own ticket terrorist, Maisie McGrane."

"Do you really think it's appropriate to refer to me as a terrorist?" I said and gripped the polyester hem of my skirt to keep from clapping a hand over my mouth.

Hank's Law Number Ten: Keep your mouth shut.

Juliana's lip lifted in disgust. "We've already heard your side, Miss McGrane. Now we're going to speak with your supervisor, Ms. Leticia Jackson."

Leticia sat up and smiled at the camera. "Good day, USA!"

Juliana bit her lip à la "aw, you're so cute." "Welcome, Ms. Jackson," she oozed.

"Call me Leticia."

"Leticia," Juliana said, "after all that's happened, how are you holding up?"

"Huh?"

Juliana pressed her palms on her knees and leaned forward. "How do you *feel?*"

"I feel like we be doing you a favor coming on your show to 'splain about how poorly we be treated as public servants. That even our own damn mayor don't give a crap about obeyin' the law and you try to"—she snapped her fingers—"what's that cowboy word, McGrane?"

"Bushwhack?"

"Yeah, *bushwhack* us like some sneaky-deke." She thrust a palm at Juliana. "Puh-lease!"

Two red circles bloomed on Juliana's cheeks. But this wasn't her first squirrel hunt. "Ms. Jackson, I think there's been a big misunderstanding here. We at *Good Day USA* hold you in no way responsible for Miss McGrane's duplicitous actions or her vendetta against Mayor Coles, do we, Alec?"

"No," Anders toadied right up. "We surely don't, Juliana."

"Maisie McGrane used you and your profession to discredit Talbott Cottle Coles." Juliana frowned at me.

Alec Anders shook his head to Camera Two in patronizing agreement.

"Obviously," Juliana said, "there is no *possible* way you could have known what she was up to."

Leticia's head began to shift from side to side, grooving into a well-oiled cobra sway. "You gonna say it, McGrane, or am I?"

What? I stared at her blankly.

A wicked light shone in her brown eyes and up came the overly stiffened index finger aimed directly at Juliana. "Oh no, you di-n't."

Now would be an ideal time to cut to commercial.

"Oh no, you di-n't just say I'm too ignorant to know what kind o' people I got workin' for me."

"Not at all!" Juliana inhaled deeply through her nostrils, hand at her throat. "Merely that you couldn't possibly have known Miss McGrane's intentions when you hired her."

Jennifer Lince hired me.

"So . . ." Leticia cocked her head. "You sayin' I too stupid to read a résumé 'cuz I'm black?"

Leticia has never seen my résumé.

Juliana Tate's eyes went so wide the whites showed all the

way around her irises. "That's not at all what I meant"—her voice stretching thin and pitchy—"and I resent that . . . that meanings . . . er, you're implying."

Ouch. Me have hard talking time with teleprompter all gone.

"Coles broke the law. He got the boot." Leticia leaned forward. "And let me tell you somethin'. McGrane is one o' the best parking enforcement agents I ever trained."

Juliana crossed her legs. "I'm sure she has done a passable job—"

"You sayin' that like you think anybody can do this." Leticia gave a bark of laughter. "That it be *easy* luggin' 'round a thirty-five-pound boot, attachin' it to a vehicle, while the whole time angry people be screamin' and hollerin' all up in your face?"

"No, no. Not at all—"

I can't believe they're not cutting to commercial.

"You wouldn't last five minutes on Patrol."

Juliana tucked her loose strand of hair curtly behind her ear and said smoothly, "I'm sure you're right."

"I am. So let's us talk 'bout what's really goin' down here." Leticia's mouth split into the hardened smile of a professional killer. "You ain't no journalistic top-shelf reporter. You just tryin' to earn your stripes off our backs and that ain't right."

Juliana gaped, unable to speak.

Karma's a bi-otch, Ju-ju Bee.

A tiny snorting giggle escaped Anders.

Leticia whirled on him, brow cocked in scorn. "What you laughin' at, Alec? You think you better than me 'cuz you on TV? Well, let me tell *you* somethin'." She stood up and planted a hand on her hip. "This"—she passed her blinged-out nail over him—"ain't working. Shaving your head like you embracin' the going bald. Nuh-uh."

Alec Anders jerked upright in his chair as though he'd been given a caffeine colonic.

"You ain't no Jason Statham, you hear what I'm sayin'?" Leticia fingered a string of beaded braid. "And cheatin' on your supermodel wife like a damn fool." She half-closed her eyes and shook her head. "Lord, what be *wrong* with you?"

The tips of Alec's ears turned bright red.

If you live in a glass house, it's probably best to change clothes in the basement.

"Go home to your woman, buy yo'self a fast car, and get a damn weave." Leticia looked over her shoulder and grinned into Camera Two. "Leticia Jackson, O.V. and out, people."

Chapter 32

Choking, fake-coughing assistants desperate to keep straight faces shuttled Leticia and me off the stage as the frantic director and producer gathered around Juliana and Alec and tried to calm the talent.

Leticia salsa-stepped next to me. "Damn, that was fun."

Yeah. A regular merry-go-round of mirth.

"Leticia," Daicen called, trotting down the hallway after us. He caught up and nodded appreciatively at her. "May I congratulate you on a drubbing of epic proportions?"

Leticia squinted at him.

"Mincemeat, baby." Daicen held up his hand and she high-fived him. He tipped his head toward me. "Would you be good enough to give Maisie and me a moment alone?"

"Tha's cool." Leticia danced down the hallway and disappeared into Wardrobe.

Daicen laid a hand on my shoulder and peered at me. "Are you all right, Snap?"

I am a human fish, drowning in oxygen.

"Sure."

He dropped his hand. "I apologize for the ambush. Sterling caught me unawares."

"Sterling?" *Try Da.*

Daicen carefully straightened his shirt cuffs. When he looked back at me, his dark eyes were solemn. "I had no idea about Da. None of us did."

Bliss popped in between us, throwing an arm around our shoulders. "Fan-*freaking*-tastic!"

Daicen's brow creased. He was not an interruption kind of guy. "Hello, Bliss."

"Oh!" She pressed two fingers to a Secret Service–style phone headset, almost invisible beneath her auburn hair. "Hang on," she said to the person on the phone and raised a finger to us. She gave us an openmouthed, head-bobbing smile, still talking, "Absolutely. Of course. I've got her agent right here. Okay, then. You bet. 'Bye."

She spun a perfect pirouette on the heel of her stiletto and threw a fist in the air. "They want her."

"Who, specifically?" Daicen said. "And for what?"

"Leticia. Hannity. Cooper. Muir. Beck. You name it."

Bliss and her five-inch heels clattered down the hall and into Wardrobe to tell Leticia the good news.

Daicen sighed and pinched the bridge of his nose. "Maisie—"

"Go. I'm fine. A-okay," I said, while my hands went independent, gesturing like a third base coach on Ecstasy. "I . . . uh need a little—" I tapped my forehead and rubbed my shoulder. "Fresh air."

"Conference Room G has been reserved for us," he said. "Any page will escort you there. Yes?"

I nodded.

I gotta get out of here.

I walked down the hallway to the elevators, shell-shocked and empty. A maroon blazer said something to me, but he might as well have been speaking Japanese. I got in the elevator and pressed the lobby button.

The actual Rolling Stones played overhead. Poor Mick Jagger. Must be rough, transitioning from rock god to Musak musician. Of course, it wasn't like his dad swiped his entire career out from under him.

Fuck.

I didn't know what hurt worse—Da's Judas routine or my own mortifying state of utter cluelessness. My entire life was family. Because the family always has your back. Except, I guess, not always.

My face itched.

The doors opened, I took four steps out into the shiny granite-pillared lobby and froze.

Apparently hallucinations are a side effect of extreme humiliation.

Six-foot-three of steel and sex appeal in a slim-fitting black suit and open-necked slate-colored shirt was simultaneously charming a maroon-blazered page and a receptionist.

"Hank?" My voice rasped like a rusty gate.

He looked up.

The maroon blazer hustled past me, catching the elevator I'd just vacated. Hank said something to the receptionist and came over to me.

"What are you doing here?" I said.

"I figured you might need me."

Pretty much the coolest moment of my entire life and I couldn't pull myself together enough to enjoy it.

"You figured right," I said.

He put an arm around me. "Let's go home," he murmured against my hair.

I nodded.

He walked me out of the studio building, put me into the backseat of a waiting Lincoln Town Car, and waited curbside as the maroon-jacketed page scurried out of the building with my things. Hank tipped him, put my purse and backpack at my feet, and slid in next to me.

The chauffeur stowed my suitcase in the trunk and got behind the wheel.

"JFK, sir?"

Hank's sleet-gray eyes scanned mine. I couldn't handle it and looked out the window. He put his hand on mine, and I started to shake.

"You're okay," he said.

I nodded and tried to swallow. *Keep it together.*

He squeezed my hand.

I am defined by my disasters.

Mine is the Hindenburg *without the girth.*

Hank let go, removed his cell from his inside suit coat pocket, sent two quick messages, and replaced it.

The drive to the airport was uneventful. Hank merciful. Cooler than glacier water, he didn't say a word, letting me find my center. People are rarely ever really quiet. I know I'm not.

Besides, I couldn't say anything without bawling, and honestly, what was there to say?

You were right. I'm an idiot.

Not like he hasn't heard that before.

Inside JFK, we walked right up the first-class line to the Delta counter, bypassing the gajillion customers who didn't think paying an extra $886 was really worth a free drink, unlimited peanuts and seven more inches of legroom.

If I'd have been able to care, I might have thought about the obscene number of miles he used to purchase my first-class one-way ticket home.

The gate clerk entered our information on a keyboard hijacked from a 1970s middle-school computer room and asked if I wanted to check my suitcase.

"No, thank you." Hank picked up the suitcase by the handle and we walked away.

"It has wheels," I said.

He smiled and shook his head. "Silly rabbit."

We hit Security and he flashed ID and some sort of pass. We bypassed the regular-schmo line and got the preferential wand treatment by the two TSA agents who never step in and help the other TSA agents no matter how busy Security is.

Fifty yards farther, Hank stopped at an unmarked door in the wall, took a card out of his wallet, and swiped us into a posh reception area.

"Hello, Mr. Bannon." The attractive woman behind the desk

smiled at him. "So nice to see you again." She nodded to me. "Welcome to the Sky Club."

Hank handed her our tickets.

"Delta flight thirteen-seventy-five, gate seven. I'll make sure an attendant notifies you twenty-five minutes prior to departure, Mr. Bannon."

We moved out of Reception into a clubby lounge with soft music, dim lighting, flat-screen TVs running close-captioned and intimate living room–style groupings.

An oasis in the airport desert of noisy, panicky humanity.

Hank set my suitcase down in front of me and pointed at a couple of armchairs in a private corner. "I'll be over there."

Huh? "And where am I supposed to be?"

"You look as cute as a button, Slim, but are you sure you want to be serving peanuts on the flight?"

Aww for cripes' sake!

I was still wearing that horrible meter maid costume.

"There's a restroom at the end of the hall."

The sky lounge's bathroom was pristine, modern, and thankfully empty. I dumped my gear on a leather bench, went to the sink, and unpinned the *Project Runway* reject excuse of a hat. I grabbed a couple of thick paper hand towels and scrubbed the pancake makeup off my face, careful to avoid smudging my triple-layer false eyelashes. No sense in wasting Chazz Blue-Hair's professional makeup magic just because my life was circling the drain.

And it wasn't entirely.

Hank came here. For me.

I grinned at myself in the mirror.

Suck-it, glass half empty!

I had an eternity to think of my family's betrayal. And I'd rather slide down a fifty-foot razor into a pool of rubbing alcohol before I was going to do that.

I shimmied out of the suffocating polyester tube of a mini, put on the skirt of my snappy Marc Jacobs I'd planned to wear in the interview, and unbuttoned the uniform shirt. The pale blue poly didn't move, clinging to my skin like perfectly hung theater curtains off the tops of my breasts.

It took both hands to free each side of the blouse from the secret-agent movie-star adhesive.

Who knew Super Glue made tape?

I looked at myself in the mirror. Not bad if I ignored the ghastly bruise spreading across my abdomen. Black push-up bra with two palm-sized pieces of double-stick tape riding on the tops of my breasts. I peeled at the edge with my thumb. Nothing doing. I worked up a lip of the adhesive and yanked. Not much.

This is going to smart.

I took a deep breath, dug my nails under both tape edges with both hands, exhaled slowly, and yanked.

"Aaaaaiih!" Tears filled my eyes. I scraped the tapes off my hands onto the counter and jammed my palms against my breasts, breathing in short pants. It stung so bad I couldn't even swear.

Cool paper towels didn't ease the sting or lower the raised red skin squares.

Super. Every nerd's fantasy. A Minecraft version of breast tattoos.

I put on my suit coat sans shirt, and found Hank. He was watching the market ticker on FBN, two vodka martinis—three olives—on the rocks on the table. I sat down in the chair next to his.

"Ouch." His eyes flickered over the exposed corners of the red squares on my chest. "They set you up with a little defibrillator action back there?"

"Ha. I could have used one after Juliana." I pulled my jacket open a little wider. "Wardrobe tape."

"Nice," he said. "Liquid soap didn't loosen the adhesive?"

"Might have." I sucked in my lips in a combination of chagrin and regret. "Except I didn't think of that, Mr. Science."

"Should've called. I'd have been happy to help."

Oooh. I wanted to say something flirty back but my throat closed up. I picked up my glass.

Hank raised his and clinked it against mine. "Here's mud in your eye."

I took a drink and didn't stop until it was gone. *Vodka. The water of life.* I planted the glass with a *clunk* on the table.

Tangible proof that God loves me and wants me to be happy.

He sat back and signaled the hostess, who immediately brought me another.

"God, you're wonderful," I said.

"Check your messages yet?"

"I can't bear to."

He tapped his finger on the table. I got the iPhone out of my purse and slid it across the table to him.

He scrolled through the text messages, listing the senders. "Mom, Flynn, Cash, Mom, Rory, Mom, Grandma, Pads, Cash, Koji, Mom, Grandpa, Lee Sharpe, Mom, Lee Sharpe, Declan, Mom, Mom."

No Da.

"And voice mail?" I asked.

Hank swiped through the screens. "Three from your mom, J. Lince, Cash, N. Peat, Lee Sharpe, and Sterling Black."

I raised the plastic sword with three olives to my mouth. "Wow. I'm practically famous." I bit one off.

He smiled. "Practically."

"Are you sure there isn't one from Coles?"

"He probably left that on Leticia's phone."

"Funny." I swiped my thumb through the condensation sweating up the glass. "Give it to me straight. Was it as bad as it felt?"

Hank tipped his hand from side to side. "Yes."

Shit.

I drained the second martini to make sure I wouldn't be bothered by it.

"Another?" Hank asked.

"It's ten-oh-five in the morning and I can't feel my teeth."

He caught my chin in his hand. "I'm the cavalry, Baby Doll. Walking, weaving, or wedged, I'll get you home."

Home.

"Hit me," I said.

Hank caught the hostess's eye and jerked his head back.

"You knew, didn't you?" I asked. "That's why you told me to quit."

"Not for certain."

I put my elbow on the table and rested my chin on my hand. "Why didn't you tell me?"

Hank's mouth went tight. "Not my place."

Ouch. I squinched my eyes shut. *I'm already down. Why bother kicking when stamping on my heart is so much easier?*

"Sport Shake," he said. "It may not feel like it right now, but you've pretty much won the lottery of life."

"Oh yeah?"

"No one has a family like yours."

"Then no one is a one hell of a lucky son of—"

Hank laid two fingers across my mouth. "Don't say it."

A snake of anger roiled inside my belly, twisting my guts tighter than a Speedo on a Euro-trash sunbather. I bit the insides of my cheeks, hard.

I'm a happy drunk, dammit!

I clinked the ice cubes from side to side in my empty glass. He slid his hand up the nape of my neck, and I almost melted onto the table. Riding the Duncan Yo-Yo string between humiliation and elation.

"Sorry to interrupt." The hostess stopped at our table. "Twenty-five minutes until your flight departs, Mr. Bannon."

Chapter 33

"Thank you, Hank. For this. For all of it."

Hank pulled the seat belt across my lap and clicked it home. "I don't mind a reasonable amount of trouble."

We took off.

Is it just me or is the first-class cabin suddenly getting smaller?

I fanned myself with the inflight magazine.

I ordered another drink. *Old enough to know better, numb enough not to give a red robin.*

The first-class flight attendant brought me my fourth martini of the morning. I got it halfway to my lips, and my hand shook so bad I sloshed a half ounce on the tray table.

Hank took the glass from my hand, flipped up the armrest, and pulled me into his side. I cried all the way back to Chicago. Not the bawling, noisy kind, but the stream of tears that just wouldn't stop.

I'm sure it was the martinis.

It had to be the martinis.

I took stock in the vanity mirror of the passenger side of Hank's G-Wagen. Only semi-hideous. Red nose, splotchy cheeks, eye makeup remarkably intact.

Cheers to you, Chazz Blue-Hair.

Hank opened the driver's-side door, and I closed up the visor. "Okay?" he asked.

"Yes."

He waited until we were on the freeway. "Call your mother. Tell her you're on the way home."

Kind of not at all how I thought this John Hughes event-of-romantic-magnitude would end.

"To my house," Hank said.

It took me a mile to calm down enough to get my phone out of my purse. I hit Home on the screen and waited as the phone rang.

Thierry, Thierry. Please let it be Thierry.

"Honey?" Mom said, "Where are you?"

"Chicago."

"Daicen said Hank was bringing you home. Are you all right?"

"Yeah."

"I'm so sorry." I could hear the hitch in her throat. "And how it happened . . . I can't believe the twins and I missed the setup. What were we thinking? Of course Dhu West would do anything to save Coles. Anyway, I'm cancelling all my afternoon appointments, and when your father gets home, we're going to sit down and—"

"I'm going to Hank's."

"You're confused and upset, but—"

"Upset? Try wrecked!"

"That may not be the wisest course of action," she said gently. "Are you sure you want the man you're not even sure you're dating to see you like this?"

Nice. "Thanks, Mom." *A low blow with a heaping side of sting, because—as always—she was right.*

"You're in a fragile emotional state—"

"And I don't know that?" I said. "You think I don't know that?"

Hank put a hand on my thigh.

I sat there, dead air humming between my mother and me, as far apart as we'd ever been. Mom spoke first. "How long will you be staying with Mr. Bannon?"

I looked at Hank. "Until he tells me to go home."

* * *

My phone started vibrating as we pulled into Hank's driveway. *Flynn.* I turned it all the way off. No way was I going to start fielding pressure calls from the Black-Irish gang.

Hank pulled into the first stall of his three-car garage. Pristine tan epoxy floor with matching cabinetry. The Super Bee was in the second stall. The third bay was extra-deep and empty except for a workbench and a line of black Craftsman tool chests.

He turned off the truck. I waited while he got my gear from the trunk and followed him inside, joy shriveling faster than a grape in the Gobi as we passed his bedroom and the living room. All the way to the other side of the house. To the guest room.

He planted my suitcase at the end of the bed. "You want some sweats?"

I had some in my suitcase, but the idea of wearing something of Hank's was more than my wretched self could resist. "Sure."

He left and I sat down on the guest bed. Midcentury modern cool, queen, graphite-upholstered headboard, with ink and gray sateen bedding. Disconcertingly recognizable. I'd seen this room before, but where?

I stood up and walked to the far corner of the room and got the full effect. Purposely mismatched nightstands. One an accent table with a mercury glass lamp, the other a steel-based ebony nightstand with a large, empty stainless-steel picture frame. And then I knew.

The catalogue.

Guest room by Room & Board, living room by Restoration Hardware, basement by Soldier of Fortune. I giggled.

"What's so funny?" Hank stood in the doorway with a neatly folded stack of T-shirt, sweatpants, and hoodie.

"Nothing." I coughed and gestured at the room around me. "So, what page is this? Thirty-seven?" I made a grab for the clothes.

Hank jerked the sweats away and scowled. "252, smart aleck."

I laughed, palms up. "I mean, it looks great—"

"Of course it does." He grinned and held the clothes out of reach. "Room and Board pay people to design their products. Then, they spend even more to art-direct those products to sell them. So why try and improve on what sold me in the first place?"

Hank logic. Devastatingly beautiful in its simplicity.

Of course, most people don't have the resources or the mentality to purchase an entire room en suite.

He offered me the sweats in a mock-football handoff. "Get changed."

I changed, brushed my teeth, washed my face again, used a healthy amount of primer under a new layer of makeup to cover the tear streaks, and sucked down three Excedrin scavenged from the bottom of my purse all the while telling myself to pull it together.

Hank was in the kitchen. "You all right?"

"Sure." I took a seat at the counter. "You ready to tell me why Da had me kicked out of the Academy?"

"Beer or vodka?"

I was finally sharpening up. Now was not the time to go as dim as an energy-efficient light bulb. "How about a Coke?"

He took a Budweiser and a Coca-Cola out of the fridge, popped the tops with a bottle opener, and handed me mine.

Hank came around the counter and sat down next to me. "I don't know why. Just that he did."

"Yeah, about that . . ."

He took a long pull from his beer. "I hinted."

"Uh-huh." *You'll have to do better than that.*

He rubbed the back of his neck. "Who am I to mix it up with your clan?"

"My friend?" *Wishing, of course, for a heck of a lot more.*

"I am." He swiped the comma of dark hair off his forehead. "I got the tip the day it happened." He shrugged. "I didn't see a copy of the paperwork for another couple weeks."

We sat there, silent. Me, tracing invisible skull and crossbones patterns on the granite countertop while Hank finished his beer. "At least"—he got up for another—"you weren't expelled."

Hold up, Mr. Wonderful. We'll have no thieving of my silver-lining-finding thunder.

"But why would he do this to me?"

"Christ, Maisie." Hank popped the cap off the beer.

"What?"

"Aside from putting your life on the line every day, the only people you come in contact with are the scum of the earth and the people they've victimized."

"I know what the job is."

"Maybe he doesn't want that for you."

"But it's fine for my brothers?"

"I don't want you to be a cop, either." He looked me straight in the eye. "But I don't have the right to tell you what I want. Because I'm not the guy for you, Princess."

The darkest day ever just keeps getting darker. Payback in some sycophantic, Philistinian, karmic way for my can-do attitude.

"How can you say that?"

Hank paused, searching for the perfect words to crush the remaining flicker of life out of me. "There are things I do that I can't tell you. And there are things I do that I won't tell you." He took my hand in his. "And while you might think you're fine with that"—he laced his fingers through mine, locked his pale eyes with mine—"I don't know how you could be. I couldn't."

"I trust you."

"Said the little lamb to the wolf." He stared down at our hands, mouth quirked in a bitter smile. "You're with me and I tell you stay out of the garage, so you just do, Pandora? No questions asked? Or how about I tell you I'm going to be gone for a week and you don't hear from me for five?"

"Wow. That many girls couldn't cut it, huh?"

His chin came up, but his voice stayed even. Implacable. "I'm sure your brothers will vet someone more appropriate."

Oh, so now I get an arranged marriage by torture commit-

tee? "They've given Lee Sharpe the nod," I lied. "You know—the Bullitt? Huh." I leaned back in my stool. "So, he's the one for me, yeah?"

Hank's jaw turned to iron. "I'm not going to spar with you, Gumdrop. Not after what you've been through."

Talk about a kill shot.

I thought I was cried out, but my eyes misted up anyway.

We spent the rest of the night tersely eating pizza, sharing Häagen-Dazs Vanilla Swiss Almond straight from the container and watching *Key Largo* on TCM.

Afterward, Hank walked me to the guest bedroom, bent and kissed my cheek. "Knowing I'm the wrong guy doesn't make it any easier."

Chapter 34

Hank's Law Number Twelve: Improvise, adapt, and overcome.
Maisie's Law of Final Desperation: Resistance is futile.

Unfortunately, I was not properly armed with a black silk Natori negligee. There's only one reason for packing uncomfortable sleepwear, and it sure as hell wasn't for the *Good Day USA* defamation tour. Instead, I was dwarfed in one of Hank's black Army tees, hem ending just above my knees.

It took me an hour to scrounge up the nerve.

What the hell? If I'm going to crash and burn, I may as well do it kamikaze-style and take him down with me.

I got out of bed and padded all the way down the hall to Hank's room. Tiny Indiglo lights lit the way like an airport runway. His door was open. "Hank?"

"Stop," he said.

I froze.

Oh God, I'm officially beyond stupid.

Next stop, Humiliation City.

I stood in the doorway, trying to recall the carefully crafted yet inane excuse as to why I was out of bed and needed to wake him up.

"I'm outta good guy, Maisie," he said in a husky growl that sent a shoal of shivers up my spine.

What?

Hank sat up and turned on the light. Bare-chested, hair rumpled, he hadn't been sleeping, either. "You come in here, you won't be leaving."

My breath escaped in a half-sob, half-laugh.

"Well?"

With a giggle of pure joy, I ran and jumped onto the bed. Scrambled up next to him and sat down, knees together, hands folded, staring straight ahead, blank-faced.

I waited a good five seconds, then glanced at him out of the corner of my eye.

He tackled me. "Jesus, you're a pill," he said, nuzzling his scruffy face into my neck until I couldn't breathe for laughing.

"But I'm cute."

He loomed over me. "No," he said, eyes darkening. "You're a knockout."

Ooooh.

He taunted me with feathery kisses across my lips and eyes and cheeks, until I couldn't bear it any longer. I wrapped my arms around his neck and pulled him down to me, mouths melding together.

His hand trailed up my thigh, fingers tracing lines of seduction across my panties. A funny little clicking noise came from the back of my throat.

Hank smiled against my mouth and slid a hand underneath my hips while the other snaked up the nape of my neck. He eased me upright against the pillows, kissing me with a sort of lazy intensity, like we had all the time in the world, while I felt like razor wire being wound too tight. I splayed my fingers across his chest and pushed.

He rocked back on his heels, the look he gave me white-hot.

With a brazen assuredness I didn't wholly feel, I crossed my arms in front of me and slowly pulled the T-shirt up and over my head.

"Oh fuck," he rasped. "Fuck."

Not exactly what I was expecting.

He was not staring at my taut and tape-hickied rack, but instead at the enormous black bruise migrating across my belly.

"Hank."

"Aw, Christ." He dragged a hand through his hair.

"Hank," I said sharply. "I'm fine. Turn off the light."

He considered for a moment, then reached back and snicked off the light.

Oh yeah.

Watery early morning light sifted between the curtains. Hank lay on his stomach, facing me.

Absolute perfection.

I watched him breathe for a while, his back rising and falling. Except for the scars, especially a really horrible one next to his scapula, his body was a flawless P90X commercial.

Jeez. What time is it?

I tugged the Army T-shirt off the nightstand clock. 5:05 a.m.

No rest for the wicked, infirm, and occupationally challenged.

I slid off the bed and crept toward the door on cat-quiet feet.

"Where are you going?" Hank said, right as I hit the doorway.

I wheeled around. He lay unmoving, just as I'd left him. "I gotta shower," I said. "Get to work."

"You don't have to do that anymore, Slim."

"Yeah, I do. For a while, anyway." I tucked my hair behind my ears. "You gonna let me borrow the Super Bee or the G-Wagen?"

He rolled over onto his back. "I'll drive you. On one condition."

"Oh?"

"Shower with me."

So that's your evil plan. "Like hell," I said and ran laughing down the hall to the guest bathroom.

Twenty minutes later, we were drinking sugar-free Amps on the way into downtown, the Super Bee traveling at speeds the muscle car was meant for.

He stopped in front of the Interceptor lot. "Call me when you're done. I'll be here in twenty."

I nodded, blush prickled my cheeks. *Shy? Now?*

Seriously, WTH?

I reached for the door handle.

"Hold up, hoss." Hank got out of the car and came around to open my door. I got out. He closed the door and jerked me to him, his mouth on mine, hot and hard, backing me up against the Super Bee, his hands sliding up underneath my shirt. He lifted his head. "Don't be late."

Jaysus. Weak-kneed and mush-minded, I walked to the sidewalk and watched him drive away, a gooby smile plastered across my face.

Time to get serious.

Chen was protecting the carts from behind the *Tribune* in the guardhouse. I stepped over the spikes and under the gate.

He slid open the window as I passed. "Where's your fancy uniform?" He leered.

"Niecy here yet?"

"In the cart." He put his hands together, bowing and laying out his best mock-pigeon English. "Oh! You big star now, Mc-Grane." He pretended to vomit and laughed uproariously. "Big star!"

Cute.

Chapter 35

I jogged up the asphalt parking lot, past Interceptor 13248. Niecy's orange hair was mashed out into a frizzy halo as she rested her head against the passenger-side window.

I entered the back door of the building and paused in the back hallway.

What the heck?

High-octane Spanish rattled back and forth in a mini La Raza rally.

Niecy and I weren't the only early worms today. *Crap.* I skirted the break room and slipped into the locker room.

Jeez. Sanchez and her lieutenants have way too much time on their hands.

My locker looked like a ProActiv before ad. A couple hundred Dramamine tablets had been taped—no, scratch that—Gorilla Glue'd to the door. The five empty boxes were adhered above the locker, in case I didn't get the joke.

Quite an effort from a bunch of no-loads. Best hustle up.

A bunch of tablets disintegrated as I cycled the combination. I unsnapped the lock, dusting a few more, reached for the handle, and stopped.

With that much effort put into the outside of the locker . . .

I took a step to the side and slowly opened the door.

Nothing.

I peeked around the edge of the door. No Santería ripped-off rooster head hung dripping blood onto my clothes.

Whew.

I stripped off my jeans and T-shirt and yanked my uniform out, the clean pale blue shirt dragging through the Dramamine dust.

Groovy. If Niecy starts feeling a little green around the gills, she can always lick my sleeve.

I put on the black poly-blend PEA cargo pants and filled the pockets from my purse. Each click of the second hand was a drip of ice water down my neck. I locked the locker, turning another strip of tablets to sand and turned to leave.

Holy cat.

The single empty wall of the locker room was her *pièce de résistance.* An über-enlarged photocopied mosaic mural. Me. Puking. A grainy screen-capture off YouTube, punctuated by a dozen cropped-in boob shots from my *Good Day USA* uniform appearance with nipples drawn in for extra artistic goodness.

For a split second, I considered ripping them down, but there was no time for a public bust and razz before Niecy and I started poaching. I poked my head out of the locker room. Sanchez's cadre of PEAs milled around the front door, anticipating my arrival.

The only avenues of escape: the break room or a fire-alarm armed exit.

I started across the empty break room and stopped at a single uninspired round of applause from behind me. *"Nuestro propio pequeño gringa vomitar."*

I didn't know what all of that meant, but the *vomitar* came in loud and clear. I turned around and blinked.

Cripes, that's one heck of a lot of makeup to be wearing in the morning. Sanchez tipped back in her chair and kicked her work boots up onto the table. "You think you some kind of movie star or somethin' now?"

"No. I don't, actually." I jerked a thumb over my shoulder toward the locker room. "Thanks for the hero's welcome, though."

Her nostrils flared. "Stay the fuck off me and *ma chavas'* routes."

"A girl's gotta do . . ." I said.

"The *mayate*'s not here to save you, *puta*."

"You say that like it's a bad thing." I turned and started toward the door.

Out of the corner of my eye, I caught something fly past and hit the wall with a *thwock*. A switchblade. Mid-blade deep in the center of the Employee Notices corkboard.

A menacing crackling sounded behind me. I spun.

Niecy held her Taser at the ready. A blue electrical arc danced between the electrodes. Her face twisted with scorn. "You're not really as stupid as you look, are you, Sanchez?"

"*Como chingas.*" Her waxy, over-lipsticked lips cracked as she bared her teeth. "You find out soon enough."

I walked over to the board and jerked out her knife. "Yeah?" I closed the switchblade and tossed it into the garbage. "We'll be waiting."

Niecy and I walked out, her rounded shoulders shaking, wheezing with laughter by the time we hit the doors.

"Thanks for that," I said.

"Fudge nuggets," Niecy said. "You didn't need me." But she walked a little taller, just the same.

We climbed into the Interceptor. She flipped on the radio only to catch the tail end of Leticia's voice and then Michael Medved's as he cut to commercial. Niecy snapped the radio off. "Danged if that gal ain't leaving the TEB to become a radio starlet."

"Why'd you turn it off?" I said.

"Jeebus. Don't you know anything? It's 5:58. Won't be back to Leticia until after commercials, local news, more commercials and traffic update. 6:06."

Maybe if Leticia became a radio personality Niecy could be her producer.

I headed over to the dead zone known as our route to get it over with before we started hijacking tickets from Marie Tufford. At 6:04, Obi Olson radioed to inform me that I had a nine o'clock meeting with Sterling Black.

Crap.

*   *   *

Sunny, the blond showgirl, led me into Dhu West's black-and-gold conference room.

"Maisie McGrane." Sterling got up, came around the desk, and shook my hand. "You were right. You are no public speaker."

"Uh . . . thanks?"

He gestured toward a chair. I took it.

"Your brother's a slippery one. Almost got it away from us with Leticia. Almost." He flashed his over-white caps. "Did you know Coles is polling even better than before the incident?"

America. The promised land of unjust reward for the infamous.

I shook my head.

"I knew he would," he said.

"That's . . . great?" *You son of a bitch.*

Sterling rolled a pen back and forth across the table. "So, Daddy didn't want his baby girl to be a cop, eh?"

Only a McGrane can mess with a McGrane. I smiled sweetly. "No, that was my decision."

"The video footage says otherwise," he said, his posture relaxed but eyes intense.

I shrugged. "It wasn't the job for me."

"Well then, you, Maisie baby, are in luck." He raised his hands, thumbs to fingertips, Mafia style. "Dhu West wants you to be the face of the Traffic Enforcement Bureau."

"Why not Leticia?"

"I'll pretend you didn't ask that." He leaned back in his chair and clasped his hands behind his head. "The Saudis want to downplay the idea they're foreigners taking over the city from within."

"Isn't that exactly what they've done with the Traffic Bureau?"

"What 'is' is irrelevant. Perception is reality, baby."

I'm pretty sure I hate you.

"And what better way to help lose the negative stereotype of misogynistic, Jew-hating, towel-head terrorists than with a sweet piece of all-American apple pie?" He pointed at me with both index fingers. "We're talking a newer, happier campaign. Mostly print ads and a billboard or two. A line or two on video. Rehearsed. With as many takes as you need to get it right."

My left eyelid began to tic.

"First photo shoot's tomorrow. You and the mayor hanging together on the streets of the Windy City."

"I'm pretty sure my contract was up at the end of the *Good Day USA* interview."

"Check the fine print. You are the chosen representative of the TEB's uniform contest, and you will fulfill your contractual obligations."

"And if I don't?"

"Maisie baby, Dhu West has the will and the way to make your life a living hell. They live for this feuding insult shit."

"Is that a threat?"

"I wish it was. See you tomorrow."

I drove all the way to our route, unable to lay off a single boot. Niecy didn't seem to notice, twirling the radio dial to pick up Leticia, now on the *Hugh Hewitt Show*.

"Don't get me wrong. I love me my Star *magazine, but you can't be atrophyin' on the couch at home, waiting for the good Lord to make you not stupid."* She chuckled. *"I took that free Hillsdale Constitution 101 class you always burblin' about. Best thing I ever did."* She clapped. *"C'mon now. Aks me somethin'. I'm ready."*

Charismatic, genuine, self-deprecating. If Leticia kept on the way she was going, she might never come back.

Chapter 36

Looking like the ultimate tough guy in jeans, a white tee, and motorcycle boots, Hank leaned against the Super Bee, waiting. He opened the door for me as I got close. "You look like hell, Hot Stuff."

Gee, thanks, honey.

I collapsed into the car, and he closed the door behind me. I was still wearing my standard-issue PEA; I hadn't seen the point in changing into the clothes in my bag while slathered in the confrontation monkey grease left over from Sterling's meeting.

Hank got in and turned on the car. "How was your day?"

"Wretched."

"Don't hold back." He gave a sardonic smile and pulled away from the curb.

I smacked my palm against my forehead.

"Forget something?" Hank asked.

Yeah. My entire upbringing. *July McGrane's Rules of Engagement Number Eight: No one falls in love with Complainey McBitchypants.*

"No. I just need a couple minutes to hit even keel."

He hit the video screen and said, "Siren mix."

Julie London's smoky lilt began "Cry Me a River." I put my head against the headrest and closed my eyes, unable to keep the curve from my lips. Nothing makes a girl feel more empowered than a torch song of heartache on the precipice of a new romance. *Not me,* you think. *Not this time.*

I snuck a glance at Hank. Perfectly still, he had both hands on the wheel, arms relaxed but there was something . . . an unease . . . pulsing between us.

He blew by the exit to my house without a mention, just changed his grip on the wheel.

And instead of delight, panic fizzed in my chest like a packet of Pop Rocks in a bottle of Coca-Cola. Too much, too soon.

July McGrane's Rules of Engagement Number Nine: Never sleep over. Ever. If you like him enough to sleep with him, you should like him enough to want to do it more than once, so get up and go home. And, as she so often elucidated, "You're not a child at a slumber party, and God willing, no child of mine will grow up to be an adult who attends sex parties."

He pulled into the garage and shut off the car. "You okay?"

Frazzle frazzle frazzle. I am a human dry-cleaning bag. Smothering you with instant move-in neediness.

"Sure." Extreme mental duress ought to cut me a little slack. *I can fix this.*

I followed him into the house, gearing up into full salvage mode. The cell in his back pocket went off. He stopped and turned to me. "Excuse me."

I nodded.

"Bannon. Go ahead."

I took a step to the left to pass him so I could go to the guest room. So did he. I moved to the right. So did Hank. Blocking my path. He shook his head and pointed at his bedroom.

Test Number One for Pandora? Bring it, baby.

I went in.

"Not possible. I'm out of town the next week, maybe two," he said into the phone, closing the door behind me.

I took a seat in the armchair next to the bed and waited. Now would be the ideal time to toss his room, but with my luck the place was rigged with pinhole cameras.

I drummed my fingers on the chair.

If Pandora sat another minute she'd cave.

I got up, went into his bathroom and took a shower. Wrapped

in a towel, I opened one of the dark wood vanity drawers in search of a blow-dryer.

Oh no.

Wrong drawer.

Shiny black Chanel compacts were nestled in a Lucite tray.

Worse, she was tidy, too.

My makeup only looked that good for the thirteen seconds it took to get it out of the package. I closed the drawer and left the bathroom.

Let's not jump to conclusions.

I panic-yawned.

Don't overreact. Armor up. Borrow a T-shirt, remember last night, and get your game face on. I went into the walk-in closet, turned right around and walked out.

Duh.

Makeup in his bathroom, of course there'll be girl clothes hanging in his closet.

I yawned and went back into his room. He's a man. A smokin' hot man. Of course, he's had a couple hundred girlfriends or so. I just hadn't considered he had one only recently dispatched.

Cripes, I hope she was dispatched. . . .

I couldn't keep my eyes open.

I got the T-shirt and jeans I'd worn into work out of my shoulder bag, put them on, and lay down on the bed. A couple of minutes to clear my head and I'd be back in the game.

I awoke with the sensation I was being watched and cracked an eye open. Hank sat across from me in the armchair, brooding over steepled fingers.

I snapped my eye shut. *Please don't let me be drooling.* I ran a hand over my face—*dry, whew*—and then into my hair so it didn't look like I was checking. Pretty damp. At most I'd been out for maybe a hard ten.

I sat up. "Hey."

"So, no?"

"What?"

"The clothes?" he said.

Huh?

He frowned. "What'd you think, Peaches?"

"I—I didn't think . . ." I went back into the closet. The sizes ranged from 2 to 6. Shirts, skirts, pants, and a couple dresses. All from Saks and Neiman Marcus, tags dangling.

Hank stood in the doorway. "Drawers, too."

I opened one of the drawers next to the rack.

Lingerie, all my size. 32C and size three panties in all shapes and colors. A racecar-red negligee.

"Oh," I breathed. "Oh."

This was beyond sexy. We're talking heavy-metal medieval-style chivalry.

I rubbed my forehead. "Hank, there's, like, five thousand dollars' worth of clothes in here."

He cocked his head. "Fifty-two hundred."

"It's too much. I can't. I . . . I just can't."

"Put something on and come to dinner."

I went back into the bathroom, found a dryer and dried my hair. The makeup, in not one but two drawers of Lucite trays, was brand-new. Identical—even down to the drugstore lip balm—to the contents of my makeup bag.

I chose a taupe satin swing dress and my own Pliner heels, which, if I'd had a fraction more cool than an ant under a magnifying glass, I would've spied next to the rest of my things that had been unpacked in the closet.

One last shaky breath of half-exhilaration, half-terror and I went out to see how unmatched I was for Hank.

Completely.

Chet Baker crooned over the sound system. The dining room table was set. Candles, flowers—the whole nine yards. Hank poured two glasses of champagne in the kitchen, then twisted the bottle into the silver ice bucket.

"It's beautiful," I said.

"You're beautiful." He came around the counter and handed me a glass.

Sounds like a toast to me. I clinked my glass to his and took a sip. So did he.

We stood there, smiling at each other, drinking champagne. Hank took my glass and set it on the counter.

"Maisie." He took my hand in his. "For me, time is a finite and precious commodity. Right now, I have it."

He can't possibly be serious. "Hank, you can't just move me in here. . . ."

He cocked his head, waiting.

Letting me do the math. My family. Mom's rules, Da's laws, my brothers' ways, and where was I?

"Do you want to be here?" he said.

"Yes."

"Then what's the trouble, Bubble?"

I started to laugh, really laugh. Giddy with the joy of it.

He grinned. "Dinner can wait."

Naked, Hank stepped into his jeans. "You want dinner in bed?"

"No," I said, pulling his T-shirt over my head. "It's too pretty not to eat at the table. Hank, the clothes and everything else—"

"The credit," Hank disappeared into the closet, "belongs to Wilhelm."

"Wilhelm?"

He reappeared in a white dress shirt, sleeves rolled up, unbuttoned. "He's an . . . er . . . spoil of war."

Barefoot, we went into the dining room.

"Tell me about Wilhelm," I said, while he got dinner.

"He butlered for royal relatives—ambassador style—in Colombia. A cartel took over the neighborhood, slaughtered the family, and kept Wilhelm as a valet for the drug lord. I found him on a housecleaning expedition, chained up in the basement. He's worked for me, sporadically, ever since."

My boyfriend is cooler than liquid nitrogen at Ice Station Zebra.

"When do I get to meet him?"

"That's up to him. He's a solitary guy." Hank set a plate in front of me. Beef tenderloin, lobster mashed potatoes, and tiny haricots verts. "Let's eat."

Chapter 37

Wednesday morning Hank came into the kitchen with damp hair and a towel wrapped around his waist. He set the keys to the Super Bee on the counter. "Let me take you to lunch."

"Aren't you sweet?" *Odds of you bargaining your way onto my photo shoot of ultimate humiliation? Zilch.* "I'll take a rain check."

He crossed the room to the sideboard, opened a cabinet door, and removed a Glock. He came back and set it on the counter next to the keys. "What's the second biggest mistake gun owners make?"

"You're kidding, right? I'm not carrying concealed to a photo shoot with Chicago's anti-gun mayor." I picked up the piece, hefted it, and laid it back down. "There will be PR people, the photographer and crew, Coles will have his staff and bodyguards . . ."

Hank looked mulish. "Coles is as dirty as they come."

"Anyway," I said, trying to be funny, "I'm armed with situational awareness."

He strode into the kitchen, opened a drawer under the microwave and waited. Instead of the assorted kitchen junk, it held a small arsenal of semi-lethal weapons.

An awfully diplomatic way to say I have the situational awareness of a dead bird.

I looked over the array. Taser, stun gun, batons, animal repellent, sap gloves, brass knuckles, Kubotans, nylon cable-tie cuffs, handcuffs, a flat sap, blackjacks, and blades of every shape and size.

The cable-ties and flat-grip sap were the most innocuous items to hand. I slipped the ties into my cargo pants and picked up the illegal-to-carry leather-wrapped flat sap.

"You sure about that?" Hank said. "The grip's too big for you."

That may be, but at least if I get caught with it I can pawn it off as one of those chichi architectural weighted bookmarks. "It'll be fine."

"You ever use one?"

"No, darling," I said. "I haven't, actually."

He slid the leather loop over my fingers and closed my hand on the grip. "Strike flat. Target elbow joint, collarbone, groin slap. Swing through the target."

I bit back a smile and nodded soberly.

He twisted the sap in my hand. "Don't let your hand roll on the grip. You'll edge your target. Laceration's not as effective."

"Got it, chief," I said.

"Sure you do."

NegativeWerks was a top-dollar photo studio in a gigantic brownstone. I entered through the blackened glass doors and was stopped by two of Talbott Cottle Coles's bodyguards.

Before I had a chance to get nervy I was carrying the illegal sap in my handbag, Sterling Black's leggy brunette stepped between them. "Let her through." She gave me the once-over. "Good. You wore your 'before' uniform."

She led me down an exposed brick hallway, chattering non-stop, "There will be seven mini-shoots. The first two with His Honor. We're budgeting a couple hours including breaks. The next five will be you, solo, in each potential meter-maid costume for the City's Choice campaign. Two hours for that, tops. I'm guessing you've never modeled?"

"Nope."

"Of course not." She puffed a long-suffering sigh. "Just stand where they tell you, do what they say, and every so often say something out loud like 'hello' so your smile doesn't get tight. And don't giggle."

Gee, that'll be tough. This is gonna be a laugh riot.

"Hair and makeup right after Sterling's apex nexus."

"Come again?" I said.

"His spearheaded effort geared to achieve amalgamation of multilevel goals."

Corporate-speak. How many ways can a man say "meeting"?

She opened one of the double metal stage doors and I entered a hive of activity.

A dozen people in black pants, black ball caps, and black NegativeWerks T-shirts were positioning lights and fans, taping down cords, clicking light meters, and testing flashes in front of a billboard-sized white wall that curved down into a spotless section of white floor.

The far wall of the studio was floor to ceiling semitruck-sized garage doors that opened out onto the waist-high chain-linked parking lot behind the building. Two men wrestled a parking meter box through the open doors.

Proof Coles's bodyguards were just for show. Only complete no-loads would leave that kind of access unattended. So where was the man of the hour?

In a screened-off section to my left, a group of Brooks Brothers suits raced for repetitive stress injuries on their Droids. Farther down, a flock of women surrounded Coles at a salon station in the corner, working on his hair and makeup while he flirted with a production assistant.

"Maisie McGrane!" Sterling Black strode across the giant cement-floored room to give me a showy hug. "How you doing?"

"Fine."

"Glad to hear it." He adjusted his cuff and rotated the silver Superman *S* cuff link to its upright position.

"So, am I next after Coles for hair and makeup?"

"Those are his own people." Sterling smirked as we watched another layer of hair spray applied to Coles's coif and patted reverently into place. "You'll get yours done off-set while we're taking some head shots of Coles."

"Where's Bliss?"

"Still touring with Leticia and your brother. Lord, the ratings have been off the charts! Unbelievable market potential." He put an arm around my shoulder and said, "C'mon. Let me introduce you to Talbott."

The production assistant saw us coming and alerted Coles. He raised his hands in surrender. "Enough, ladies. No matter how much magic you work, there's no turning this ugly phiz into George Clooney."

The hair and makeup staff giggled and gooed all over him.

There are always women desperate enough to misinterpret slime for allure.

Talbott Cottle Coles rose, waiting for the production assistant to remove the paper makeup bib from his collar and straighten his tie. He walked out into the center of the room and waited for us to come to him. "Well, well, well. Maisie McGrane." He put out his hand. "Where do we begin?"

I could start by kicking you in the shins and work my way up.

I took his hand. A perfect political handshake, dry, firm with two pumps, while maintaining eye contact the length of the shake. "Please, call me Talbott. I believe I may owe you an apology. I lost my temper at our first meeting, and for that I'm sorry."

But not for the felonious assault?

I smiled. I'd die before I'd say "water under the bridge."

Sterling did it for me, clapping us each on the back. "Bygones and bullydogs. All in the past. And now? Symbiosis, baby." He stepped away from us and held up his hands. "People! Can you give us fifteen?"

The photog and his assistants were wise to Sterling's SOP and hit the bricks. The guys struggling with the parking machine set it down and left. Coles's staffers naturally thought they were exempt, so Sterling went over to remind them of their inferiority.

Coles reached in his pocket and pulled out a gold cigarette case. He took a cigarette out, closed the case, tapped it on top, and replaced the case in his jacket pocket. Next came a gold

Colibri lighter. "I *almost* ought to thank you." He lit the cigarette. "Except Sterling's the one who spun it my way." He blew a cloud of smoke in my face.

"You know they make electronic ones now," I said, flexing my fingers, itching to pop him.

"Yeah. For all the little law-abiding lambs holding their little law-abiding balls."

What I wouldn't give to have that on tape.

His lips rolled back in a leer, showing teeth so unnaturally white they looked like dentures. "My polling numbers are through the roof, campaign contributions rolling in."

Then why are you trying to sell off the Local #56?

"Good for you," I said.

"It is." He exhaled a column of smoke toward the ceiling in exultation.

Having cleared the shoot bay, Sterling joined us.

A thin guy in black jeans, tee, and cap walked toward us from the open garage doors.

"Hey, buddy! You can't be in here now." Sterling threw a thumb toward the steel stage doors. "Beat it."

Instead of veering toward the doors, the guy came closer. He ripped the black ball cap from his head and pulled a double-edged serrated blade from behind his back. "I have a message for Coles."

The first reaction to evil is confusion.

And we were all freaking confused.

There are only two directives when confronted with a knife. Distance and mobility. I dropped into a defensive stance.

He was five-nine, one-hundred-fifty, late thirties. Black hair turning gray, with a weird little half-beard, half-mustache that accentuated his ferrety features. There was a fanatical look in his brown eyes, but he wasn't buzzing with crazy.

Not good. Not good at all.

He moved in close to Coles. "You think you can screw with the Local #56? Sell them out to the Traffic Sheik Bureau like you did the meter maids?"

"Let's calm down," Sterling said, hands up. "Talk about this."

Ferret pressed the tip of the knife beneath Coles's chin. "The Transit Union's never gonna let that happen."

"Then why are you here?" Coles scoffed.

Unsure, Ferret lowered the knife.

Coles slapped him. Hard, open-palmed.

Whoa. Didn't see that coming.

Neither did Ferret.

"Who the hell do you think you are?" Coles followed up with a backhanded return that echoed through the studio. "Threatening me—the goddamn mayor of Chicago—with a goddamn blade?"

Ferret fingered the blood at the corner of his mouth, straightened, and spat. He waved the knife in my direction. "You think beating up a meter maid makes you tough?"

Sterling took a step closer to me. To protect or for protection, I wasn't sure. I turned into him, reached across my body into my purse, and eased the sap out. Gripping it in my right hand, I hid it along my side.

Coles eyed Ferret like a maggot in a baby crib. "No. What makes me tough is that I fucking own Chicago Labor. And selling a small-potatoes bullshit sub-union of overpaid bus drivers to private industry is going to make me a goddamn national hero."

Ferret's face went white with fury. "You'll burn for killing Nawisko."

"Who?" Coles scoffed. "The Amalgamated Transit Union doesn't give a mouse's shit about that blue-jacket asshole." Coles's eyes glittered. He leaned down and put his face close to Ferret's. "So you can go fuck yourself on the bus you rode in on."

The knife flashed.

Coles's jacket split apart over his left breast. His face crinkled in confusion.

Sterling's hands went to his head. "Holy—"

Ferret whirled from Coles and thrust the knife at Sterling, who lurched backwards.

Collarbone. I stepped up and swung the sap. Ferret turned, my grip rolled, and I landed an edge blow against the side of his head.

It was like hitting a flower pot full of pudding.

His knees buckled. The knife fell from his fingers and bounced away on the cement floor. He wobbled for a moment, then fell facedown, landing with a wet and awful-sounding *thunk*.

I had the cable ties out of my cargo pocket and between my teeth before the air left Ferret's lungs. I dug my knee into the middle of his back, jerked his deadweight arms behind him, and secured the cables on his wrists. The *thwip* of the zip tie sweeter than a tiger's purr.

Wristed. In less than forty seconds.

I stood up.

Sterling stared at me with eyes as wide as a couple of silver-dollar pancakes. "Holy Mother of God!"

Coles stood looking down at his immobilized and unconscious attacker, fingering the sliced breast of his suit coat, directly above his heart. A dark mottled red crept up his neck. "You come here and threaten me in my house, you insignificant fuck?"

Coles shrugged off the jacket, wadded it up in a ball, and threw it on the floor. "I'm gonna burn your house to the ground!" He drove a black Bruno Magli into Ferret's belly. "And piss on your goddamn ashes!" Coles planted his foot and drew back for Ferret's head.

"Enough already." I grabbed Coles by the back of his shirt and yanked him back hard. He stumbled backwards and landed on his can, sweating and swearing and shaking.

The puddle of blood beneath Ferret's head was spreading at an alarming rate.

Oh my God, oh my God.

I got the iPhone out of my bag. "I'm calling an ambulance." *And Flynn.*

"Stop!" Sterling raised a finger. "I need a minute." He walked in circles, talking to himself.

I let out the breath I hadn't realized I'd been holding. *Of course they're going to want to "handle" this.*

Coles got to his feet and leaned against the parking meter box, breathing heavily. Still pacing, Sterling pressed his fingertips to his eyes. "Christ, I need a drink."

"I'm buying," Coles said.

"Hello?" I waved my hand in front of their faces. "No cops, no ambulance? What do you want to do here, guys? You got some secret magical band of cleanup elves waiting in the wings?"

"Right," Sterling said, and dragged a hand over his face. "We gotta get him out of here. On the QT."

Both men looked at me expectantly.

Why? I had no idea. "Uh . . ." *Think, Maisie.* "Coles, is your limo driver here?"

He nodded.

I ran out the open garage doors. At the far end of the NegativeWerks parking lot sat the black Lincoln stretch limo in all its rescue glory. I sprinted across the lot and skidded to a stop in front of the driver's-side window. I rapped on it.

Poppa Dozen flinched, closed his copy of *Penthouse*, and rolled down the window.

"Yo! Bluebird." He leaned way out and took me in slowly from top to toe. "Why ain't you wearing that fine outfit from TV?"

"You looking for a little time and a half?" I asked. "The Tallywacker stepped in something."

"Talbott Tallywacker Coles!" He gave a whinnying laugh and smacked his gloved hands on the steering wheel. "You've gone and proper-named the motherfucker."

"Yeah, well, time is of the essence, as they say."

He popped the locks, and I slid into the passenger's side. I filled him in as we backed up to the open bay doors.

Dozen shook his head. "I told the Tallywacker not to hire them mail-order bodyguards." He puckered his lips and made a weird sucking noise. "I also told him selling off the union to aspiring terrorist assholes is a good way to get killed." He gagged slightly.

"You okay?" I asked as he put the car in Park.

"Yeah. It's these goddamn Crest whitening strips."

We got out and went into the bay. Coles was in the makeup chair drinking bottled water and practicing his smiles. Sterling, percolating with anxiety, paced around the Ferret—still face-down and out cold.

At our approach, Sterling gave a shaky smile and stepped back.

"Damn, girl. You chunked his ass. Remind me not to piss you off." Poppa Dozen rolled Ferret over with his foot to inspect the damage. The wiry guy had a giant egg on the side of his head and his face was covered in dark red, congealing blood.

"He got most of that finding the floor," I said.

"Yeah?" Dozen said. "Then where's his ear?"

Well, that explains the blood.

Ferret's right ear, or at least the upper half of it, lay a few feet away.

Eeewwrrgh.

I hustled over to the makeup station, grabbed a washcloth, and gingerly picked up the piece of ear. I folded it up and wedged the washcloth in Ferret's shirt pocket. So utterly awful, it didn't bother me at all.

"Ain't you sweet." Poppa Dozen fingered his soul patch. He looked at Sterling. "You got a blanket or somethin' for the trunk?"

"This isn't *Goodfellas*," Sterling said.

Sure feels like it to me. "I'll find something."

"You cannot put an injured man in the trunk!" Sterling shouted.

Dozen pointed at Ferret. "If you think I'm letting this janky-ass fool anywhere near the inside of this ride, you crazier than he is."

Even Sterling saw the logic there.

"I also ain't letting him leave no CSI trail behind, neither."

A spattered canvas tarp lay behind some trash cans. I dragged it over to the limo.

Dozen clicked the remote. The trunk opened. "Hold up." He got out the spare tire, toolbox, and tire iron and set them inside the bay. "I'll pick up this shit when I return for His Honor."

I spread the tarp in the Lincoln's spacious trunk.

Dozen picked up the unconscious Ferret and stowed him inside. "Where to, boss?" he called to Coles, still primping at the makeup station.

"The Local #56." Coles caught my eye in the mirror. "Where else?"

Surreal.

Poppa Dozen shut the trunk muttering, "Bus-drivin' mutherfuckers ain't never gonna learn."

"Okay then," Sterling said, swinging his arms. "Time's money." He glanced down at the puddle of blood. "I'm going to get someone in here to clean this up." He started toward the stage doors.

"Yo. Bluebird." Dozen pointed at the serrated survival knife on the ground, a few feet away from where Ferret had lain. "This his?"

"Yup," I said.

"Anybody touch it?"

"Doubt it."

He picked up the blade between his two gloved fingers. "Bitch might come in handy some hifee morning, know what I mean?"

A jolt of electricity zipped up my spine. *I think I did know. Exactly.*

I rushed after him. He opened the driver's-side door and reached across the seat for the *Penthouse.*

"Like the hifee morning you merked Nawisko?" I said.

Dozen stilled for a two-count. Then he slipped the knife between two pages of the magazine, jammed it under the seat, and turned to me slowly. "Where'd a nice girl like you learn a word like that?"

He did it.

I tried to speak, but my mouth wouldn't move.

"You want to get up close and personal with me, Bluebird, all you had to do is ask." Dozen smiled, the plastic from the whitening strip shimmering across his teeth.

I step-tripped backwards, bumping up against the rear of the limo.

He moved in with a menacing chortle. "Your heart's thump-in' now, ain't it?" He slid his tongue over his plastic-covered teeth. "You payin' attention?"

I nodded.

"I was with the mayor. Whenever it happened. Plenty of staff around to co-rrobor-ate."

I stepped away from the limo with an injured man in the trunk and a killer behind the wheel.

Dozen started the car. The window slid down. "Be seein' you, girl." He threw me a two-fingered salute from the brim of his cap. "Fo-sho."

Chapter 38

The photo shoot passed in a miasma of lights, pop music, posing, fake compliments, and crocodile smiles. Coles, getting off on his near-death escape, spread a thick layer of overcharged libidinous charm on every female in proximity.

I am a worm on a hot plate.

"How about you take five and walk Talbott to his car, Maisie?" Sterling said after Coles's portion of the shoot had finished.

"Okay."

Coles and I fell in step as we walked toward the opened bay doors where Poppa Dozen had parked and was supervising Coles's chastened bodyguards as they reloaded his trunk. "You brought a blackjack to my photo shoot, Ms. McGrane."

Uh-oh.

"No, sir." *It's a sap, actually.*

Talbott stepped in front of me and gave me a slow skin-crawly once-over. "They're illegal in Illinois."

Duh. "It's a book weight," I lied.

"Of course it isn't," he said smugly. "I'd say we're Dutch."

Oh yeah? I save your emaciated ass from Ferret and his Ginsu and we're square because I used a sap to do it?

He pretended to frown, muscles warping around his Botoxed forehead. "Now, why do I think the last thing you want is a felony arrest and the media circus that'd accompany it?"

Because you don't want it, either? I bit the insides of my cheeks. *Hank's Law Number Ten: Keep your mouth shut.*

This was not a pissing contest I could win. With a cross between a chuckle and a snort, Talbott Cottle Coles turned on his heel and walked to the limo. Dozen, in his ludicrous uniform, held the passenger door open.

Coles got in. Dozen closed the door behind him, tipped his aviators down, and winked at me. As the limo drove away, I jammed my hands in my pockets to keep from flipping them off.

Finally alone inside the Super Bee, I started panting. My hands were shaking so badly I couldn't get the key in the ignition. The keys slipped from my fingers, and I bent over to retrieve them, honking the horn with my head.

Real smooth.

I laughed until tears leaked from my eyes, which helped. When the stitch in my side eased, I picked up the keys and started the muscle car, sure of two things. One, I had no intention of telling Hank what happened, and two, my brothers were going to join Hank in the inky black darkness of my None-the-Wiser cave.

Hank's house was empty. I went to the wet bar and poured a generous Stoli on ice. I finished it and poured another.

Dozen killed Nawisko.

Even if I could explain it, telling Flynn and Rory would be an exercise in futility. The case belonged to the BOC. If Hank was right and they knew who did it, maybe they were going to squeeze Dozen to rat out Coles.

Couldn't happen to a nicer guy.

I undid the button on my cargo pants pocket and took out the black sap. It looked clean enough at arm's length.

I tossed back a big slug of my drink.

Please please please don't have some stringy-bit of ear goo attached.

Closer inspection revealed nothing, which didn't mean there

wasn't trace DNA left behind. How exactly did one clean a leather sap?

I opened the cupboard under the sink. I'd start with detergent and go from there. I plugged the sink, filled it with scalding water, and added the drops of dish soap. In a sort of daze I watched them sink to the bottom. After a bit I put my hands in the sink, swishing them around in the hot, soapy water.

I cut off a man's ear today.

"Wrist rolled?" Hank said from behind me.

My hands flew up, splashing water and suds all over the counter, the floor, and me. "Jaysus criminey." A few tiny soap bubbles floated down between us.

"Want to tell me about it?"

"No." Color crept up my neck. "Not really."

"Sit down."

I didn't dare not to. He followed me over to the dining table, and everything that had happened that afternoon poured out of my mouth like sand through a sieve.

His expression never changed. Not even during the almost-funny bits. "Have you told your brothers?"

"No. I was . . . um . . . kind of freaked." I gave a breathy half laugh he didn't return. "If I can ID the ferrety-looking guy, I might tell them some of it. But if the BOC is going after Coles, I don't want anyone, including my brothers, to get in their way."

He dragged a slow hand over his face. "You're planning to go to work tomorrow?"

"Ferret was there for Coles, not me."

"You sure about that?"

That sounded like a trick question. "Uh . . . yes?"

I had the feeling he was going to say something else. Instead, he pinched the bridge of his nose, then smiled a not-happy smile at me. "Let's go to bed."

Niecy and I had been out on patrol for a couple of luckless hours when I was summoned to Jennifer Lince's office. We putt-putted over to the Dhu West building. Niecy, God help her,

wriggled in her seat with delight at the prospect of an uninter-
rupted hour of talk radio.

Lince's surly secretary showed me in. Jennifer, texting, didn't
look up. I sat down on one of the red fabric chairs and waited.

And waited. Trying not to freak as my workday vaporized
before my eyes.

She set her phone aside and rolled her chair up to the desk.
"My-my. Aren't you just the lucky one? Sterling gets you on *Good
Day USA,* your performance is, frankly, less than adequate, and
still he chooses you as the face of the new Traffic Enforcement
Bureau campaign." Jennifer blinked in disbelief. "Unbelievable
good fortune."

"Yeah, I'm a regular lil' amputated rabbit's foot."

Jennifer trilled a pointed miniature laugh. "I'd be a bit careful
of how I say things, Maisie. Not everyone has your acrid sense
of humor."

"I appreciate your input."

"You're welcome." She folded her hands on the desk. "On
another note, your short absence had a noticeable impact on
Ms. Peat."

"Oh?" *Oh shit, more like.*

"Agent Peat failed to write a proportional share of tickets on
the days you were absent." Jennifer shrugged her pale pink–
suited shoulders, and *tsk-tsked.* "Odd because the single day of
your return she did relatively well. Now, why is that?"

"I'm a great motivator?"

"It's no matter," Jennifer said. "There's no possible way for
her to achieve the requisite number of violation vouchers. The
month will end in her termination, and I couldn't be happier."
She smiled. "What can I say, Maisie? You're the gift that just
keeps on giving."

Just call me Maisie McClaus.

A shave-and-a-haircut rap sounded at the door.

"Come in," Jennifer said in a gooey voice.

I got up, started toward the door, and almost fell over.

My brother Cash walked in, a pasted-on smile on his face and eyes as hard as black ice.

"Hi-eee!" Jennifer's voice hit the shrill happy of a middle-school tween. She jumped up, ran on tiptoe in her heels, and threw her arms around my brother's neck. Cash screwed up his face at me over her shoulder, then patted her rump to let her know cling time was over.

She stepped back. "You're early!"

"Jennikins, can you give us a few minutes?" Cash said.

Jennikins?

"But I thought we were going to have lunch and talk about the Gala and Maisie's date and the limo and—"

My brother held up a finger. "No."

"But, Caiseal—"

"I need a little alone time with my sister, darlin'."

Western accent, aka the kiss of death.

"I suppose I can forgive you . . ." Jennifer's lower lip pooched out in a pout. "If you take me out for Starbucks."

"You bet. Now scoot."

Cash should have been an actor. Or an escort.

She left, closing the door behind her. Cash none-too-gently jostled me with his shoulder as he passed to take a seat behind Jennifer's desk. "Where you been?"

"Hank's."

"Jaysus, Snap! Did you take a wallop to the melon or what? I thought Flynn was kidding. You moved in with the fucking *mercenary*?"

"Back off."

"Cripes! Way to follow Mom's rules," he said. "You're doomed."

I adjusted my PEA ball cap. "Hank's different."

"Sure he is." Cash snorted. "The ones we fuck up the rules for always are." He picked up a pen and rapped it on the desktop. "What about Lee?"

"What about him?" I asked.

"News flash, Galileo. The universe doesn't revolve around you. It revolves around *me*." He folded his arms across his chest. "Two months of Jennifer Lince equals some serious *quid pro quo*." His chin jutted forward. "You're going to go to this goddamn gala and you're going to give Lee Sharpe the fecking night of his life. Are we clear?"

"Crystal," I said, bridling. Which was wrong. I owed him. Big-time. But that didn't make it any easier to take.

"Call him."

I fished my phone out of my cargo pocket and scrolled through the directory to find Lee's number.

Cash caught sight of his own face grinning from the eight-by-ten frame at the side of Jennifer's desk. "Shite," he muttered and snapped his fingers. "Hustle up."

I hit Call and left the phone on speaker, holding it a good two feet away from my face like those arguing reality show slatterns do.

Ringing.

Please please please, message machine.

"Lee Sharpe. Leave a message."

The picture of innocence, I lifted my hands in helplessness. *Oh no, what should I do?* Cash glared and jabbed a finger at the phone.

"Hey, Lee, this is Maisie. I'm back in town and was wondering how you want me to sign my head shot. To Lee, The Sharpest Tack in the Box?" I paused. "Maybe not. Talk to you soon."

My brother dragged a hand through his dark hair. "Jaysus. Why does *any* guy like you?"

After promising *Jennikins* he'd come right back, Cash and I rode down the elevator together. "I'll tell Mom and Dad you'll be home for dinner tonight," he said.

"Not happening."

"Don't go against the clan, Snap. C'mon." He hit me in the arm. "We're a family."

"Not right now we're not."

He didn't like that. Not one bit. We walked out of the lobby to the Interceptor. He opened my door, leaned in, and smiled at my partner. "You must be Niecy." He stretched out a hand. "Cash McGrane, Maisie's brother."

Niecy grasped it in her pale little claw. "Niecy Peat."

"From the brat's description, I'm a little surprised to see you don't have two heads," he said.

Thanks a lot, drongo.

Niecy screeched with laughter. "Back atcha, boy."

The next six hours Niecy and I did what we do best. Sniping tickets and pre-filling guns. We barely hit the low end of quota.

A dull throbbing started behind my eyes. Niecy's benefits were slipping through her fingers and she didn't even know it. *Fuck.*

I turned the Interceptor around to take us back to the lot.

"Stop!" Niecy pointed a trembling finger at a bright yellow Volkswagen Jetta. I pulled over. "I got this," she said. "You don't look so good, kid."

I watched her struggle to open the door, get out, and approach the car one shaky step at a time.

Sweet Jesus. She's about to lose her job, her benefits, and after that, all her savings.

Niecy wedged the ticket under the wiper blade and gave me a thumbs-up.

I needed to think of something. And fast.

Chapter 39

Sick to my stomach over Niecy's imminent termination, I spent an exhausting and unsuccessful night of searching for Ferret through the memorial service photos I'd reprinted from Walgreens again, before climbing in next to Hank.

I woke up half-crushed in his bear hug at 4:45 a.m. knowing exactly how to save my partner's job.

Who would've thought This Gun for Hire was a sleep-cuddler?

I eased out of his arms and hustled into the shower. By the time I was dried and dressed, Hank was out in the kitchen, pouring Lucky Charms into a bowl. "Hey," he said, grabbing a couple Xenergy Cherry Lime drinks out of the fridge, popping the tops, and handing me one as I came around the counter. He clinked his can against mine. "Cereal?"

"Uh, no thanks."

"Most important meal of the day."

"Yeah." I made a face and waited until he ate another bite. "I didn't notice any pepper spray in your light-arms kitchen drawer. You wouldn't happen to have a can I could borrow, would you?"

"Uh . . ." He ran a hand over the back of his head. "Check the junk drawer."

"Which is?"

"Next to the fridge."

I pulled out the top drawer. Odd-shaped utensils.

"No," Hank said. "The big one."

What I thought was a cabinet door was actually a large drawer. Filled to the top. "Whoa."

"Sure you don't want the sap?" he teased.

"No, thank you."

I started taking out items and setting them on the counter. An Army ball cap, a dog-eared Dick Francis novel, several screwdrivers, road maps, an expired driver's license with Hank's photo and someone else's name, a DVD of 1939's *Gunga Din*, a bottle of gun oil, two hammers, a pair of scissors, raggedy T-shirt, six permanent markers, and more. A lot more.

I held up a Beretta. "Maybe I should borrow this."

"Firing pin's broken." He came up behind me and set his Lucky Charms down next to the growing pile. "I'm not a tidy guy. Anything Wilhelm doesn't know what to do with ends up in there."

"Hmmmm." I held up a lavender Cosabella thong. "Like this?"

"Like I said—" He yanked it out of my hands and threw it in the trash compactor. "It's the junk drawer." He hip-checked me out of the way and dug around in the drawer until he came up with a small black canister. "Call in sick today?"

"You wish."

I closed and locked the Dispatch gate and pulled the Interceptor around to pick up my partner.

Niecy opened the passenger door. "Holy shrimp! Where the hell am I supposed to sit?"

We were locked and loaded with nine boots, one in the passenger side. "You're not that big. Let's go."

She wedged herself around the orange metal anchor and tried to turn. "Jeebus, McGrane. I can't reach the dang door."

I got out and went around to her door. "You in?"

She pointed a trembling finger and sniggered. "I ain't seen one o' them tin cans since The Dead broke up."

I turned. A faded electric-blue Suzuki Samurai was legitimately parked half a block up the street.

Whatever.

"Let's focus on cars that are illegally parked, okay?" I closed her door and got back in the cart.

"Where to, kid?"

"Butch's. Then we're gonna go have us a couple of bacon breakfast sandwiches, listen to a little Prager, then go say hi to Leticia's old boyfriend."

I stood in the doorway, letting my eyes adjust. Radio waves carrying Leticia's voice echoed across the bar.

"Like I be sayin', Glenn. Jesus was a capitalist. Check it. The Parable of the Talents. It's all there. Mmm-hmm."

Niecy, who could have found her way around Butch's in a blackout, bellied up to the bar. "Ginger ale, barkeep."

The Glenn Beck show cut to commercial. "Hey," I said. "Could we get a little Dennis Prager?"

Wiping out a glass, Butch rolled his eyes at the tin ceiling. "Leticia was on Prager *yesterday.*" He threw a thumb toward the kitchen. "I have it on podcast in the office, if you'd like."

"Nah, the kid wouldn't like," Niecy said. "We're havin' an effin' powwow."

We took a seat at a faux wood–grained Formica round. Butch brought over her soda and a bag of chips.

He looked at me. "What can I get for you?"

A double whiskey. "A Coke, please."

Butch left.

"You're thinking so hard I can see the smoke comin' out your ears," Niecy said, fighting with the potato chip bag. "What gives?"

I waited the interminable forty seconds until she got the package open. "This is a make-or-break day for us," I said softly.

"I figured as much." Seemingly unconcerned, she munched a couple of chips. But her rheumy eyes wouldn't meet mine, and she had a hard time swallowing.

"How'd you get Obi to issue us nine boots?" A teasing leer cracked her smear of peach lipstick. "You threaten him with sexual harassment?"

"Nope. I just said please."

"The hell you did."

"Keep an eye on the kid, Niecy," Butch said, putting the soda at my elbow. "I don't want her checking out my package."

"That's why we come here"—she gave a croupy laugh—"for the scenery."

We finished our sodas and left, drifting around writing tickets on Leticia's route until 12:20 p.m. I pulled over around the corner from the golden alley and turned off the Interceptor.

"What gives?" Niecy said.

I unzipped the yellow-green reflective vest and reattached my radio to my shirt. "Can you drive?"

"Of course I can drive."

"Now?" I folded up the vest and wedged it in a cargo pocket of my pants. Perfectly legal according to the *Parking Enforcement Agent Manual*, which explained that while the Loogie was "critical to the employee's safety, it is not a mandatory component of the uniform as such."

"Yeah." Niecy squinted at me. "Why?"

"We're poaching the Brotherhood."

"You got guts, kid." Niecy dug in her purse. "Not much in the brains department, but you've got guts."

Hank's Law Number One: You are defined by your disasters.

"I need a minute," I said.

Niecy pulled out a pair of binoculars. "Preloading."

I got out of the Interceptor, typed 555-0162 on my phone, hit Send, and climbed into the hurt locker.

Eleven rings. "Narkinney."

"Hiya, Tommy," I said. "It's Maisie."

Nothing.

"McGrane," I said.

"I can read caller ID."

Good for you, window licker.

"Whaddya want?" he said.

"I thought I'd call you directly, seeing as you're the TEB's police liaison. Interceptor 13248 is requesting immediate police backup at the Brothers of Allah Prayer Center for multiple booting."

"You gotta be shitting me."

"Not really, no," I said, a little stunned. I'd pretty much figured he'd come full-speed with sirens blaring for the chance to rub my face in it.

There was a scuffling sound as I heard him cover the mouthpiece of the phone and say something to Peterson. He came back on the phone. "Liaison is subject to interpretation, grunt. First and foremost, we're patrol officers. With a beat."

WTF? "So?"

"We're eating."

"Eat and drive."

He snorted. "So that's how you think it is, huh? You snap and I say how high?"

Hank's angry bear lesson flashed in my mind—*Don't insult. Don't challenge. Don't threaten. Give him an exit.* "Not at all, Tommy. My partner and I need you." I shuddered with revulsion. "Those Brotherhood guys are really scary."

"Well, now, whatcha wanna do, Molly Maid, is send it through Dispatch and wait for us to show."

I stifled a humongous sigh of annoyance. "I'll do that. Thank you for your assistance, Officer."

I hit End and kicked the curb hard enough to feel it through my steel-toed work boot. Then radioed Obi for backup. When I finished, I got back on my phone.

"What the friggin' ficky-fick are you doing?" Niecy squawked from the window.

"Saving our ass." Just to be a pain in the ass, I sent Tommy a text, asking him politely for backup. Traceable insurance aka a little sand in his salad.

Niecy and I swapped places. The Interceptor's clock read 12:42. "Let's roll." The street looked as though Godzilla had walked down the street during rush hour, swipe-kicking the cars out of his path, like a mother trying to say good night in an eight-year-old's bedroom.

The very first car on the block was a boot. Three-hundred-dollar unpaid on a green Chevy Citation.

How apropos.

I got the orange Wolverine anchor on in forty seconds and

sprinted back to the Interceptor, where Niecy held an enveloped ticket out the window. I slapped it on the hatchback parked full-on in the yellow zone.

"Two boots," she barked. "White Rio and the dog-crap tan Tahoe three up from it."

I booted the Rio. It'd be a hassle for the Boot Removal and Tow crew. The nose of the Rio was in the guy's driveway, body across the sidewalk. A battered Monte Carlo blocked the Rio's rump as well as the driveway egress.

I hit Print on my AutoCITE, jammed the ticket in a wrinkled envelope, and slid it under the Monte's windshield.

"Quit writing tickets," Niecy said. "Gimme your gun and boot the Tahoe."

I got that sunshine-and-lollipops feeling. Tahoe secured, six to go.

The next three cars were philanthropists for the Save Niecy's Benefits fund. Starting off in a no-parking zone. They were each multiple violation tickets. I walked them, confirming with the tape on my boots. "Off eighteen inches," I said. "On curb. Water main."

We were smack-dab in front of the converted apartment building that housed the Brothers of Allah Prayer Center.

Blood pulsed in my ears as I dropped the boot at the rear wheel of a red Caprice street side.

"What do you think you're doing?" shouted a man from across the street. And then the protests. A chorus of it.

I put the plate against the hubcap. *Here we go.*

But Niecy was no Leticia. "Call Obi," I said over my shoulder.

"Eh, they're still on their own side of the street."

The wrench slipped twice. My hands were shaking from adrenaline. *Shit.* I exhaled a slow breath from my nose and finished tightening the plate. "Call!"

"Wuss."

It's really one of life's joys, having a partner who has your back.

An angry man popped up across the Caprice's hood. "Didn't you learn from last time, daughter of a whore's shoe?"

I recognized him immediately. The miscreant I'd had kissing the car hood. The one who broke my radio. He smelled like he hadn't had a bath since our last encounter.

Good times. Good times.

Boot secure, I stood up and moved toward the front of the Caprice. No-Bath kept his distance. "You ticket us to embarrass us," he spat. "To persecute Allah's faithful."

Over his shoulder, the rest of the block looked like a bunch of Driver's Ed kids had dropped acid before their first parking lesson. I tried not to smile. "I ticket cars that don't follow the traffic laws of the state of Illinois."

No-Bath rushed me.

I cringed toward the car, let him in close, then sidestepped into the street. No-Bath caught the Caprice's driver's-side mirror in the chest. It folded over and cracked against the window. That dampened the misogynistic banter coming from across the street. For about half a second.

Niecy shrieked with laughter and pulled the Interceptor up behind me. No-Bath bent over the Caprice's trunk, trying to recover his desert wind.

"Green Versa." She held a ticket out the window.

With a glance at No-Bath—still prone—I grabbed it, trotted ahead to the car, and jammed it under the wiper.

"Boot!" Niecy called, the Interceptor idling in the center of the street as she ran tickets for the pair double-parked on her right. "Rusty Mercury six cars up."

I glanced up the block. A faded electric-blue Suzuki Samurai revved its engine. Hadn't we just seen that thing? The Brothers of Allah's flock now lined both sides of the street, cranking the obscenity volume up to a Spinal Tap eleven.

Cripes. When is Narkinney going to show up?

"Get the friggin' boot, McGrane!"

I jogged over to the Interceptor's trunk and halted. Four men, one with an aluminum baseball bat, approached the rear of the cart.

Shit. Hank's pepper spray was in the Interceptor.

"We gotta get out of here," I said, backing around the front of the cart.

"A little too fuckin' late for that, bitch."

I spun around. Leticia's archenemy, Marcus, grabbed me by the shirt with both hands and propelled me like a tackling dummy up the middle of the street.

I got my arms inside his grasp, popped my fists up, and slammed my arms down on top of his. He let go and I staggered backwards. "It's a felony to touch a parking enforcement agent, Marcus."

He stiffened. Surprised I knew his name.

"Yeah?" He leered. "I don't see no witnesses around."

Whatever.

Through the windshield, I saw Niecy on the radio. *Thank God.*

An earsplitting squeal sounded at the end of the block. I did what Hank taught me never to do. I took my eyes off the nearest threat and glanced at the Japanese Jeep bucking in place at the end of the block.

Marcus shoved me in the back.

I took a header onto the asphalt, shredding my hands and knees on the pavement. I scrambled to my feet, ready to give Marcus the what for.

The Suzuki Samurai dropped into gear and charged me.

I faked left, the Suzuki swerved. I stutter-stepped to the right and froze as I got a good look at the driver. He had a big white bandage over his ear.

Ferret.

I cut back left again. Ferret cycled the wheel as I threw myself toward a pickup truck, smacking the back of my head on the running board as I rolled underneath the truck bed.

The screech of rubber combined with the crumpling of steel and explosion of glass and plastic was one of the worst sounds I'd ever heard.

Oh no. Oh no.

I pushed myself up onto my hands and knees and forced myself to turn around and look. The Samurai lay on its side, wheels spinning, engine whining, the Interceptor crushed between the Jeep's nose and a red Ford Taurus.

I got to my feet and ran toward the wreck. "Call nine-one-one!"

The men backed away. No one lifted a finger. *Jaysus!*

The glass face was cracked on my phone, but it still worked. "We need an ambulance, police, and fire truck at the Brothers of Allah Prayer Center."

"Stay on the line, please."

"I can't!" Leaving it on, I jammed it in my back pocket and climbed on the hood of the Taurus. "Niecy? Can you hear me?" The windshield of the Interceptor was a mangled but intact spiderweb around her. "Niecy!" I couldn't see her. "Niecy, help's on the way!"

Fifty yards away, Ferret fought his way out of the Samurai's passenger window. He glared at me, flipped me off with a latex-gloved finger, and disappeared into the welcoming crowd.

Not a sound. Not a movement from the smashed cockpit.

I couldn't get to her, much less get her out.

Far off in the distance, the faint aria of emergency vehicles sounded. I sank down on the hood. The blare of sirens came closer. I lay back on the Taurus's windshield, waiting for the bright blue and red lights, certain that Niecy was going to be okay.

Had to be okay.

Chapter 40

The CPD in its officious blue and white, two ambulances, and the sublime scarlet fire truck arrived all at once. Men of all shapes and uniforms spread out and took over in a display of true American efficiency, freeing the crumpled soda can of an Interceptor from the Samurai.

I swayed.

"Are you hurt?" a detective asked me.

"No," I said.

He eyed me up and down. "You look a little dinged up to me. Why don't you sit down on the curb and I'll get one of the EMTs to check you out."

I scanned the paramedics, looking for Ernesto. *Not this call, I guess.*

"I got this one," Tommy Narkinney said from behind me, fingers closing on my arm.

He hustled me away from the noise, bumping and nudging me past the ambulance and the firemen. "Always gotta be the goddamn center of attention, dontcha? Fucking showboat."

He was too imbecilic to respond to.

Tommy opened the rear door of his squad car and shoved me in, pressing my head down perp-style. "For once in your life, you're gonna stay quiet." He closed the door and went back to the fray.

The emergency crew peeled back the Interceptor roof like the top of a sardine can. I sat watching from the back of the squad car and realized I couldn't open the damn door.

Paramedics surrounded the Interceptor. One mouthed okay with a thumbs-up and motioned for a stretcher. Between the broad-shouldered navy uniforms, I got a glimpse of Niecy's tiny white hand gesturing to them.

Thank God.

I got my broken phone out and called Hank.

"Maisie? Are you okay?"

"Um . . . yeah. Yeah," I said, not really knowing. "I'm in the back of Nark's squad car. They're taking me to the station and loading Niecy in an ambulance and Nark—that bastard—"

"Who?"

"Tommy Narkinney. Oh my God! The guy. The Union guy I sapped at the photo shoot. The Ferret. He tried to kill me—*with a Jeep!*"

"Say again."

"Ferret! Idiot Narkinney should've been here after I called him and—"

"Maisie."

I looked down at my skinned knees peeking through the torn polyester-blend cargo pants. They were shaking.

"Cripes, Hank. A freaking Suzuki Samurai. He tried to kill me with a goddamn high-school shop project! He missed and hit the cart and Niecy's hurt and they're Jaws-of-Lifeing the Interceptor and—"

"It's going to take me two hours to get to the police station."

"Okay okay okay," I said. "Jaysus! I'm gonna tear Narkinney's goddamn head off—"

"Maisie!"

My spew of chatter ceased.

"Do not say a single word. No name, rank, and serial number bullshit. Nothing. Can you do that?"

I nodded furiously at the phone.

"Maisie? Say yes."

"Yes."

"Not another word."

He hung up. I switched my phone off and put it away.

The driver's door opened. Narkinney got in behind the wheel. He cracked his knuckles in that riffling fist-at-a-time way and caught my eye in the rearview. "Now would be a good time to call your daddy, Maisie-Daisy."

You'd love that, wouldn't you? I ducked my head and latched the seat belt. *Hank's Law Number Ten: Keep your mouth shut.*

Peterson got in, smelling of onions, Afta, and dirty socks. "Where we takin' her?"

"To the station," Narkinney said. "Where else?"

Keeping your mouth shut is surprisingly hard to do. Especially when you're trying to come down off a fight-or-flight adrenaline overload. Tommy knew it, and revved his sweet self up to moderate dick, laying out some easy lines that were hard to pass up.

I thought about what Hank told me. Nothing different from what anyone in my family would have said to anyone in the squeeze. Still, I wasn't the one in the vise. . . .

I sat for thirty-five minutes on a chilly metal folding chair in a squalid interrogation room. Two hours till Hank was starting to seem like a *Waiting for Godot* retrospective.

I hadn't made a sound.

Narkinney was fuming. Thoroughly pissed. Peterson couldn't quite figure it out, staring across the steel table at me like I was some sort of circus freak.

The courtesy knock at the door didn't help.

A uniformed officer ushered in a slim, six-foot-four, red-headed, freckle-faced man-boy, with an "aw-shucks" smile and laser-bright blue eyes.

"Good day, y'all. I'm Beau Stadum. Miz McGrane's legal representation."

"Huh?" Peterson said. Which was pretty much what I was thinking.

"I'm her lawyer." His molasses-sweet Southern drawl thickened. He set his briefcase on the table. "Now, I just moved on up here from Alapaha, Georgia, an' I'm findin' y'all do things a lil' bit different 'round these parts."

"Yeah." Tommy sat back and put his hands behind his head. Using a fair bit of restraint not to prop his feet up on the table. "Here in Chicago, witnesses don't lawyer up."

Beau didn't seem to hear Narkinney. "Miz McGrane? Gracious! Are you shiverin'?"

Before I could decide if I was, he'd slipped out of his suit coat and slung it around my shoulders. The jacket was warm and carried the faint scent of pine needles.

"One o' them cultural differences, I s'pose," he said. "Down South, we don't normally take a witness's statement in an interrogation room, neither."

"She hasn't said a fucking word," Peterson spat.

Beau smiled and squinted across the table at his nameplate. "Officer Peterson, is it? I thought I spied a couple of vending machines down at the end of the hall. Do y'all think you'd mind fetchin' Miz McGrane a Coca-Cola?" He sat down next to me, removed his billfold and took out a couple of five-dollar bills. He set it on the table in front of Peterson. "Maybe bring back a round for us all?"

Peterson looked at Narkinney, then snatched the money and lumbered out of the interrogation room.

"Miz McGrane." Beau eyed my ripped cargo pants and scraped hands. "Why, you sure do look all tore up." He nodded at me slowly. Hypnotically. "Am I right in thinking you took a knock to the head in whatever altercation it was you witnessed, ma'am?"

I nodded.

"And not even a Band-Aid." Beau shook his head and shifted his attention back across the table. "Funny thing 'bout cultural differences, Officer Narkinney. Down in the Peach State, we don't take a shiverin', tore-up, head-banged *victim* into an interrogation room to make a statement until she's been seen by a trained medical professional. Why, I'll wager my client's suffering from a concussion and non-progressive shock at the very least."

Tommy looked away, tongue popping out his cheek.

"I think we all know we're done here." Beau rose and helped me from my chair. "I'll be damned if this ain't exactly the kind of tiddlywinks that would stir up a hornets' nest of unwanted media attention back home." He opened the door for me. "Miz McGrane will make a statement next week. Y'all have a nice day, now."

Peterson met us in the hallway, four cans of soda in his arms.

"Thank you kindly, Officer, but I'm afraid we can't stay. Y'all enjoy those." Beau raised his briefcase, effectively blocking Peterson from comment, guiding me toward the exit. "This way, ma'am."

We rounded the corner. Beau smiled at me. "Good golly and a gray cat, it's one of life's simple pleasures working with a client who takes direction."

I took his suit coat from my shoulders and handed it to him. "Thanks."

"My pleasure, Miz McGrane."

Hank stood waiting in the lobby. Beau met him with a two-handed handshake. "Bannon, ain't you a sight for sore eyes."

"Appreciate this, Beau." Hank put an arm around my shoulders.

"Nothing doing. Happy to be of service. This here gal's tough as whit leather."

"I owe you," Hank said and we started toward the door.

Beau chuckled. "Y'all don't be strangers now."

The Super Bee was double-parked in front of the police station. No ticket.

Hank opened the passenger door and tucked me into the car. "Your partner's going to be fine," he said. "Northwestern Memorial. Broken wrist, broken femur, concussion. They're keeping her over the weekend."

I closed my eyes, feeling as wrung out as a Cello Mop. When I opened them, we were on the freeway.

"You all right, Buttercup?" A tic pulsed at the base of his jaw.

Not by a long shot. "Yeah," I said, my voice weirdly hoarse. I rubbed my forehead.

"Sure you are." He sliced across four lanes of traffic and hit the exit. Anger rippled off him in waves.

Hank marched me into his office, hooked an additional chair around the corner of his desk—a glass-topped airplane wing of a B-25 bomber—and sat me down in it. He flipped on a couple computer monitors and after several clicks and password entries, a program titled Solomon EFIT-V v5.6 popped up. "Ready?"

I felt grubby and sick. "For what?"

"To show me the guy who tried to kill you."

Talk about a little perspective. Game face back on. Check.

The program was a marvel, really, generating sets of faces that progressively evolved as I answered Hank's questions. "Wow," I said.

"Yeah. EFIT's effectiveness is based on recognition versus recall. The program corrects from the rejected features as well as the ones you've chosen."

Within an hour, a disturbingly accurate composite photograph of the hired gun spat out of the printer. Ferret definitely hadn't attended Nawisko's memorial service.

Hank slipped the picture into a manila envelope and pulled open a drawer from the credenza behind us. A dozen cell phones were jumbled together. He selected one.

"What are you doing?"

"Making a phone call." His face was stony. "Stay or stay blind. Up to you."

I don't know how to answer that.

He took pity on me. "Why don't you go get us a beer? Take your time."

It took me all the way to the kitchen to realize I wanted to stay. I ran-walked back two Buds. Hank had moved to the couch across the room. I sat down next to him. He reached over, twisted the tops off both beers, and took one.

"Okay." He pressed Call on the cell, hit Speaker, and set it on the coffee table. It rang three times.

"What?" whined a male voice.

"I want to talk to Eddie."

"Yeah? So does the president and my old lady. Who the fuck are you?"

"A friend of Vi's."

The voice sneered, "How *friendly* are you?"

"Not very. I'm the electrician."

The attitude evaporated instantly. "One moment, please." The phone muted.

Hank took a swallow of beer.

A click, then, "This is Eddie."

"You got a live wire," Hank said. "Needs to be grounded. Or clipped."

"I didn't think you black-bag boys worked local. Are you bidding the job?"

"No. I'm sending over a schematic."

"And if I don't want to fix it?"

"Up to you," Hank said, "but it's the kind of thing that can burn a house down."

There was a pause. "Thanks. I'll let Vi know you called."

Cripes. Did I just wake up in a 1940s detective novel?

Hank flipped the phone over, pulled the SIM card, and snapped it in half.

I took a swig of beer, choked, and rested my elbows on my knees, trying not to look like the complete rube I was.

He put his hands on my shoulders and massaged my shoulder blades with his thumbs. It felt so good I started to pass out.

I let my head loll forward. "Oh my God!" I snapped upright. "I gotta call my mom."

My mother answered on the second ring. "While I understand the difficulties of your situation and I appreciate Mr. Bannon's keeping me abreast of what's happening, I expect to hear from my baby's own mouth that she is okay."

"I know, Mom. I'm sorry. And I'm okay. Perfectly fine." I prattled on, cringing at my inability to stop. "Great, in fact."

"That's nice for you, honey," she said in a flat voice that made my stomach clench. "You do realize the rest of us are choosing up sides in the McGrane Civil War."

"What?"

"Your father and I expect you tomorrow night. Whether or not you bring Mr. Bannon is up to you."

I squinted at the clock. 2:37 a.m. "Hank?"

He padded out of the closet in jeans and a T-shirt. "Shhh."

I was too sleepy to stop myself from asking questions. "Why are you up?"

He sat down on the edge of the bed and laced up his boots. "A CUB needs rewiring."

"Huh?"

"I'll be back before you wake up."

And before I could remember that CUB stood for completely useless bastard, he was gone.

Chapter 41

I hesitated in the foyer. "I'm ready," I said and I was, clad in a scarlet Ella Moss tunic, black Alexander Wang cigarette pants, Prada mules, and a face full of Chanel war paint. *When meeting the firing line, it's best to present a confident target.* "Are you?"

"Always," Hank said and followed me into the kitchen.

Thierry was preparing a *mise en place*, yammering into the Bluetooth headset. "She is here, Cash. With Mr. Bannon. I send her upstairs." He put his hand over the mouthpiece. "Maisie! You are okay after your crash-up, yes?"

I flipped him a salute. "Tip-top."

"'Allo, Mr. Bannon."

"Hank," he said. "Hello."

Thierry pointed a knife at a giant bouquet of hot-pink roses at the far end of the bar. "The flowers, they come for you." He returned to his conversation with my brother.

I walked over to the three dozen long-stemmed in a cut-crystal vase. The card in the holder was engraved with *Dhu West*. I flipped it over.

> *Maisie,*
> *Take the week off. I want you looking your*
> *best when Coles gives you the award for best*
> *new recruit at the Gala.*
> *Sterling*

*   *   *

I flashed Hank the Dhu West side. "Work. I've got the week off."

Thierry smiled at Hank. "You stay for dinner? I prepare pork with morel-calvados sauce."

"Maybe." Hank took a seat at the bar and said to me, "Go see your brother."

I found Cash in his room, lounging on his beanbag, playing Xbox. "Finally smartened up and came home, huh?" he said, eyes on the screen. "Got any butt left? Or did Mom chew it off?"

"I don't think she's home yet. And anyway, what are you talking about?" I said. "She's on my side."

"Ha! The only thing Mom's on your side about is being pissed off Da kept her in the dark, too."

"Hardly."

He hit the Pause button and craned his head way back so he was looking at me upside down. "The McGrane Civil War stacks up as follows. Your side—me and Daicen. Straddling the fence—Mom and Flynn. Against—Da, Rory, and Declan. Although I'm pretty sure Dec's just bent out of shape you chose Daicen as your agent."

"That's not funny."

He rolled over onto his stomach. "I didn't say it was. All I know is that my slide into SWAT is gonna be so smooth it's fluidic."

"Yeah? I used to wanna be a cop, but then I took an arrow to the knee."

"Aw, c'mon, Snap. Don't be like that."

Thierry's voice sounded on the intercom on Cash's phone. "Maisie? Your father is home."

"Batter up." Cash squirmed back into gamer position.

Wasn't it Agamemnon who said delay isn't avoidance? I'll buy that for a dollar. I squared my shoulders.

"I'd wish you luck," Cash said, clicking the controller, "but I don't see the point."

I stopped short on the stairs when I heard my mother's voice. "Mr. Bannon, I find you to be a canny, intelligent, and perceptive man. But do not mistake my admiration of those qualities for acceptance."

Jeez, Mom. I sat down on the steps and gritted my teeth to keep from screaming.

"Your *relationship* started while my daughter was in the midst of significant turmoil. Some might say you stepped up to the plate when she needed you most. Others, however, might interpret your highly romanticized actions as opportunistic. . . ."

"I've known Maisie for twenty-two months," Hank said pleasantly.

"And after a single date she's residing in your home?"

There was a long silence.

Good luck trying to sweat him, Mom. The man has the patience of a spider.

She broke first. "I don't approve of this living arrangement—in either the short or long term."

Who needs self-tanner when you can wear a permanent blush?

"She's an adult," Hank said.

My mom gave a patronizing little laugh-snort. "She's a Mc-Grane."

I scooted down three steps and peeked around the wall into the living room.

Uh-oh. Mom had that wide-eyed doe-sweet expression on her face. The one she got just before she crucified a witness. "I have the distinct sensation that the attempt on my daughter's life was more than a random hit-and-run." She leaned forward. "Why don't you enlighten me as to the other forces at play?"

He cleared his throat. "Not my place, ma'am."

That's it, Hank. Run what little goodwill your coolness banked right through the meat grinder.

I trotted down the rest of the stairs. He didn't deserve to be on the fire just because I couldn't take the heat.

Hank stood when I entered the room, but it was long past the time when good manners scored points.

"Thank God, you're all right." Mom came over and hugged me. "You look tired, baby."

More like sick with apprehension. "Yeah," I said. "Da's home."

The three of us adjourned to the kitchen, Mom leading the way. "Thierry, could I have something to drink, please?"

He'd been ready with a chilled bottle of Diatom Hamon. "Of course, July." He poured a glass and handed it to Mom. He flipped a white towel over his shoulder. "Maisie? Hank?"

"A tray of Jameson in my study," Da said from behind us. "Two glasses."

We watched as Thierry poured our whiskeys, placed the tray and bottle on the sideboard, and left, closing the door with a quiet *click* behind him.

My father ran a hand through his thick, dark hair. It seemed to have gotten grayer in the last few weeks. The lines at his eyes deeper, more defined. "I never wanted you to be a cop."

Twenty-four years of right-between-the-eyes. Don't know why it surprised me now. "I must have missed the memo."

"You didn't hear it because you didn't want to."

"I'm an adult," I said, somehow managing to hold back "*and I can do what I want.*"

Da shook his head, and when he spoke his voice was tinged with brogue. "You'll always be my wee gel."

Not so fast, silver tongue.

He took a swallow of whiskey and tipped his glass, watching the amber liquid slosh back and forth. "You always believe the best possible version of yourself when you're young," he said. "Pride yourself that there are things you'd never do, lines you'd never cross. And then one day you do. Without a second thought or a twinge of conscience." He looked up. "Reskor owed me. I called it in."

My knee started bouncing. "Did he tell you I was at the top of the class? That I would be Top Cadet?"

"Yes."

"And that meant nothing to you?"

"It meant I *had* to scotch you. You'd be the worst kind of up-

and-comer. Taking every risk and opportunity to keep on proving it."

Wow. That hurts so bad I can't even feel it.

My jaw slid forward. "I guess Flynn, Rory, and Cash are just
natural Top Cadets? Born with some magical anti-risk-taking
caul?"

"This isn't about your brothers. Just look at the shite you've
rolled in with Coles. And you're only a meter maid."

I felt that one.

A sigh hissed from his lips like air from a knifed tire. He said
softly, "You're the spitting image of her. Of Moira."

I didn't like it when he talked about her. I had no connection
to her. And I didn't want one. July was the only mother I've ever
known. Ever had. Ever could want.

"I thought it couldn't get any worse, the night she was killed.
The night you were born." He finished his whiskey and closed
his eyes. "But it did. Every time I looked in your face, in your
brothers' . . . Dear God, it got so much worse."

I flexed my fingers. They felt puffy and cold, but they didn't
look any different.

"The night the bastard's family settled, I brought July home.
Christ, we were bloody wrecked," he said, growing hoarse.
"Sitting in the kitchen having a drink. Mrs. Shiely was keeping
house back then. She'd laid you in a laundry basket of warm
clothes from the dryer to calm you. But in those days nothing
calmed you for long. You needed your ma. You started
squalling. By the time I got to my feet, July'd scooped you up
into her arms. You stopped mid-wail."

Dad's dark eyes were unfocused, faraway. "July looked up at
me, crying Moira's tears for you, and I knew. Moira had sent
her to me. To us. Only an angel could make July Pruitt fall for
some dumb Mick with six kids."

My chest ached.

"I don't want you on the job, Maisie."

"Because you don't think I can handle it?"

"No. Because I know I can't." The pain etched around his
eyes and mouth was unbearable to look at. "Losing you—" He

ran a hand over his eyes and cleared his throat. "I'd wrap you up in cotton wool and bunting if I could."

"I'm going to be a cop."

Da got to his feet and laid a hand against my cheek. "Then I'm sorry, luv. Because I'm going to do everything in my power to stop that from happening."

He left.

I couldn't find my bearings. After a bit, Hank came in and closed the door. He looked at me. "You okay?"

"I can't tell. I've never had the glass-completely-empty feeling before." The puffy feeling in my hands had spread to my head. "Let's get out of here."

Chapter 42

Hank drove us straight from my house to see Niecy at Northwestern Memorial. We stopped in the gift shop, where I charged an enormous and exorbitant arrangement of sunny orange and yellow flowers on my father's credit card. When we got upstairs, Hank rapped on Room 412's open door.

"Come on in!" Niecy called.

I felt a surge of relief at her normal-sounding voice. We stepped inside. The window ledge already held a bunch of daisies, Dhu West's three dozen fuchsia roses, a balloon bouquet anchored to the neck of a large stuffed elephant, and a lacquered vase of white Chinese narcissus.

"Well, look who's here," my partner said from behind a gray tray table laden with chocolates and every tabloid off the rack. A leopard-print satin robe was slung over her hospital-gowned shoulders, cast-free arm through one sleeve.

"Hi, Niecy. This is Hank—"

"C'mere." She gestured him forward. Hank complied. "Let me get an eyeful." After an uncomfortable ogle, she turned to me and wiggled her brows. "You got yourself a friggin' piece of Grade A beefsteak, McGrane."

"How are you feeling?" I asked.

"Fan-freaking-tastic."

My eyes blurred with tears. "I'm sorry, Niecy. So sorry. And I—"

"Holy shrimp!" Niecy let out a scratchy belly laugh. "Are you friggin' kidding me? Injured on the job means workman's comp, disability, insurance—I hit the gol-dang jackpot!" She motioned toward the pale blue plastic pitcher and Styrofoam cups on the table next to me. I filled one with ice water, attached the lid, inserted the bendy straw, and gave it to her.

She took a sip. "I'm not frickin' retiring until I'm seventy."

Hank cocked a brow.

"That's the morphine talking," I said.

"Whooo no!" Niecy hooted. "Did the cops catch the friggin' jag-off that did this?"

"Not yet," I said.

"Cuz when they do, I wanna send them a thank-you card." She took a noisy slurp of water from the straw. "Holy crap! There's gotta be a court case. Gotta be. I mean, the cops haven't talked to me yet, but holy crap! I could be on *TruTV*, dontcha think?"

"Um . . . maybe?"

"Jeezey Creezey, I could be as big as Leticia! I'm telling you, kid, you're the second best thing to come along since the AutoCITE."

As Hank drove us back to his place, the more irrationally angry I became. If I didn't release a little heat, rage would spew from me like napalm from a flamethrower, obliterating every-thing around me. "Niecy could've been killed."

"No," he said in an iron voice. "*You* were almost killed. Niecy Peat was collateral damage."

Talk about dumping diethyl ether on the fire. Color seared my cheeks. I stared out the window, trying to stay quiet.

It didn't take a behavioral scientist to recognize that focusing on Hank's interference was an ego-protection measure. One that distracted me from dealing with the Union thugs as well as my da.

By the time we got home, I didn't like him.

"Are you *angry* with me?"

In response to that ridiculous question I got out of the car and stomped to the door. He beat me there and opened the door for me.

"You planning on staying that way?"

I hadn't been until now.

I stormed past him into the house. He caught my wrist and jerked me to him, backing me into the wall, his mouth hard on mine, kissing me until my hands fisted in his hair.

Just because I don't like you, doesn't mean I don't want you hell-bad.

He lifted his head. The unrepentant spark still flashed in his eyes. He edged me back into the bedroom, picked me up, and tossed me onto the bed.

Wow. I ought to get mad more often.

Afterward, I lay across his chest listening to the steady *thump* of his heartbeat, his fingers grazing across my bare back. We stayed that way a long while. I floated, wondering exactly how long it takes to get mojo back, especially after it's been surgically removed with a rusty ice-cream scoop.

"Still mad?"

"Not at you." I nuzzled my face into the dark hair dusting his chest.

"That's good. Because you're not going back to work."

I groaned. "Please don't."

"I'm not asking." Hank gripped me by the shoulders and lifted me off his chest so we were eye to eye. "Listen, sweetheart. You chose to go swimming with Coles. Now you're underwater with a target on your back."

I tried to wrest from his grip. Impossible.

"You're going to play this my way," he said. "No work."

"Fine." I sagged into his chest. "Okay."

"Thank you."

After a bit, Hank got up, stepped into some jeans, and disappeared into the bathroom. I could hear the tub running. He leaned against the door frame and rubbed his hand on the back of his head. "Take a bath and I'll make you a drink." He said it sweet as pie, but it was an order all the same.

Too tired to argue, I went into the bathroom, put my hair up in a twist, and got into the Neorest Toto bathtub. Five by seven feet of superb Japanese luxury. Pale blue LED lights cast a mellow glow. I sank chin-deep into the warm water.

Hank's words, *"Take a bath. I'll make you a drink,"* bounced around in my head like a bowling ball in Crate and Barrel's open glassware aisle.

My whole life I'd searched for the guy who'd treat me the way Da treated Mom. The man who'd know I was upset and instead of telling me everything would be fine, would offer me a bath, a drink, and alone time. And now that I'd finally found him, Da wasn't the man I thought he was. At all.

I cried a little in the tub.

Hank knocked and I splashed some water on my face. He came in bearing gin and tonics, handed me one, and sat on the side of the tub. "Want to talk about it?"

"No . . . Maybe. I don't know."

He reached out and tucked my hair behind my ear. "Let me be your Atlas, Peaches."

Chapter 43

Seven o'clock on Monday morning, the police station was a fre-
netic termite mound of activity.

Hank was taking Atlas duty dead-serious. Before we left, I
asked him for a copy of the EFIT composite photo IDs of the
Union bus drivers to take to my interview.

He looked at me like I was a puppy trying to climb the stairs.
"You're adorable."

"Yeah?"

"The way you think all cops are as honorable as your clan."

My smile went as brittle as spun sugar.

"They don't need the EFIT." Hank ruffled my hair. "I've got
your six."

I sure hope so. I rubbed my eyes and took a deep breath.

Lanky Beau Stadum waved and strode over. "The drums are
gathering along the Mohawk," he said with a handshake and a
smile.

A plainclothed female cop with a chic auburn bob waited
until our greeting was finished and then approached.

"Ms. McGrane? I'm Detective Barbara Pearse, traffic division. I'll be interviewing you this morning." She started toward
the steel gray doors set in brick at the opposite end of the lobby.
"This way please."

The three of us trailed along behind. Detective Pearse stopped
at the gate and pointed at the upholstered benches in the lobby.

"You gentlemen can wait right there. She'll be out in a half hour or so."

"I think Miss McGrane would rather we come along, ma'am," Beau said.

Her eyebrows disappeared beneath her thick fringe of bangs. "And you are?"

"Beau Stadum. Maisie's attorney." Beau stretched a hand forward, forcing her to shake.

She did, briefly, with a polite smile. "While it's nice to put a face to the name, Mr. Stadum, a witness has no need for an attorney. Your presence here is unnecessary."

"Well, I'm not here to jerk a knot in your tail, Detective, but Ms. McGrane's a *victim* as well as a witness." Beau raised his palms and turned to me. "Last time I checked, it's up to her."

Hank gave an almost imperceptible nod.

"I'd like them to stay," I said to Detective Pearse.

The detective's smile thinned to a knife's blade. "If Ms. McGrane would feel more comfortable with you present, so be it." She gave Hank the once-over. "And you are?"

"My associate, Mr. Bannon," Beau answered. "Shall we?"

Detective Pearse led us into the gray and tan halls to a bland and frigid windowless conference room labeled Interview Room D. She gestured us to one side of a conference table and excused herself.

"That was only slightly uncomfortable." I slid into the seat. "You know her?"

"Of." Beau sat next to me, Hank on his left. "Hell on wheels. And too big to be sittin' in on a lowly lil' non-fatal hit-and-run."

"Looking forward to this?" I asked.

"Like a house afire."

"I wouldn't mind a little heat right now." I rubbed my arms. "It's freezing in here."

Hank started to take off his coat.

"No," Beau said, flipping through his notes. "Keep her shudderin'. A heap more pathetic-looking."

The door swung open and Detective Pearse and Peterson entered, followed by Tommy Narkinney moving so slowly, it was painful to watch. He pulled out a chair and eased into it, face white and drawn, dark purple circles under his eyes. He looked like shit. And not the hungover kind.

Detective Pearse gave him a sideways glance, then poured a glass of water and pushed it in front of him. "Are you sure you should be here, Officer Narkinney?"

"Yes, ma'am," he croaked, hand shaking as he raised the glass to his lips.

"Golly." Beau scratched the back of his head. "This does seem a lil' bit like a conflict of interest, don't it? Seeing as these are the very officers who held my wounded client for hours after her near-death escape."

Peterson started to say something. Detective Pearse moved her hand slightly and he shut up. "I hardly think a pair of skinned knees qualify as wounded."

"I beg to differ, Detective," Beau said. "Why, the poor thing was so shook she didn't hardly know which end was up."

Pearse nodded sympathetically toward me. "And what hospital were you treated at, Miss McGrane?"

Crap. She knew I hadn't been seen. She'd clearly nosed around HR to see if I'd had any medical billing activity on the day of the accident. Not exactly legal, but a common enough technique.

"Mr. Bannon treated her," Beau said. "She was concussed and suffering mild shock."

Pearse's eyes narrowed. "And your qualifications?"

"Army 68 Whiskey," Hank said.

Pearse sucked her upper lip. She hadn't seen that one coming. Neither had I, although Hank passing training as a combat medic wasn't exactly a shocker. "And you dropped everything to come to her aid, Mr. Bannon?"

Hank's lips twitched in a hint of a smile, but his eyes never wavered from Narkinney. "I don't mind a reasonable amount of trouble," he said flatly.

Tommy's water glass exploded on the linoleum floor. He was

on his feet, shoulders hunched, eyes panic-wide. "'Scuse me," he mumbled and rushed out of the room.

Hank turned his Sphinx-like gaze on Peterson.

"These new recruits . . ." Pearse tried to play it off. "Can't stand to take a sick day."

"I can understand that. So much to do, securing attempted murder as well as aggravated assault and battery charges against"—Beau paged through a legal pad gone almost black with cramped handwriting—"the unknown assailant driving the Suzuki Samurai."

Pearse took a settling inhale and said pleasantly, "After we have collected all the evidence, the ASA will decide what charges should and will be filed."

"Y'all have a ballpark on that timeline?"

"Not long." She opened a manila folder and set out eight police artist sketches. "Ms. McGrane, do you recognize the driver from these drawings?"

I was surprised they weren't in crayon. Stick figures with beards would have been equally useful. I tapped one with the barest resemblance. "This one's closest."

"I told you she didn't get a good look at him," Peterson muttered.

She collected the rest of the sketches and put them back in the folder, not asking me to sit with a sketch artist. I didn't volunteer. "The Samurai was reported stolen that morning," she said. "Evidence techs are examining it as we speak."

"They won't find any fingerprints," I said. "The guy wore gloves."

"Are you certain?" The detective turned to Peterson. "None of the witnesses mentioned that fact."

"Positive."

For the next fifteen minutes Detective Pearse, Beau, and I navigated the tedious minefield of interview questions. Masterful really, how fast Beau set her back on her heels.

Peterson, under Hank's still and watchful eye, began to squirm like he had sand in his shorts.

"I'm chugged full of the basics." Beau sat back from the table. "How 'bout we get down to brass tacks, Detective."

"Oh?"

Beau spread out several photos of tire tracks. "Intent."

Her chin popped up. "Where did you get these?"

"The sweetest lil' gal from one of them insurance companies. She was more than happy to pass on her findings." He frowned. "But this here less-than-aggressive pursuit of said murderin' assailant sets me to wondering if maybe y'all aren't trying to sweep this whole thing under the rug."

"And what possible reason would we have to do that?" Pearse said.

"Because the CPD's own designated liaisons failed in their responsibility to protect Ms. McGrane and Ms. Peat." He laid down several sheets of paper in front of the detective. "Miss McGrane's cell phone records and texts for the day in question."

Supplied by Hank, no doubt.

Detective Pearse didn't even glance at them. "As well-intentioned as you may be, Mr. Stadum, I don't need you to tell me how to do my job."

"Why, I'll be damned if you ain't wound up tighter than an eight-day clock, Detective." He tapped a slender finger on the cell records. "Now, I'm not much of a gambler, but I'm betting when your computer experts triangulate the coordinates of where Officer Narkinney and Officer Peterson were at the time of the call and subsequent text, you'll find they were only three blocks away at Fatburger."

The blood seemed to drain from Detective Pearse's face into Peterson's.

"It's only fair to warn y'all," Beau said. "I'm preparing to file a negligence lawsuit on behalf of Miss McGrane and Miz Peat against the Chicago Police Department."

What the what?

This interview is spinning out of control faster than a toddler trapped in a washing machine.

Peterson looked at me with the kind of hatred I couldn't imagine carrying for anyone and folded his arms across his chest. "How's your father?"

"Very well, thank you." *You prick.*

"Conn McGrane's a Homicide captain." His lip pulled back in a sneer. "She's got three brothers on the force, too."

You deserve a high five, Peterson. In the face. With a chair.

Detective Pearse saw daylight and cut for it. "You looked surprised, Maisie, when Mr. Stadum mentioned a lawsuit. Maybe you'd like to talk that over with your family before things are said that can't be unsaid."

"What makes you think she hasn't?" Beau chuckled in delight. "Half her kin are cops, sure enough, but the other half are lawyers." A grin split his face. "Y'all can bet your bottom dollar there's due cause."

Peterson huffed short, bullish breaths through his nose.

I shivered. The room was so cold I couldn't think straight. "I'm . . . er, not feeling well." My voice went convincingly hoarse. "Could we continue this at a later date?"

Pearse slumped in relief. She didn't believe me, but she didn't much care, either. "Absolutely."

"Sure this is how you want to play it, Slim?" Hank said.

"Yeah."

Everyone got to their feet. I walked toward the door. Peterson got there first and yanked it open. "See you around, *meter maid.*"

Hank's cement-colored eyes met Peterson's and I saw in that look that Hank could kill him, would kill him with as little effort and afterthought as it took to slap a mosquito.

Peterson saw it, too, and stepped backwards into the door, bouncing it noisily against the rubber stop. The alarm in his eyes exactly like Narkinney's only minutes before.

Hank had done something to Tommy.

A true Southern gentleman, Beau gestured for Pearse to walk ahead of him. "Detective, would you care to partake of a little bourbon and branch with me this evening?"

She blinked in surprise. Beau was a good fifteen years younger than Pearse. She held up her left hand, wedding ring glinting in the light, and wiggled her finger.

"Must be those years of training that allowed you to see my impure intentions," Beau said.

In spite of herself, Detective Pearse's lips twisted in a wry smile.

"Your husband's a lucky man." Beau pressed his palm over his heart. "I sure do hope he's treating you right."

Criminey.

The rest of the day passed in a whirligig of activity. We had lunch at Blackie's with Beau, hit Joe's, and swung by the shooting range before heading home.

I followed Hank into the great room, wanting to ask what happened to Tommy in a neck-and-neck with not really wanting to know.

"You're thinking hard," he said. "What about?"

"It's not important."

"I think it is, Angel Face."

"You put Tommy Narkinney in the box, didn't you?"

"Yes."

"When?" I asked.

"A couple days ago."

"Show me."

He cocked his head, and considered for a long while.

"Close your eyes." Hank moved in tight behind me and laid the chilly steel barrel of a gun alongside the edge of my jaw, muzzle pointed away.

I hadn't even heard him pull it.

He lifted the gun, the sight digging into the soft tissue beneath my jaw, forcing my head back. I rocked back on my heels, straining to remain motionless and keep my balance, imagining what I thought it must have been like for Narkinney.

Blindfolded, off balance, physically stressed, enveloped in loud pulsing noise. Basic disorientation techniques. I felt a vague sense of pity for Tommy-the-gutless-wonder.

It didn't last.

Hank's Law Number Thirteen: Anyone can endure expected pain.

The trick—he'd told me once—the skill the very best ones cultivated, was to make each action meted out unexpected by type, frequency, and intensity.

He gripped my elbow above the pressure point and jerked it partway up my back, giving me the feel of it without the pain. Hank's voice turned guttural and cruel. "I don't mind a reasonable amount of trouble. I prefer not to kill children and policemen." He paused and I could hear my own breathing, short and shallow. "But they pay me because I do."

He let go and returned the gun to his shoulder holster.

Asked and answered. I stood there, trembling. "Effective."

"Narkinney thought so."

"I'm sure," I said, completely disconcerted by the primitive, mad-sexy awareness that Hank had done something bad—very bad—to Tommy Narkinney to please me.

And it had.

Chapter 44

Hank and I spent the next morning sprawled on the couch, playing Ghost Recon on Xbox. I couldn't shake the sensation I was playing house with a pet tiger—carefree and wonderful as long as you ignored the dark danger lingering beneath the surface.

"I got a line on Sox tickets. Third base. Box seats. Friday afternoon. Sound good, Rally Monkey?" he asked without asking, knowing I live for the Nirvana of an afternoon baseball game.

Aiiigh. Friday.

The Gala.

He hit his controller and a fireball streaked across the screen. "You could take Pads. Or a brother."

Talk about dodging a bullet. "Oh?" I asked, careful not to sag in relief. "And where will you be?"

"Someplace . . . chilly," he hedged. "I leave Wednesday. Yes for the game?"

Bullet undodged.

My phone rang. I snatched it up off the coffee table. "Hello?"

"Maisie? Lee Sharpe."

My life is a daily example of the bait and switch. "Uh . . . Hey," I said, my voice weirdly dropping an octave. "What's up?"

"Heard about what happened Friday. How you doing?"

"Great."

Hank continued to slaughter man after man in purposeful nonchalance.

"You sound . . . different," Lee said. "You cool to talk now?"

"Not so much."

"We still on for Friday?"

"Yeah. You bet."

"I'll call you later, then." The tease was clear in Lee's voice. "Say hi to the guy. His time's almost up."

Everybody's a comedian. I hung up.

I picked up my remote and pressed Play. *Gah!* I was lost in the stupid lower level of the cargo ship. *Great. Dead in more ways than one.* "Um, Hank? I'm . . . I can't go to the ball game."

He paused Ghost Recon and flipped his remote on the table.

I put my remote down too. "The, uh, Gala's on Friday."

He squinted at me with a bemused smirk that turned me to Jell-O. "No."

"What do you mean no?"

"It's the perfect place for a hit. Coles will be there. He may be the Local #56's prime directive, but you're running a tight second. You're not going."

"What about your call to Eddie V?" I asked carefully. Now was not the time to go into the whole electrician thing.

"Eddie V's gonna do what's best for Eddie V. I want you safe."

Me, too. "If I don't go, I'll be fired."

"Your father blackballed you, Sugar Pop. No job's gonna change that." A stubborn glint showed in his eyes. "You're not going."

"I told you I wouldn't go back to work." *For a while.* I crossed my fingers behind my back. "And I meant it. This is a party. I'll be totally safe. Coles will have bodyguards and a TV crew. For God's sake, I'm going with Cash and the head of SWAT."

Hank's face went perfectly blank.

"If you recall, you didn't exactly jump at the chance when I asked you." The silence stretched and frayed. "Besides, I promised Cash I'd go. Not Lee."

"And that makes it better?"

Well, yeah, actually, I thought it might. I opted for the only correlation I could come up with. "Hank, it's like the prom."

"Oh. So you're getting drunk in a limo and having sex in a hotel room?"

"What?" I said. "What are you saying?"

"That's what my proms were like."

"For your information, Mister Dance-Party-in-Your-Pants, the *single* prom I attended was with Ernesto Padilla, who was furious he had to take me when he wanted to go with Polly Ringdahl. His mother drove us. There and back."

The iron mask cracked and a single bark of laughter escaped. "*Pads* was your prom date?"

My cheeks were on fire. *Last stop: Loserville. Everybody off.*

He covered his mouth with his hand, face serious, but his eyes were laughing too loud.

"Knock it off." I punched him in the arm. "It's not funny."

"Yes, it is." A warm rumble came from his chest. "Nothing but funny."

I went to sock him again and he caught my fist, pulled me in, and kissed me. Hard. Leaving me breathless and hazy.

"You're not going."

"Hank . . ." I scrambled to pull my head together. "I don't have a choice."

His eyes went opaque. "This feels like a game I'm not interested in playing." He stood up.

What?

"Get your gear," he said.

May I have a paper bag for the road, please? I'm starting to hyperventilate.

He drove me home in the G-Wagen, eyes on the road, radio on a classic rock station. The Gala sat like the Gaza Strip between us.

He can't actually be breaking up with me over this. Not over my stupid job. And a date that's not a date. Not possible. No way.

Hank pulled smoothly up to the driveway gate, punched in the code, and we drove through. My knee started bouncing.

He put the car in Park and unlatched his seat belt.

"Hank." My voice went thready. "This isn't a big deal. Really, it's not."

"I can't be distracted. Not when I'm working." His face, lit from the dashboard, was as tight as a fist. "You wanna play cops and robbers? I'm out."

"You can't mean that." I shook my head, desperate to say something else but terrified I'd make it worse.

He got out and opened the door for me.

I wanted to touch him—kiss him—something . . . but he was granite.

July McGrane's Rules of Engagement Number Thirteen: Take it in stride, act like it was your idea, then go home and regroup.

"I'll call you," I said and went in the house.

Chapter 45

Light glowed from beneath the door of Mom's office. I knocked and went in. Surrounded by case files and paper, she sat staring off into space. *The Kelly File* ran muted and close-captioned on TV.

"Mom?"

She blinked at me in mild surprise. "Hi, baby. When did you arrive?"

"Hank brought me home a few minutes ago."

"Oh? How did that go?"

"Not so good." Tears were dangerously close.

"Don't fret. There's something decidedly sexy about a hard case doing a slow burn. Revel in it."

I would if I could. "How?"

"I doubt Mr. Bannon is familiar with jealousy." She tapped the tips of her fingers together. "Useful to see how he handles it."

Except he isn't jealous. He's pissed off I'm taking chances. "Hank's a serious guy. And what I'm doing is pretty much unredeemable."

"You know best," she said easily.

Yeah, right. "How are things going for you?"

"No better. I could murder your father for withholding from me, much less for what he's done to you." Mom sighed. "And if that wasn't enough, I'm relatively confident I'll get our complete and utter asshole defendant off scot-free. Every day I come home from work and see your father, I'm so happy to be around a decent man that I start to forget I'm furious with him. The constant re-amping up into righteous indignation is exhausting."

"The stuff between Da and me is just that, Mom. Between us."

"Don't be naïve. What happens to one McGrane affects us all."

I slouched in my seat, waiting for the inevitable.

"Any thoughts about Loyola?"

"Actually, Mom, I'm just trying to make it to Saturday."

"I heard Detective Pearse sat in to take your statement. The CPD's sending in the big guns." She picked up a pen and tapped it against her palm. "I think it's time we had a little 'come to Jesus,' baby."

"Hank thinks the hit-and-run was the Local #56's way of sending a message to Coles."

"My-my," Mom said. "Your Mr. Bannon is a dark horse, isn't he?"

That's one way to put it.

"What did he do?"

"Uh . . ."

Mom leaned forward. "If a girl can't tell her lawyer, who can she tell?"

"He called Eddie Veteratti."

"The Mobster?" Mom blinked, sat back in her chair, and smiled. "Oooh. I like that."

Not the response I was expecting. At all.

"There's more than one way to take up the gauntlet, Maisie."

Wow.

Mom laughed. "Don't look so surprised. One of the first things you learn at the state's attorney's office is that justice is served in a variety of ways. The Veterattis may be criminals, but they operate with a semblance of honor." She moved her pen in a circle. "So, what happened at the station?"

I filled her in on the interview.

"How did it end?" she asked.

"I bought some time, but"—I sucked in my cheeks—"I don't know that I can screw Niecy over again by crushing her shot at a legitimate civil suit against the CPD."

"Again?"

"The crash was my fault. I knew it was a hot spot, and I made the call to go ahead without backup. I should have never taken her there."

"Aside from the fact that she is your very senior partner, criminals commit crimes, not their victims." She frowned and shook her head. "A lawsuit against the CPD. From any angle, a vile and mirthless future lies ahead."

My mother mandated a three-day respite of spa and shopping to get my head on straight. It hadn't been enough to stop my fingers from dialing Hank's number on my leg every twenty seconds or checking my phone minute to minute like an OCD.

Zip. Zed. Zero.

My lower lip wobbled. *Snap out of it!*

I stepped into my Halston Heritage halter cocktail dress in blackest black. The neckline crisscrossed to a plunging back and shirttail hem. I took a final look in the mirror. My hair was swept back into a sleek high ponytail, makeup—heavy, smoky eyes and nude-colored lips.

About as cat's pajama-y as I can get.

Hank. Hank. Hank. If only . . .

Ignoring everything my mother had ever taught me, I picked up the phone and called him.

"Good evening, Ms. McGrane." The steamy lilt of his girl Friday scorched my ears. "Mr. Bannon is not available at this time."

Big surprise.

"He did, however, leave a message for you."

I bit back a grin. "Go ahead."

"Eddie's electrical problem unresolved. Don't be the blow-dryer in the bathtub." She paused long enough for me to know he hadn't left a sweet send-off. "Would you care to leave a response?" she drawled, as long and sweet as warm taffy.

"No." Unable to say anything else, I hung up.

I caught my reflection in the mirror. *As I don't look crushed to smithereens, I must be fine.*

I hit the landing. Mom waited holding her Canon EOS Rebel, Da beside her, hand at her waist.

"Looking pretty biscuity, Snap." Cash, wearing a black suit, flipped Jennifer's pink and black striped tie accusingly at me. "Almost as good as me."

"Pictures." Mom waved me over to stand by Cash with an overbright smile.

"No time," Cash said. "Car's waiting."

"It can wait another minute," Da said with a sad smile at me.

I looked away. Forgiveness wasn't something I could muster right then. Maybe not ever.

Cash groaned and drag-marched me over to the stone entry wall.

"I'm having a memory overload. You two are so cute." Mom hit the shutter and Cash and I played along.

"Enough. We gotta go, Mom. See you guys." He jerked open the front door and I followed, stopping on the porch steps.

You gotta be kidding me.

A white stretch limo waited in the driveway, courtesy of Dhu West.

"Sweet, huh?" Cash said as we climbed into the prom-mobile. "Know what's even sweeter?" He settled into the seat across from me. "Jennikins is already there."

"Where?"

"At the Gala. Been there since early this afternoon. She's em-ceeing and had to practice. Why, I don't know. What's she gonna do? Hand out trophies for the most tickets?" Cash flipped his dark hair out of his eyes. "She's freaking out 'cause Coles is gonna be there." He started laughing. "Maybe he'll give you an award for puking yourself."

"Thanks." I wondered if I had time to choke him uncon-scious with his hideous pink tie before we got to Lee's. "It's such a blessing to have such a supportive brother, said no younger sister ever."

"Don't go all wah-wah–wet blanket tonight. You got us into this, and I for one am going to make the best of it and get totally obliterated. Party bus!" Cash cracked his knuckles, leaned over, and pulled a beer from the mini fridge. "Want one?"

"No thanks."

He cracked it. "I'm warning you—those SWAT guys can party. After tonight, you'll be like 'Hank who?' "

A half hour later, we pulled up in front of a tidy bungalow. The driver opened the door, and Lee Sharpe got in wearing a navy suit, white shirt, and red and navy rep tie.

He sat next to me and cracked a smile. "I feel like I should have brought you a giant carnation wrist-corsage." He glanced at his watch. "There's still time to swing by a 7-Eleven."

I laughed. "I think I'll pass."

"You look terrific," Lee said.

"Thanks, I think I do, too," Cash said and handed him a beer as we drove off.

Chapter 46

The Jake was a swanky downtown hotel from the 1920s. Its name was Prohibition slang for excellent. And it was—a gorgeous brown brick château secreted away in its own private park.

Lee whistled long and low as we were waved through the wrought-iron gates and driven up the narrow, winding cobblestone drive. "A lot of property for downtown."

The limo stopped. Cash groaned. "We're here."

We entered through the massive wood entry doors. A tuxedoed staff member escorted us into the cocktail room, apparently carved from a mahogany forest.

Jennifer Lince, prim and officious in her tailored pale pink dress, fingertip-clapped, scurried over to Cash in mincing steps and gave a tiny squeal of delight. "Darling, you look perfect." *Frigid librarian meets God-Squad cheerleader.* Oblivious to us, she adjusted Cash's tie and began murmuring directives into his ear. The look he shot me was murderous.

"What's our plan of attack?" Lee asked out of the side of his mouth. "Dog and pony meet and greet?"

"Nope." I smiled. "That's my brother's department. We're just witnessing the wreck."

A waiter held out a tray laden with champagne and vodka martinis. "Would you care for a drink?"

Death by a thousand bubbles or a couple of quick shots.

I chose champagne. Lee and Cash—who stepped around the still-talking Jennifer—opted for martinis.

Jennifer took Lee and me in with a critical eye and rewarded us with a polite smile and matching nod. "Maisie, Mr. Sharpe."

Apparently we passed the not-complete-losers test.

"The rank and file won't arrive for another hour," she said. "Everybody who's anybody is here now. Mingle, enjoy your-selves—just not *too* much." And with an oh-so-subtle two-handed cling to Cash's arm, Jennifer led him away to a bunch of corn-fed business suits in the corner.

Lee and I chose a couple of chairs at a small table and ban-tered about SWAT, family, and baseball. The insides of my cheeks were raw from biting back the urge to pose hypothetical Hank breakup questions.

"Aiigh!" An ice cube went down the low back of my dress. I arched out of my chair and shimmied awkwardly. "Jeez! You can't behave for more than five minutes. . . ." I whirled around ready to smack Cash.

And saw Dacien.

"Tell me about it." Bliss Adair, poured into a scandalous silver-sequined sheath that would have had any supermodel re-thinking the half a tomato slice they'd eaten for lunch, snuggled up to Daicen.

Good Lord. Are my brothers carriers of clinging vine dis-ease?

She let go of Daicen and introduced herself to Lee. Already up, I went and hugged my brother.

"Hello, Snap," he said.

"I didn't know you were back in town."

"We flew in for this."

We, is it?

Daicen read the look on my face and raised a palm. "Strictly casual."

"Better tell her that," I said.

"I've been briefed on your . . . situation." He put his hand on my shoulder. "Quite a burden for you to manage on your own."

My nasal passages opened as if I'd taken a hit of Afrin. *Alert! Tears ahead.*

Daicen tipped his head at the waiter exchanging my empty champagne flute for a full one. "It might be prudent to stop after that."

"Why?"

"Aside from the fact that Sterling and Coles have something in mind for you onstage, Narkinney and Peterson are here."

Of course they were. As the police liaisons to the Traffic Enforcement Bureau, Narkinney and Peterson would probably be getting some shiny worthless awards for their shiny worthless performance. I smiled and nodded at Lee, who was saying something I couldn't focus on.

A hotel attendant paused at our table, murmured that the Gala was about to begin, and moved on to the next set of guests.

Feeling no pain, Lee and I registered, received our table card, put on our name tags with the gold foil stars signifying our drinks were comped for the night, and wandered into the ballroom. Cash caught my eye from across the room. He saw Lee's hand at my back and flipped me a thumbs-up.

Lee led us to our table. Right near the front of the stage. *Delightful.*

He pulled out my chair and we both sat down. I turned to him and he did the lean-in to hear me. *Irritatingly charming.*

"Remember when I told you I was getting out of something?" I said. "Well. I didn't. I'm still in."

"Yeah?" He shrugged a wide shoulder. "I ran out of milk this morning."

"What?"

Lee smiled. "I thought we were talking about things that don't matter."

I'm so not up for this. "Do you think you could tamp down the Captain Adorable bit a little?"

"Why? Is it working?"

I rolled my eyes.

"Okay, okay." His voice softened. "Hey—" He held his arm

out to me and ran a hand over the sleeve of his suit coat. "Feel this."

I ran my hand over the smooth, dark fabric. "Nice," I said. "What is it?"

"That's boyfriend material, baby."

"Dude," I groaned, unable to stop myself from laughing. "That is sooo bad."

"Hey, I'm under a lot of pressure here, Little Miss Celebrity." Lee drummed his hands on the table. "So tell me, what's it like being famous?"

"I wouldn't know. No one's recognized me yet."

"Riiight."

"Having the week off didn't hurt," I said. "But let's face it. I'm no Leticia Jackson."

A thin claw of a hand seized my arm. "Maisie?" Jennifer asked frostily. "May I speak with you for a moment?"

It was not a request. "Uh, sure."

Lee stood up while I got to my feet and mugged me a *what's her problem?*

I grimaced and went after Jennifer. She marched us a few feet away to a semi-private corner, stopped, and stamped a pink heel. "Just look at your brother!" she scream-whispered. "Look at him!"

Cash was flirting with five women at the same time, in the way only a talented few could do. All wives and dates of the higher powers of Dhu West. Which, according to at least two glowering significant others, was not well received.

Jennifer's cheeks were fuchsia with fury. "Do something."

Sorry, Jennikins. That's above my pay grade. "Like what?"

"I don't care what you do. Fix this. Now." Without waiting for a response, she stomped off.

Aw, heck. I went back to the table.

Lee handed me another glass of champagne. "Drink up. For Monday you may be unemployed."

"The infamous puking PEA? Never. How about we talk a little SWAT?"

He cocked a brow. "Have something in mind?"

I got my iPhone out of my clutch and tapped open an IM to Cash. "Cash's chances."

Lee bared his teeth in a lazy smile. "Fair to poor if he pisses off my date."

I shot Cash off a short warning, set my phone on the table, and said in a sweet Southern twang, "I knew there was a reason I was partial to you, Mr. Sharpe."

Lee flirted the fast and furious forty-five seconds it took for my brother to cross the ballroom and flop down into the chair next to me. "Lighten up, Snap." Cash leaned back in his chair, tipping it up onto two legs. "Jennifer's about as fun as a wet sock."

I slipped my toes under one of the unanchored feet of Cash's chair and lifted up.

He wobbled, caught himself, and set his chair down hard. He gave me a dirty look and stood up. "It's a little too *chilly* over here." He went over and sat down on the other side of Lee and started talking baseball.

Unable to help my despondent self, I snuck a peek at my phone. *No text, no call, no Hank.* Not exactly a surprise from the guy who could keep the devil on ice. Instead of putting it in my purse, I took an etiquette mulligan and slid the iPhone under the far edge of my charger.

"Hiya, Maisie."

I flinched.

Obi wheeled up beside me. "Didn't mean to scare ya." He was wearing an ill-fitting black tuxedo jacket with white piping over a *Star Wars* T-shirt. "You look really hot."

"Thanks. Uh . . . you, too."

He pointed at the star on my name tag. "Big shot, huh? Drinking for free." He gave me a gap-toothed smile.

"Want me to score you something?"

Obi brightened. "Yeah, totes! A fuzzy navel?"

Too girly of a drink for even me to order. I peeled the foil star off my name tag and stuck it on his.

"Oh no." He shook his head so hard, I thought his hair would fall out. "That's yours."

"Good side of the force and all that."

"Thanks." He pushed his glasses up with an index finger, adding another fingerprint to the left lens, and glanced at Lee, who was still talking smack with Cash. He leaned a little closer, but instead of whispering, his voice got louder. "Is that *the* guy?"

"No," I mouthed and straightened as Lee put his warm hand on my bare back.

"Yes," Lee said. "She just doesn't know it yet." He extended a hand. "Lee Sharpe."

Obi shook it. "Obi Olson."

"As in Kenobi?" Cash asked across Lee. Obi nodded. "Dude, c'mere." Cash waved him over. "I gotta hear this."

Obi maneuvered his way around me and squeezed in between the guys.

Talk about feeling like the odd man out.

My iPhone gave a quiet *Predator* growl. A text.

Look to your right. Far right.

I did.

Ernesto Padilla raised a martini glass at me from one of the mobile bar stations.

What the what?

I excused myself and left Obi to Lee and Cash. Ernesto held out his arms as I approached.

"What are you doing here?" I asked. *Oh please, oh please, say Hank sent you to keep an eye on me.*

A *harrumph* sounded behind me.

Leticia Jackson stood leg out, arms folded across her ample bosom in a skintight canary-yellow satin dress with matching six-inch stilettos, yellow rhinestones in her gravity-defying updo and on her fingers. "Don't you go Bogartin' my date, Mc-Grane."

Chapter 47

Well, that accounts for the quiet on the Western Friend Front. I raised my palms to Leticia. "Wouldn't dream of it."

"Easy, baby," Ernesto said. "Maisie and I go way back."

"All the way to preschool."

Leticia raised an index finger and waved it between Ernesto and me. A little yellow diamond—dangling from a tiny gold chain drilled through the tip of her nail—swung back and forth. "I don't wanna be hearin' no nekked stories about the pair o' you playing doctor."

I watched the diamond as she gestured, hypnotized. Not nearly as hip as I wanna be, all I could think was, *how does she do anything with a little necklace hanging off her fingernail?*

Ernesto laughed. "Maisie's a McGrane. She's like a dude that's been snipped."

"Gee, thanks, Ernesto." I smiled at him. "Sensitivity. An important quality in a best pal."

"Best pal, my ass." Leticia dropped a hand to her hip. "If there's one thing I know for sure, it's that men and women cannot be friends."

"Bullshit," Ernesto said.

Leticia looked at him like he'd lost his mind. "What, you think I'm dating you for your sparklin' communication skills?"

Enough with the lovey-dovey. "Seen Hank?"

"What's the matter?" Ernesto said. "You having second thoughts about dating SWAT?"

Nice. Last time I checked, you were in the "owe" column of our friendship. I turned to Leticia and pulled the pin on the grenade. "Did he bring you 'round to meet his mom yet?"

Ernesto winced.

"Damn, that's cold, McGrane." Leticia nodded at me in approval. She cozied up to Ernesto and trailed a finger around his ear. "Talk to her all you want, Man Blanket. Ain't no mad love for you in her heart."

"Thanks," he said wryly.

"Man blanket?" I asked, because I really needed to know.

"Oh yeah." The tip of Leticia's tongue came out and wet her upper lip. "On account of he's so hot, and I want him on top of me all the time."

Careful what you wish for. . . .

"Maisie, baby," Sterling Black said from behind me. "Looking good."

"Feeling good," I said, complete with a half wink and cheesy smile.

He leaned in. "Play nice, Coles is doing you a favor coming here."

"Oh?" My brain disconnected from my mouth. "How so?"

Sterling pointed a finger at me. "You slay me." He raised an arm. "Talbott! Over here."

Glad-handing, the man of the moment made his way over. His salt-and-pepper hair had recently acquired more pepper, his teeth still as unnaturally white as ever. Two staffers and three bodyguards lagged behind at an appropriately subservient distance. His throwback preppy wife, who only accompanied him to heavy photo-op events, was nowhere in sight.

Oh yeah. I'm getting out of this with a hop, skip, and only a couple of cringeworthy pictures.

And then I saw them—six of the slimiest bottom-feeding gits. Talbott's personal public relations squad, aka the local news media.

"Maisie McGrane." Coles came over and gave me an all-for-show hug complete with kiss on each cheek. "Stay the fuck out of my way," he said in a low voice, then spun us around to face the cameras.

"Yessir." *Elitist ass.*

A microphone feedback whine cut through the camera shutters. "Good evening, Dhu West employees, members of the Traffic Enforcement Bureau, and guests." Jennifer beamed down at us like a Miss America contestant from the stage. "I'm Jennifer Lince, and I'd like to welcome you all to the first annual Dhu West Gala."

Polite applause sounded, reminding me to clap, as well. "We have a tremendous evening planned, so if everyone could please take their seats . . ."

Luckily we were well away from Coles, Sterling, and the Dhu West hotshots. Obi and his empty chair date, and Ernesto and Leticia rounded out our table of eight. It didn't take Lee long to size Ernesto up. Of course, the fact that Ernesto was doing the same might have clued him in.

"McGrane," Leticia said in a harsh whisper. "Call Niecy. Lince is gonna talk about her."

I dialed. "You awake?"

"Yeah," Niecy said.

"Lince is about to talk about you."

Jennifer raised the microphone to her lips. "This has been a dramatic and vastly improved year for the Traffic Enforcement Bureau under the new ownership of Dhu West."

Cash made a snoring noise.

"Tonight we'll be discussing some fantastic new innovations in parking enforcement. After dinner we'll hear from our guest of honor, Chicago's own illustrious Mayor Talbott Cottle Coles, and conclude by recognizing individual achievements. But right now, I'd like a moment of silence for one of our own." Jennifer smiled down broadly at our table.

The lights dimmed and the words *Eunice Peat* came up on the movie-sized screen behind Jennifer. "Parking Enforcement Agent Eunice Peat."

"A moment of silence?" Niecy's voice squawked from my iPhone. "Jeebus crispies. I'm not dead!"

Lee and Cash started coughing.

"Let's remember Eunice's commitment and service to public safety." Jennifer began clapping. "She would be so honored to see so many celebrating her retirement."

A small smattering of applause drifted across the ballroom.

"I'm gonna kill that friggin'—" I covered the phone in my lap, muffling the screaming.

Leticia, having none of it, stood up. "Stop your bawlin', peeps. Niecy Peat is one hundred percent Terminator. She'll be back!"

Jennifer gave an involuntary shudder. "Thank you for the update, Ms. Jackson."

The parking enforcement agents broke into cheers—more at Lince's distress than Niecy's return. Jennifer handed the microphone off to a suit-wearing duo extolling the virtues of new uniforms and the public relations campaign that would be unfurling in the fall.

On screen, three pictures of me clad in the hideous new uniform popped up.

Sweet Jesus. This night cannot get any worse.

Like trying to break up with a girl in a fancy restaurant, Sterling and Dhu West seemed to think rolling out the new uniforms at the Gala would keep the PEAs quiet and decorous. They had another think coming.

Sanchez jumped to her feet. "Yo! What the hell kind of uniforms is this?"

This is gonna get ugly.

Niecy was still on. I handed my phone to Lee. "I need a little air."

"I'm sure you do." He winked.

I snatched my clutch off the table and got the hell out of Dodge.

I should have listened to Hank. After those uniform pictures, I'd be lucky to make it out of the hotel tarred and feathered. Instead of using the restrooms off the ballroom, I took a coward's furlough, crossing through the main lobby all the way to the other side of the hotel. I followed a discreet sign down a dim hallway, rounded the corner, and ran face-to-chest into Tommy Narkinney.

Where's a wooden stake when you need one?

His ruddy face froze with fear.

"That guy—" he wheezed, edging away from me. The hint of what Hank had shown me hadn't been close to the hellfire he'd rained down on Tommy. "I—I don't want any trouble, McGrane."

"I didn't want any, either, but I got plenty," I said.

I almost felt bad for him.

Almost.

Sweat beaded on his upper lip. He gave a couple birdlike darting glances down the corridor. "Look, I—I'm sorry about your cart."

I folded my arms across my chest, waiting for the *I'm sorry you almost got run over and your partner got hurt.*

It didn't come.

Tommy sidestepped around me, talking in fits and bursts. "I didn't mean it. I mean I did it, but I didn't plan it, you know?" He wiped his mouth on the back of his hand. "How about I swear to stay out of your way? From now on and always?"

Whiskey Tango Foxtrot.

"You trashed my cart," I said slowly.

He nodded.

My eyes dropped to his waist. The corner of his service Glock showed from his holster. I held out my hand. "Show me your backup piece."

"What?"

I snapped my fingers. "Now."

He bent and raised his pants leg to expose the butt of a 9mm Beretta in his ankle holster.

"Stop."

He let his pants leg drop and stood up.

Just call me Sam Spade Jr.

I knew who left the wadcutter—who killed the mayor's staffer.

"Maisie?" Tommy said.

"Go," I said. "Just go."

He scuttled down the corridor and away to the lobby. I dug in my clutch for my phone, only to remember I'd left it with Lee. *Great.*

At the end of the hall, past the restrooms, was a guest phone bank—three wall-mounted open partitions each with their own phone. I chose the phone at the far end and called Flynn. "How fast can you get to the Jake Hotel?" I said.

"Why?"

"I think Wesley Peterson of the CPD killed Thorne Clark. And he's here now."

"Where are you?"

"I'm by the bathrooms at the north end of the hotel. I don't have hard evidence, but Peterson was the guy who vandalized my cart and left the bullet. The killing fits. His father's a bus driver, and he was at the memorial service."

"How do you know this?"

I almost said *Narkinney spilled his guts.* But for some reason I answered, "A little dog pissed on my leg."

"What about the guy that tried to run you over? Are they working together?"

"Jeez, how would I know?" I said, rocking back and forth on my toes. "This is where you guys come in and connect the dots detective-style."

"Rory and I will be there in under ten. Do me a favor, will you? Go in the bathroom, lock yourself in a stall, and wait until we get there."

Are you frigging kidding me? I thunked my head against the partition. "But Cash and Lee—"

"Maisie, please. For me," he said, managing not to say *or else.*

"Fine."

I pressed the metal button on the cradle to hang up, then

dialed the first three digits of Hank's number. I pressed the metal button again. *What's there to say, anyway?*

A meaty hand landed on my shoulder. I turned to see Peterson, nostrils flared, huffing like a bull.

Uh-oh.

"You think you're so goddamn smart, dontcha?" He jabbed a thick finger into me, hard, right below my collarbone. He dragged his finger up my throat and leaned in until we were almost nose to nose. "You don't have shit."

What I wouldn't give to step back.

"Oh yeah?" I said, praying he hadn't heard my conversation with Flynn. "Once our negligence lawsuit hits, you'll be lucky if the CPD ever lets you write a parking ticket."

"And you wonder why you're not a cop, you stupid whore." Peterson grabbed me by the throat, dragged me out of the partition, and slammed me against the wall. He grunted and pressed himself against me. "I know you know."

Since I'm already in hot water, I may as well start cooking.

"Narkinney told me everything," I rasped.

Peterson's face darkened. His hold loosened, and he gave a bark of laughter. "That rookie ass-wipe doesn't know shit."

Hank's Law Number Fifteen: Get tighter to get loose.

I lunged, grabbing him around the girth.

"What the—?" He let go of my throat and spun off the wall, trying to push me off. I let him, getting enough space to land two sharp pops to his kidney.

"Bitch!" He grabbed my ponytail and yanked my head back. I tried to spike my foot down into his calf. My heel glanced off his shin and tangled in his ankle holster. I pitched backwards, falling, taking him down on top of me, crushing the wind from my lungs.

Peterson straddled my chest, pinning my arms with his knees.

I bucked and squirmed.

"I've been restraining jacked-up dust junkies for twenty years." He laughed. "Keep trying. It's turning me on."

He wasn't kidding. *Yuck.* I quit moving and started to scream.

He slapped a sweaty palm over my mouth and pulled a small switchblade from his pants pocket. He was breathing hard. Harder than me, even. "What to do, what to do?" He tapped the tip of the blade against my forehead over and over. "There oughta be a warning label for cunts like you."

Trapped beneath a wing-puller. Not good.

A horrible light danced in his eyes. "My first choice is *cunt*, but *bitch* has more letters."

Maybe if I squirm, it'll be less legible. Icy sweat trickled down my neck.

He smiled. "You gonna cry now?"

Hank's Law Number Thirteen: Anyone can endure expected pain.

I'd be damned before I made a sound for that fat fuck.

His small porcine eyes narrowed in concentration, tongue poking from between his teeth like some special-ed sadist. He creased my forehead with a straight downward cut.

Bitch it was, apparently.

The single, searing slice felt exactly like a curling iron burn. Except for the thin trickle of warm blood slicking down into my ear.

Peterson leered. "Not laughing now, are ya?"

"Nh-nn," I said into his hand.

"That's right. You're gonna shut the fuck up. About everything. Or else I'm gonna—"

A human bullet knocked Peterson off me.

My brother Rory was on his knees beside me, pulling me upright, shaking my shoulders. "Maisie? You okay? Maisie?"

The unpleasant squelching sounds of fists hitting flesh filled my ears.

"Jaysus, you're bleeding." Rory felt around in his jacket pocket. He removed a handkerchief and pressed it to my head. It smelled of gun oil. "Oy!" He shouted at Flynn, "Don't croak him."

I looked over.

My brother had Peterson in a chokehold, face stop-sign red.

Flynn slackened his hold and forced him to the ground, cuffed him, and removed the Springfield Armory service pistol from Peterson's holster. "I'm thinking attempted murder, assault with a deadly weapon, battery . . ."

Peterson started swearing. Flynn dug his knee into his spine. Peterson groaned and stilled.

Rory helped me to my feet.

"Where's his backup?" I asked.

Flynn frisked him and found a Smith & Wesson K-Frame revolver in his ankle holster. He grinned at me. "Give her a pair of gloves, Rory."

Rory, who'd been in the process of putting on his own gloves, waited until I jammed his handkerchief down the front of my dress. He tossed me a pair, then picked up and bagged the switchblade.

I snapped them on. Flynn handed me the gun and I opened the cylinder. Five Buffalo hardcast lead wadcutters. "One short," I said.

"I'm betting the one I have at the station is from the same lot." Flynn hauled Peterson to his feet.

"Doesn't prove anything," Peterson snuffled through his broken nose.

"True, but the morgue still has the ones you left in the mayor's staffer. I'm guessing a mutt like yourself is too goddamned cheap to have bought a new piece. Or even changed the barrel." Flynn grinned at me.

Peterson blanched.

"Nice feckin' police work, Snap," Rory said. "Want to come downtown with us and book him?"

Not really, no.

"Uh . . ." I glanced at my watch. Only twenty-three minutes had passed. "I think I'm going to stay. I'm pretty sure I'm getting an award."

"For what? Blowing Coles?" Peterson spat a mouthful of blood on the carpet. "Have a nice ride on your knees in the limo."

Rory walked over and punched Peterson so hard in the stomach he fell to his knees and started to retch.

Flynn stepped around him. "Get a couple of Band-Aids from the front desk and don't drink too much." He kissed my cheek. "Trust me, there's nothing worse than a comedown and cocktail hangover."

Chapter 48

The concierge of The Jake took one look at me and marched me straight into the office. After two minutes of swearing I did not want an ambulance and would not be filing charges against The Jake, he had one of the sous-chefs clean me up and apply four pieces of barely noticeable skin-colored stitch-tape from the first aid kit.

I walked into the lobby exhausted and jittery. Goddamned Peterson.

There was no way I was ready to go back into the ballroom. Hoping to take the edge off my adrenaline in the dank Chicago air, I pushed through the heavy wood front doors.

A red-jacketed valet sat at his empty station, playing with his phone, back conspicuously to the drive.

Fifty yards away, at the far side of the circle, parked tail-up on the curb, in front of a fire hydrant and blocking the egress, was Coles's black Lincoln limo.

Of course it was.

I walked over to it, angling for a peek into the illegally darkened driver's-side window.

Empty.

I turned on my heel. Dozen came around the outside of the hotel, cigarette pinched between his lips, zipping up his jodhpurs.

"They have bathrooms inside, you know," I said.

He spat. "No pissing on the Tallywacker's dime." Dozen

took a long drag on his smoke and waved the cigarette in the general direction of my head. "Mixin' it up again, Bluebird?"

I dropped into a three-point boxer stance and threw a couple quick punches. "That's me."

He shook his head. "Yo, that shit go dumb last week."

"You're telling me."

"I laid that whacked-out sumbitch all nice and cozy at the Local #56." Dozen smacked his lips and smiled. "Shoulda seen the office girl. Man, did she lose her shit."

"I'll bet."

"Yo, well that's what a mutherfucker gets for interfere'n." He sucked the cigarette down to the filter, plucked the burning tip from his lips, and flicked it in a graceful arc toward the rear tire.

The glowing ember fell like a fading firework. A tiny reflection glimmered in the wheel well. A glint of something that didn't belong there.

Dozen moved toward the door.

"Freeze!"

His hands shot up. "Christ, you sound like a fuckin' cop!"

"Step away from the vehicle," I said, feeling equal parts ridiculous and scared.

Arms still up, Dozen stepped back onto the curb. "Now what?"

Praying I was wrong but full of the gut-twisting foreboding I wasn't, I fished a compact out of my clutch.

"You lookin' a lil' pale," Dozen said.

"Catch." I tossed him my bag. Compact in one hand, I hiked my Halston cocktail dress high on my thighs with the other and dropped gingerly to my knees. I peeked up under the rear wheel of the limo. Nothing.

"Damn, girl, I could break you off something proper."

Nice. On my hands and knees in the gutter and you're checking out my ass.

I opened the compact and reflected The Jake's lights up into the wheel well. Three galvanized pipes with caps, cable-tied together.

Jaysus H.

My hand began to shake.

Hank's Law Number Six: Don't fear fear.

Fighting the urge to drop the compact and get the hell out of there, I slowly moved the mirror closer to me. A woven strand of black, yellow, and red wires protruded from the cap of one pipe. The wires ran into a small plug at one end of a glass vial with a shallow puddle of silver fluid at one end, duct-taped to a magnet. A mercury switch. Motion activated.

Ballsy, stupid, and goddamn serious.

If Dozen slammed the driver's door hard enough, it might've gone off. Probably could've when he closed the door behind the mayor. Definitely would've when he pulled off the curb.

I tilted the mirror to a different angle and ran the back up the length of the bomb. Scrawled across the bottom pipe in black Magic Marker was the ultimate "screw you." A message—*Courtesy of the #56.*

Only cocksure idiots would sign a bomb. But how could they be so sure with a mercury switch?

I adjusted the mirror again.

A tiny red light blinked at the opposite end of the mercury switch. They'd doubled down with a remote.

I slowly removed the compact.

Dozen loomed overhead. "You a'ight, Bluebird?"

The three words I learned at the Police Academy blared front and center in my brain—*recognize, retreat,* and *report.*

Dozen held out a hand and my clutch to me. I took them both, and he pulled me to my feet. "Car bomb," I said. "A whomper."

I surveyed the deserted cobblestoned courtyard, hotel entrance, and tiny slice of street visible through the gates. Depending on what the pipes were loaded with, it could take out more than the front of the hotel.

I opened my clutch and closed it. Stupid phone was *still* in the dining room.

Dozen marched in place without lifting his feet. "Goddamn motherfucker sonsofbitches asshole—"

"Give me your phone."

"It's in the goddamn ride!"

I grabbed him by the arms. "Look at me."

He stilled and I let go. "Don't let anyone out of the hotel."

I sprinted across the courtyard to the valet station. "Hey, you!" I shouted, startling the red-jacketed kid off his stool. I grabbed a silver luggage cart and pushed it over. "Give me your phone. Now."

Startled, he handed me his phone. I dialed 911, hustled behind the station, and tossed orange road cones onto the cart. The phone kept ringing. The valet stared at me. "Car bomb," I said. "We've got to block off the drive."

The valet kept staring.

"Now!" I shouted. "Move!"

The kid jumped as if stung and started loading sandwich boards and wet floor signs onto the cart.

The operator answered. "Nine-one-one. What's the address of the emergency?"

"The Jake Hotel. Car bomb in the front drive."

"Please repeat," the operator said.

"Car bomb at The Jake Hotel. This is Maisie McGrane. My father is Captain Conn McGrane. Homicide. The bomb's on a mercury switch and on remote. . . . Pretty sketchy handiwork."

"*A-course* it's sketchy!" Dozen shouted. "Some janky-ass fool rigged my ride!"

"Please stay on the line."

"I can't. But I'll give you to someone who can." I handed the phone to the valet and waved Dozen over. "You two—block off the drive and sidewalk—hell, block off the whole street. Do not come back to the hotel."

Dozen took hold of the cart with a running start. The valet sprinted alongside, phone at his ear. "What you gonna do?" Dozen called over his shoulder.

"Keep everyone inside the building."

Chapter 49

Lee and Cash shot out the massive lobby doors with guns drawn and Talbott Cottle Coles sandwiched between them in full protective bodyguard detail. A TV crew complete with a couple of photographers were tight on their heels. Sterling, Bliss, and Daicen brought up the rear.

Cash and Lee halted at the pillars on either side of the door, pinning Coles between them, scanning the courtyard.

I sprinted toward them, arms out wide. "Stop!" I shouted. "Freeze!" The limo was twenty yards behind me. The hotel twenty yards ahead. "Car bomb!"

"This?" Talbott snorted. "This is my so-called assassination attempt? Let go of me!" He jerked his arm from Cash's grip and shoved past Lee. He stormed toward me with fierce brows and flared nostrils. "You." He pointed. "It's always you."

"Hey!" Cash shouted.

"Sir," I said. "There's a bomb—"

"Sure there is. The ad campaign's not enough, eh?" He jostled past me, knocking his shoulder into mine, heading straight toward the limo.

You stupid son of a—

I launched myself at Coles and took him down in a flying tackle that would've done J. J. Watt proud. We hit the cobblestone drive with a heavy thud.

I lay there, on top of the mayor of Chicago, listening to the faint chatter of camera snaps from the front door.

At least I'm not wearing a thong.

Mind bending, really, how thirty underwear-flashing seconds can feel like thirty thousand.

Finally, Coles grunted and pushed himself onto his forearms. "There better be a fucking car bomb, you stupid little publicity slut. This is a six-thousand-dollar Versace tuxe—"

White lightning burst through the limo.

Whoomph!

The blast wave whip-slammed us into the drive.

It felt like a giant spoiled child had stomped on me, wanting every concussed inch of my flesh to know exactly how furious he was.

And then it was gone.

Dust and grit misted over everything. Thick black smoke turned the mist to noxious fog.

Coles and I lay facedown on the cobblestone drive. My ears were ringing, pulsing with blood. My entire body loose-limbed and numb.

I lifted my head and looked back at the hotel.

Cash and Lee were on their feet, shaking themselves like a couple of big dogs after a swim.

"Remote!" I yelled. "It was set off by remote!"

Cash lifted his chin and hit Lee in the chest. The two of them took off at a run, sprinting down the drive, scanning the area for the triggerman.

Daicen and I exchanged thumbs-ups and then he and Sterling began to untangle the mayor's unhurt and terrified entourage.

Coles struggled beneath me.

I was still on top of him. "Sorry." I rolled off and knelt beside him. My body throbbed like I'd been strapped to the speaker at an AC/DC concert.

I put my hand on his back. "Are you okay, sir? Can you hear me?" My ears were ringing so loudly I couldn't even hear myself.

With the smallest of purposeful motions, Coles scooped handfuls of dust and grit off the ground before clenching his head as if in pain. Camera-ready trauma testimony, disheveled but not distressed.

Oh, he's fine, all right.

I supposed he deserved it. The bomb was under his limo, after all.

Bright lights glared from the hotel doors.

Cameras rolling. Nifty.

I sagged and sat back on my heels. Coles got up on all fours, opening and closing his mouth wide, trying pointlessly to pop his ears.

"Sir?"

He rose up on his knees and stared me right in the eye. "You saved my life, McGrane." He put his hands on my face and kissed me hard on the mouth.

Bleah. I need a wet wipe and Listerine.

"I owe you," he said, in full-on Mobster. "A big one."

"I'm sorry?" I said. *For cripes' sake. He's looped.*

"Jesus! You do this—thing. You save my life." Coles shrugged a single shoulder, complete with moue, and looked to the heavens. "Now I do for you."

Do what, exactly?

He grabbed my arms and the both of us struggled to our feet. It would have been a lot easier if I hadn't had to lift him.

Coles pulled me in tight to his chest.

Ugh.

But instead of pivoting toward the TV crew, he faced us toward the limo. A hulking shell, the bulletproof windows of the warped armored doors were crisscross crackled, bulging outward like glowing spiderweb balloons. Bright yellow flames tongued the edges of the melted roof as the viscous black smoke roiled into the air.

"We're going to wait," he said.

"For what?"

"The patriotic backdrop of flashing lights and scores of Chicago's finest." He tipped his head until it was touching mine. "Hear the sirens?"

I stood there, waiting for the convergence of EMTs, hating him. The limo continued to burn.

"Fucking armored car." Coles gave a derisive snort. "I bought the thing to save my life."

"It did," I said. "Without the armor, we'd be a pile of shredded beef shrapnel in a puddle of blood."

Coles's face tightened. "Let me do the talking."

"Yessir."

The Jake was ablaze with sirens and lights and men and women from every possible city service: police, fire, ambulance, gas and electrical, building inspectors, and of course, more news crews. It was like someone had shaken open an ant farm and every ant immediately set to work to rebuild their city.

A full-staged press conference in less than thirty minutes after the explosion.

Look out, Domino's.

Satisfied, Talbott Cottle Coles stepped forward and raised his arms, revival preacher–style, basking in the tension while giving the news reporters time to set the stage. "It is moments like these that define us as Americans. As Chicagoans."

He took a deep breath, held it, and released it with a serious nod. "I'm here tonight because an ordinary person—a humble meter maid—spotted something unusual and did something about it."

He smiled down at me. "Allow me to introduce my Irish angel, Maisie McGrane." Coles put his hands together and, like a bunch of trained seals, the crowd started clapping.

Slicker than a scuba diver in a sea of lube.

"Her quick thinking and fast action turned what could have been a life-ending tragedy into an inconvenience." Coles put his hand to his heart. "It is for this reason that I am meritoriously promoting parking enforcement agent Maisie McGrane to Chicago police officer on my personal security detail, effective immediately."

I stood there, dumb.

My brass ring.

Slathered in an indelible layer of political grease and bat shit. At least I didn't wince.

"Miss McGrane!" shouted a reporter. "How do you feel?"

Coles's fingers crushed my shoulder.

"Uh . . . flattered." I glanced down at my skinned knees. *Did he think my baby butt just fell off the milk truck?* I smiled. A syrupy one full of treacle. "And . . . filthy." *In more ways than one.*

The reporter and crowd laughed. Coles let go of my shoulder and stepped slightly in front of me. "I promise you, Chicago, we will catch the perpetrators of this horrific and senseless act of violence. . . ."

The news crews gushed righteous starlight and gumdrops all over his brave self.

Time to take a powder.

I cut around the rear bumper of a CFD fire engine. My skin was cold and tight, and my mind was a blur.

I need a phone. I need to get out of here. I need . . . Hank. My legs trembled like a newborn fawn's.

"Maisie?" Ernesto laid a hand on my shoulder. "Where you think you're going, *chica?*" He wrapped me in a foil shock-protection blanket. "I'm checking you out."

Daicen was waiting at a nylon camp stool in front of a paramedic truck. I sat down and he put his hand on my shoulder. "Heroic, Snap. Truly."

Ernesto took my pulse. "How you feel?"

"Fine," I said. "A little drifty, maybe."

Ernesto flashed a light in my eyes. "Follow my finger."

He went through a laundry list of checkpoints. I complied, not fully paying attention, floating instead as I listened to Daicen on the phone, reassuring the family. He walked across the courtyard, palm against his open ear.

Antiseptic stung my knee. "Yikes! Take it easy."

Ernesto moved to another palm-sized abrasion I didn't recall getting.

"Could you call Hank?" I asked.

He took his phone from his jacket pocket and held it out to

me. I shook my head. Ernesto looked at me sideways, wondering if I was concussed. "You want me to let him know you're okay?"

I nodded.

"Okey-doke." He smiled and handed me a bottle of Gatorade. "Drink this and don't move. I'll be back in a few minutes."

I nodded and he took off, cell to his ear. I rubbed my eyes with my dirty hands, making my eyes itch even more.

I'd pretty much sell my soul to take a shower.

Leticia sashayed up next to me and surveyed the scene. "Damn, McGrane, what a mess."

"How'd you get out here?"

She threw her chest out. "I am a supervisor with the TEB. Ain't no one gonna tell me I can't check on my weebles."

I nodded and pulled the foil blanket tighter, not feeling so hot.

"So tell me, that out-of-pocket TV shit true, McGrane?"

"What?"

"You're gonna slave for that fascist peckerwood?"

I'd rather hit every red light for the rest of my life than work for a sleazoid like Coles. "What?" I said. "And leave all this?"

"I didn't think so." Leticia laughed. "Dhu West opened the bars. The party's gonna be sick!"

In more ways than one, I'm sure.

"Don't go letting my Ernesto babysit you all night, hear?"

I nodded and she reached in her banana-yellow satin bag and handed me my iPhone. "You owe me. Obi was tryin' to pocket it. And I *know* you don't want that little perv trifling in your private business."

"Thanks," I said. I hit the Home button. The screen lit up with an unopened text from Hank from an hour and forty-six minutes ago.

Hank: *Wire live. Leave NOW.*

"Whassup?" Leticia frowned, with a nod at the phone. "You lookin' ghosty."

"Nothing. Just a message from my . . . electrician." I tried to swallow, but my mouth had dried to dust.

Leticia gave a little shimmy. "You hear *The Five* is considerin' me for a guest spot?"

Unable to speak, I gave her a thumbs-up.

"I gots a great agent," she said and salsa'd across the courtyard to Daicen and Bliss.

I sat in the chair, shivering in my tin foil blanket, drinking Gatorade, trying not to think.

"Yo, Snap." Cash plunked down on the ambulance's bumper step. "We found him. Lee and I."

"Who?"

"The fucktard who tried to kill Coles. In an alley across the street. Dead. Remote at his feet." He dug his cell phone out of his pocket.

"Oh?" I squeaked. *Jaysus, Mary, and Joseph.*

"Throat crushed, neck snapped," he said absently, scrolling through his phone. "I know how it's done, just never seen it before."

A one-second kill. Small dots of light danced in front of my eyes. The very first hand-to-hand combat kill Hank had shown me.

He'd been here. And at what cost?

"What the—? It's gone." Cash's iPhone screen showed ones and zeros. "It's gone!"

I swayed. "What is?"

"The text. Lee and I each got one. An attempt was gonna be made on Coles, complete with a photo of the rat-faced, one-eared skell in the alley. Jaysus, why else do you think we came crashing out of the hotel with Coles? Lee thought for sure he'd be a shooter."

I put my head between my knees and sucked air. *Hank tried to warn them, too.*

Cash squatted down next to me. "You okay, Snap?"

No. Not even a tiny bit.

Lee said, "She all right?"

"Sure." Cash patted me on the back, none too gently.

"Can I have a minute with her?"

Lee took the seat Cash left. "SWAT doesn't run investigations. Still, an encrypted text and a murdered and guilty perp sets a guy to thinking." His brown eyes narrowed. "Somehow I'm guessing you'll tell me it's just one of life's little mysteries, right?"

"Yeah." My mouth lifted up at the corner. "I mean, who could possibly want to kill Talbott Cottle Coles?"

Lee nodded, thinking it over. He shrugged, leaned forward, and kissed me on the cheek. "One of these days we're going to have a real date, Maisie. And that guy of yours will be nothing but a hazy memory."

That guy of mine.

I wish.

Chapter 50

My phone buzzed. "Hi, Mom," I said. "I'm fine."

"Thank God, baby." I could feel her tears over the line. She gave a giant sniff. "Talk to your father."

"Hi, Da."

"What the hell were you thinking?" He didn't wait for an answer, his voice low and furious. "You weren't. Jaysus, Mary, an—You could have been splattered to kingdom come."

"I'm fine."

"You're not working for Coles!"

That got my back up. High enough so a sizeable part of me didn't want to come clean. But I was too damn tired. "No. I'm not. I want to be a cop, not work for a criminal."

"For the love of Christ—"

"Although I'll admit the shine's come off. A bit," I said, getting cagey. *Of everything, really. Peterson and Ferret were another talk for another day.* "For the time being, Parking Enforcement suits me just fine."

Before Da could reply, the phone was nicked from my fingers.

I stared up into Hank's face, brutal and grim. His pale gray eyes were hard, and the tic at the base of his jaw pulsed double-time. "Mr. McGrane? Hank Bannon. I'm taking Maisie home." He clicked off the phone and slipped it into his pocket.

"Fourteen," he said in a voice colder than anything I'd ever heard, telling me what I already knew.

Hank's Law Number Fourteen: A good plan violently exe-cuted immediately is better than a perfect plan executed later.

He held out his hand. "Let's bounce."

I took it and he led me away from the hotel, the noise and lights and smoke.

"I should have listened—" The words tumbled free-fall from my mouth. "I'm sorry, Hank. So very sorry."

He slowed and put his mouth to my ear. A sexy shiver rippled down my spine.

"Never look backwards, Peaches. Or you'll fall down the stairs."

I have got to start reading Kipling.

Maisie McGrane will return in

CHOKED UP

A Kensington trade paperback and
e-book on sale January 2016!